Warmaster 6: The Lonely Tor
A LitRPG Fantasy Adventure

Melissa McShane

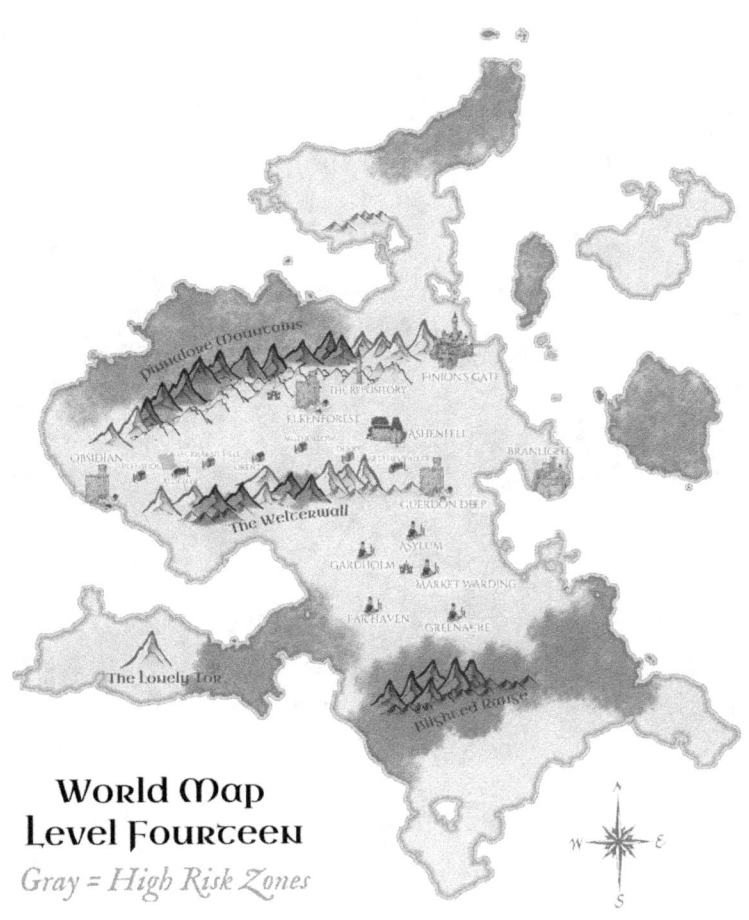

World Map
Level Fourteen
Gray = High Risk Zones

CHAPTER ONE

Aderyn cupped the <**Wayfinder**> in both hands and closed her eyes. She didn't normally need to shut out distractions when she used it, but she'd never tried to find anything so abstract before. The chilly wind blowing from the west brought the scent of dry grasses to her nose. She thought it should have smelled of the Lonely Tor as well, whatever that smelled like, which was stupid because it wasn't as if mountains had a scent.

And now she was stalling.

She let out a long breath and relaxed her shoulders. As she inhaled slowly through her nose, she filled her mind with thoughts of shelter and let them resonate through her body. Not a specific shelter like one of the many inns her team had stayed at over the months they'd been together, or the houses of the wealthy in Finion's Gate, or her own home in Far Haven. She didn't need to be drawn to any of those, which were weeks' and weeks' travel away. No, she needed the *concept* of shelter. A roof overhead, food on the table, a warm fire and a cozy bed. It was warmer in this part of the world than the one they'd left behind just half an hour ago, but still chilly enough at sunset that warm beds and cozy fires were desirable.

In a sense, they didn't need shelter. They had the <**Soldier's Friend**> for that. But with a dragon roaming above, nobody wanted to be a target out in the open. Nobody wanted to approach the Lonely Tor in darkness, either. So Aderyn's desire for shelter was more fervent than anything she'd wanted before. With luck, the <**Wayfinder**> would respond to that.

She opened her eyes. The metal remained cold and dark.

Blowing out her breath in frustration, she said, "I guess there really wasn't much chance that would succeed."

"It was worth trying," Owen said. He gave her a one-armed hug and rested his head against hers for a moment. "It's not like we don't have options."

"Yes, but the <**Soldier's Friend**> has that campfire that's as good as a beacon," Livia said. "It never goes out until camp is broken."

"We'll figure something out." Owen released Aderyn and turned to gaze at the distant mountain. "And the dragon didn't attack us before. Maybe we're too small to be interesting."

"Your optimism astounds even me," Weston said. "Come on, let's set up camp and I'll see about concealing the fire, if we can't douse it."

Aderyn backed away from Livia to give the <**Soldier's Friend**> room. To Isold, standing beside her, she said, "Should we have known about the dragon?"

"There are no legends of a dragon living on Lonely Tor," Isold said. "Though rumor says it holds great treasure, which suggests it could be a giant dungeon. If it's a dragon's lair, that seems plausible."

"I love this idea," Weston said.

They all stared at him. Livia, holding the bronze cube, lowered it slowly without activating it.

Weston shrugged. "All right, not the dragon thing. But a dungeon no one's entered in centuries? It could have all kinds of treasure."

"And all kinds of monsters guarding the treasure," Aderyn pointed out.

"What, living in the dungeon all this time?" Weston pointed at Owen. "Owen's the one who said it's unlikely there are monsters living in the rooms, all waiting patiently for adventurers to enter. They'd die of starvation."

"I said that's the tedious and impossible scenario," Owen said. "I didn't say that meant there couldn't be monsters. They might have developed their own societies by now."

"Monsters aren't that smart," Weston said. "And it's just as likely, if there were different kinds of monsters there to start, they've all killed each other off by now. This is going to be—"

"*Don't* say easy," Livia warned. "Optimism is a jinx."

"I was going to say 'exciting,'" Weston said, pretending wounded feelings.

"Let's all hope for 'rewarding,'" Owen said. "It's the quest we care about, after all."

Livia snorted and raised the cube again. "Getting through the night safely is my concern right now," she said, and pressed the side of the cube showing three stylized tents. A whirlwind rose up around her in which small figures could barely be seen as they flashed from one spot to the next. In a few seconds, the whirlwind died, the figures disappeared, and three elegant white tents surrounded a merrily-burning fire in a spot that had been cleared of grasses.

Weston walked forward and put his hands on his hips. "Maybe we should try the obvious way first."

"What's that?" asked Aderyn.

"Livia's spell *drench*."

"Hmm," Livia said. She snapped her fingers, and an enormous gout of water fell out of the sky, hitting the firepit and splashing Weston. Weston let out a yelp as the freezing water struck him.

"Sorry, dearest," Livia said. "But it worked." The fire was extinguished, the ground beneath it saturated.

"Perhaps we might have done that *after* we had a meal," Isold murmured to Aderyn, who giggled.

"I wonder, though, if the fire will come back once the ground is dry," Livia said. "It's something to consider, anyway. Let's eat—oh." She looked chagrined.

"It's fine," Owen said. "We shouldn't take chances on any fire drawing unwanted attention, even if it only burns for a little while and before sunset. It won't kill us to eat cold food."

They sat in a group in front of Isold's tent, well away from the wet ground, and shared out bread and hunks of cheese bought in Finion's Gate that morning, as well as grapes and beef jerky from the <Forager's Belt>. Aderyn's fear at seeing the terrible bronze shape of the enormous dragon faded, though not so much that she wasn't going to stay alert for its possible return. "Has anyone checked to see if the [Fire and Ash] quest has changed at all since we arrived here?" she asked.

Silence fell as all of them checked the Codex.

[Fated One's Destiny: Fire and Ash]
A threat from the Lonely Tor puts the surrounding communities in danger. Find and eliminate the threat to proceed. This quest is automatically activated upon acceptance. Recommended minimum adventurer level for this quest is 16. WARNING: A solution that puts the communities in danger from a different threat is not considered a success. Reward: [50,000 XP] plus any XP gained through actions taken to complete the quest.

"That does seem definite," Weston said. "Kill the dragon, don't do it in a way that hurts the communities."

"Then why wouldn't it say 'a dragon' instead of 'a threat'?" Aderyn silently read the lines again. "And why the warning? Doesn't that imply that there's a solution that does more harm than good?"

"I agree," Owen said, "but I'm not sure that means anything to us right now. I mean, all we know is that there's a dragon and it might be terrorizing the villages all around here. We don't know anything about dragons, their strengths and weaknesses, and we don't know what else the Lonely Tor might contain. We'll have to investigate first, and be wary of implementing the first solution we discover."

"I wish I hadn't panicked, and had Assessed the dragon when it flew past," Aderyn grumbled. "Who knows if I'll get another chance like that? Next time it gets that close, it might not feel like leaving us alone."

"Or it might have been angry about being Assessed," Livia said, "and decided to attack anyway."

"**[Improved Assess 3]** doesn't have a tangible effect."

"Not to ordinary monsters. Dragons might be different." Livia idly ran her fingers up and down her stone arm, her habit when she relaxed. "The point is, we don't know what might have happened, so no point getting upset about lost opportunities that might have worked against us, right?"

Aderyn sighed. "You're right."

She glanced at the Lonely Tor, silhouetted against the western sky. Clouds massed on the horizon, turned purple and pink and gold by the setting sun, and the glorious backdrop made the mountain look even more dramatically stark. "I wish I was close enough to try **[Improved Assess 3]** on the Lonely Tor. If it now gives me terrain assessments, whether it's a dungeon or a volcano, we'd learn more. But I still need to be within three miles."

"Tomorrow," Owen said. He rose and offered Aderyn a hand up. "We'll set watches tonight, though these plains are bare enough we should have plenty of warning if something attacks."

Weston put up a hand. "Quiet. I hear something."

They all froze. Aderyn listened, but she couldn't hear anything but the wind in the tall grasses and the lazy flap of a tent door that a breeze stirred and Owen's quiet breathing. Weston stood up and turned to face north, his chin raised and his eyes narrowed as he listened intently. He still held his hand high, asking for silence, but as Aderyn watched, his hand gradually lowered and he leaned forward like a pointer hound scenting prey.

In the next moment, he recoiled and put a hand to shield his eyes, then cursed. "Where did I put the <Cat's Eye Goggles>? It's almost too dark to see—but they're moving fast!"

Now Aderyn heard it, the noise of rapidly running feet thrumming against the hard earth like stampeding horses. Something moved on the northern horizon. She couldn't make out details either, but it was coming up fast and it was definitely headed for them.

Well, she didn't need to see clearly to use [Improved Assess 3] on an enemy.

Name: Waspnettle Drone [57]
Type: Magical beast, intelligent
Power Level: 5
Attack(s): special
Immune to: none
Resistant to: bludgeoning damage, mind control
Vulnerable to: trip attacks, *daylight*, *sunburst*
Special attack: trample

Waspnettles are centauroid hive creatures with a strict hierarchy. Though the females have vestigial wings, they don't get any use from them because waspnettles live underground in elaborate burrowed-out cities centered on their queen's lair. They're intelligent, but only just—you won't catch a waspnettle graduating from a university. Like many subterranean creatures, they can see in the dark and are vulnerable to bright light.

Waspnettles are connected to their queen and to one another by a low-level version of [Bonded Mind] that allows

them to share perceptions when they're within one hundred feet of another waspnettle. This connection gives them a resistance to other forms of mind control.

Waspnettle drones lack the poison stingers of other waspnettle castes, and they aren't allowed weapons, so about the only danger they pose is trampling you to death. Don't be in the way of a drone stampede if you can help it, but knowing you, this advice will come too late.

"Crap," Aderyn said under her breath. She didn't know what the bracketed number next to the name was, but she had a very bad feeling about it. She shouted, "There's nearly sixty of them coming! They won't stop—they're going to overrun us!"

"Strike camp," Owen commanded. "How soon will they reach us?"

The whirlwind of the <Soldier's Friend> breaking camp drowned out Aderyn's reply. "Less than two minutes," she repeated.

She now clearly saw the oncoming horde of waspnettle drones. There were dozens of them, bugs the size of ponies with dull brownish carapaces that blended with the grasses. The creatures ran on their back two pairs of legs and snapped their forelimbs with their terrible claws in the air before them. Aderyn's heart beat faster at the sight of vicious pincerlike jaws and hind claws that dug chunks out of the earth with every running step. It was hard to believe **[Improved Assess 3]** when it told her the jaws and claws weren't a threat—just the inexorable oncoming horde.

"Do we fight?" Weston said.

"They're vulnerable to bright light, but that doesn't mean *daylight* or *sunburst* will kill them," Aderyn said. "We need to get out of their way."

"Even if we run now, they're spread out far enough we won't get out of their reach," Owen said.

"Then I know what to do," Livia said. "Everybody gather around me."

The sound of thrumming feet on the ground was so loud now Aderyn could barely hear Livia's words. She continued to face the rushing horde of waspnettle drones, feeling helpless to look away.

"We're out of time!" Owen shouted.

"Not quite," Livia said, and took a solid stance and shouted the nonsense words of a spell.

CHAPTER TWO

With a roar and a lurch, the earth between them and the horde shifted and rose. The ground shook, and Aderyn and Owen clung to each other to keep from falling down. The moving earth rose to curve over the five friends until they were in a cave barely lit by the sunset's rays finding a way in through the human-sized opening.

Only seconds after the earth stopped shaking, new tremors started, and dust and dirt clumps fell from the ceiling of their impromptu shelter as dozens of waspnettle drones stampeded over it. Livia's eyes were closed, her face contorted in a grimace of pain, and she stood with her arms akimbo and her fists clenched like she was facing down a terrible threat. Aderyn clasped Owen's hand, watching Livia as if she could pour her own strength of will into her friend.

They all waited in silence for the drones to pass. Through the narrow cave entrance, Aderyn saw the rapid, blurred motion of far too many brown carapaces. Then the noise abated, and finally stopped.

Nobody moved for a few moments. Then Livia relaxed, sagging so deeply Weston grabbed her shoulders to keep her from falling.

"I'm fine," Livia said weakly. She gestured, and the earth reversed direction, opening up around them until the wave of dirt and stones flattened back into the ground. Aderyn shook dust out of her hair and brushed off her shoulders.

"Quick thinking," Owen said.

"I was counting on Aderyn being right that they wouldn't stop to come back for us," Livia said. Sweat beaded her forehead, but her voice was strong. "If they had, we'd have been stuck inside that cave, unable to spread out to fight."

"That was bracing," Isold said. "And odd. Waspnettles are nocturnal, yes, but they're also subterranean. And the drones are always supervised by a warrior or two. I can't explain what that horde was doing aboveground and alone."

"There might have been warriors," Aderyn said, "and maybe [Improved Assess 3] didn't happen to notice them. If it's just a couple of warriors, they could blend into the crowd. But you're right, it makes no sense."

"Unless they're migrating," Owen said.

Aderyn stared at him. "What do you mean?"

"Just that. They looked like wingless bees—bees in my world, and I'm betting here, leave their hive when it gets too crowded and found a new hive elsewhere." Owen was staring after the waspnettle horde, which was distant enough now to be barely visible. "And look where those are headed."

Aderyn's heart lurched. "The Lonely Tor."

"What are the odds we'll arrive just as a hive of waspnettles decides to colonize our quest location?" Weston said.

"This is good, though," Isold said. "Not the waspnettles, but what they mean for the quest. It said not to create a situation that will threaten the settlements in a different way, and expelling a hive of waspnettles to where they can prey on human settlements is definitely a threat of that kind."

"You mean, we have our first clue of what we have to avoid," Livia said.

"Precisely." Isold was staring in the same direction as Owen. "I'm trying to control my impatience."

"Right, because going to the Lonely Tor in the dark just got twice as dangerous," Owen said. "We need to rest up and set out early tomorrow morning. I can think of a couple of possibilities for what we might encounter there."

"Other than a horde of waspnettle drones?" Aderyn said.

Owen nodded. "If their hive is migrating, then either the drones were the first wave of settlers, if you can call them that, or they're a later wave, and there are more powerful waspnettles waiting for them. And for us. What other kinds are there?"

"Waspnettles have a hierarchy," Isold said. "Drones, warriors, elite, and queen, in rising order of importance. I'm afraid my Herald's knowledge doesn't include details about what attacks they might bring to bear on us. They can see in the dark, they dislike bright lights, and they are all devoted to the safety and health of their queen."

"**[Improved Assess 3]** says the other castes have poison stingers, but since I wasn't Assessing one of them, it didn't tell me the effect of the poison," Aderyn said. "But they're resistant to bludgeoning damage, probably because of their carapaces, and they are easy to trip, which means if you can get them on the ground, they have trouble defending themselves. And they—oh."

"Oh, what?" Owen asked.

"Just that the Assessment compared the waspnettles' hive mind connection to our **[Bonded Mind]** skill," Aderyn said. "I kept forgetting to find out how that works."

"If it gives us insight into the waspnettles, I say find out now," Owen suggested.

Aderyn brought up her Codex and Assessed the skill, reading aloud.

[Bonded Mind]: Allows partners to share brief messages through telepathic communication when they are out of sight of one another. Higher skill ranks increase the length of the messages and the ease with which they are sent.

"Telepathy!" Owen exclaimed. "That could be useful."

"Limited telepathy," Aderyn reminded him. "And it's sort of the reverse of the waspnettles' hive mind. That is, they have to be close together, and we have to be relatively far apart."

"It just says 'out of sight of one another,'" Weston said. "Turn so you're not facing each other and give it a try."

Aderyn shrugged and turned her back on Owen. She waited. Nothing happened. "I didn't hear anything."

"I was waiting for *you* to send *me* a message," Owen said with a laugh. "This time I'll try it, okay?"

Aderyn waited again. After several seconds, she said, "I guess the system knows when we try to game it. There's no loophole. Though, we have **[Read Body Language]** to communicate when we can see each other, so maybe the system figures our skills shouldn't be redundant."

"I'm fine with however it ends up working," Owen said. "And now we really ought to camp. I'm impatient for morning to come."

"So am I," Aderyn said.

Despite her impatience, she slept soundly until Owen woke her for her turn at watch, and then paced the perimeter of the camp, watching and listening for another horde of waspnettle drones. Nothing stirred on the plains. Near the end of her watch, she thought she heard the flap of great wings, and stared madly into the sky, Assessing the blackness in the hope she might catch the dragon. But she saw nothing, and eventually decided she'd imagined it.

The night was cold enough she kept herself in motion to stay warm, and was grateful for her increasingly battered coat, with its faint stains from old wounds and the grubbiness of its hem. She was even more grateful when it was time to wake Weston for the final watch and she could duck back inside her tent and cuddle up with Owen.

Owen jerked awake when she slid into their shared bedroll. "Aaah! You're freezing!"

"Oh, I'm so sorry, I didn't think!"

Owen drew her into his arms. "It was just a surprise, that's all. Let's get you warmed up." He kissed her, slow and sweet, making her temporarily forget the world as she kissed him back.

"I don't know if I can fall asleep," she said when they separated. "I love setting out on a new quest, and that makes me eager to get going."

"Well, the ice statue in my bedroll is going to keep me awake—no, don't leave, sweetheart, that was a joke." Owen breathed out heavily across Aderyn's forehead. "I've slept enough I think I'm done, too. And I have the same feeling about starting something new. Forget what I said about giant dungeons. I'm excited no matter what the Lonely Tor throws at us."

"You don't think we're being overconfident, do you? The quest does say sixteen is the minimum recommended party level for this quest."

"I know. But it's not overconfidence to recognize that we've accomplished other quests we were theoretically too low a level for." He rolled over and propped himself on one elbow so Aderyn could just make out his face in the low light. "Look, the system assumes that adventurers will have skill levels that match their experience level progression, right? But we all have skills that are higher than they should be—some, a lot higher. So even though our technical party level is fourteen, we have abilities that make us able to go toe to toe with monsters that ought to be too much of a challenge for that level."

"I hadn't thought of it that way, but you're right. It's like how in the Glory Games you defeated opponents who should have beaten you easily. And now I think about it, all of us do have high ranks in key skills." She blew out her breath. "That eases my mind that we're not going into this recklessly."

"I never take chances like that, not with my team and especially not with my wife." Owen settled back down and put his arms around her. "I can't help imagining what the inside of the Lonely Tor looks like. I know I shouldn't make assumptions about a dungeon, but those waspnettles have me picturing an ant farm."

Aderyn blinked. "An ant farm? Why would anyone farm ants?"

"No, it's like the ants are farming—you set two sheets of glass in a frame so they're just far enough apart for ants to fit, and you fill it with loose earth or sand, and then you can watch the ants make tunnels."

"Ordinary ants?"

"Sure. Little black ants."

"You're making this up."

"I swear I'm not."

Aderyn's mind blanked for a moment as she tried to picture an ant farm. Finally, she said, "People in your world must be seriously starved for entertainment if that's the sort of thing they come up with."

Owen laughed. "It's supposed to be educational. Learn about insect biology and behavior, that sort of thing."

"I guess that's what you'd have to do if you couldn't Assess things." Aderyn returned Owen's embrace. "I know your world has indoor plumbing, but this world is superior anyway."

"It has you in it, so I totally agree," Owen said, and kissed her again.

As if they'd discussed it, all five of them rose before dawn, even Livia, who downed the coffee Weston made for her without any of her usual comments about needing more of it to get going. They packed swiftly and set out just as the sun lit the landscape, casting their shadows so they pointed the way to the Lonely Tor like guide markers. Though nobody could miss the enormous mountain, which dominated the landscape in its nearly-perfect conical shape. Aderyn had seen drawings of volcanoes in her parents' books, and this looked like it had been plucked from those pages and set down in the middle of the plains.

Aderyn examined it in between attempts at Assessing it. It looked nothing like the other mountains she'd seen in her travels, which were mostly gray or grayish-brown; the Lonely Tor was black shading to charcoal where the light struck it. Its rough surface reminded her of an anthill, which brought her back to thinking about Owen's ant farm and how odd a notion that was. Maybe that was why the wasp-nettles were drawn to it, if they were basically giant insects that lived underground. The mountain looked like a haven for monsters.

After about twenty minutes' walk, her attempts at Assessing paid off. She stopped walking in order to read the information to her team.

Name: The Lonely Tor
Type: Themed, giant, victory condition variant B
Power Level: 16
Inhabitants: population currently in flux
Traps: occasional
Environmental hazards: structural deterioration
Reward: coin and mundane items worth a total of 9,458 gold at current rate of exchange; assorted minor and major magic weaponry, armor, and items
Built centuries ago by a high-level community of Spell-crafters, the Lonely Tor is an abandoned compound comprising several levels joined by devices that represented the pinnacle of the Spellcrafter's art at the time. Their ultimate construction was the defense mechanism shaped like a dragon.

Aderyn broke off in her reading aloud. "*Shaped* like a dragon?"

"It's mechanical?" Owen exclaimed. "I mean, not mechanical, but—it looked alive."

"Keep reading," Livia urged.

Drawing on legends of real dragons, they created a Forged dragon that would protect their compound and the neighboring villages, linked to the compound's operations so they maintained control over it. After the imposition of the level cap, and the eventual deaths by old age of the original creators, no new Spellcrafters were able to attain the high levels required to maintain the compound, and it was abandoned and left to fall into disrepair.

The current inhabitants of the Lonely Tor are a mix of magical beasts, abominations, anomalies, and vermin, as well as the remaining Forged left behind by the Spellcrafters. While not all are by nature hostile, any creature will fight to defend its home, so you're advised to tread lightly. More dangerous are the networks and devices still containing magical energy, as their corruption over time means they function erratically. There's no malice in them, but you should consider them as dangerous as traps.

"That's not at all what I expected," Owen said. "What's a Forged?"

"Something built and imbued with energy to give it a semblance of life," Isold said. "Forged can range from the mere mechanical to constructs that react just as living creatures do. We've seen how life-like that can be, thanks to the dragon's appearance."

"So, like a robot—yeah, I know you don't know that word." Owen's brow furrowed. "What does that all mean for us?"

"Victory condition B means we have to defeat the dragon," Aderyn said. "But we already knew that."

"No," Isold said, drawing the word out as if he was thinking about it, "no, that's the victory condition for defeating the dungeon. Our quest isn't the same."

"I don't get it," Livia said. "The dragon is the threat, so we have to kill the dragon to accomplish the quest *and* the dungeon. Or am I wrong?"

"I'm not sure," Isold said. "It's just that when Aderyn told us the victory condition for the dungeon, it occurred to me that we're only guessing the **[Fire and Ash]** quest requires the same thing. But that quest wants us to eliminate a threat, and it doesn't specifically say the threat is the dragon."

"You mean we shouldn't jump to conclusions," Owen said. "And you're right. If the dragon was meant to protect the Lonely Tor and the communities around it, that means it *isn't* the threat, or at least might not be. Maybe killing the dragon is the opposite of what the quest demands."

"I say we enter the dungeon, and figure all that out later," Livia said. "Even with **[Improved Assess 3]** we're making a lot of guesses."

"So sensible," Weston said. "And this time I agree with you that the impulsive approach is the wrong one. If we can avoid going head to head with a dragon, I'm in favor."

"Right," Livia said. "Now let's go before Weston comes to his senses."

Chapter Three

The closer they got to the mountain, the more trampled and torn up the landscape appeared. The tall grasses were ground into the earth, which looked like it had been the site of a battle between farmers' plows and then trampled by a herd of wild horses. Aderyn remembered the oncoming horde of waspnettles and tried not to picture her teammates' bodies, her own body, ripped apart by clawed feet.

But when the mountain was close enough that it blocked out the sky to the west, she exclaimed, "Look at that! The waspnettles turned right." The plains ahead were unmarred by the passage of the horde, but to the right, the devastation continued.

"We don't want to follow them, do we?" Livia asked. "Unless they have instincts that led them to an entrance, and we *should* follow them to get inside."

"Any entrance they know about will be crawling with waspnettles," Weston said. "I think it should be our last resort, if we can't find another entrance."

"Sensible," Owen said. "Let's get to the mountain's base and circle it in the other direction. It's a dungeon, so it has to have an entrance."

"Unless the entrance is at the top, where the dragon enters and leaves," Livia said.

Isold clapped her on the back. "So practical."

"Climbing that thing would be virtually impossible," Owen said. "I choose to believe there's something more accessible down low."

By the time they reached the base of the mountain, the sun had risen fully, and it was clear Owen was right about not being able to climb the Lonely Tor: the conical, steeply-sloping sides, completely free of hand- or footholds, were also gritty with black gravel that occasionally rattled and slid to the ground. Even an Earthbreaker would have trouble getting up those slopes.

Weston walked up to where the mountain rose out of the ground and ran his fingers over the surface, dislodging more grit. "This is surreal. No foothills, no rising ground. It's like someone dropped a giant cone on the plains."

"That's what I was thinking," Aderyn said, "except I didn't realize it wasn't an illusion of distance. Dropped, or maybe raised from the ground—Livia, is that possible?"

"Not for me," Livia said. "Not for anyone, probably. *Move earth*, even for a level twenty Earthbreaker, is limited to about a mile in radius, and it's intensely draining. Making that cave was a strain for me. Making something this size would probably kill the Earthbreaker who tried it."

"It doesn't matter," Owen said. "We already know it's not a natural mountain. Let's look for a way in."

"I have an idea," Aderyn said. "I bet **[Spot Weakness]** could reveal the entrance."

"Because a door is a weakness in something meant to protect?" Owen said. "That's a great idea."

Aderyn took a step back and Assessed the wall in front of her. Immediately, the slope took on a reddish tinge that meant it was strong against attack. "There's no door here, but that would be too much of a coincidence. Let's back up about fifty feet so I can Assess more of the wall at once, and keep walking around to the left."

They continued circling, with Aderyn stopping every twenty or thirty feet as new sides of the mountain came into view. It was more than an hour before blue lights gleamed in a line against the mountainside, a line that became an arc like the outline of a door as Aderyn rounded the curve. She ran toward it, fearing irrationally that the door might disappear if she didn't hurry, but the lights only grew brighter as she approached with the others behind her.

"It's here," she said, running a finger along the line. Gravel fell, obscuring the mark she'd made.

"Use this," Owen said, handing her the <**Deadly Blade**>. It wasn't a particularly high-level magic weapon, but its edge never dulled and it could make marks in stone.

Aderyn dragged the blade's point awkwardly around the curve revealed by [**Spot Weakness**], sending more little stones rattling around her feet. The line was jagged rather than smooth, but still easy to see. "There's no door. I mean, I don't see any groove that would indicate a concealed door."

"Let me take a look," Weston said.

Aderyn stepped back, and Weston felt all along the line she'd cut. Then he leaned closer and, with his eyes closed, inhaled deeply and blew out his breath in a long, thin stream. His left hand, pressed flat against the center of the imaginary door, shifted like he was stroking something upholstered in velvet, moving steadily downward. His hand came to a stop left of center, and he stepped back without pulling his hand away.

"I don't know what this does," he said, "but we can't just stand here forever." He pressed down, and a flat circle of stone shifted and depressed about half an inch. Weston rotated his palm a quarter turn to the right, moving the stone disc until it gave a barely audible click.

With a puff of air that blew dirt and gravel out of the line Aderyn had drawn, the section of the mountain inside that line sank back-ward and then dissolved, raining down larger chunks of earth. Aderyn's incautious gasp of surprise drew dust into her lungs, and she coughed hard to clear them. "It exactly matched what I carved," she said when she could breathe again. "How is it possible that my awkward tracing of [Spot Weakness] managed to mark exactly an irregular, ancient door?"

"I think there isn't a door until someone makes one," Weston said. "Carving, painting, drawing, whatever." He was looking at the inside of the door "frame." "This looks like the whole section is primed to create an opening. Whether that means someone could batter it down, I don't know. But it's a level of Spellcrafting I've never heard of."

"Let's get inside quickly, in case it re-forms and we have to open it again," Owen said.

The door opened on a short, low-ceilinged tunnel of red earth, lit not just by the light from outside but by dim, flickering lights strung on lines along both sides of the tunnel. Aderyn reached to touch one of the lights, but hesitated. When they weren't flickering, they burned a white so clear it couldn't be natural.

"That looks like electricity," Owen said. "See, they're glass bulbs connected by wires. Except the wires aren't connected to anything that might power the bulbs, so it's Spellcrafting rather than technolo-gy." He gingerly touched one of the dim bulbs, then curled his hand around it. "They aren't warm."

"Should they be?" Isold said.

"I don't know. Incandescent bulbs get hot over time, but these look more like LEDs." He let go of the light and reflexively wiped his hand on his trousers. "I need to not make assumptions. I bet a lot of what we find in here reminds me of my world, and I can't assume those devices work the way I expect. That could get someone killed."

"Everybody look at this," Weston said. He was standing some twenty feet away, looking at the wall at the end of the tunnel. It was made of a single sheet of black metal that gleamed dull pewter where the lights struck it. A door in the center bore a brass plaque a foot square, covered with engraved writing small enough not to be readily legible.

Isold bent over and squinted at the plaque. "It says, 'WARN-ING. Entering the decontamination chamber locks both doors until the cycle is complete. Exit by this door is prohibited. Do not proceed beyond this point unless authorized.' What do you suppose it's meant to decontaminate someone of?"

"Maybe anything that would compromise what they do inside?" Owen said. "This is spooky surreal. It's like entering a Fallout Vault. You're sure your world doesn't know anything about mine?"

"I thought the point was that this is the origin world, and it's your world that remembers bits and pieces of ours," Aderyn said. "Whatever that thing is you just said probably was inspired by this or other places like it."

"Okay, true." Owen ran a hand through his hair the way he did when he was stumped. "I don't like the sound of being locked into a decontamination chamber. Especially when we don't know if we're considered authorized."

"It's an ancient compound," Weston said. "The locks might not work."

"Or they do work, but the decontamination process is broken, and we'll be trapped inside a metal box that sprays acid or poison," Livia said. "Hey, somebody has to imagine the worst-case scenario," she added when Weston frowned at her.

"That's sort of what I fear, too," Owen said. "On the other hand, if both doors have to lock until the process completes, we can't go any farther until that happens."

"Let's at least open the door and look inside. We don't have to go in until we're ready," Weston said. He rested one hand on the short metal handle, gripped it firmly when nothing bad happened, and turned it with some effort. The latch engaged with a grinding of metal on metal, and the door swung inward a few inches and stopped.

Weston pushed. "It's caught on something down low. Something blocking it." He shoved harder. The door resisted for a few more seconds, then abruptly swung forward, throwing Weston off balance. He took an involuntary step over the threshold, and lights came on in the room beyond, brighter and steadier than the ones in the hall, but still burning a clear, white light.

Weston let out a surprised grunt and went perfectly still. "What?" Owen demanded.

"Well," Weston said, "it's a dead body."

CHAPTER FOUR

Aderyn stepped involuntarily closer to Owen. "A dead body?"

Weston crouched to examine the thing Aderyn still couldn't see. "Long dead," he told them. "Come and see, but don't let the door close on you. I'm still not sure this thing isn't trapped." He rose and stepped cautiously all the way through the doorway, grabbing the edge of the door and hauling it open wider.

Isold followed Weston, but stood in the doorway looking down. "I wish I had actual healing knowledge," he said. "There's no way to tell how long ago this fellow died. He's more desiccated than bony, which I suppose makes sense if this chamber is airtight when sealed."

Livia gently pushed past Isold and entered the room. "More bodies," she said. "Looks like it might have been an adventuring team."

"Go ahead," Owen said to Aderyn.

Aderyn's heart thumped harder. "I—no, you go ahead," she said. "I'll see if I can Assess the room, and if that's possible, it won't work if I'm inside." She didn't want to tell him the thought of being trapped in that little room, with all the weight of the Lonely Tor bearing down on her, frightened her in a way nothing else ever had. She hadn't thought she was claustrophobic, because she'd been in small spaces before, but maybe she'd just never been in the right situation to trigger it.

To distract herself, she took a few steps back and Assessed the room.

Name: Decontamination Chamber
Power Level: Exceeds authority limit
No further details available

The stark finality of the Assessment scared her more. She was used now to the almost chatty nature of the information the system gave her, like it was—well, not a friend, but a kindly older relative who was amused by her youthful enthusiasm. That it wouldn't tell her anything about this room unsettled her, and she couldn't help imagining terrible reasons for the system's silence. Or, worse, that her skill wouldn't work in this kind of dungeon.

That last thought woke her out of her fear. Skills worked or they didn't. They weren't conditional on dungeon or monster types. She was being ridiculous because she didn't like small, enclosed spaces, and she was letting that fear affect her.

"Aderyn? Did you learn anything?" Owen's voice sounded like he'd tried to get her attention before.

"Sorry," Aderyn said. "No. Whatever this is, it's extremely powerful, and it's beyond my skill with **[Improved Assess 3]**. It just repeated the thing about it being a decontamination chamber. That's helpful, I guess."

"It implies that the compound beyond is sterile, or wants to be," Owen said. "In my world, places that require decontamination have things in them that will be affected by germs or other microorganisms. Do those words mean anything to you?"

"I know what germs are, Owen," Aderyn said. "Do you think the Lonely Tor is still sealed, though? I mean, do we care about contaminating it?"

"I think we should worry more about letting out whatever's inside." Owen scanned the inside of the room. "Imagine what might have mutated over centuries."

Aderyn shivered. The thought of strange new monsters was a more normal fear she welcomed. It didn't freeze her joints into paralysis, for one. "Let's just see about getting in, and worry about— mutated means changed, right?"

"Right. And an environment created by Spellcrafters might have had any sort of effect on monsters that found their way inside... and that tells me the Lonely Tor can't still be sealed off, so I have no reservations about forcing our way through. Weston, what have you found?"

"I can guess what killed these people," Weston called out. "The walls are riddled with holes, and when I looked behind this loose metal sheet, I found hoses that lead to reservoirs of some potion or other. Not acid, but even a benevolent potion can degrade over time."

"I believe it used to be some kind of germ-killing solution," Isold said. "I wonder..."

Owen stepped into the room, and Aderyn followed as far as the doorway, feeling she shouldn't step through until they knew how to disable the locks. "We all have germs on our skin and inside us," Owen said. "Some of them are beneficial. What if the potion became more potent, and killed *all* the germs?"

"That is exactly what I was thinking," Isold said.

"I think I can disable the potion sprayers," Weston said.

"Couldn't that be a problem?" Aderyn said. "It sounds like the far door unlocks when the room finishes its decontamination process. So shutting this first door engages the locks, the spray does its job, and then the far door opens. If the room can't spray, maybe that door will stay locked."

"We can't survive being sprayed with this stuff," Isold said. "We'll just have to work out the locking mechanism for the door as well."

"And then we can loot these bodies," Livia said.

They all fell silent, staring at her. Livia shrugged. "They're dead, and they might as well benefit fellow adventurers. But let's make sure we can move forward before we worry about that."

Weston glanced over his shoulder. "I was about to say, someone needs to block the entrance in case the door closes automatically, so good thinking, Aderyn."

Aderyn didn't want to admit it was fear of the little room that had motivated her. "Is that what triggers the spray, then? Both doors being closed?"

"It seems so. There's a lot about this place I don't understand. Those Spellcrafters must have been an insanely high level." Weston crossed to the room's far end and tried the door handle. "Locked, of course. I'll see if I can force it."

As Weston dropped to one knee in front of the locking device, Owen said, "What about your *air bubble* spell, Livia? That provides clean air, right?"

"Yes, but it's only good against gases, not sprays or mists," Livia said. "There's a spell called *wind wall* that makes a barrier of moving air that sweeps anything lightweight away, and I think as I improve at casting *air bubble,* I can make a hard shell containing fresh air around my target. But air spells aren't really my thing."

"What if—no, the floor would have to be earth," Owen mused. "I was thinking about if you could create an earth barrier like the cave that protected us from the waspnettle stampede."

"I don't know. If we pulled up the floor panels—" Livia said.

Aderyn used [Spot Weakness] on the floor, which glowed with a red aura. "There's no weak spot where we could pry any of them up. And I bet they're heavy, too."

Weston grunted and came to his feet. "The lock is beyond me. Literally beyond. I think the mechanism is on the far side."

"So should we look for another entrance?" Aderyn asked.

"Because I have a feeling this may be the only one that isn't controlled by waspnettles."

"It's not time to give up," Owen said. "*Transport*?"

"I have to see—oh." Livia sounded embarrassed. "I don't know why I never think to use *clairvoyance*. It's too sneaky. I'm a straightforward thinker. That's why I keep Weston around."

"That's not what you said—" Weston said with an arch smile.

Livia waved him to silence. "Let me take a look." She faced the door, and her body stilled. In only a few seconds, she said without moving, "It's too dark. I can tell there's space there, but there's no light, so I can't see anything that would give me a reference point to *transport* to."

"You managed it at Tarani's memorial, though, and that was dark inside," Isold said.

"That had very faint light, coming through the cracks in the boards. This is pure darkness like the inside of a sealed canister." Livia's brow furrowed. "If we could get light out there..."

"I think our only option is for me to disable the sprayers, then step inside and take our chances." Weston was already examining what lay behind the loose wall panel.

"That's insane," Aderyn said. "We might be trapped. That would kill us slower than the poison, but we'd still be dead."

"Of course we wouldn't. Livia would *transport* us out. To the wrong side, sure, but we'd be free." Weston stopped working and turned to look at Aderyn. "Are you all right? You sound a little on edge."

"I'm fine," Aderyn snapped, and instantly felt guilty. "I mean... sorry. This little space frightens me."

Owen put an arm around her shoulders. "I didn't know you were claustrophobic."

"Neither did I. I think it's just this room specifically." She buried her face against his chest. "It's fine. I'll be fine. There's nothing to worry about. Let's figure this out and move on."

"It doesn't have to be all of us," Livia said. "I can *transport* myself, and the rest of you will—"

"Don't even finish that sentence, sweetheart," Weston said. He'd gone back to fiddling with whatever was behind the wall panel and didn't turn around, but there was steel in his words.

"That's right," Owen said. "We face this together, or not at all."

A squeaking, sighing noise came from behind every wall panel, and a hiss of air arose from all the little holes. Aderyn jerked away from Owen. "It's activating!"

"No, I think that's just what air was in the system from the last time it sprayed." Weston adjusted the loose panel so it almost fit back into place. "I'm sure it's safe now."

"Gather around Livia, just in case," Owen said.

"Wait," Isold said. He'd been kneeling beside one of the bodies as Weston worked. "We should see if these fallen adventurers have anything worth taking."

"I was distracted by trying to think of a spell to get us out of this," Livia said. She bent to examine the body nearest her. "Let me see if they're carrying magic items."

Aderyn continued to hold the door open, superstitiously fearing it would close on them. Maybe the chamber was safe now, but she didn't want to be locked into it any longer than she had to be. She gazed at the bright, irregular arch of the doorway she'd made in the outer wall. Pale shadows passed in front of it, like clouds were massing.

"Nice weapons," Owen was saying, "though no improvement on ours. Livia?"

"I don't see any magic. Funny, they would have been fairly high level to get this far, so why no magic?"

The shadows were moving faster now. Aderyn squinted. They looked too angular to be cloud shadows. On a whim, Aderyn Assessed them.

Name: Waspnettle Elite [10]

Type: Magical beast, intelligent
Power Level: 14
Attacks: weapon, claw x2, bite, special
Immune to: none
Resistant to: bludgeoning damage, mind control
Vulnerable to: *daylight, sunburst*
Special attacks: trample, [Overrun], stinger (poison)

Waspnettle elite fighters are centauroid hive creatures with a strict hierarchy, in which they are surpassed only by their queen. Elites are powerful not only with their natural abilities but with the weapons they take from their fallen foes. Their intelligence surpasses that of lesser waspnettles, though they are still not very intelligent. They can see in the dark and are vulnerable to bright light.

Waspnettles are connected to their queen and to one another by a low-level version of [Bonded Mind] that allows them to share perceptions when they're within one hundred feet of another waspnettle. This connection gives them a resistance to other forms of mind control.

Waspnettle elites have a stinger that delivers a poison attack on a successful hit. Their poison paralyzes a foe temporarily, but that "temporarily" is usually longer than the time it takes to disembowel a victim. That means you'll be alive and conscious when they tear out your liver. Not the most reassuring image, is it?

Aderyn sucked in a breath. Maybe the monsters wouldn't notice the doorway. They still seemed to be far away. "Um," she said, and as she spoke, the distant figures changed direction. They were closer than she'd realized. And they were coming straight for her.

Instinct took over. She stepped into the tiny, horrible room and slammed the door shut.

CHAPTER FIVE

Owen shouted, "Aderyn, we're not ready!"

A hissing noise went up from all the little holes. Livia grunted. "I'll *transport*—"

"We can't go that way," Aderyn said. "There are ten waspnettle elites approaching. They're each power level fourteen. Beyond our capabilities."

"Yes, but this could kill us too!" Owen said.

"Look," Isold said. "It's just air." Faint greenish rings accumulated around each hole, but no potion sprayed out. The air near each hole quavered with something like heat haze.

Livia gestured, and a clear membrane surrounded all five of them where they were gathered at the center of the room. "Just in case there's any lingering potion," she said. Her voice echoed a little within the bubble.

Owen put his arms around Aderyn. "You're shaking," he said. "Is it that bad, being in here?"

"I was startled by the waspnettles—it was so unexpected. I'm trying not to think about this place." Aderyn closed her eyes and pretended they were in a vast hall with a vaulted ceiling. It didn't work. The sounds of everyone breathing pressed on her, reminding her that this was a very small room with a very low ceiling that might have any number of other traps because maybe Weston had stopped looking after finding one—

Owen drew her closer. "How do you know there were ten wasp-nettles?"

Aderyn swallowed and tried to steady her voice. "It's part of **[Improved Assess 3]**. I saw it with the drones, too. It tells me how many of a particular monster are present. I'm sorry I reacted like that. I should have warned you all, and we could have decided together whether to face them. It's not like we didn't have the advantage of that bottleneck, forcing them to approach no more than two at a time—"

Owen chuckled, cutting her off. "It's your Warmaster's vision we count on to make those decisions, Aderyn. If you reacted like that, it's because you knew it was too difficult a fight for us. Don't be sorry for protecting everyone."

Aderyn nodded. "What is it you always say? Don't freak out? That means running and screaming, right?"

"Technically, it means having an extreme emotional reaction. You're still thinking about this room, aren't you?"

"I don't know why it bothers me. It's no smaller than my old bedroom back in Far Haven. But—"

Owen rested one finger gently against her lips. "Don't dwell on it. I may not have any idea how to stop the fear, but I'm sure of what will make it worse."

"I think it's stopping," Weston said. "The hissing isn't as loud."

The hissing didn't sound any quieter to Aderyn, but after a few more seconds, the noise trailed off. Another second later, the welcome *clunk* of a bolt disengaging echoed through the chamber.

**You have received [5000 XP] for defeating the
[Decontamination Hazard].**

Aderyn closed her eyes and let out a long, slow breath. "I'm sorry, everyone. I let myself be rattled, and because **[Improved Assess 3]** said 'no further information' I didn't Assess the inside of this room to see if there was a trap. Or I guess it's a hazard."

"It's understandable if you were surprised at learning how you feel about small enclosed spaces," Owen said. "It won't catch you off guard again."

"I wonder what the difference is between a trap and a hazard," Weston said. "**[Improved Assess 3]** said there are environmental dangers, right? Maybe a hazard is one of those, and we can get experience for avoiding or defeating it even though it wasn't intentionally set by the Spellcrafters."

"I'm glad to get experience either way," Livia said.

"I am still curious about why these adventurers had no magic items on them," Isold said. "I doubt they came here without being fully supplied, but nothing could come through that door—" He pointed at the second door, which now showed a hair-thin crack around its edges— "to loot the bodies."

"Maybe it was an adventuring team that didn't get caught by the poison, but couldn't get through the second door, either," Aderyn said. "They could have taken anything valuable... except that doesn't explain why the weapons are still here."

"It's a mystery, but not one that matters to us," Owen said. "Let's move on. Cautiously."

Weston led the way through the door. The moment he set foot on the floor beyond, lights sparked and flared into life on both sides of the corridor, long strings of the same kind of bulbs they'd seen before, but burning steadily rather than flickering.

They all gathered in a tight group just outside the chamber, and

Owen shut the door. When the lock engaged again and Livia exclaimed, he said, "We can't get out that way, remember? So it's just as well we lock this door in case someone else wants to test themselves against the hazard."

Aderyn ran a hand over the smooth metal of the walls. This space wasn't small enough to worry her; the hall was wider than she was tall, the walls rose to a height of ten feet, and the ceiling was curved rather than flat, making the corridor feel spacious. "Why metal, I wonder?"

"Reinforced against the earth," Livia said. She had her head tilted back and was staring at the curved ceiling. "I wonder..." She pressed her palm against the wall and closed her eyes. "I can feel something above and around us," she said. "Empty spaces like tunnels. This place is *enormous*."

"Can your skill guide us to the way up?" Owen asked. "Our first goal ought to be to find the dragon's lair so Aderyn can Assess the construct."

Livia shook her head. "[Tremorsense] is better for sensing movement. All those corridors—it's more like knowing a room is big by hearing echoes. You wouldn't know exactly how big the room was unless you had some other specialized skill."

"I'm in favor of [Tremorsense] telling us when monsters are approaching," Weston said. He was scanning the floor in front of him. "This floor is clean. Maybe too clean."

"Sealed or not, there's not a lot in here that can produce dust," Owen said.

"True, but this looks polished." Weston crouched and ran a finger across the floor. Metal panels with raised crosshatch patterns fit together closely enough the cracks between were virtually invisible. "Which is stupid, because these patterns are meant to make footing secure, and polishing would do the opposite."

"Is it safe to move forward?" Isold asked.

"Yes. I see no evidence of traps." Weston rose and rubbed his hand on his trousers. "Of course, if their trap makers were as high a level as everything else here, I might not see anything until it's too late. But if we fret about that, we'll stand here until we die of starvation."

"Good point," Owen said. "Let's move, then."

The lights kept pace with them, as Aderyn discovered when she glanced back once and couldn't see the door because the lights were extinguished. It felt like traveling in a bubble of light, one that extended only fifty or sixty feet ahead and behind them. Even more disconcerting was the lack of smells aside from what they carried with them. Maybe the decontamination was more effective than she realized.

They rounded a corner and almost immediately found another hall branching off from theirs to the left, identical to the first in size and shape and construction. "What do you think?" Weston said. No lights burned in the new hallway, but its first ten feet were visible, revealing nothing of interest.

"There's a door there, down the way we were going," Isold said. "Perhaps we should examine that before taking any side paths. If that is what it is. It might be the main path for all we know."

"It's a good idea," Owen said. "We can always backtrack."

The door looked like wood, dark brown with a deep grain, but when Weston checked it for traps, he said, "Strange. It's metal. And it slides into the wall rather than swinging open. There's no handle."

"Let me try *clairvoyance*, though the room is probably as dark as the hall was," Livia said. "And I can't do that forever, or I'll be useless with any other spells." She squared up to the door and closed her hands into fists. "No, it's too dark. Sorry."

"At the very least, that information rules out about three-fourths of the monsters who might possibly live here," Isold said. "Though we can't do anything about the ones who can see in the dark."

"It's not locked. But that's because the lock is damaged." Weston put both palms flat on the door and eased it open.

When the door slid halfway open, lights went on in the room, revealing a wide, high-ceilinged space. Aderyn followed Weston inside, astonished. Her first impression was of cubes, lots of cubes in bright colors. She blinked, and everything fell into place—the cubes were actually blocky chairs upholstered in patterns of red and blue and green. "It's a sitting room, sort of."

"What's that?" Owen said.

Aderyn turned, startled, to see a man standing to the left of the door. A second glance told her it wasn't a man, but a bronze statue of a man. The statue's metal clothing didn't look familiar at all, but its facial features, cast in a subtle smile, were so perfectly rendered every eyelash was clearly delineated.

She took a step closer and gasped when the statue's eyes opened. They had no pupil nor iris, but were hemispheres of bronze. "Owen—"

Owen swiftly put himself between Aderyn and the statue. "Who are you?"

The statue's mouth opened, and again its construction wasn't perfect, because the lips didn't move. Instead, the jaw opened and shut in time with the words the statue spoke. "Welcome to the Enchanterium at the Lonely Tor. Are you expected?" The voice was tinny and flat, the words slightly slurred as if the statue was speaking more slowly than normal.

"Um," Owen said. "No, we're not expected." He glanced at Aderyn as he spoke, looking for agreement. Aderyn thought honesty was the best idea, given that they didn't know what the creature believed. Maybe it didn't know all its masters were long gone.

The statue blinked. When it opened its eyes again, the bronze orbs glowed red. "Unexpected guests are not authorized. Leave now, or prepare to be dispatched with prejudice."

"Ah," Owen said, taking a step back and moving Aderyn with him. "We're not—"

The red glow brightened. "Failure to comply will be seen as

aggression. Prepare to be dispatched with prejudice." Its right forearm twisted a half-turn to the side and retracted into its upper arm. With a metallic hiss, a sword blade extended in its place. The statue, its expression frozen in an amiable smile, raised the blade and struck at Owen.

CHAPTER SIX

[R]ead Body Language] jerked Aderyn to the side before Owen, backing up, could trip over her. Owen dodged the swinging blade and drew his sword, shouting her name, but she had already Assessed the creature.

Name: Minion, Hospitality [1]
Type: Forged
Power Level: 3
Attacks: slashing x1, bludgeoning x1
Immune to: mind control
Resistant to: weapons damage, precision damage
Vulnerable to: elemental electricity damage

The minions constructed by the Spellcrafters of the Lonely Tor come in varying sizes, shapes, and power levels, but all are immune to mind control, as they don't technically have minds, and all are vulnerable to electric shocks, which confuse the instructions that make a Forged creature work.

Hospitality minions were created to welcome invited guests in and to see uninvited guests out. This one's been standing

around for centuries, so it's probably confused about the difference.

"It's not very high level, but it's resistant to weapons damage," she shouted, drawing her own sword. "And it has no mind to be controlled."

Owen caught the minion's sword blade on his own and shoved it out of the way, then ducked as the minion's other hand, clenched into a fist, swung heavily at his head. Owen took a step back, then another, drawing the creature away from the wall so Aderyn could take a position for [Outflank]. Weston circled around, looking for an opening, which prompted Aderyn to say, "Weston, I think [To the Heart] won't be as effective!"

"I guessed," Weston said. "It's not like it has real eyeballs. But—" He swung at the Forged's left shoulder joint, making the arm hang limply at the creature's side. "It does have joints like anything else with humanoid anatomy."

Aderyn thrust at the minion's spine, but the point of her blade slipped uselessly along the bronze curve of its back. Injuring it hadn't been the point, though. As the minion swiveled to face her, Owen took its head off with a powerful sweep of his <Twinsword>. The bronze head hit the wooden floor with a thud and rolled a short distance away. The minion staggered, took a few steps with its hands outstretched as if groping for its missing head, then sagged limply, though it stayed on its feet.

Aderyn prodded it with the tip of her sword, making the Forged's headless body teeter and fall with a much louder crash. "Is that—"

A system message appeared.

**Congratulations! You have defeated [Minion, Hospitality].
You have earned [195 XP]**

"I guess it is," she finished.

"That was a surprise," Owen said. "Robot servants."

"Is that what they're called in your world? Robot?" Aderyn examined the stump of the minion's neck. Masses of slender silver wires like stiff threads quivered, their ragged ends looking like torn fabric.

"Sort of. Most robots in my world aren't human-shaped, and the ones that are aren't as sophisticated as this one." Owen sheathed his sword. "I feel bad about killing it when it was just doing its job."

"Its job was to kill intruders," Weston said. "We're intruders. I don't think we should lie down and be killed just so it can do its job."

"True. I must have been infected by Aderyn's inappropriate sympathy for monsters." He winked at Aderyn. "What is this place? It looks like some kind of waiting room."

"I don't know," Isold said. He had his hands full of slick sheets of paper. "The writing on these suggests that the Spellcrafters who lived here sold their services to those who could afford it."

They all gathered around Isold to look. Aderyn touched one of the papers. "It doesn't feel right. Too slippery."

"But it's not plastic, either—a manmade substance in my world," Owen said.

"These Spellcrafters were such high levels they might have created any number of things we can't manage now," Isold said. "Look at how the colors haven't faded, not even the slight amount reasonable for these sealed conditions."

"I don't recognize more than a few of these listed items," Weston said. "Wands, scrolls, but even most of those have effects I've never heard of. What is a <**Scroll of Hilarity**>?"

"No idea," Livia said. "A lost spell, maybe? Or possibly they were able to create items that did unique things instead of replicating a known spell effect?"

"This tells us the Enchanterium sold magic items, so we know the Spellcrafters here weren't just researchers," Aderyn said. "It would be nice to imagine finding samples of what they made, but my

Assessment of the Lonely Tor suggested they didn't leave in a hurry, and probably everything valuable was taken. Anyway, I don't know if this helps us at all."

"Only in the sense that more information is good." Owen tapped the sheaf of slick papers. "I think we should take these with us. They might be useless, but they're also the only key we have to the former contents of this dungeon."

"I'll study them when we come to a resting place," Isold said. "It's not urgent." He squared up the thin stack and slipped it into his knapsack.

Back in the hall, Owen said, "There's a turn up ahead, and the side passage behind us. Any preferences?"

"I hate leaving unexplored territory at our backs," Weston said.

"Fair enough." Owen stepped back to let Weston take the lead back the way they'd come.

The side hallway lit as they entered it, just as the other halls had. Aderyn found the slightly metallic sound of their feet on the floor panels strange and a little unsettling. Every other dungeon her team had explored had been created by the system. This one had been created by people and had only become a dungeon after its abandonment. Why that made a difference, she didn't know, but it felt almost like intruding on someone else's house—someone who might object to their being there.

The hallway ended in another of the metal doors made to look wooden. Weston examined it. "Also not locked," he said, and dragged it open with some effort.

Again, lights came on when he entered, but this time, it was only the lights in the back half of the large room. They glowed brightly enough to cast the front half into a semi-gloom, enough for sight. More of the boxy, brightly-upholstered chairs filled the room, all of them oriented on a podium on a small dais at the darkened front.

Aderyn drifted between the chairs, not touching them. The patterns weren't all the same, which might mean each chair belonged to a specific person. Or maybe it just meant the ancients had strange tastes in interior design.

"Seventeen chairs," Livia said. "Not a lot."

"I think this was a meeting room, or an instruction room," Owen said. "Look at how all the chairs are pointed where the sitters could watch whoever stands at the podium."

"I agree," Isold said. "And that implies there weren't many Spell-crafters living here. More possibly useless information, but I don't think we should disregard anything we learn."

"Three more doors," Weston said. "One locked, two not. I don't expect to find traps on anything unlocked. If they left this place in an orderly manner, they wouldn't have added traps to the doors they used frequently, meaning the unlocked doors. And yes, I'm still checking everything. I'm just saying that's more information about this place."

"Smart," Owen said. "What about the locked door?"

"Also not trapped." Weston pointed at the door he stood in front of, on the far side of the room from the dais. "These locks are unusual. Whatever they used for keys didn't look anything like our keys today. They had the strangest shape."

"But you can open it, right?" Aderyn said.

Weston grinned. "Thanks for demonstrating faith in my abilities. I can open it, but if we could find an example of one of those keys, even if we don't know what lock it opens, it would give me a better idea of how the locks work."

"Well, I for one want to see what they thought was important enough to lock up," Owen said. "Let's try that door first."

Weston fiddled with the lock for a minute, and finally slid the door open on darkness. He moved to step inside, but Livia grabbed his arm. "We've been incautious so far, walking into unknown rooms. Let me light it up first." She lobbed a couple of floating lights through the door, and they all gathered around to look inside the room.

After Livia's warning, Aderyn had expected something dramatic. Instead, the white-walled room was empty except for several counter-tops lining the walls and a big white butcher block table at the center. Cabinets attached to the walls above the counters were all latched shut with shiny black metal toggles. Aderyn Assessed the room, hoping not to see the green fire of a trap.

To her surprise, a single line of a system message appeared, floating some distance away from her:

Laboratory A11

"[**Laboratory A11**]," she read aloud. The others all turned to stare at her. "It's what it's called. Except I don't think that was [**Improved Assess 3**]. It's like the message is attached to the room—why don't you all try Assessing it?"

"Weird," Owen said. His eyes unfocused, and he jerked in surprise. Then he stretched out his arm to its fullest length and wiggled his fingers. "It's like a VR display. Don't ask me to explain VR, please."

"I see it," Weston said.

"I don't," Livia complained. "What are you all talking about?"

"I can see it as well," Isold said. "Livia, what is your [**Assess**] skill rank?"

Livia frowned. "It's 6. I don't exactly use it often."

"Mine is 10, and I'm sure Weston and Owen's are around that level. That must mean there's a base skill rank requirement to trigger the message." Isold's eyes narrowed as he regarded the room description. "I had no idea it was possible to make a dungeon Assessment visible to anyone but a Warmaster."

"It looks different, though," Aderyn said. "All my Assessments show up right in front of my face, just like anything. I think this is something the Spellcrafters did, not the system. It—" She Assessed the room again to take another look at the message. "Is it strange that this awes me more than the hospitality minion did? Because this is like tapping into the power of the system, and that ought to be impossible for any person."

"Now I'm annoyed that I can't see it, if it's that impressive," Livia groused. "I'm going to check these cabinets. They aren't trapped, are they?"

"There's no magical trap in here," Aderyn said.

Livia flicked open the first set of toggles and swung the doors open. "Empty."

They spread out to search the room. All the cabinets were empty. The butcher block table turned out to be on wheels that locked to keep it from rolling. Aderyn stared a while at the floor, which wasn't metal, but was made of squares of some rubbery white substance that softened the floor and made their footsteps nearly inaudible. She liked it better than the metal plates, and she couldn't imagine why the builders hadn't wanted it for all the floors.

Finally, Owen said, "I know I said I wasn't going to compare things in the Lonely Tor to my world, but this really does look like an abandoned lab, especially given the system label. It's probably just as well there isn't anything here, because lab experiments can be dangerous, never mind the ones that have been unattended for centuries."

"Aren't we curious about why this was attached to that meeting room?" Aderyn said. "And locked?"

"Demonstrations?" Weston said. "Maybe it was a place all the Spellcrafters could use. It *is* a big room."

"I get your point, though," Owen said. "I feel like... well, this is silly, but almost like we owe it to those Spellcrafters to understand their lives. Like that will make us better able to figure out the secrets of the Lonely Tor. Especially since we don't know for sure what it takes to complete the **[Fire and Ash]** quest. It might require us to repair some system, or operate their Spellcrafting tools."

"Now I'm hoping we do find an undisturbed room," Livia said. "We won't learn much by guessing. No offense, dearest."

"Of course not," Weston said. "But making many guesses that fit together will take us closer to the truth." He closed and latched the nearest cabinet. "Let's take a look at that other door."

The second door from the meeting room, which Assessment revealed was tagged [**Meeting Room A**], led to a short hall that terminated in another locked door and a hall to the right. Weston knelt before this door, muttering, for more than a minute before saying, "There's no trap, but this lock is more complex than the other. I feel like there's something I'm missing." He rose to his feet.

"Anything that locked up is worth trying for," Owen said.

"I agree. I just need to think about it another way." Weston backed up and leaned against the far wall, crossed his arms over his chest, and closed his eyes.

Aderyn tried Assessing the lock, though she felt she'd pushed the system enough for one day, between the new developments of [**Improved Assess 3**] and the room description tags. Nothing happened. She ran a finger over the mechanism, which to her looked impenetrable—a lock plate with a grooved hole, and no sign of what lay within.

"Huh," Weston said without opening his eyes. "Livia, what's that spell you have that lets you open doors in stone?"

"It's *pass through walls*," Livia said. "But it only works in stone."

"All right, but you have affinity for metal, too, right?"

"Yes, but like I said—"

Weston stood upright. "I'm not asking you to create a door in solid metal, just to take advantage of the door that's already there."

Livia chewed her lower lip in thought. "I could use *telekinesis*."

"That might ruin the door. What I want is to see if we can encourage it to open. That will bypass the lock, and it might give me better understanding of how the locks work. Will you try?"

"Sure." Livia pressed her palms flat against the door and took a solid stance. Chanting a series of nonsense words that sounded like gargling gravel, she pushed against the door like someone sliding a panel open.

Metal squealed against metal. The door shuddered. Then, as smoothly as if it hadn't protested, it slid sideways and disappeared into the wall, leaving an open doorway into a darkened room. Livia drew in a deep breath and flexed her fingers. With a flick of her wrist, she launched several *orbs of light* into the room. "Let's see what's here."

CHAPTER SEVEN

Dim lights flickered on when they entered, making Aderyn grateful for Livia's brighter lights. This was the biggest room they'd found so far, twice the size of [**Laboratory A11**]. The sight of rows of unoccupied beds separated by tattered curtains told Aderyn immediately what it had once been, without the need for [**Improved Assess 3**], though she did that anyway, just in case. "It's an infirmary. I didn't think Spellcrafting was such a dangerous class, for them to need one this size."

"With the kind of Spellcrafting objects they made, I'm surprised it's not bigger," Weston said. "Don't tell me you didn't imagine those hospitality minions going mad and attacking innocent bystanders."

"Spread out and search," Owen said. "There might be some valuable items here, if they weren't thorough in cleaning it out."

Aderyn knelt to look beneath each bed. She found no lost objects, and the curtains disintegrated when she touched them, falling in dusty shreds at her feet. She sneezed.

"I don't think we should take a chance on any potions we find in this place," Owen said. "Not after what happened to that germicide in the decontamination chamber."

Aderyn drifted over to where he was searching several glass-fronted cabinets. "I wonder if they knew other healing options beyond potions. Those are something a Spiritsmith brews, and they were all Spell-crafters. So if they had potions, they had to buy them from outside, and suppose they learned other methods that didn't depend on potions?"

"I'm not seeing any potions, anyway." Owen closed a cabinet and surveyed the room. "Anyone find anything?"

Livia opened a cabinet low to the ground and gasped. "Wands!"

They all clustered around her. Isold bent to examine the three wands hanging in a row from a wall-mounted rack clearly designed for that purpose. "These are all useful in treating injury. A <**Wand of Limited Paralysis**>, a <**Wand of Deep Slumber**>, and a <**Wand of Minor Healing**>. All of them low on charges, which might explain why they're still here."

"How does paralyzing someone help heal them?" Livia asked.

"This wand immobilizes only part of the body. It would be used in treating broken bones, or in caring for an injury that should not be moved, such as spinal cord damage." Isold gently lifted each one out of the rack. "A <**Wand of Deep Slumber**> is like your <**Wand of Sleep**>, Livia, but the effect lasts longer and is not disturbed by anything short of an aggressive blow. Putting a patient into a deep sleep while performing healing treatments is sometimes valuable."

"How many charges? Is it worth taking them?" Owen asked.

"Four charges for the paralysis wand, fourteen for the sleep wand, and twenty-nine for the healing wand." Isold handed the <**Wand of Deep Slumber**> to Livia. "An upgrade, if you will. I will keep the <**Wand of Minor Healing**>."

"That leaves the paralysis wand. Anyone interested?" Owen asked.

"You said it paralyzes only part of the body?" Aderyn said. "I can think of ways to use that."

Isold nodded and handed it over. It didn't look like any wand

Aderyn had seen before. It was carved from a translucent blue stone Aderyn thought was aquamarine, and silver wire wrapped in a tight coil around its base and then spiraled loosely to the tip, where it connected to a silver cap. She touched the wire and got a tiny shock, like touching a doorknob after shuffling across a rug. "Are you sure this is safe? It's not defective or anything?"

"Very sure," Isold said. "My **[Identify Magic Items]** skill is still growing, true, but it works like **[Improved Assess 3]** in the sense that if there is something wrong or unknown about an item, I usually discern that." He hesitated. "And now I am wondering about the possibility of a magic item capable of concealing its true identity or nature."

"Don't start doubting yourself, Isold, that leads nowhere good." Owen took the wand from Aderyn and touched the silver cap. "It didn't try to bite me or anything, so I'm sure it's fine."

"I suppose you're right." Aderyn found a place to put the wand where it would come easily to hand. "Did anyone find anything else?"

"Just that the construction is unusual," Weston said. "Like how the cabinets and so forth are metal, but the white coating isn't paint, it's some kind of hard substance they glued on." He pointed at where he'd picked away at the corner of a cabinet. "It flakes off if you work hard enough at it, and I admit I was curious."

Owen looked at the scattering of white flakes. "Enamel," he said. "I saw it on some guy's YouTube channel—it's a powder you spray on the metal surface, and then you bake it and it hardens. I bet that's not how the Spellcrafters did it, though."

"Let's keep going," Aderyn said. "Finding those wands was exciting. Maybe there are other things left behind! Those Spellcrafters were high enough level they didn't care about abandoning those wands, but we'll get use out of them—there could be more Spellcrafted items like that."

"That's an invigorating thought," Owen said. "We have a choice of two doors besides the one we came in by."

"They're both locked," Weston said, "and in the same way this door was." He stood near the door they'd entered by. "After I got bored with picking at things, I investigated this lock. I still wish I had an example of a key, but I have a better idea of how the lock works now, and I'm sure I can open the others."

"Then... that one," Owen said, pointing at one of the doors.

Weston didn't seem to do much of anything at first, but after a while he got down on one knee and peered at the lock plate, then brought out his lock picks and carefully probed the lock. From Aderyn's position, it looked like he was trying to pry a coin out of a deep crack in the pavement, something that might fall deeper if he wasn't cautious.

Minutes passed. No one spoke, though Livia created a few more light orbs and made them spin in a flat circle in the air in front of her. Finally, Weston said, "That should do it," and with a loud, grinding clank, the door popped open, retracting into the wall about halfway.

"Sorry. That won't take as long next time," Weston said, tucking his lock picks into his belt. "I have the feeling I'm doing this the hard way. Like my lock picking is the exact opposite method the Spell-crafters used in opening locks."

"You got it open, and that's what matters, dearest," Livia said. With a flick of her hand, she sent the spinning *orbs of light* into the next room. Weston manhandled the door open the rest of the way, and they all stood around the entrance, looking in.

"Wow," Owen said. "What a mess."

Aderyn Assessed the room and again saw what she now thought of as a description marker, hovering out of arm's reach. "[**Laboratory A12**]," she said aloud, in case the others didn't think to Assess. "I'm not sure there's anything left worth taking. Somebody thoroughly destroyed this place."

[**Laboratory A12**] was the same size and shape as A11, and the cabinets and countertops and flooring were identical, but where that had been empty and pristine, this looked like the site of a battle. Shards of vials and bottles littered the rubbery white floor, marking it in places with long slashes from the broken glass. Stains of different shades of brown spattered around the glass. Aderyn leaned close to take a look, but didn't touch—the glass looked sharp.

"I think these were potion containers," she said. "Meant for offensive use, probably—my mother the Spiritsmith says when she was an adventurer, she used thin glass vials for any potion meant to shatter on impact. Except I can't explain why someone would store a bunch of harmful potions right next to the infirmary."

"What about test tubes?" Owen said. "For collecting blood samples and testing for disease or illness. Those aren't very thick, at least not in my experience."

"Oh." Aderyn nodded. "If these stains are blood... the samples might have been stored here, and someone destroyed them when they smashed the room up."

Isold carefully crossed the room, but he couldn't avoid every shard of glass, and his boots made crunching sounds as he trod the broken vials underfoot. "I am trying and failing to come up with an explanation for Spellcrafters keeping blood samples. Medical experimentation, perhaps?"

"If they were Bonemenders or Spiritsmiths, maybe," Weston said. He followed Isold, making less noise than the Herald, and examined the door on the far side.

"Or it was for health and safety reasons," Owen said. "Maybe they were worried about contamination or exposure to radiation or something. They might have tested themselves frequently to make sure they hadn't contracted a disease." He turned to examine the cabinets nearest him.

"True, but after what we've seen, do you think the Spellcrafters were the ones who tore this place apart?" Livia stood with her hands on her hips, watching Weston.

"No," Aderyn said. "It's more likely they left everything, because why would they need to carry blood samples when they were leaving forever? And someone or something else got in here and destroyed it." She tugged open a cabinet with some force after it stuck the first time she tried. "And see? There's still unbroken vials here. So it was opportunistic destruction."

Owen joined her. "Full vials, too. What should we do with them?"

"Not drink them, obviously. Livia, what do you think?"

Livia crunched over to Aderyn's side. "They aren't magic. I bet they're leftover blood or other bodily fluids." She made a face. "Let's shut them away and forget about them."

Isold let out a startled breath and stepped back from the cabinet he'd been examining. "That one moved—back up!"

Aderyn spun to face Isold, who was retreating at speed from a flat-bottomed glass beaker that rattled and shivered. Instinctively, she Assessed it just as the green-tinged brown translucent contents boiled out of the glass.

Name: Bilious Ooze [1]
Type: Formless
Power Level: 5
Attacks: special
Immune to: mind control, precision damage
Resistant to: slashing weapon damage
Vulnerable to: elemental fire damage
Special attacks: drain, infectious touch, stench
Oozes are bags of viscous fluids with barely enough aware-ness to hunt their next meal. A bilious ooze is formed when human bodily fluids are left alone in a magically-rich environ-ment with no supervision for a hundred years. It has no mind to target and no anatomy for one attack to do more damage than another.

In addition to causing damage, a bilious ooze's attack

lowers the victim's maximum health level, and its touch can cause a virulent disease that leaves the sufferer's corpse looking like a bilious ooze as well. Also, they stink when they're cut open. You're going to cut one open anyway, aren't you? Bet you wish you had a flamethrower right now!

"Don't let it touch you!" Aderyn screamed. "And it will stink—"

Owen slashed the bilious ooze as it poured out of the cabinet, scoring a solid hit that tore through the creature's membranous hide. The stench of a hundred thousand rotting eggs filled the air, sending each of the team staggering back. Aderyn gagged, forced herself not to vomit, and choked out, "No mind control, no **[To the Heart]**— I'm not sure what we can do!"

Livia shouted the words of a spell. Fat tentacles of rich black earth emerged from nowhere to wrap around the ooze. The formless creature quivered and stopped moving, hanging halfway down the cabinet and half sprawled across the floor. "*Greater immobilize*," Livia said through gritted teeth. "It doesn't have enough mind to fight me, but this spell isn't meant to contain a formless, so we only have a minute to figure out what to do with it."

"I don't think we can get it back into the bottle," Aderyn said. "It already looks too big to have fit there in the first place."

"We need fire," Owen said.

"Sorry," Livia ground out.

"That wasn't a criticism." Owen pulled out his <**Matchlighter**> and circled the bilious ooze. He flicked the starter and then bent to apply the flame to the edge of the quivering mass. Aderyn expected an animal squeal of pain, but the flame merely flickered along the edge of the creature and then went out.

"I didn't expect that to work," Owen said, "but I'm still disappointed."

"Think faster," Livia said. "I can't hold it much longer."

"We could run, but that just makes it someone else's problem," Aderyn said.

"Try this," Isold said. He held one of the sheets of strange paper they'd taken from the welcome room. With his other hand, he applied his own <**Matchlighter**> flame to the edge. The fire caught and burned brightly without consuming the paper. Isold gingerly extended the burning page to touch the wound Owen had inflicted. This time, the fire caught and spread across the bilious ooze's body.

"Quick, hand them out," Owen said. Isold passed pages around that the others lit rapidly. Aderyn caught sight of Livia's exertion-reddened face before she wedged her burning sheet of paper between the formless and the floor. The papers continued to burn slowly but strongly, and to the stench of the bilious ooze's innards was joined the sooty smell of burning paper smeared with fat.

With a gasp, Livia sagged, and the tentacles disintegrated. The bilious ooze started moving again, but erratically. Parts of its shapeless body folded to try to encase and extinguish the flames, but the movement only made the fires burn hotter and spread faster.

Weston took Livia by the shoulders and steered her back, and Aderyn and Isold joined them. Owen stood near the bilious ooze, his sword at the ready. No one spoke. The combined smells were almost unbearable now, and Aderyn covered her nose and mouth in a futile attempt to block the stench. Maybe the system was right, and a flamethrower was what they needed, but Aderyn doubted that would have improved the stink.

After more than a minute, the bilious ooze stopped moving, but Aderyn didn't relax until the system defeat notice appeared.

Congratulations! You have defeated [Bilious Ooze]. You have earned [500 XP]

"That could have gone a lot worse," Owen said. He made as if to wipe his blade on his shirttail, but changed his mind when he saw the disgusting greenish-brown goo coating his sword.

Livia waved at him to hold the sword away from his body and

then summoned a gout of freezing water to wash the <**Twinsword**> clean. "I hope there aren't a lot of those in this place. I specialized in stopping fires, not starting them."

"We did just fine," Weston assured her. "Though I don't know if we'll eventually regret burning those pages."

"They were a whim, and unlikely to be more useful to us than they were just now." Isold tucked the two unburnt pages into his knapsack. "I suggest we leave this room immediately, before my sense of smell is entirely destroyed."

CHAPTER EIGHT

The second door exiting **[Laboratory A12]** wasn't locked —worse, the lock had been torn free from the door. They all hurried into the hallway, and Weston swiftly slid the door shut so no trace of the reeking miasma could follow them.

No lights came on when they entered, so Livia made a handful of *orbs of light* and tossed them into the air. They illuminated the same kind of hallway they'd seen everywhere else: metal walls curving to a high, arched ceiling, metal floor embossed with a rough crosshatch pattern. Owen drew in a deep breath of clean air. "So, we know something got in and wrecked that room, and then couldn't bypass the other lock. We need to be careful going forward. There's no way to know how long ago that happened."

Aderyn pointed. "Doesn't that look like an opening up there? There's a patch of wall that isn't as dark."

Livia gestured, and two lights sailed down the hall. "They can't go too far from me or they go out."

"Then let's follow them," Owen suggested.

They hadn't gone far when Livia said, "You were right, there's an opening at the end of the hall." In the distance, the little lights hovered, illuminating an arched opening onto darkness.

"If there's anything in there, it's either blind or not interested in attacking," Livia went on. "But we should be cautious. It's not just the broken lock and wrecked room. I don't like that there's no door."

"Form up, then," Owen said. "Weston, take the lead. Isold and Livia behind. Aderyn and I will watch the rear."

They shuffled around into new positions and then walked, slowly so Weston could keep an eye out for traps, toward the opening. Aderyn tried Assessing the hall, but nothing happened. It was almost a relief to find [Improved Assess 3] had limitations. All these new abilities unnerved her as much as excited her.

Weston stopped at the entrance. "Lights, please?"

More lights sailed past him through the arched opening. Weston still didn't move, but he craned his neck to look upwards. "It's a shaft, I think. The ceiling rises well above what I can see, and it feels open. There's a draft, too."

"It might open to the outdoors, then," Isold said. "Do you see any creatures?"

"None."

"Spread out, and let's examine it," Owen said.

Aderyn's first instinct was that this almost couldn't be called a room. It was circular, a good hundred feet across, and Weston was right, the walls extended up farther than the limits of their lights. As they entered, tiny blue-tinged lights not strong enough to illuminate anything gleamed along the walls, making strange constellations in the darkness above their heads.

Her Assessment produced the description tag [Shaft No. 2] and nothing else. Reassured that it wasn't a trap, she circled the room, occasionally touching the walls and feeling nothing but cool metal. Her feet made soft metallic echoes against the flooring, which was made of steel like the floor of the hallway, but was smooth underfoot. She stopped to examine a place where one of the panels was loose.

Each panel was fastened to the ground by fat nails driven through holes at the corners, but this one was missing a nail and the corner lifted up slightly. She pulled up on it and discovered concrete slabs beneath. No wonder this place had held together so well.

"There are levers here," Isold said. He was standing next to a panel on the wall that had several rods sticking out of it. "And instructions."

The others hurried to his side. "Instructions for what?" Owen asked.

"For moving between levels of this dungeon." Isold trailed a finger along rows of text engraved on a brass plaque like the one on the decontamination chamber. "The center of this room is a device for lifting or lowering cargo or people. I gather the Spellcrafted device generates a levitation field that can be altered by the configuration of these levers, and this button here gives it the command to operate."

"So we just found our way up," Weston said.

"If we can make it work," Livia said. She looked very pale. "I'd rather climb the sides of the room into who knows what kind of danger than have to levitate up."

"Let's see if it's still operational before we freak out, all right?" Owen said, gripping Livia's shoulder in reassurance. "Does somebody have something they don't care about destroying? We can try levitating that first."

A quick search produced half a loaf of nearly-fresh bread. Aderyn walked toward the center of the room and stopped before she was halfway there. "The flooring changes. There's a big circle of that same weird rubbery stuff, only light gray instead of white. I think it's the outer dimensions of the levitation field."

"Try setting the bread just inside the circle," Isold suggested. "That should prove if you're correct."

Aderyn put the loaf down and hurried away, though she knew the circle wouldn't spontaneously activate and toss her screaming toward the still-unseen ceiling. When she returned to the others,

Isold and Owen were speaking in low voices and gingerly shifting one of the levers. Weston had his arms around Livia, and they both stared at the loaf.

"Let's try that," Owen said, stepping away from the levers.

Isold pushed the button. A high-pitched squeal, too high to be human, filled the air, making each of them clap hands over their ears. After a few seconds, the noise ceased, though Aderyn still felt the pressure of it on her eardrums, like a phantom echo.

"Well, that didn't work," Livia said. The bread still sat where Aderyn had left it.

"Yes, but we don't know if it was our maneuvering the lever that did it, or that the field is broken." Owen eyed the row of levers again. "We could be here for a while."

"Let's not give up," Aderyn said. "What if this is the only way into the upper levels?"

"I hate to say it, but she's right," Livia said. "But I haven't given up hope that there are stairs. Those Spellcrafters thought in practical terms, and I can't believe they depended solely on a device that might break down and trap them up higher. I'll keep looking while you all figure the device out."

"I'll join you," Aderyn said.

They continued to circle the room—the shaft, Aderyn reminded herself, because that meant it was probably accessible from every level and was therefore an important landmark. Sheets of metal covered the walls, fastened in place the way the floor panels were, but much, much bigger, at least ten feet wide, Aderyn judged.

"Wait," she said. "I think this is a door. It looks like it slides into the wall." She traced the faint outline of a door, barely visible. "And this little sheet of metal moves to reveal the keyhole."

Livia opened her mouth, then shut it again. "Let's not go haring off after the first thing we find. We've still got a third of the wall to examine."

"You're so sensible." Aderyn continued to walk, though she

couldn't help casting a glance back at the mystery door. "Do you think there are more like that? I admit I wasn't looking for anything like it before."

"I was thinking more about some kind of hatch," Livia said, "something small to access the levitation device."

"I thought the levitation device was those levers."

"No. If the field is as big as that circle, the device is enormous." Livia let out a snort of derision. "Listen to me. Who knows what those Spellcrafters were capable of? It might be as tiny as that panel of levers. I'm just hoping to find something that will mean I don't have to leave the ground."

"Don't you think it's funny that we're opposites in that way? I mean, you love being encased in earth, and to me that sounds like a nightmare."

"It is a strange coincidence." Livia's steps slowed. "There's something there. It might be another door." She gestured, and half a dozen lights flew toward the dark patch in the wall. Aderyn and Livia followed them.

It wasn't a door. It was a hole in the wall. Something had peeled back two sheets of steel from where they had once joined, making the four-foot-tall irregular hole visible. Livia put a hand against the exposed earth, above the hole, and said, "I don't feel movement. But there's no way to tell how recently anything has used it." She crouched and peered inside. "It's a tunnel, not a straight one."

"Don't you dare go in there," Aderyn said. The idea set her heart racing with fear as if she was the one asked to enter.

"I'm not stupid, Aderyn. Besides, there's no point me *burrowing* through there if we can't get everyone in." Livia dusted off her hand and called out, "Can you men come over here and take a look at this?"

When they were all gathered around, Weston said, "I guess we know how whatever destroyed [Laboratory A12] got in."

"We assume," Livia said.

"It's a safe assumption. There are no other doors out of here—"

"Actually, we did find another door," Aderyn said. "But it was hard to see, and I think you're right that if it was undisturbed, no one's used it for a long time, certainly not anything that would rip through that laboratory."

"Exactly." Weston scratched his head in thought. "You know what worries me?"

"That whatever tunneled into this compound could bend steel?" Owen said.

"Yes. That is precisely the worry at the top of my list. However, the creature obviously isn't still here, so I choose to believe it crawled in, wrecked the laboratory, couldn't find a way forward, and crawled back out." Weston felt along the edge of the hole. "This isn't fresh digging. Too compacted."

"Then we have nothing to worry about," Isold said. "Except the fact that we can't make the levitation field work. But even that is not a disaster. We've barely explored a fraction of this dungeon."

"Yeah, it's too soon to fall into despair." Owen took a step back. "Where's the other door?"

Aderyn showed Weston the door and the keyhole while the others finished searching the walls. Weston looked grim when he saw the lock. "I don't know. Like I said before, I feel like I'm going about this the wrong way. Using brute force. But I don't know how else to unlock these doors."

"Can you tell what the original keys did?"

"Only from speculation. My instinct is that it has something to do with communication. Like the lock wants a... a code word, or passphrase, that the key whispers to it. But there's no way—" He stopped and put a hand over his mouth, thinking. "I have an idea," he said, and pulled off his knapsack to root around inside.

"A way to talk to the lock?" Aderyn asked.

"Sort of. I'm going to try disabling it as if it was a trap rather than picking it like a lock." Weston withdrew a coil of uncut candlewick and a couple of brass objects Aderyn didn't recognize. "It might not work, but no sense not trying."

"Will I disturb you?"

"No, working through distractions is part of the skill set, and you're hardly a distraction. Though I suppose you could Assess the lock, just in case."

Aderyn focused on the lock as Weston began assembling something from his items. The lock flashed with pale blue light, but she saw nothing more. "It's not a trap, at least. I mean, not that your approach is wrong, just that it won't bite your fingers or blow up if you mess with it. But it's more than just a lock. I'm sorry, I can't see more than that."

"That's fine. Reassuring, even." Weston pressed the brass object against the door next to the lock. It was shaped like a flat cup, and Weston had tied something that looked like a long-billed brass bird to its upper curve with the candlewick. He threaded the loose end of the candlewick into the keyhole. He flicked the cup with his fingernail, causing it to ring with a high note just at the edge of Aderyn's hearing. Weston shifted the bird's long, skinny beak a fraction of an inch to the left and flicked the cup again. Now the note was a little lower in pitch. Aderyn breathed as quietly as she could, hoping Weston was right and she wouldn't interfere with his work.

After half a dozen repetitions of moving the bird and flicking the cup, Weston's face lit with a smile. Without adjusting the bird again, he slid the cup over the lock and felt around in his knapsack, coming up with a metal fork. He struck the cup hard with the fork. This time, the note echoed off the walls, a loud, clear tone that made Aderyn shiver.

With a quiet click, the door slid sideways.

To Aderyn's surprise, a system message appeared.

You have received an [Ingenuity] bonus of [3000 XP] for

solving [Element 16] of the Lonely Tor mysteries. Experience bonuses increase with each element solved.

"A secret bonus!" Aderyn hugged Weston. "That was amazing!"

"It's still not the same as what an actual key does," Weston said with a grin, "but it's not like I'm beating at the lock with a lump of metal and an iron spike anymore. And it will be faster even if the tone to open each door is different. But the system approves, so I'll take it as a win."

"Did you find anything else?" Aderyn shouted at Owen. "Weston got the door open."

Owen jogged across the chamber to join her, followed more slowly by Livia and Isold. "What was that about an Ingenuity bonus?"

Aderyn shrugged. "It means there's more to this dungeon than just defeating it. Isn't that exciting?"

"More like worrying," Livia said. "What if we don't find all these elements?"

"The dungeon Assessment didn't say anything about them, which means they're optional. Like a secret quest. It's nothing to fear." Aderyn didn't know why she felt so confident in saying this, but in her heart, she knew she was right.

"Then let's keep it in mind, and move forward," Owen said. "We already wanted to learn as much about the Enchanterium as we could, and this just means we could gain experience for doing that. Weston, what's behind that door?"

"Another hall, and it's lit up." Weston stepped through the door. "Let's see where it goes."

CHAPTER NINE

The new hall went only a short distance before turning right. Aderyn noticed the difference right away. "Look at the floor. It's black, and it feels springy."

"And it's made us all as silent as Weston," Isold said. "Curious."

"Wonder what the Spellcrafters wanted silence for." Owen bounced gently on his toes a few times. "Is there such a thing as a silence spell?"

"There is, but it only lasts a few minutes," Livia answered. "Though I think there are ways to extend the curation of a spell if you're a high enough level. Maybe even make it permanent. But nobody did that here, so either they weren't all that concerned about noise, or their system has broken down. Either way, it doesn't matter to us."

They walked a short distance to where the hall ended at another of the wood-appearing metal doors. "It's not locked," Weston said. "I wish I understood their logic."

"Maybe solving that is another one of the mysteries that will earn us experience," Aderyn said. "Though I don't know how we'd figure it out."

Weston opened the door a crack, then slid it open wider. "Look at that," he said. "It's a library."

They all crowded in quickly, staring in astonishment. Unlike the rather austere laboratories and the odd, alien furnishings of the waiting room, the library's warm lighting and soft, undamaged purple and gold carpet welcomed them in. Even the air smelled of dry paper and leather and a pleasantly nose-tickling cedar scent. It was a room that embraced tired visitors and encouraged them to stay a while.

Aderyn knew about libraries. Her parents had a small one in their home in Far Haven. She'd seen bigger ones on their travels. But this room was immense, filled with bookcases of oak and cedar lining the walls and freestanding bookcases making aisles for readers. Every bookcase Aderyn could see from the entrance was jammed full of books, with more books piled atop those.

"This place could be worth a fortune," Isold breathed. He pulled a book from a nearby shelf at random and flipped it open, skimming the pages. "Well, worth a fortune to a Spellcrafter. This appears to be a rather technical tome about Spellcrafting theory. I'm sure their library was collected with an eye to their specific needs."

Aderyn, who'd started to feel excited about the possibility of finding lost stories, said, "What about magic books? Or scrolls?"

"I don't see any magic on the shelves," Livia said. "But let's explore. This room is huge."

They spread out, surveying the shelves and checking the walls for secret doors on Owen's suggestion. "There's this great tradition of hiding doors behind bookcases in my world," he said. Nothing magic appeared, no secret doors. The books were in excellent condition, though Isold was right and their contents were boring. Aderyn reminded herself that a modern Spellcrafter would be ecstatic over them. Since she and her friends didn't have any idea which of these books were most valuable in those terms, though, hauling them back to civilization was pointless.

They made their way through the room to an open doorway leading to another room they examined without entering. This one had only a few short bookcases, with most of the space being given over to tables and chairs. Isold stepped inside and immediately recoiled. "Another minion," he said, his voice high-pitched and startled. "But I believe it's inert."

The others followed him. There were actually two minions, one to either side of the doorway. Both had the same detailed bronze construction as the hospitality minion, down to the sculpted clothing, but these appeared female. Their faces were smooth and beautiful, a triumph of the sculptor's art, and their eyes were closed as the hospitality minion's had been.

Owen waved a hand in front of one of the elegant faces and got no response. "Librarians, maybe?"

Aderyn Assessed them, as curious about whether [Improved Assess 3] worked on inactive Forged at all as to learn more about these. She was only moderately surprised when she saw silver letters flash into existence before her eyes.

Name: Minion, Research [2]
Type: Forged
Power Level: 5
Attacks: none
Immune to: mind control
Resistant to: weapons damage, precision damage
Vulnerable to: elemental electricity damage
You already know the minions' limitations. Research minions were created solely to help in searching for information, which is why they won't attack if aggressed on. These had the entire catalog of the library in their knowledge reserves, so it's unfortunate they're inoperative.

"That is unfortunate," Isold said when she relayed these facts to her team. "They could have identified which books would be useful to modern Spellcrafters."

"The **<Knapsack of Plenty>** has a limit to its capacity," Livia said, "and I'd rather not fill it with books. Not when there are other magic items we could take." She pointed at the short bookcases, none of them taller than waist high. Miscellaneous objects filled the shelves. "Those are all magic."

Isold knelt in front of the nearest bookcase. "Interesting. None of these are part of my Herald's knowledge, and **[Identify Magic Items]** gives information on only one—or, rather, one type, because there are many of them." He picked up a pair of brass-framed spectacles with very thick lenses that distorted the appearance of his fingers when they passed behind them. "I don't know its name, but these are designed to help find a particular book. I think they had a connection to the research minions, back when they worked. There are at least three dozen of them."

"Find a book in this library, or in any library?" Owen asked.

"I have no idea. I suspect just this one, if they work the way I believe. Letting them be attuned to all libraries would confuse the magic." Isold put the spectacles in his knapsack. "I'll take one of these to a Spellcrafter when we're finished here and see what they can make of it."

Aderyn picked up a brass cylinder with four sliding switches circling one end that tapered at the other. The cylinder was about the diameter of a silver coin and a little longer than her hand. "This looks like a fat pen, except there's no nib."

"Try sliding one of those switches," Owen said. "My world has pens that work like that."

Aderyn awkwardly moved the black switch with her fingernail. A small silver nib slid out of the tapered end. "Amazing," Aderyn said, holding the pen close to her eyes. "It's got ink already on it. I guess it's a fountain pen—you know, the kind you can fill with ink, not a dip pen?"

"With four nibs," Isold said. "Four magic effects?"

"Or just four colors of ink," Weston said. He pulled out his diary and tore a blank page from the back. "Go ahead and try it."

Aderyn made a loose scribble to test the ink flow. The pen moved smoothly, without catching on the slightly rough surface of the paper at all. When she set the pen to the paper again, she let out a surprised squeak. "Look at that!"

They all examined the paper. "It's a couple of scribbles," Owen said.

"Yes, but I meant to write my name next. And *look*. The scribbles are identical!"

"So, it makes a copy of whatever you wrote first," Isold said. "That's incredible." He held out his hand. "May I try?"

Aderyn handed the pen over. Isold moved the white switch, which disengaged the black one before locking into place. He wrote a few lines. "This switch doesn't seem to do anything. Possibly they wanted an ordinary pen option."

"We need to take these," Aderyn said. "How many are there?"

"I didn't count," Livia said, "but only two of them still have magic on them. We'll take those."

Aderyn took one and Isold took the other. "What else?" Isold said. He wore the stunned look of someone who'd fallen down a hole onto a pile of gold.

"These goggles," Livia said. There were three sets of them, with soft leather cups holding brass-rimmed lenses. Instead of a single lens, each eyepiece had a stack of lenses of decreasing size, like a round pyramid. Isold prodded one stack, and a lens rotated out and away from the others. Isold kept pressing until the lenses looked like a dandelion puff, each pointing in a different direction.

"I have no guesses," he said. "Are they all magical?"

"The magic aura is faint, but it's there." Livia picked up another of the mysterious goggles and held the device up to her eyes without putting it on. "I can't see anything. Meaning it's black."

"Worth taking," Owen said.

"Isn't anyone going to ask the obvious question?" Weston said. "Why was all this left behind?"

"Aside from how difficult it is to crate and move tens of thousands of books, as I estimate this library contains?" Isold said. "We know the Enchanterium was abandoned when there were no longer high-level Spellcrafters to use it. That suggests that their knowledge was useless to those who came later. Why not leave the unusable library here?"

"And maybe they thought of it as a memorial to what they'd lost," Aderyn suggested. On a whim, she Assessed the room. Only the description tag [Scriptorium] appeared, but it was tinged with the same pale blue that had hovered over the lock Weston had successfully picked. "I think this room, maybe this and the library both, are one of those Lonely Tor mysteries."

"Which could take forever to figure out," Owen said. "Let's explore some more, and keep this room in mind for a safe place to rest if we need one."

There was a second door in the library that was also unlocked. It opened on a hall extending left and right. Owen pretended to flip a coin. "Right."

"You always sound so decisive," Aderyn teased.

"It's part of my leadership strategy. Confidence in the face of uncertainty." Owen grinned. "Plus I can see light ahead to the right, and I'm curious."

They slowed their steps as they approached the light, which came from beyond a door that was open a crack. "Weird," Owen said. "We need to be cautious. That might mean someone else is here."

But the room beyond, tagged [Laboratory A02], was as empty as [Laboratory A11]. Nothing indicated that anyone else had been there in the past several centuries. Another door led to [Laboratory A01], also empty.

"This door is locked," Weston said, pointing at a third door in [Laboratory A02]. "Let's see where it goes before we continue. I tell you, leaving unexplored territory at our backs makes me feel like someone's holding a knife to the base of my neck."

"Do you have a map of where we've been, Isold?" Owen asked.

"I do." Isold's eyes briefly unfocused. "It fills in almost reluctantly, and gives me no hint as to what lies in the unmapped sections. But it is complete as far as our explored territory goes."

"I wish we could see it, too," Aderyn said. "I'm all turned around, and even having the compass and knowing which way north is doesn't help much, not with how these corridors turn."

A click, a clunk of moving metal, and a quiet beep preceded Weston saying, "That's it. I don't know why it beeped. I don't like it."

"You're not normally the pessimistic one, dearest," Livia said.

"That's not pessimism, it's good old fashioned paranoia." Weston stood with his hands on his hips examining the unlocked door. "I think something important is inside. Which could mean treasure. How's that for optimism?"

"Nice," Owen said. "Let's see if your treasure has a guardian."

Weston opened the door. The moment he stepped inside, lights went on, not all at once but in sections spreading out and up from the door. Not everything lit up, giving the vast room a patchwork appearance of light and dark. Aderyn stood beside Weston and Assessed the room. She saw only the tag [**Central Control 1**]. "No monsters, and no traps—at least, not any room-sized ones."

"Are you sure about no monsters?" Owen said, pointing.

The floor was covered with the same metal cross-hatched panels as the halls, but not smoothly. Panels over most of the circular floor were dislodged, lying at angles across one another, and broken pieces of concrete jutted between the panels. Walking across them would be slow and difficult. Aderyn took one step toward the mess and stopped, feeling uncertain. "It looks like something came up from beneath and took the panels and under-floor with it, except there's no hole."

"Central control, though," Owen said. "That sounds important. There might be an override for the levitation shaft in here. Look, there are instrument panels all around."

"I see no instruments, Owen," Isold said.

"Not musical instruments, more like controls for devices." Owen began circling the room, staying off the destroyed floor.

Aderyn followed him, but stopped when Livia said, "Wait." Her voice sounded strained. Aderyn looked back. Livia crouched with her hand flat on the floor, eyes closed. She seemed to be listening.

Weston abruptly said, "I hear something. Like a cart rumbling over a rough road."

"Something's coming. And it's *big*." Livia's whole body was tense.

Now Aderyn heard it, too—a rumbling noise, so deep and quiet that she heard it more with her bones than her ears. She hesitated, unsure which way to go: return to the door, or follow Owen, who'd crossed most of the room between their entrance and another door.

Livia shot to her feet. "*Run!*"

With a titanic roar, something huge and purply-black erupted from the center of the room, scattering metal panels and concrete chunks in every direction. Aderyn barely heard an *oof* of breath from Isold as a head-sized hunk of concrete caught him a glancing blow across the chest and knocked him back a few steps. The thing rose higher and higher, its segmented body seeming endless. Its round mouth opened, showing jaws like rows of serrated knives and a thick, saliva-coated tongue. It roared again, and lunged.

CHAPTER TEN

Aderyn threw herself backward to press against one of the instrument panels, whose tiny levers caught at her ponytail and sent twinges of barely-noticed pain through her scalp. Ignoring the part of her that wanted to scream and run away, she Assessed the creature.

Name: Deep Delver [1]
Type: Abomination
Power Level: 18
Attack(s): slam, special
Immune to: mind control, *blindness*
Resistant to: weapons damage, elemental earth damage
Vulnerable to: elemental fire damage, elemental ice damage, *sunburst*
Special attacks: swallow whole, slime vomit

Deep delvers burrow through earth and stone in search of their next meal, which fortunately for lesser creatures doesn't have to happen often. This colossal monster can see in the dark and avoids the sun and open ground. It tracks its prey through its ability to sense even tiny vibrations in the earth. Its stomach acid is particularly potent, and being swallowed by a deep delver is generally a death sentence.

Speaking of its stomach acid, a deep delver can vomit the slimy contents of its belly, causing damage as well as making it difficult to move and impossible to run. That means it's a good idea to run now.

The lines of [Discern Weakness] slid over the purplish hide. Rather than coalescing into points of blue light, a sheen of blue tinged with red covered the deep delver's body from the base of its jaw down to where it emerged, and kept emerging, from the ground. Aderyn observed this in horror. Then she shouted, "We have to run! It's got the high ground and we're not prepared!" She was painfully aware they were lined up between the two doors like beads on a string, out in the open and vulnerable.

"Back this way!" Weston yelled.

Aderyn ran. She stayed close to the wall, well away from the broken ground and the hideous monster. Owen came up fast behind her and then passed her. Her calves immediately felt the strain of [Keep Pace] taking effect.

The ghostly image of the deep delver striking gave her enough warning to grab Owen and pull him back just before the vast bony maw slammed into the wall right where he'd been, blocking their way to the others and the exit. Owen took hold of Aderyn's arm and towed her backwards. The deep delver shook itself as if the impact had dazed it, but Aderyn's hope that they were safe died when it immediately turned on them.

She heard the others shouting. "Get out!" she yelled, [Amplify Voice] making her words echo off the walls and ceiling.

"We can't leave you!" Isold shouted.

The deep delver struck again, hitting the floor hard enough it buckled and threw Aderyn off balance. Owen's grip on her arm let her scramble to her feet. "Go to the library! We'll find you!"

"If the door's locked—" Weston called out.

"Just *go!*"

Owen stopped, and Aderyn fell against him and again had to catch herself. "The door's locked," Owen said, his voice tense but even.

"Shit," Aderyn said. The deep delver had stopped lunging and instead reared up, high above them. Its terrible toothed jaws worked like it meant to cough something up. "Owen, we have to run. We can circle the chamber—"

"It will get us before we reach the unlocked door." Owen was slapping the door all along its frame. "Come on, damn it, this room of all places has to have one."

"What are you—Owen!" Aderyn shrieked as the deep delver's body convulsed. She cringed away as if that would protect her from the monster's slime vomit.

Owen's hand came down on a part of the panel that depressed. The door slid open. "Door override," Owen said, and dragged Aderyn through the opening.

The two of them slid the door shut just as the monster's slime struck it. Splashes of pale purple ooze made it through the opening before it shut. One of them landed on Owen's hardened leather brigandine and immediately began to smoke and sizzle.

"Get it off!" Aderyn said. "It's spreading!"

They tackled the buckles and straps and swiftly removed the armor. Owen scrubbed it across the floor, scraping off most of the slime, but it was too late. The brigandine now had a fist-sized cavity over the right breast going almost all the way through the leather. The remaining traces of slime continued to widen the hole. Owen dropped his now-useless armor and drew in a deep breath. "That could have been us."

"I hope the others got out," Aderyn said. "They wouldn't have tried attacking it on their own, right?"

"They're too smart for that." Owen took Aderyn in his arms and held her close. His heart was beating rapidly in time with hers. She hugged him and closed her eyes, but the image of the deep delver rearing over her filled her vision.

"How did you know about the door override?" she asked.

"I didn't. It just suddenly came to me why almost all the doors are locked. Remember what the hospitality minion said about whether we were expected? In my world, there are doors that require authorization to open. Usually a badge or card or something. Without the badge, you have to hack the door lock, like what Weston was doing, but with the badge the door opens automatically. I think that's why the keys are strange, according to Weston—they're not keys, they're badges."

"But you didn't have a badge."

"No, but sometimes there are systems in place to keep people from being locked in. Overrides. They're on the inside, not the outside, and it didn't occur to me to look for them before even though the sliding doors should have given me a clue. I took a chance." He hugged her more tightly. "I'm so glad I was right."

They stood like that without speaking for a while. "Now what?" Aderyn said when they were both a little calmer. "We have to find our way back to the library. But I have no idea where we are. [**Basic Map Access**] only maps terrain, not dungeons."

"Let's see your compass." Owen took the compass from Aderyn and oriented it. "We entered on the north side, or at least mostly north, and the hall beyond the entrance took us east. We kept going roughly east until we got to the shaft, and then we turned south and west. We're now west of the central chamber." He handed the compass back. "That means we need to go east if we want to find the library."

"Those hallways turn so much we can't just walk east," Aderyn pointed out. "It's going to take careful navigation." She squeezed her eyes shut. "Or the <**Wayfinder**>. I'm sure it will direct us to the others."

"We were both rattled not to think of that immediately," Owen said with a grin. "And no wonder. What *was* that thing?"

"A deep delver. Looked like a bigger, meaner, nastier version of a chaos worm." Aderyn dug the <Wayfinder> out of her <Purse of Great Capacity>. "Power level eighteen. Maybe we could have fought it, but it would have been a dangerous fight even if we'd been prepared."

"Let's just ignore it, then." Owen's eyes unfocused briefly. "It says [Laboratory A09]. Three possible exits, so I'm glad we have the <Wayfinder>. Not much else here. Just—" He froze. "Did you hear that? Something rattled."

"I did." Aderyn turned slowly. "It sounded like it was inside one of those cabinets."

Like the other laboratories, white cabinets lined the walls at ground level, with more of them hanging on the walls at head height. The rattling sounded again, louder, and this time Aderyn saw one of the lower cabinet doors shake as if something had struck it from inside. "I hope it's not another bilious ooze," she whispered.

Owen crept silently to the cabinet and gestured to Aderyn to take a position on the other side of its door. He put a hand on the latch and raised his other hand with three fingers spread. Aderyn waited with her sword drawn for him to count to zero, and when he flung the door open, she leaped forward, brandishing her weapon.

There was nothing there.

Aderyn lowered her sword and looked at Owen, who shrugged. He bent to look inside, and stiffened. "There's a hole. It looks like the one in the shaft. Take a look."

Aderyn stuck her head inside the cupboard. Just like before, the steel plating had been peeled back around a hole maybe a little smaller than the other one, dug up through the floor. "It looks like something burst through from beneath and tore the plating open when it bored through. That's unsettling." She leaned back and squatted in front of the open cabinet. "Though we knew things might be living in here."

"If nothing else, that deep delver needs something to snack on." Owen rose and shut the cabinet door and latched it. "I don't see what we can do about it. Something to worry about later. Let's get moving."

Aderyn cradled the <**Wayfinder**> in both hands and focused on her knowledge of her friends. The magic item began to glow a faint, warm pink.

A door opened, startling Aderyn out of her concentration. "How did you get—" she began, and stopped mid-sentence.

It wasn't Weston, Livia, and Isold. It was four total strangers.

CHAPTER ELEVEN

Aderyn swiftly dropped the <**Wayfinder**> into her purse. Owen moved to put himself in front of Aderyn and just to her left. "Who are you?"

"I think you ought to answer that question first," said the man in the lead. He looked like he was in his late twenties, older than Owen and Aderyn, with a blue knit cap pulled over his bald head and a full red beard and mustache as if to compensate. He held his oak staff at the ready to attack, but by the way he stood, the staff wasn't his only means of defense. Aderyn guessed he was a Swifthands, and a quick Level Assess of the group proved her right.

Name: Revelin
Class: Swifthands
Level: 13
Name: Cyanne
Class: Flamecrafter
Level: 12
Name: Embrus
Class: Pathseer
Level: 12

Name: Inaya
Class: Moonlighter
Level: 13

"I'm Owen, and this is Aderyn," Owen said curtly. "And we're higher level than you, so I don't see where you get off making demands."

Revelin lowered his staff, but didn't return it to a resting position. "Fair enough. I'm Revelin, and this is my team. Embrus, Cyanne, and Inaya."

Aderyn surveyed the other three. The tall brown-haired woman, Inaya, relaxed immediately, as did Embrus, both of them lowering their short swords. The Flamecrafter, Cyanne, didn't look happy, glaring at Aderyn as if Aderyn had done something to insult her, but she didn't look poised to attack, either.

"Can I ask what quest you're pursuing?" Owen asked. He'd sheathed his sword and looked relaxed, but **[Read Body Language]** told Aderyn he was still prepared to leap to the attack if this new team proved dangerous.

"Do you know about the dragon that lives on Lonely Tor?" Revelin said. "We're here to defeat it so it will stop harassing and burning the nearby settlements. What about you?"

Owen twitched in the way Aderyn recognized meant he was about to lie. "Exploring the dungeon. We saw the dragon, but we didn't know it was attacking people."

"It's a dragon," Cyanne said. "Of course it's attacking people." She sounded so disdainful it set Aderyn's back up. She'd been prepared to treat the new team as potentially amiable, if not friendly, but Cyanne's dismissive attitude irritated her.

Owen's body language said he felt the same, but he only said, "We considered the dragon a major challenge."

"Meaning we're not strong enough to take it on?" Cyanne shot back.

Revelin raised a hand to silence her. "I'm sure that's not what he meant. As it happens, one of the villages asked us to take on the dragon, and we consider it our duty to help others. We're not concerned about glory or treasure, just doing the right thing."

Aderyn held back a laugh and made it sound like a cough—successfully, because no one took it as an insult. "Is that your goal? Helping others?" she asked.

"Of course." Revelin looked her over as if searching for hidden flaws. "I'm sure that seems strange to you."

"We've done our share of humanitarian quests," Owen said. "It's not like we're heartless bastards. And usually we take on quests that are level appropriate. You must have had strong feelings about this one to tackle it at your level."

"You're not much higher level than us," Embrus said abruptly. His voice was a light tenor nearly as beautiful as Isold's. "And there's only two of you. How is this dungeon any less dangerous to you?"

"We were separated from the rest of our team," Owen said. "In fact, you should avoid that door and steer clear of everything around it. There's a power level eighteen monster inside. It's what split our team. We're on our way to join them."

"Is there," Cyanne said dismissively. "I suppose it's actually treasure you don't want us to have? We aren't motivated by money."

"Cyanne, enough," Revelin said. He sounded so much like Owen did when he was exercising leadership Aderyn found it eerie. "They have their own motives, true, but let's not ascribe evil where there isn't any."

"Thanks for that." Owen sounded sincere, something he was good at when dealing with hostile or antagonistic people. "It's true, we came at this in different ways, but I hope we can deal fairly with each other."

"Then you're not trying to kill the dragon?" Embrus's words echoed with disbelief, as if Owen had admitted to a crime.

"We haven't decided. As I said, we're here to explore. We

intended to Assess the dragon to see if it was something we could tackle." Owen didn't react to Embrus's near-accusation.

"We got here first," Cyanne said. "This is our quest."

"Oh, please, Cyanne, give it a rest," Inaya said, rolling her eyes. "It doesn't matter who kills the dragon so long as it stops attacking, right?"

"I hope we don't stumble over each other," Owen said. "If you get there first, you're welcome to try to kill it."

Aderyn started to protest, but a look from Owen shut her up. She still wanted to say something. They might need to kill the dragon to satisfy the Fated One quest, and what if these others got there first?

"'Try'?" Revelin smiled. "We're more experienced than our team level implies. We'll be fine."

That sparked interest in Aderyn. She quickly did a Skill Assess on Revelin, scanning his skills and ranks, and saw nothing unusual except the skill **[Heron Style]**. That was probably a Swifthands specialty, but Revelin had started talking again and she didn't have time to Assess the skill to learn more about it.

"At any rate, good luck finding your team," he was saying. "Do you need help? We have a **<Traveler's Aid>** that's guided us so far." He indicated Embrus, who held up a faceted peridot stone in a silver bezel, hanging from a silver chain.

"How does it work?" Aderyn asked, intrigued.

"Whenever we reach an intersection, it pulls us in the right path to our destination," Embrus said. He flicked it with his fingernail, making it twirl.

"I see," Aderyn said. "No, we—"

"We just have to backtrack," Owen overrode her. "That way. I take it you haven't found a way up? How did you get in here, if I can ask?"

"There's a tunnel to the northeast that leads from a hidden

entrance to a big round room with a high ceiling," Revelin said. "We've been searching for stairs, but so far we've found nothing."

"Neither have we," Owen said. "Well, good luck. Maybe we'll see you around." He turned on his heel and approached the door behind them. Aderyn followed him, hoping his dramatic exit wouldn't be spoiled by a door that refused to open. But Owen patted the wall up and down for a second or two and eventually pushed on a spot that looked no different from everywhere else. The door slid open.

"Wait!" Inaya said. "Wait. How did you do that?"

Owen exchanged glances with Aderyn, hesitated a moment, then said, "There are override switches on some of the doors. They open them from the inside only. I take it you've been brute-forcing the locks?"

"I couldn't figure out what else to do." Inaya moved as lightly as Weston, almost bouncing as she hurried to Owen's side. "Will you show me? Please? I promise not to use it against you." She smiled, a cheerful expression that showed off two dimples.

"Well, yes, I probably should." Owen demonstrated, and the door slid shut again. "Like I said, if there is one, it's only useful if you're on the inside of the room. Keeps people from being locked in."

"That is *amazing!* Isn't it amazing? Wow. I could kiss you, but I'm sure your wife wouldn't approve." She smiled so impishly Aderyn didn't take offense. It would be like hating an inquisitive kitten.

"Um, well, you're welcome, and I hope that information is helpful." Owen reddened slightly.

"Thanks for the help," Revelin said, sounding sincere for the first time. "And good luck to you both." He moved to the final unopened door, the one opposite the central control chamber, but had to step back to give Inaya room to open it. Owen and Aderyn waited for all four to exit before leaving **[Laboratory A09]** themselves.

The door led to another empty laboratory. Aderyn let the door shut behind her before leaning against it and saying, "Now what? If they get to the dragon first, and it turns out to be what we need to kill to complete the [**Fire and Ash**] quest—"

"I couldn't think of anything to stop them," Owen said. "If they're the kind of lawful good stick-up-their-ass adventurers they seem to be, they won't care that I'm the Fated One. They might even think they ought to do something to stop us achieving the quest, since Fated Ones are well known to be self-centered and arrogant."

"They aren't any better or more generous than we are, Owen."

"No, but they certainly believe they are. I don't trust anyone that altruistic." Owen ran his hands through his hair in a frustrated gesture. "We have to hurry. If we can find our way to the top first, it won't matter what they do."

Aderyn retrieved the <**Wayfinder**> and held it in both hands. Instantly, the spike glowed a warm, rosy pink when she pointed it at the two other doors opposite the one they'd entered by. Both doors looked identical, and the glow didn't change when she shifted between them, so Owen opened the door on the left. His shoulders relaxed. "It's the sitting room, the one where we killed the hospitality minion. We really do just have to backtrack."

Aderyn Assessed the room, which revealed the description tag [**Lobby**], and then realized the <**Wayfinder**> had dimmed and cooled when her concentration lapsed. "I think we should go on using the <**Wayfinder**>, though. It might show us a shorter path."

"Good idea." Owen led the way through the lobby and found the override switch to make the door slide open easily. "I think it's unlocked now, but I kind of like using the button. It makes me feel like we're winning against the dungeon."

Aderyn stepped in front of him into the hallway and turned left, following her guide. "Don't you feel this place isn't antagonistic, though? I mean, after Sorrowvale, no dungeon acts like it wants us dead, but so far the only awful things have been monsters, not traps or puzzles. And the thing with Element 16 of the Lonely Tor mysteries was almost cheerful. As if the dungeon was hoping we'd discover it."

"I've been too busy worrying about finding a way to the next level to pay attention to that, but you're right." Owen opened the door to the room with the podium, which turned out to be [Meeting Room A]. The <Wayfinder> directed them to one of the unlocked doors they'd ignored the first time. This one led to a long hallway. "We're going south, toward central command," Owen said.

"I hope the <Wayfinder> is smart enough to steer us around the deep delver," Aderyn said.

"If not, we'll go back and see if it can light up a second path," Owen said. "It's like GPS that way, right?"

"I refuse to answer on the grounds that I have no idea what GPS is, and you know it," Aderyn said, pretending haughtiness.

"It's—well, look at that," Owen said, opening the door at the end of the hall. "It's [Laboratory A01]. The <Wayfinder> really did find us a shortcut."

"Oh, I hope so much they all did as I said!" Aderyn dropped her magic item into her purse and hurried after Owen.

They ran through [Laboratory A01], into the hall, and from there to the library door. It didn't open. Owen pounded on it. "Weston? Open up!"

A few seconds later, the door slid open, and Livia dove past Weston to hug Aderyn. "That would have been terrifying without the team roster showing you were unhurt. It was blasted scary even so. I can't believe you found us again!"

"I did say the <Wayfinder> would be effective," Isold said, clapping Owen on the back. "Even so, we didn't know it would find its way past other threats."

"That's what I said." Aderyn hugged Livia back and added, "It was a hidden blessing, though. We discovered we're not alone here. There's another team, trying to kill the dragon."

"That's not good," Weston said. "We have to stop them. We still don't know if the dragon is our goal."

"I know," Owen said, "but these people aren't evil, and we shouldn't kill them just because they might get in our way. Of course, if *they* attack *us*..."

"Which they might, because they think they're noble and virtuous and we're petty treasure-grubbing villains," Aderyn groused. "I didn't like how snooty that Cyanne was."

"Then it's even more urgent that we find a way up," Livia said. "I'm almost ready to tackle the levitation field."

"If there's a way to make it work, it's in the central chamber with the deep delver," Owen said, "so let's make that our last resort, okay? Time to search for stairs."

"Deep delver?" Weston said. "That sounds so harmless. It should be called something more accurate, like Jaws of Death or Putrid Slime Beast."

"I'm just as happy to avoid it," Aderyn said.

CHAPTER TWELVE

They made their way back along the path Aderyn and Owen had just taken. Despite the memory of the other team and her new feeling of urgency over the dragon, Aderyn's cheerful mood filled her with optimism. Maybe it was having avoided death by slime acid, maybe it was being reunited with her friends, but she felt like they could conquer anything.

When they reached **[Laboratory A09]**, Owen showed the others the hole behind the cabinet. Livia knelt before it and ran a hand over the exposed earth, then gingerly touched the steel sheets. "The edges aren't sharp. It looks like the plates buckled at the seams. I can't imagine what would do that, other than the deep delver, and it's way too big."

"That does make me curious about why the deep delver doesn't break out of the central control chamber," Weston said. "It was strong enough to tear up the floor and a sublayer of concrete."

"It wouldn't fit anywhere else," Aderyn said. "But, yes—why didn't it pursue us directly?"

"I could feel the walls and floor of that chamber are especially thick," Livia said. "No, it's more than that. They felt... I'm not sure how to describe it. Denser, maybe. Like the metal had been compacted. I wouldn't be able to *transport* past it."

"I thought *transport* could move through anything," Aderyn said.

"The range is determined by how many thicknesses you want to go past. I can teleport through half a mile of gauze, a hundred feet of wood planking, twenty feet of stone..." Livia's gaze turned pensive, calculating. "That stuff is the equivalent of a quarter-mile of solid mountain."

"That sounds a lot like radiation shielding," Owen said. "Though why that room would be a radiation hazard, I don't know. From what little I saw, that room was where the Spellcrafters managed the entire compound, so they'd spend a lot of time there. It wouldn't make sense for them to be exposed to radiation."

"I don't know what you mean by radiation, except it sounds like something other than the sun's rays or a *daylight* spell. Those radiate." Livia scooted back from the cabinet.

"Yeah, you guys don't have nuclear power in your world. Radiation is like tiny particles, too small to see, that come off certain substances, and too many of them hitting your body can make you sick or kill you, like being poisoned. But superdense materials can block the radiation, so people can use those substances for power. Like creating electricity, or bombs."

"Bombs?" Aderyn made a face. "I'd rather the electricity."

"Same," Owen said. He got a peculiar look on his face. "Unless it's the rest of the compound that's radioactive, and the shielding was to protect that room... in which case—" He stopped and shook his head. "No, that's ridiculous. I'm sure **[Improved Assess 3]** would have revealed a threat like that."

Aderyn had no idea what he meant, but it sounded like he'd changed his own mind through talking to himself. "Can we go on, then? Or are we in danger?"

"I'm babbling. Ignore me." Owen pursed his lips in thought.

"Okay, we have to make a choice. We can either go south, which is the door that other team came through, or we can go west, which is where they went after we talked. Ideas?"

"I say we follow them," Weston said. "Not *follow* them, but go in that direction. I'd like to meet them and get a sense of what to expect."

"I was going to say do the opposite, but Weston makes a good point," Livia said. "And I'm never going to use those words again."

"What, even if I'm right?"

"I don't want you to get a swelled head and go haring off after crazy notions." Livia pretended to scowl at him. "You'll drag us all along with you, and that's the sort of thing that leads to bloodshed."

"True, but it's not usually our blood that's shed, dearest."

"Let's stay on topic, all right?" Owen said with a grin. "The other objection to going south is that they'll have had the chance to clean everything out along that path. On the other hand, I am sort of curious about how they got here from [Shaft No. 2]. That's a long way in the other direction."

"But we've been to [Shaft No. 2], too, and we don't need to go back, we need to find new territory," Aderyn said. "I can't say I want to run into that team again, but I think Weston is right that the rest of you really should meet them. At the very least, it might intimidate them into taking us more seriously if they know we are powerful and outnumber them."

"If we are going to follow them, we should do it quickly," Isold said, "because we don't want them stripping the rest of the dungeon bare before we get a chance to."

"Then we're agreed," Owen said. "Weston?"

"Show me how the door override works," Weston said.

Weston was quicker to identify the right place to press than Owen had been. The door slid open on a dark hallway, one whose lights flickered wanly when Weston stepped through. They gave enough light to show the hallway was identical to the others. There was no sign of the other team.

"This reminds me of Sorrowvale," Weston said, leading the way. "Dark and foreboding, except it doesn't have that ominous presence hovering over us."

"Yeah, this is more SF horror than classic," Owen said. "Hope there aren't xenomorphs hiding in the ceiling."

"Stop doing that," Aderyn said. "I swear you get more pleasure out of saying things we don't understand than anyone should."

"It's because you're cute when you complain—ow! All right, I deserved that punch." Owen grinned at her. "Seriously, this does remind me of a movie, but I think we could take the monster. I do have this epic sword."

"The <**Twinsword**> worries me a bit," Aderyn said. "When you were fighting in the Glory Games, I know there were times you hesitated because you were used to getting my tactics through the link. That could be dangerous if I were ever unable to provide that."

"How likely is that going to be, though?" Owen glanced behind them as the door slid shut on its own.

"I think, if the [**Bonded Mind**] skill is available, it must be there for a reason. We ought to be thinking of what we'll do if we're separated. Like, suppose it had been you and Isold caught on the wrong side of the deep delver?"

"There's a door," Weston said. "Let's leave the theoretical discussion for later, in case those adventurers didn't get very far."

There was no override on this side, proving Owen's theory right about where the mechanisms were located. Weston got out the brass cup, then said, "Someone damaged this lock. It looks like they brute forced it open."

"I bet that was them. That Moonlighter, Inaya," Aderyn said. "Does that mean you can't open it?"

"It means it isn't locked, and it won't lock ever again." Weston's irritated frown deepened. "I hate seeing this compound damaged. It's an amazing construction, and people shouldn't go around breaking it only to get where they want to go."

"Let's see what's there," Owen said. "You can have words with Inaya if we meet her."

The door didn't move smoothly despite the broken lock—or maybe, Aderyn thought, because of it. Weston shoved it open with a series of jerking halts and starts, then stood in the doorway, his neck craned to look up. "Another shaft," he said. "The tag says **[Shaft No. 1]**."

"Any threats? Or people?" Owen asked.

"It's not well lit, but it seems empty. I don't hear anything." Weston stepped inside. Lights came on in the same patchwork pattern as in the central chamber, illuminating the room to a height of some fifteen feet, while tiny blue lights again made patterns in the darkness above.

Aderyn walked to where the circle of gray rubbery stuff lay. "I wonder why this room's lights came on when the other's didn't." Gingerly, she scuffed a toe over the line as if it was drawn in chalk and she could rub it out. Nothing happened. She stepped over the line, curious to see if it felt as spongy as it looked.

Some force grabbed her leg and hauled her off her feet. She shrieked as the force swung her upside down and dragged her rapidly upward. She screamed again, visions of being carried to the unseen top of the shaft and then falling from that height filling her imagination.

But after only a few seconds of acceleration, her ascent slowed, and soon she came to a halt and floated midair, roughly even with where the room's lighting ended. She struggled to right herself, moving her arms and legs like she was swimming, but there wasn't anything to push against except air, and after a while she gave up and hung there mostly head down, panting from exertion.

She now heard the shouts of her friends from below. "I'm not hurt," she called out, and waved both hands to prove she was still conscious. The others were grouped around the edge of the circle, and as she watched, Owen made a move as if to enter it.

"No, don't!" she shouted. "We don't need more of us stuck up here."

"We have to get you down," Owen said. "Livia?"

"I know." Livia took the solid stance that meant she was going to cast *telekinesis*.

"Wait, let me look around here first," Aderyn said. She flapped and kicked and managed to rotate to see the center of the field. From here, it was possible to see what had been invisible from the ground: chunks of metal, oddly-shaped tools, and a couple of desiccated rodent bodies, all floating at the same level she was.

"It looks like this is as far as the field goes, and it lost strength the higher I got. Like it couldn't push me higher than this." She worked her way back around. With her head lower than her body, she should have felt the pressure of blood rushing to her head, but instead she simply felt disoriented, like if she closed her eyes, she would have no idea which way was up.

She stretched out one leg, wondering what would happen if it left the field, though she still wasn't sure where it ended. As she did, her foot suddenly felt heavy, no longer supported. With a jerk, her whole body regained weight, and then she was falling.

She had time for one strangled scream before the invisible hands of *telekinesis* gripped her, dragging her away from the field's influence and slowing her fall. She spun gently so when she landed, she was on her feet. Immediately Owen was there, pulling her into his embrace. "That was stupid," he murmured.

"I know. I was careless. I'm sorry." She kissed him in reassurance. "I was lucky, too. I think the field has lost potency over the years."

"Still." He held her close for a few more moments, then sighed and released her. "Nobody touched anything, so either the field's been on for centuries, or that other team found the right switch."

"There are dead creatures up there, so I'm guessing it's the former. Mice or rats that ran into the field and got stuck." Aderyn grimaced. "At least now we know for sure how the Spellcrafters got from this level to the next."

"I intend to test these levers," Isold said. "If the shaft still contains some magical energy, it may be enough to help us, assuming we can figure out how to manipulate the field." He was examining a brass plate screwed into the wall next to the row of levers and a big blue button.

"Unfortunately, this doesn't provide any more information than the other shaft did," Weston said. "It's just those same instructions, plus a warning that users should be careful when exiting and entering the levitation device. Though the levers are in a different configuration here."

Isold maneuvered one of the levers halfway down its groove. "Nothing."

"Try pressing the button," Owen suggested.

Isold pressed the button. Aderyn peered up at the tiny floating objects, waiting for them to fall. Still nothing happened.

"Keep trying," Owen said. "The rest of us will search the room. There's got to be another door out of here. The other team clearly didn't figure out the device."

Aderyn circled the room, moving slowly now. She didn't want a repeat of the levitation incident, though that was unlikely. Still, there could be any number of other dangers. But the walls remained smooth and uninterrupted by doors, hatches, holes, clever poison needle traps... She shook her head to clear it of stupid notions and moved on. Buckled slabs of steel lay here and there, not like what the deep delver had done to [Central Control 1]'s floor, but as if they'd fallen from high above. Now the fear of being hit by falling steel joined the other irrational images.

"Here's the door," Livia said. "It's still locked."

Aderyn hurried across the chamber, skirting wide around the

levitation circle and stepping over loose hunks of steel. "Then they couldn't have gone this way," she said.

Owen felt around the frame. "I can't find an override switch. I guess, if they could levitate out of here, those Spellcrafters weren't worried about people being trapped inside. Did either of you find anything else?"

"I stopped looking once I found this," Livia said.

"That's all right, I covered half the chamber, and I think Aderyn searched the other half." Owen stared at the lock as if he could open it with the power of his thoughts. "So. No weird wall-bursting holes, no stair rungs—"

"I didn't even think of that!" Aderyn exclaimed.

"Neither did I until we came in here. Anyway, there aren't any. And only this door and the one we came in by. So, where did Revelin and his team go?"

"I have no idea," Weston said as he and Isold joined them. "We managed to alter the field, but don't get excited, we could only narrow it within the circle. That increased its range, but not enough to get us up the shaft."

"And the moment we stopped actively meddling with the levers, it reverted to its original dimensions." Isold sounded affronted, as if the field had insulted him personally.

"Well, that other team will have to stay a mystery, because if that messed-up lock was Inaya's work, and they used this door, this lock would look the same." Owen stepped back to give Weston access. "Let's see where this goes."

CHAPTER THIRTEEN

The new door opened on a long, dimly-lit hallway, this one with green-tinged bulbs that made Aderyn feel like she was underwater. Fortunately, the hall was as wide as all the others, and the underwater feeling didn't unnerve her. They followed Weston's slow progress for more than a minute, their footsteps on metal the only sound.

Eventually, the long hallway ended at another locked door. "I've observed some trends in the different doors," Weston said as he got down on one knee to unlock it. "The ones that look like wood have only casual locks, or none. The sliding doors like the ones to the laboratories are sturdier in addition to having better locks. And the ones to the central chamber were for serious security."

"What is this one like?" Isold asked.

The lock clicked, and the door slid noiselessly open. "Somewhere in between the first two," Weston said. "Like the difference between an external house door and the doors inside a house. I predict we're going to discover bedrooms here. Some kind of living quarters, at least."

Weston was right. The room they entered had more of those

strange boxy chairs that might have been someone's weird idea of armchairs, but there were also tables and more conventional chairs and a couple of bookcases and a drinks cabinet. It was carpeted, too, though it was a thin carpet laid down over the ubiquitous metal floor panels.

"Funny," Owen said, examining the drinks cabinet, which was empty. "Add a pool table and a dartboard and you'd have a real rec room."

"Wreck room?" Aderyn said before she could stop herself. "To destroy? Those things sound like entertainment."

"Short for recreation." Owen shut the cabinet. "This is definitely where someone would come to kick back after a long day of Spell-crafting."

Isold was examining the bookcases. "Nothing valuable," he said, "and from what I see, nothing magical."

"That's true," Livia said. "I don't see any magic in the room."

Weston was already looking at the other door. "I was right again," he said. "This one's not locked at all."

"I'm not sure we care about bedrooms, but if they lead to a way up, I say we take a look." Owen idly pushed a chair closer to the table, sending up a puff of dust as its legs scraped across the timeworn carpet.

Aderyn expected an orderly series of halls, with doors opening on identical bedrooms. It would fit the mental picture she'd built up of these Spellcrafters: hardworking, driven men and women who didn't spend a lot of time sleeping or hanging out in their bedrooms. But instead they found a warren of twisty passages, with doors spaced randomly. Sometimes there would be three close together, and then the hall would snake on until it sprouted a single door. It didn't at all look the way she thought it should.

All she had guessed right about was that every room was a bedcham-ber, and all the bedchambers were small and identical. The bedframes were empty of mattresses, the wardrobes smelled like dust and dry rot, and while the bedrooms all had wooden-frame rocking chairs, about half the chairs had fallen apart. Aderyn amused herself by Assessing each room. She did that anyway out of habit, in case of traps, but perceiving the description tag made it more interesting when the room was empty.

"I like that each bedroom is labeled with its occupant's name," she said. "It makes it feel like we're meeting them, centuries later. Raisha, Wylter—there was even an Isold. Doesn't that give you a feeling of connectedness?"

"It was unsettling to see my own name among the others," Isold said. "I'm not one for the belief that names give us a relationship with the others who've borne ours, so my feeling was, superstitiously, as if that name was a warning."

"Am I right that there's only ever one living person at a time with a given name?" Owen asked. "It's how the system keeps track of us, right?"

"It is," Isold said. "When a child is born, the parents offer their chosen name to the Codex, and it's rejected if it's currently in use."

"You can see how things would be confused if there were several Aderyns, or several Westons," Aderyn said. "We couldn't have marriage bonds, for one—imagine if the system couldn't identify which Aderyn you were married to!"

"My world is more complicated with naming," Owen said. "First names, middle names, surnames—and even then there can be more than one person with all those names, and they get mixed up. Sometimes mixed up in government records or credit histories, which is a hassle."

"Well, here you're the only Jacob Owen Lindberg, and doesn't that feel nice? Not being one of a thousand Jacobs, like you said?" Aderyn took his hand briefly and squeezed it.

"It does, really." Owen returned the gesture. "Isold, where are we? I'm so turned around I can't tell which direction I'm facing."

"We are still southwest of the central chamber," Isold said. "I'm afraid we've been going in circles."

"This new hallway is straight, though," Weston said, returning from where he'd scouted out a turn in the hall. "Three doors, and they're farther apart. Maybe the leaders had bigger quarters."

"We don't know if there were leaders," Livia said.

"No, but if those rooms are bigger, I can't imagine they wouldn't go to people of higher rank, or higher level." Weston looked thoughtful. "In any case, I'm curious."

"Let's check them out," Owen said.

The first door, unlike the rest of the bedroom doors, was locked, but Weston had it open in a flash. "Still not much more than a token," he said.

The room beyond wasn't a bedroom. Aderyn crossed the carpet, which looked like it would have been expensive when it was new, to where a chair was pulled up in front of a fireplace. "This is impossible. There's no chimney, so how could you have a fire?"

"This," Isold said, kneeling in front of the hearth. "It is an **<Everburning Log>**, a much larger version of an **<Everburning Candle>**, and they are among the rarest of magical items. I understand they are difficult to craft, and since fuel is generally not scarce in settled areas, most Spellcrafters don't bother. We have to take this with us."

Aderyn slipped off the **<Knapsack of Plenty>** and opened it for Isold to put the log inside. "Do you know how to activate it? We don't need it, thanks to the **<Soldier's Friend>**, but whoever buys it will want to be able to use it."

"I do, don't worry." Isold dusted his hands off. He looked as if he'd encountered a long-lost friend. "If there are more—"

"Let's make sure there aren't any surprises first," Owen said. "Where does that door lead?"

"It's a traditional door, not a sliding one," Weston said, "and it opens on a bedroom. Somebody important occupied these rooms once."

"I get it, don't be smug, love," Livia said grouchily. "We still don't know if these were leaders."

Aderyn Assessed the room. "[**Fynn's Sitting Room**], it says. We should remember that name. Whether he was a leader or just a high-level Spellcrafter, it might matter."

"You mean, like a password, or a key to a code?" Owen said.

"Something like that." Aderyn shrugged. "It's a thought."

Weston was staring into space, moving his lips in silent calculation. "I bet we'll find two more of these setups, based on the spacing of the other doors. Let's go."

"They left the log behind," Livia said. "Like we needed more evidence that they were used to magic on a level none of us can imagine. Maybe there's more."

"You're catching the vision," Weston said, hugging her around the shoulders.

"I am? What vision?"

"The vision of finding enough magic items we can retire on the proceeds from selling them." Weston grinned. "Big dungeons are exciting like that!"

"You may have a small point," Livia said, pretending to frown. "And I'm never saying that again."

"That's what you said the last time," said Aderyn.

"Well, this one is it for certain." Livia kissed Weston swiftly and added, "Let's see what else we can find."

The second room was, again, a sitting room. "[**Dulcia's Sitting Room**]," Aderyn read. "It's not like the other one, not exactly. The furniture is different, and so is the rug. All the carpets in the other rooms matched each other."

"There is, however, another <**Everburning Log**>," Isold said with pleasure. He opened Aderyn's knapsack.

Weston said, "Wait. Be quiet."

They all stilled. Weston turned slowly, tilting his head. "I hear something in the next room," he said in a low voice. "A humming sound, or a low buzzing."

Owen drew the <**Twinsword**>. "That's the bedroom, if we're right about the pattern. It's not conversation?"

Weston shook his head. "It sounds like a small, quiet version of the machines that hauled the elevators up and down the terraces of Finion's Gate."

"Livia, take a look," Owen said.

Livia was already tiptoeing across the carpet to stand in front of the door and cast *clairvoyance*. Her body tensed. "The room is dark. Not pitch blackness, but like there's a dim light somewhere out of range of the spell. But I can see movement. People, or creatures, shifting around and going back and forth."

"There isn't anywhere to go," Aderyn whispered. "Unless that's not a bedroom."

"We have to investigate," Isold said.

"Agreed," Owen said. "It's a normal door, right? Which way does it open?"

"Swings inwards. Inwards toward the other room, not toward us," Weston corrected himself.

Owen cast a glance at Aderyn. Aderyn considered the tactical situation. "Livia, stand back and be ready to send some light in there. If that room is like the other bedroom, there's not a lot of room to maneuver, but we could be wrong about what happened to the other team, so we shouldn't start with an area attack in case it's them. Owen, you charge the room, I'll follow to Assess, and Weston can see about hitting them from range. Isold should keep an eye on our rear."

"Got it," Owen said. "Weston, are you ready?"

Everyone moved into position. Weston, standing beside the door, nodded. Livia created half a dozen lights and held them in front of her with *telekinesis*. Aderyn drew her own sword and waited. It occurred to her that if this was nothing, a broken and humming magic item or something, bursting in there was going to be anticlimactic after all this preparation. But she'd never regretted being over-prepared.

Weston shoved the door open. It stuck halfway as if blocked. Livia flung her lights into the room, and Owen turned sideways to fit through the gap, deftly avoiding Weston, who leaned back just in time. Aderyn darted past and through the doorway, Assessing whatever lay beyond the moment she crossed the threshold.

A confusion of messages crossed her vision in silver lettering. Distant, beyond arm's length, was the description tag [**Dulcia's Bedroom**]. Much closer, and more worrying, were not one but two system messages.

Name: Waspnettle Drone [3]
Type: Magical beast, intelligent
Power Level: 5
Attack(s): special
Immune to: none
Resistant to: bludgeoning damage, mind control
Vulnerable to: trip attacks, *daylight, sunburst*
Special attacks: trample
You already know about these creatures. Time to learn that a monster will defend itself in any way it can, even if it's not technically an attack.
Name: Waspnettle Warrior [1]
Type: Magical beast, intelligent
Power Level: 9
Attack(s): weapon or claw x2; special
Immune to: none
Resistant to: bludgeoning damage, mind control
Vulnerable to: trip attacks, *daylight, sunburst*
Special attacks: stinger (poison)
Waspnettle warriors are stronger and more aggressive than

the drones. While they are usually armed with javelin or short sword, they are equally dangerous with their claws. The attack you need to watch out for is the stinger, which does terrible damage in addition to the poison. If you've forgotten, their poison paralyzes a foe temporarily, but that "temporarily" is usually longer than the time it takes to disembowel a victim. I don't have to remind you to avoid this, right? I've gotten you all this way, it would be such a waste if you let a waspnettle kill you.

Aderyn didn't waste time exclaiming over the system's new and even more personal mode of address. "Waspnettle warrior," she shouted, letting [**Amplify Voice**] carry her words through both rooms. "Watch out for the stinger!"

The bedroom was larger than the other had been, but it felt cramped with several waspnettles as well as Owen and herself filling it. One of the waspnettle drones clung to the ceiling at the mouth of a large hole. Scatterings of earth lay on the carpet beneath it. The other two drones froze, staring at the humans intruding on their new domain. Both were laden with backpacks and lumpy sacks.

The fourth waspnettle, the warrior, stood blocking a second large hole, this one in the wall. Unlike the reddish-brown drones, its carapace shone black like obsidian in the light from Livia's orbs. It held a javelin loosely in one hand, slack with its surprise.

Owen shouted a challenge and lunged at the warrior, swinging the <**Twinsword**> at the creature's slim neck. The warrior took a step back and brought its javelin up to block the blow. The sword hit the javelin and kept going, taking its metal point off.

The waspnettle drone on the ceiling disappeared into the hole. The other two dropped the sacks they held and approached Owen, clawed fists raised. Aderyn shouted, "Weston!" and went after the nearer drone. [**See It Coming**] showed her Weston's thrown dagger in time for her to duck as it flew past and embedded itself in the monster's thorax.

Aderyn's first hit glanced off the drone's brown carapace, doing no damage, but all she'd really wanted was to keep it from raking Owen's unprotected back. The drone jerked, swiveled, and came at her, swinging wildly with both fists like a child striking out at random against an adult. It wasn't all that much smaller than Aderyn, but the image persisted as the monster lashed out again, not coming close to connecting with her body.

She swung, parried a blow, then thrust for the blue spot revealed by **[Discern Weakness]**, right at the point where its thorax connected to its lower body. Her attack impaled the creature, sending clear-whitish fluid spurting from the wound. The drone backed away and then collapsed, clutching itself.

Aderyn took a moment to Assess the situation. Weston had finished the other drone. Owen was still fighting the warrior, who had drawn its short sword, but he'd landed a couple of solid hits and hadn't taken any himself. "Owen, hit the body joints!" she shouted. "Throat or abdomen!"

Owen had already begun to move as she spoke. He dodged a wild swing that told Aderyn the warrior was close to panic and then brought his sword around in a two-handed blow aimed at the creature's abdomen. The <**Twinsword**> bit deep, and the warrior threw its head back and chittered. It was an eerie sound, nothing like the howl of pain Aderyn expected. Owen twisted the blade, and the warrior dropped its sword and folded, its upper body hitting the ground and its lower pairs of legs locking so its hindquarters stayed frozen in place.

"We need to get out of here," Weston said, grabbing Aderyn's arm. "The drone that escaped may bring friends. Come on!"

Owen wiped his sword on the ruined carpet and shooed them all out of the room. Livia looked tense. Isold was watching the outer door. He still held the <**Everburning Log**>, but in an attack position. "You said one escaped?" he asked.

"Yes, and I want us gone," Owen said. "Individually, those waspnettles are a pushover, but a lot of them together could overwhelm us."

"That room was ideal for fighting a group of them, though," Aderyn said. "Just those two holes, and they weren't wide enough for more than one waspnettle—they'd be caught in a bottleneck—"

"Not a risk I want to take," Owen said. "Let's see where the next door leads. And hope it's stairs."

CHAPTER FOURTEEN

The next door was another two-room suite belonging to someone named Laralyn. They stopped long enough to pick up a third <Everburning Log> and were off again. Aderyn, despite her cavalier remarks about bottlenecks and fighting a horde, found herself listening for the sound of scuttling clawed feet echoing on steel.

"They burrowed through the walls," she said as Isold stowed the log in her knapsack. "But they weren't the ones who made the entrance in [Shaft No. 2]. That hole was too small for a waspnettle to fit."

"Which means we have two creatures capable of tearing steel running around this place," Livia said. "I know, probably the one in the shaft is long gone, but supposing it isn't?"

"It's a good thing to be alert to, but we shouldn't let possibilities get to us," Owen said. "We saw the waspnettles range to the north, and we're on the north side of the compound now, right, Isold?"

"That's right. The waspnettles found a way through the steel, and they've burrowed into the upper levels." Isold sounded grim. "Which means we may end up facing a horde of them, after all."

"If we ever find a way up," Weston muttered.

"Stop being pessimistic, dearest, that's my thing."

"I feel pessimistic. All these corridors and rooms—maybe we're wrong, and there isn't a stairway." Weston stooped to look at the latest door. "That's something, anyway. This door is more secure. I think we're leaving the living quarters behind."

On seeing that the room beyond was labeled [Laboratory A05], Aderyn had to agree with Weston. "It does feel like we're making progress. Isold, how much of this place have we covered?"

Isold's eyes unfocused as he looked at his map. "There are blank spaces where we didn't go, but the largest empty section is right here, the northwest corner. If there are stairs, they must be here."

[Laboratory A05] was empty, but the room beyond, [Laboratory A06], showed the same destruction as the one where they'd found the bilious ooze. Aside from shattered potion bottles and wand racks wrenched from the walls, though, the room was empty, devoid of life. Aderyn nudged the broken lower half of a fat beaker and said, "I don't get it. This looks like it was done for fun, but why were these empty vials and beakers left for anyone to have destructive fun with?"

"Is this another of the Lonely Tor mysteries?" Owen asked.

Aderyn shook her head. "Those glow pale blue to show there's something important. This is just empty. Let's move on."

But there were no rooms past [Laboratory A06], just another long hall, this one unlit. They walked for several minutes, turned a corner, and walked for several more minutes before Weston said, "I can't believe this was the ideal layout these Spellcrafters came up with. Walking forever between laboratories strikes me as a waste of time."

"Oh!" Aderyn exclaimed. "What if the place this hall leads to is where they did dangerous experiments, and it had to be kept far from the other labs in case of disaster?"

"That's possible," Owen said, "but I'm not sure why you're excited about the idea of us walking into a place like that."

"Because it's where they would have kept interesting and poten-tially valuable items, of course. And maybe they left them behind because they were too dangerous to transport." Aderyn hesitated. "Which would make them too dangerous for us. Well, crap."

Owen laughed. "It's not bad logic. And we have found some valuable loot so far. Besides, that reasoning cheered me up. Walking forever is easier when you anticipate coming to something worthwhile."

"And I think we're about to do just that," Weston said. "There's another door ahead."

Aderyn controlled her pace. The door wasn't going anywhere, and running was pointless. Even so, she couldn't help feeling excited.

"It's another one of those extra-reinforced doors with the diffi-cult locks," Weston said when he examined it. "And the lock's undamaged. Give me a second."

"Did you hear anything moving around in there?" Owen asked as Weston busied himself with his brass contraption.

Weston shook his head.

Livia laid a hand flat against the door and closed her eyes. "The door is dense, like the walls of the central chamber. It might block sound."

"Good point," Weston said. "Let's take extra caution here." He put a hand on the door to keep it from sliding open more than a crack, and recoiled when light shone in the gap. "The lights are already on."

"That doesn't mean anything. The lights have been erratic through the whole compound," Owen said. "What do you hear?"

Weston pressed his ear to the opening. Aderyn held her breath, superstitiously fearing the small noise would interfere with Weston's keen hearing. Finally, Weston said, "If anything's in there, I can't detect it. We have to take a chance sometime." He pushed on the door, which retracted smoothly into the wall.

Bright light spilled out into the hallway, clearer and stronger than any lights they'd yet found, almost as bright as daylight. The smell of dampness and green growing things filled the air. Aderyn peered around Weston's bulk. "It's—is it a garden?"

Owen moved past Weston into the room. "It looks like one. Everything's laid out in trays and on tables. Come in and see."

Aderyn and the others followed him. Rows of steel tables filled the enormous room, each of them bearing a variety of plants. Aderyn knew a bit about herbs thanks to her mother's garden, so she recognized much of what grew there: rosemary, thyme, woundwort, mint. A few of the others were in flower, jasmine, holly—

"This is impossible," she said. "Forget that it's been hundreds of years and the plants should all be dead. None of these ought to flower at the same time. They're all out of season."

"There's no dirt, either," Weston said. "These roots just dangle in the water or stick up into the air. What kind of magic is this?"

Aderyn Assessed the room. "It says [Hydroponics Laboratory No. 1]. I don't know what that means."

"Hydroponics is growing plants without soil," Owen said. "I dated a girl who was an agronomy major and she was obsessed with getting hydroponics to operate on a large scale. The idea is to use special nutrient solutions so you can grow plants in places where the soil is poor. Either the Lonely Tor has the wrong kind of dirt for growing plants, or this is another one of their Spellcrafting experiments."

"If the Lonely Tor really is a volcano, it's not the wrong kind of dirt," Livia said. "Volcanic soil is the most fertile in the world."

"I don't know the answer to that, but [Improved Assess 3] says this room is one of the Lonely Tor mysteries," Aderyn said, observing the pale blue glow that surrounded most of the plant trays. "We should be careful."

"We don't have time to solve mysteries," Owen said, "especially now that we have competition."

"I'm not sure that's true," Weston said in a slow, contemplative way. "Figuring out the secret to opening the doors without a key has helped us move more freely. I wonder if getting the compound on our side isn't going to benefit us in the long run."

"How are plants supposed to help us?" Livia asked.

Weston shrugged. "I have no idea, but it's worth spending a few minutes investigating, don't you think? If the reward means an advantage later?"

"That makes sense," Owen said. "We can spare some time. And if we don't find anything immediately, we can always come back if we get stuck elsewhere."

They spread out, exploring the hydroponics laboratory. Aderyn focused her attention on the plants as she paced the aisles, Assessing them occasionally but seeing only the faint blue glow. "It's amazing that they're even still alive after all these centuries, you know? Imagine if we could take this growth solution back with us. But I bet it requires specialized knowledge to use."

"That was my thought," Isold said. "We could easily bottle some, but we have no idea whether the water alone produced the plant growth. It might be something in the light, or the boxes, or there might be a magical field generated by some other magic item that influences the plants' survival."

"Which could be the mystery we solve," Livia said. She dipped her stone finger into one of the little cells a larger planter was divided into and sniffed the liquid.

"Livia!" Weston exclaimed.

"It's not acid, or the plants would all be dead," Livia said placidly, "and anything else won't have an effect on my stone hand. Besides, all the planters are made of marble, and nothing bad has happened to them." She shook the droplets off her finger. "It smells like water and burnt sugar, but in a good way. Almost too good. I'd want to drink it if I wasn't sure that was a worse idea than touching it."

Owen had moved faster than the others and had reached the back of the room. "There's another lab through here. No door, just an opening, but the tables and plants all look the same. And I found a minion."

"Deactivated, I assume," Isold said.

"Falling apart, so yes. Some of its limbs are dangling loose, and it's got a big hole in the top of its head."

Aderyn hurried to join him. The minion wasn't human shaped; it looked more like a dog-sized bronze crab with six legs spaced evenly around its circular carapace. One of the legs lay on the floor beneath it, and two others hung loose in their sockets, joined to the body by silver wires. "The hole in its head is regular enough I think something might have been there originally. Something meant to be there, I mean." She Assessed the creature.

Name: Minion, Laboratory [1]
Type: Forged
Power Level: 1
Attacks: none
Immune to: mind control
Resistant to: weapons damage, precision damage
Vulnerable to: elemental electricity damage
Remember what I said about minions coming in all sizes and shapes? Laboratory minions were built to perform menial or repetitive tasks in the Spellcrafters' experiments. They don't attack and can't defend themselves, though they share the same resistances and vulnerabilities of all minions.

"That's so strange," Aderyn murmured.

"What is? Is it going to attack?" Owen demanded.

"No, it's just that it—" Aderyn stopped. Normally, she told Owen everything, not just because he was her husband and her partner but because he often saw details she missed. But this new development with her Assessments, how they'd gone from impersonal to friendly to seemingly having a person behind them, confused her even as it thrilled her. It was like making a new, unusual friend, and she wanted to think a little longer about what it meant before sharing it, even with Owen.

"It's nothing dangerous," she said. "But I assumed, when **[Improved Assess 3]** said minions come in all shapes and sizes, it meant people shapes and sizes. Not bronze crustaceans."

"I told you robots—minions—in my world generally don't look human," Owen said. "The jobs they do don't require it. Seems like that's true here." He nudged the minion with his toe. "Too bad it's broken, though that does confirm the plants don't need active tending."

Aderyn swiveled, Assessing the room, and froze. "There's something alive over there."

"Aderyn, the room is full of plants that are all alive."

She grabbed his arm. "I mean a creature." She read the information **[Improved Assess 3]** told her, speaking in a low voice in case the thing heard her.

Name: Vagabond Creeper [2]

Type: Plant

Power Level: 8

Attack(s): tendril whip, special

Immune to: mind control, elemental poison damage, suffocation

Resistant to: elemental water damage

Vulnerable to: elemental cold damage

Special: throttle, swallow whole

The vagabond creeper gets its name from its ability to uproot and "walk" from one location to another. It mimics the plants in its vicinity so well even the other plants don't know

it's a fake. It feeds on unwary animals or even humans, since the latter incorrectly assume it's too small to be a threat. However, not only is most of its body underground, its maw can enlarge to swallow whole creatures bigger than your average human, so wariness is advised.

Watch out for its tendrils, which strike lightning fast. The vagabond creeper knows enough to wrap its tendrils around a mammal's throat, choking it unconscious before swallowing it. If you're asking yourself why something like this is living in an underground hydroponics lab that hasn't been entered in centuries, well, that's a very good question!

"Only power level eight, though," Owen murmured when she finished.

"What worries me is I can't make out which of those plants it is," Aderyn said. "And there are two of them. They could be anywhere."

"We don't have to go over there. It's not an issue." Owen was moving his head like he hoped to spot the vagabond creeper when it moved out of concealment.

"They can move themselves, Owen. We should stop them before they come after us." Aderyn drew her sword and walked slowly forward, scanning the planters with [**Discern Weakness**]. She'd never used that skill on a monster she couldn't see, but if [**Improved Assess 3**] worked on concealed monsters, so should that.

She spotted the vagabond creeper almost immediately as blue lines of light skimmed across one of several low, spreading pumpkin plants whose trumpet-shaped yellow blooms bobbed in an air current coming from a slit in the ceiling. The vagabond creeper looked exactly like all the other pumpkin plants, though she thought its flowers might be bobbing a little more vigorously than the real pumpkins'. The entire plant glowed with blue light, indicating that it didn't have any particular vulnerabilities.

She gestured at Owen with her sword. "See if you can go around—"

"*Aderyn!*" Owen shouted.

She caught a flash of **[See It Coming]** and half-turned just as the second vagabond creeper whipped a thin but steel-strong tendril around her left wrist and yanked her toward its gaping maw.

CHAPTER FIFTEEN

Aderyn struck the tendril with her sword. It felt like hitting a steel cable wrapped in thick cotton wool; the blade bit deep, but it didn't sever the thin tendril. Still, the vagabond creeper released her, only to strike with three other tendrils that slashed sharply across her face and arms. [See It Coming] showed her the attack, but it was faster than anything she'd ever encountered, and her excellent reflexes weren't fast enough to avoid it. Aderyn cried out in surprise and pain and turned [Discern Weakness] on the bank of plants where the enemy lurked. She didn't care about the weaknesses so much as she wanted to see the thing attacking her.

"Right there!" she shouted, lunging with her sword. She impaled the plant near where it emerged from the nutrient solution, causing a thick greenish goo to burst from the wound and leak into the water. The vagabond creeper thrashed as if in pain and whipped more tendrils at her. This time, she dodged two of them, then got her left hand in front of her face in time for another tendril to lash around her neck and wrist. The maneuver bound her arm to her throat, but it saved her from strangulation.

Then she felt the unmistakable pull of **[Outflank]** as Owen flung himself over the table, jostling the other plants, and slashed at the base of the vagabond creeper where Aderyn had stabbed it. The <Twinsword> sliced the plant monster in half. It thrashed again, and then the tendril around Aderyn's neck loosened and fell.

**Congratulations! You have defeated [Vagabond Creeper]
You have earned [3600 XP]**

Gasping out of fear and shortness of breath, Aderyn turned to face the other vagabond creeper just as an identical system notice appeared. Weston had gotten there first and the thing was dead. Then Isold was at her side, touching her wounds with the **[Wand of Healing]**, and the stinging pain vanished.

"Thanks, all of you," she said. "I assumed, since **[Improved Assess 3]** said there were two of them, that they were physically close to each other. That was a stupid mistake."

"A natural assumption, though," Weston said, wiping green goo off his sword. "And look at it this way—you won't be caught off guard by a monster you didn't see, right?"

"That's right," Owen said. "Though I think we should address the other issue, which is that the system told you it was strange these monsters were here."

"It did," Aderyn said. "They're carnivorous, so they'd need prey, not just a nutrient solution. And all the rest of these plants are just plants, right?"

"My knowledge of herbalism isn't much, but it's enough to tell me everything in the first room is the sort of thing a Spiritsmith or herbalist would typically grow," Isold said. "Granted, I can't identify most of the plants in this second room, but none of them have attacked us. This suggests to me that the Spellcrafters were interested in beneficial plants, not monstrous ones. So, yes, it's strange that the vagabond creepers were here."

"Sounds like we've found what Lonely Tor mystery is in this room," Weston said. "Let's look a little more closely, shall we?"

Aderyn Assessed the rooms again, just in case, but still saw nothing but description tags and the odd faint blue glow. Then she examined the dead vagabond creepers, gingerly picking them up and moving them to an empty table so they didn't continue to leak goo into the nutrient solution. The one had stopped imitating a pumpkin plant, and both now looked like scraggly, limp weeds, the way weeds get when they've been uprooted for an hour. They had stalks covered in sharp, hair-fine bristles she avoided, and their bodies bulged unnaturally about halfway down. Aderyn hoped this was the way they looked naturally and not the result of their last meal. Rats did live here.

She took a look at the table where the first monster had hidden. Thin marble partitions divided the planters into cells, each cell containing a single plant. These looked more randomly arranged, though. In the first room, each planter had only one kind of plant—pansies, or lemongrass, or mint. Some had more plants than others, but those plants weren't mingled. Not like here.

"Why so mixed, I wonder," she mused aloud.

"It's strange, I agree," Owen said. "They couldn't reproduce if they weren't near others of their kind. And it's not like cross-pollination across species is at all possible."

"How do you know about all that?"

"That agronomy student, remember?" Owen grinned. "We didn't have much in common, so it wasn't more than a couple of dates. But she sure did talk a lot about plants."

"Dates," Aderyn said, wondering whether he meant calendar days or those odd, sticky fruits her father had bought from a traveling merchant. "I'm—"

"Wait," Owen said, raising a hand. "Hold on. This world has magic, and you people do things I would swear were impossible. Why not that, too?"

"What?"

"Pollinate one species of plant with the genetic material from a totally different species. Like crossing wheat with a marigold. Or a dog." Owen chewed his lower lip in thought. "I have no idea how to prove it. But what if they made all these plants, all the mixed-up ones, receptive to any pollen, not just pollen of its own species?"

"I don't under—no, I see what you mean. You think they did that on purpose?"

"I don't know. But suppose they wanted to find out where plant monsters come from? Or discover new types of plants by letting them mingle freely?"

The others had gathered around as Owen spoke, listening. Isold said, "That could be extremely dangerous, as we just saw."

"And dangerous in more subtle ways," Weston said. "What if one of their new plants looked like an ordinary ear of corn, but was deadly poisonous?"

Aderyn shuddered. "That didn't occur to me. How awful!"

"I thought the idea was to solve the mystery," Livia said. "How do we do that?"

"Well, with the door locks, I discovered an understanding of the principle behind them," Weston said. "So it could be solving the mystery means learning something about the Enchanterium."

Livia frowned. "What did we learn? That these Spellcrafters were brilliant, but not wise?"

A system message appeared.

You have received an [Insight] bonus of [4000 XP] for solving [Element 14] of the Lonely Tor mysteries. Experience bonuses increase with each element solved.

Everyone fell silent. Then Owen said, "I don't know if that helps us, but I feel good about having figured it out. And not just because I love experience."

"The bonuses increase as we solve more elements," Aderyn said. "Maybe that means we'll understand how the mysteries link together better, too."

"Well, I'm going to finish searching for treasure," Weston said. "It's not safe to bring any seeds from this place back to civilization, but if there are magic items in here, maybe in hidden compartments, I want to at least take a look."

"All right, but after this, we'll have to tackle the shaft," Owen said. "This place is a dead end."

Aderyn searched with the others, but her heart wasn't in it, not after nearly being killed. She ended up sitting next to the laboratory minion, idly trying to figure out how to reattach its limbs. Like the plants, the minion might be too dangerous to bring back to civilization, if only because they didn't know what it did when it was functional. Maybe some of its abilities were harmful when someone couldn't operate it properly. But it was beautiful, if strange, and she kept going back and forth between telling herself to leave it alone and contemplating putting it into the <**Knapsack of Plenty**>.

Finally, she stripped off the knapsack and stuffed the minion and its loose parts into it, cinching up the flap vehemently as if ending the argument with herself. She'd give it to her grandfather, who was an experienced Spellcrafter, in thanks for the <**Wayfinder**> he'd given her.

A whoop from the back of the second laboratory brought her to her feet, scanning the room for enemies. Then Weston exclaimed, "It's a secret door!" and she ran with the others to join him.

When she got there, Weston was standing in front of a wall that looked like all the others, steel with that hard white coating Owen said was baked on. "I am a genius," Weston declared. "I defy any other Moonlighter of my level to find this door. Seriously, you should all bow before me."

"You'll grow a long, gray beard before that happens," Livia said, poking him in the stomach. "Show us this mysterious door."

"The thing is, it's not really all that mysterious." Weston pressed a patch of wall, and a hair-fine outline of a rectangle the size of a pack of cards appeared. Weston withdrew his hand, and the wall within the outline vanished, revealing rows and rows of tiny buttons. "I imagine the Spellcrafters who used these laboratories knew about it and used it all the time, because this panel is built like the door over-rides. Same principle." He pushed several buttons apparently at random, and an otherwise invisible door slid into the wall, revealing a room with the first few feet lit by the white light of the laboratory and blackness beyond.

"How did you know the code?" Owen asked.

Weston grinned. "The buttons have letters and numbers on them, the whole alphabet and zero to nine. I remembered what Aderyn said about the names of the Spellcrafters maybe being pass-words, and I spelled out their names with the buttons until I found one it liked. Thank you, Dulcia, whoever you were."

"You win," Owen said. "I officially bow before your greatness."

"Thank you," Weston said grandly. "Now, forget what I said about this door being common knowledge. It was hidden well enough that something amazing ought to be back here. Let's find out what."

Livia's lights extended their field of vision farther, enough to show an empty box of a space from which a hall led. The hall was narrower than the others and floored with the same rubbery material as the levitation circle. That made them all nervous until Owen pointed out that the ceiling was only ten feet above, and if the hall did levitate them, it wasn't like they could go very far. Then they arranged themselves in their usual marching order and set off.

The hall went on farther even than the ones leading to the hydro-ponics laboratories, long enough that Aderyn started imagining lights at the far end, anything to keep her from feeling like they would never emerge from this place. "This is even worse than before."

"I have to say, again, that this doesn't seem like the best layout," Weston said. "We must be halfway under the mountain by now."

"I lost track of what direction we're going," Aderyn complained.

"South, now," Isold said, "and according to my map, we're farther west than anywhere we explored."

"And since the hall doesn't slope up or down, it's not taking us to a different level," Livia said. "So I agree with the musclebound Moonlighter. This is a stupid way to design a dungeon. Even if they didn't know it was going to become a dungeon."

"We're coming up on a turn," Weston said abruptly. "Stay alert."

"No traps?" Owen asked.

"Nothing yet. But I suspect we won't find any. People don't bother with traps in places they've hidden as well as this. Waste of resources." Weston paused, then added, "People who are sane, that is."

"We don't have reason to believe the Spellcrafters were mad," Aderyn said. "Just unwise."

"Still, it's a good reminder that they might not have thought the way we do." Owen gripped Aderyn's hand briefly.

Weston's steps slowed as he reached the turn. "There aren't lights. Livia?"

Livia shot two of her *orbs of light* around the corner. Weston peeked after them. His shoulders tensed. "Guess what?"

"Monsters?" Aderyn and Owen asked at the same time.

"Better than that." Weston gestured to them to follow him around the corner. Livia's lights lit up the short hallway, and beyond it, rising out of their range of vision, a beautiful, wide staircase.

CHAPTER SIXTEEN

O wen walked forward to stand at the foot of the stairs. Handrails on both sides of the stairs angled gently upwards. "I can't believe this was here to be found."

"Why wouldn't it be?" Aderyn asked.

"I don't know. It makes sense—have a backup in case the levitation stops working. I guess it's that it's just what we need." Owen put a hand on the nearest rail. "And they're not steep. The Spellcrafters must have taken cargo this way."

"That seems unlikely, if they had levitation available," Isold said. "But I agree that's what the construction implies."

Weston crouched to examine a groove in the wall near the floor. "I think you're right. This looks like it was designed to fit wheels. It's a track like the one in the Repository that those horseless carts ran on. See, there's one on the other side."

"If they needed to take things out of the hydroponics labs to other floors, this is a more direct route than going all the way across the compound to the levitation shafts," Livia pointed out.

"Now I'm wondering about that long hall," Weston said. "That hidden door was really well disguised. There might have been a dozen more I didn't see because I was focused on the end of the tunnel."

"It doesn't matter now," Owen said. "We need to focus on our quest now that we've found a way to the next level. Might-have-beens are a distraction."

"I know, but imagine all the loot we might have missed!"

"What about the face-eating acid monsters?" Livia said.

Weston frowned. "What acid monsters?"

"The ones we might have missed in bypassing the rooms you can't prove are there. 'If' goes both ways, right?" Livia tucked her stone hand around Weston's elbow. "Think instead about what we might find upstairs."

"So sensible," Weston said with a fond smile.

Aderyn Assessed the stairs. "No magical traps, and no description tag."

"I doubt there are traps here at all, but since this is where traps could do the most damage to us, I'll take extra care." Weston took another look at the steps, then cautiously put a foot on the lowest one. The step didn't collapse, or turn into a steel-jawed bear trap. Tiny lights bloomed along the walls just above the grooves Weston called a track, like beads of light on a long string. Weston took another, surer step, and the others followed him as he continued up.

The tiny lights were barely enough to illuminate the stairs and the curved ceiling. To Aderyn, the passage felt like a tunnel, one that seemed to narrow in the distance until it closed in on anyone fool enough to keep going. She told herself that was impossible, that the Spellcrafters hadn't been stupid enough to build a staircase that went nowhere, but a remembered fear of being trapped in a tiny space built within her until her breathing was ragged and she had to stare at Owen's back to give herself perspective.

Desperate for a distraction, she surveyed the walls and ceiling. "Huh. Look at that," she said, pointing.

Everyone came to a halt to look at the flat circle of glass fitted into a brass ring embedded in the ceiling. "It reminds me of Gamboling Coil," she went on. "The lights puzzle room. I bet it's a light."

"Not turned on, though," Owen said. "Must be another damaged system, because there are many of them, and none of them are lit."

"If they generate as much heat as Gamboling Coil's did, that's for the best." Weston reached up on tiptoe and was able to brush his fingers across the glass. "This ceiling is shorter than I realized."

Aderyn swallowed. "Can we move on now? I feel like we've been climbing forever."

"There's no immediate hurry," Owen said. He took a closer look at her. "Are you all right? You're sweating."

"It's nothing. This space is too small for my comfort. Or maybe it's knowing how much mountain is above us." Aderyn took a deep breath and let it out slowly. "I'm fine. I refuse to be controlled by irrational fear."

Owen took her hand and drew her into his embrace. "You never are, sweetheart. It will be fine. And you're right, we should keep going."

Another hundred steps brought them to the end of the stairs and a door outline in an otherwise blank wall. Weston strode confidently to it and felt around briefly. After only a few seconds, he pressed down on a spot that went *click*. The wall slid open, not just one door but two sliding away from each other and disappearing into the walls to either side.

Weston walked into the new room, which lit fitfully at his step. "Storage," he said. "Lots of shelves and cabinets. All empty, as far as I can see. Maybe some of these closed cabinets contain treasure." He sounded disappointed.

The others followed him inside. Aderyn could picture the room when the Enchanterium was occupied: boxes and bags of Spell-crafted magic items, pots containing plants grown downstairs, all of it waiting for transport to its buyers. Now, empty like this, it depressed her.

"It's sad they all left, isn't it?" she said abruptly. "This place represented the hopes and ambitions of so many, and now it's empty. And yes, I know there was no point to staying when it turned out the new Spellcrafters couldn't reach a high enough level to run it. It's just sad."

"I get it," Owen said. He opened a cabinet and checked inside, then shut it again. "They did amazing things here, and they made it beautiful, in a minimalistic way. And now it's too dangerous for the average person to be here, even if there weren't any monsters."

Weston was opening and closing cabinets more rapidly. "It feels uncomfortable to me. Too hard and angular. Though I guess it's beautiful the way those buildings in Guerdon Deep are, if you like that kind of thing."

Aderyn Assessed the room again and still only saw [Storage B-3]. "There's nothing here. Let's see where that door goes." The doors to the stairs had slid shut a few seconds after they entered the storage room, and from this side it was invisible. The other door was the kind they'd encountered throughout the Lonely Tor, complete with override panel. Weston opened it and discovered—

"Another hallway," Livia said. "Why couldn't these rooms be connected directly?"

"They're not one of the mysteries, are they?" Owen said. "Maybe there's a reason for the halls and the indirect passages and the long paths between some places."

"I checked before. It's not the halls." Aderyn Assessed the hall again, just in case.

"It was just a thought."

The hall was dark enough to require Livia's lights. It turned at right angles several times, always heading the same direction like taking a back-and-forth path across a hill too steep to climb straight up. When they finally reached a T-junction, Weston halted, looking both directions. Then he strode rapidly to the left. "We found familiar territory. It's [Shaft No. 2], unless I'm more turned around than I thought. See, there's those tiny blue lights."

Aderyn hurried after him and discovered he was right. The door led onto, not a solid floor, but a walkway wide enough for five people that circled the shaft. Surprisingly bright lights that came on as they entered illuminated the space, which ended some thirty feet above. Aderyn held onto the railing marking the inner perimeter and leaned out. With the lights still burning below, she could see all the very long way down.

"Strange, though," she said. "My feeling is the levitation circle is smaller than this open space. If they transported people and things with it, they'd end up floating midair, unable to reach the walkway or the door."

"And what do you suppose the gaps in the railing are for?" Weston said. "Five of them... actually, let me take a closer look."

Livia, Isold, and Owen examined the wall panels, which had more switches and levers than the ground floor. "Same brass panel warning about using the levitation field responsibly," Livia said.

"There's another one warning people to stay away from the edges," Owen added. "I guess people are the same everywhere. Wonder if they had a version of OSHA regulating their compound? Covering their butts by posting unnecessary warnings?"

"I guessed right," Weston said from where he knelt by one of the ten-foot-wide gaps in the rail. "There are extensions of the walkway that can slide out so someone can walk all the way to the levitation field. I don't know how to make them work, but I can tell they're there."

"Isold, you're being quiet. Something wrong?" Owen asked.

Isold shook his head. "I am trying to work out what this means." He stood in front of a steel plaque bolted to the wall, a rectangle some three feet wide and half that tall. Beside it was a lever, painted in a cracked, worn red instead of the black of all the other levers. "It reads 'For Emergencies Only. Activation may interfere with normal working conditions. Do not use unless the levitation pad is deactivated.' It seems straightforward enough, but I have questions."

"Like 'what if we wreck this place more than it already is'?" Livia said.

"Yes, exactly. And we don't know for sure that the levitation pad, as they call it, is deactivated. It might just be broken."

"You mean the switches may be in the right position still, but it's not getting power," Owen said. "Okay, so there's things we don't know. But I think an emergency is exactly what we have right now." He put his hand on the lever jutting out from the plaque and pulled it down.

A system message appeared, startling everyone.

You have received an [Intrepidity] bonus of [4500 XP] for solving [Element 10] of the Lonely Tor mysteries. Experience bonuses increase with each element solved.

A clunking, rattling sound filled the air, and then a rush of air like wind blowing through a canyon. The sound came from beneath the walkway. Aderyn leaned over again, thought better of it, and dropped to lie on her stomach and poke her head over the edge.

Along the shaft, circling it, slabs of steel were emerging from the walls, starting at the walkway a short distance from where she lay and continuing in a great spiral downward. "It's a staircase. Sort of," she said. She rolled on her back to look up, but the walls all the way to the ceiling were flat and undisturbed.

"Amazing," Isold said. "And I see why it would be for emergencies. That would be a frightening route to take. No handrail, nothing to stop your fall."

The same clunking rattle sounded, and the stair steps began retracting from bottom to top, reversing their path. "Did that turn it off?" Owen asked. "I can't see from here."

"Yes," Weston said. "And I don't think it's all that scary. Steel is solid, and those steps are broad. Stay close to the wall and it's perfectly safe."

"This gives us another route down, in any case, and a shorter one than that long hallway," Isold said.

"I like having options," Owen said. He released the lever and walked to the nearest handrail. "Intrepidity, huh? I think that means 'courageous.' I'm not sure what finding the emergency staircase has to do with courage."

"You'd need courage to take that path, whatever Weston says," Livia said, punching Weston lightly on the shoulder. "And it tells us that the Spellcrafters who built it believed taking risks was better than being trapped."

"I like them better all the time," Aderyn said.

CHAPTER SEVENTEEN

"We should leave the emergency stair turned on," Weston said. "This shaft is still the most direct route between the first and second levels."

Owen pulled the lever again. Over the sound of the steel slabs grinding out of the walls, he said, "Did you all notice the shaft ends here? I doubt this is the highest level. What's the point of having an elevator shaft that doesn't go all the way up?"

"*Levitation* isn't all that powerful a spell," Livia said. "There are limits to how high you can lift things, even for higher-level spellslingers. Remember the Repository? Their highest level was lower than this. It's possible the Spellcrafters here couldn't make the levitation pads work better than casting the spell. That explains the field in **[Shaft No. 1]**, how we could alter its shape and its maximum lifting power, but it still had a limit."

"At least now we know how the emergency stairs work." Weston snapped his fingers. "That's where the other team went! They figured out the stairs and then shut them off so it looked like they disappeared."

"I'm going to feel stupid if it turns out there was one of these levers at the bottom," Aderyn said.

"There wasn't," Isold replied. "More likely their Flamecrafter cast *fly*. And it doesn't matter except to confirm they're somewhere on this level with us."

"Let's go back to the T-junction and see where that hallway leads," Owen said.

This time, lights in steel cages hanging on the walls lit as they passed and darkened again when they went a few feet past. The lights burned with a dim red glow, barely bright enough to show the cross-hatching on the floor panels and the joins where the metal walls connected.

They walked for a few minutes before reaching another door. "This would be tedious if not for the need for constant vigilance against dangers," Weston grumbled as he examined the lock. "This one's unlocked. Not smashed, just unlocked."

"I'm trying not to see that as ominous." Owen pushed on the door, and it slid open.

Only a few lights flickered on at their entrance. Aderyn saw several long wooden tables with high-backed chairs pushed up to them. **[Improved Assess 3]** revealed the description tag **[Dining Hall B]**.

The team spread out, searching, though there were no cabinets or drawers to contain treasure, just the furniture. Dusty tapestries hung at intervals around the room, softening the metal walls. Aderyn paused to look closely at one. Dust aside, the colors hadn't faded over the centuries, and no moths or other insects had eaten the fabric, which showed a landscape with a waterfall and a wide river. Deer at the riverside bent their heads to drink. Aderyn didn't have experience with sewing or needlework to know how good the craftsmanship was, but she liked it.

"Lots of doors," Owen said. "South, west, and east where we came in."

"And one to the north," Weston said, pushing one of the tapestries aside. "It's not exactly hidden, because it was obvious this tapestry, unlike the others, is on rails."

"That one should be interesting," Aderyn said.

"I think we should eliminate the other doors first, then," Owen said. "Save the exciting one for last." He was standing next to the west door. "This one looks more sturdy than the south and east doors."

"I'm guessing south leads to more living quarters, then, or a kitchen." Weston busied himself with the lock. "Yes, someone wanted to discourage people from using this door casually. It might be as interesting as the tapestry door."

The door latch clicked, something beeped, and the door slid open on a well-lit room. "See?" Livia said. "Sometimes the rooms connect directly. None of these ridiculous long hallways." She marched into the room and surveyed it before Weston could stop her.

Aderyn hurried after her. "If this was a trap, you could be badly hurt now," she said.

"It's not a trap. The room is empty. But look at the walls." Livia pointed.

Aderyn Assessed the room anyway and got [**Testing Chamber B05**]. The others gathered around her. "It's not a trap," she said, feeling mildly annoyed at Livia making her job irrelevant.

"They didn't scrub the walls when they left," Owen said. "This must have been used for research."

Brightly colored writing covered the walls from waist high to a few feet below the ceiling, which was lower than they'd seen in other rooms in the Enchanterium. Weston touched the letters. "It's not paint or chalk, and it's carved into the wall. Not deeply, but enough that I don't see how they could use this place for study after they filled the walls with their research."

"If they left behind their writing tools, we could find out," Owen said.

"That's not likely," Livia said. "Can you imagine how valuable that sort of writing instrument would be?"

"That reminds me." Isold dug the fat pen they'd found in the scriptorium out of his knapsack and tried writing with it on the wall. It didn't make a mark. "The ink doesn't stick to the surface. That might be the key. If this substance is magic—"

"It's passively magical," Livia said. "Like it absorbed magic over the years. Or it could be I'm detecting magic in the writing."

Weston prowled the room searching as they talked. "I don't see any secret compartments. What I do see is a door like the one leading to the central chamber below. Definitely more reinforced and secured than the others." He pointed at the other doors exiting the testing chamber. "Those are basic doors. This one might as well have a sign reading 'Keep Out, Peasants, That Means You.'"

Owen grinned. "Then that's where we want to be."

"It's going to take a minute." Weston set his knapsack on the ground and crouched to look at the lock.

Aderyn examined the walls again, running her fingers over a line of bright blue script. "Several different handwritings here. I can't read any of them."

"Are they too old?" Owen asked.

Isold answered for her. "Too old, but also not legible. They look like the kind of shorthand specialists develop for use in communicating with other specialists. If we had some way of recording or copying what they wrote, we could take it to an expert in handwriting analysis to puzzle out."

"Yeah, it's too bad no clever Spellcrafter has invented photography." Owen stopped to look at where several lines of script in different colors overlapped each other. "This looks like an argument. I wonder what they were testing?"

"Something dangerous, probably," Livia said. "I can't stop thinking about the hydroponics lab. That behavior is incredibly careless."

"You have to take risks if you want to learn anything," Aderyn protested, though she didn't know why she was defending the Spellcrafters whose experiments had nearly killed her.

"Risks with precautions, though. They left their experiment going and didn't care about what might happen centuries down the line." Livia shrugged. "It seems stupid to me."

"I agree." Aderyn considered the broken minion in the [Knapsack of Plenty]. Was she being irresponsible in bringing it back to civilization? "Um, maybe—"

A click, a beep, and the sound of a door retracting cut her off. "We're in," Weston said. "And Livia, don't you dare enter this room until Aderyn says it's safe."

"I'm not reckless!"

"You just now walked—"

"Save the arguments for later," Owen said. "Aderyn?"

The room was lit in the patchwork way Aderyn had seen before, as if some panels still had magic and others didn't. She stood in the doorway and took a moment to look with her natural eyes. The room did resemble the central chamber from the first level, though its floor was smooth and unmarred except for—

She grabbed Owen's arm. "There are bodies. It's—" She counted the fallen lumps swiftly. "Six of them. It's not Revelin's team."

"That's a relief," Owen said.

"That team might be our rivals," Livia reminded him.

"Yeah, but they're not evil, and I don't wish them dead. Is there a trap, Aderyn?"

Aderyn Assessed the room. After seeing the bodies, she expected to see the room light with the green flames that indicated a magical trap. But nothing happened except the description tag [Central Control 2] popped up in silver letters at arm's length. "No trap, but look at what's left of those bodies. They didn't just fall asleep in here, something attacked them. Something they weren't fast enough to avoid."

"Let's be careful, then," Owen said, stepping into the room. Aderyn sucked in a frightened breath, then let it out slowly when nothing happened to him. She followed him, not staying too close. If there was a hidden danger, they needed not to get in each other's way.

Like the other control room, this one had what Owen called instrument panels covering about a third of the wall space. Aderyn left Owen to look at those and continued to where the plain metal sheets began. "Livia, are these walls the way you said the others were? Extra dense?"

"They are." Livia had a hand splayed flat against one of the steel panels. Her head was tilted as if she were listening to some distant sound. "It's strange. There are two layers to the walls and floor. One is the steel paneling and the sections with levers and buttons and so forth. Then below that is a thicker layer of that strangely dense steel. Like they slapped down the paneling over the substructure."

"So strange." Aderyn Assessed again, just in case she'd missed something before, but found nothing unusual.

She finished circling the chamber, observed that the door was still open, decided that was a mystery she couldn't solve, and neared Weston and Owen, who were looking over the instrument panel nearest the door. "There's a bigger version here of the letters and numbers box in the hydroponics lab I'm not sure I want to fiddle with. I don't think it's trapped, but it doesn't have to be trapped to be dangerous," Weston said.

"No, it just has to be an ancient magical device that did who knows what," Owen replied. "Too bad the Spellcrafters weren't obsessive enough to label all the controls. Maybe we should take what we can from the bodies and head out. Though I was hoping..." He tapped a glass window that looked out on darkness, the first window Aderyn had seen in the entire Enchanterium. "This looks like a monitor. A, hmm, what would you call it? In my world, sometimes they're used as scrying tools, and sometimes they show pictures or information."

"Like a <Scrying Bowl>," Livia said, approaching from the other side. "But flat."

"I don't know all that a <Scrying Bowl> does, but that's likely right." Owen tapped the glass again. "I was hoping there might be a map—damn it, I need to stop thinking like I'm in my world."

"What are you talking about?" Aderyn said.

Owen sighed. "This looks like a really old computer, the kind that takes up a whole room. A computer is a device that stores and processes information. This device, whatever it really is, has monitors, switches, even a keyboard, just like a computer. Anyway, looking at it made me think about the possibility that there's a map in there of the whole compound. That's the most useful thing I can think of that the Spellcrafters might have had. Except this *isn't* my world, and I shouldn't make assumptions. What if it's only sort of like a computer, and my assumption breaks something important?"

"I guess that's possible. But you sound more sad than frustrated. What else is wrong?"

Owen's lips quirked in a self-deprecatory smile. "Sometimes it hits me that my world is lost to me, that's all. It's stupid."

Aderyn took his hand. "It's all right," she murmured. "That's natural. It's only been a few months, Owen. But—look. Just because it's not your world doesn't mean you don't have a good idea. Isold, what's the name of that academy in Guerdon Deep? The one you went to for information on the Repository?"

Isold was crouched beside one of the bodies. He glanced up when Aderyn spoke. "The Postern Academy."

"Don't they have an unusual library? Or maybe I mean an unusual filing system."

"They do." Isold rose and walked toward her. "The library's books and documents are stored deep below the academy buildings, in a room designed to preserve them in top condition. Even the librarians don't go there. Instead, they have a number of Spellcrafted items that retrieve requested documents to be read on the library premises in specially secure rooms."

"That's what I remember!" Aderyn hugged Owen. "If the Spell-crafters of the Enchanterium stored documents that way, then it's possible they arranged to display them where the scrying, um, window could reveal them."

"The library we found wasn't restricted, though," Owen said.

"No, but that library was just for books on Spellcrafting, remember? We didn't see any magical books, and we didn't see anything mundane like a map, either. I think it's worth investigating, because like you said, a map of this place would be a huge benefit."

Owen put his arms around her and sighed again, this time in pleasure. "That's a much more positive way to look at it. All right, let's see if we can fire this baby up."

Aderyn was so relieved at Owen's change of demeanor she didn't challenge him on his use of strange idioms. She hoped it was a strange idiom and not something that would require setting fire to an infant. No, that was ridiculous. "What should we do?"

"Take a look around." Owen was feeling around the edges of the scrying window. "We need—hey, there we go." There was a click, and the scrying window turned pale gray, like a window looking out on thick fog. "It's a start."

Weston, who'd examined the adjacent panel while they were talking, said, "I think I know how all these controls connect. They lead over here." He pointed at a thick disc twice the size of a gold piece that looked like a sundial. "And if you turn this disc—"

Aderyn held her breath as Weston gripped what would have been the gnomon of the sundial and twisted. It made a series of small clicks, but nothing else happened.

"Anticlimactic, sorry," Weston said. "Anyway, from what I can tell, each panel is its own Spellcrafted device. This one's probably out of magical energy, but I can see about yours, Owen."

Owen stepped back with a gesture to indicate Weston should go ahead.

It only took a minute before Weston, after peering over the different controls, said, "It's this one," and turned an identical disc.

All over the panel beneath the scrying window, tiny lights barely bigger than the head of a pin kindled, blue and amber and red. Their intensity grew slowly until they glowed as brightly as the blue lights decorating the shafts. A few of them flickered, but most burned steadily.

Owen whooped. "That's it! Nice work, Weston."

"Don't cheer until we've figured out what these all do," Weston warned, but he was grinning. "All right. This one here connects to the scrying window." He pressed a switch next to an amber light.

A jagged line of white flashed across the window, moving too fast to be more than an afterimage by the time Aderyn focused on it. Then letters rapidly appeared, one at a time as if an invisible hand wrote them at three times normal speed. The slanted white letters made the window look like a painted sign board.

Central Control activation in process
Present identification to proceed

"That looks *exactly* like a computer," Owen said. "And we don't have identification."

"We can try the names again," Weston suggested.

"Good idea. What were those names?"

"I'm going with what I think were the important ones." Weston carefully picked out the letters L-A-R-A-L-Y-N.

The message vanished like the invisible hand wiped a cloth over the letters. A second later, a new message appeared.

> *That individual is no longer authorized to use Central Control*

"No longer?" Livia said. They were all gathered around Weston now, watching.

"Weird, but all right." Weston tapped the letters F-Y-N-N.

> *That individual is no longer authorized to use Central Control*

"I'm starting to get nervous here," Livia said. "Maybe we shouldn't poke around on this thing. It's such a powerful item it doesn't have a name."

"It's just a matter of time, dearest." Weston tried I-S-O-L-D.

> *That individual is no longer authorized to use Central Control*

"Who remembers—" Weston began, but another message appeared on the window.

> *You have made three failed attempts at identification Security protocols require immediate evacuation of Central Control*

"Evacuation? We have to leave?" Aderyn said.

With a hiss and a clang of metal on metal, the door slammed shut. The patchwork lights turned red, casting an ominous glow over the five friends and the instrument panels and the remains of the other adventurers. A louder hiss and a sudden fast-moving current of air drew Aderyn's attention to the ceiling, where previously unseen vents opened.

Owen's hand closed convulsively over Aderyn's. "Shit," he said. "It means evacuate the air."

"What does that mean?"

"It means," Owen said, "in a few minutes we'll be breathing vacuum."

CHAPTER EIGHTEEN

"No air," Aderyn said. "We have to stop it!"

"How?" Weston exclaimed. He flipped the switch back and forth, but the scrying window didn't change and the air flow didn't stop. "Livia, can you *transport* us out of here?"

"The walls and floor are too dense, remember?" Livia laid a hand on the wall in emphasis.

"Right," Owen said. "Let's stay calm and figure this out."

"I can cast *air bubble*, but that won't cover all of us for more than a minute," Livia said. "Let me think."

"We need to get the door open," Owen said. He felt along the door frame until he reached the override and pressed it. The door didn't open. Owen swore again. "It feels broken. Like it's not attached to anything."

"Try one of the others," Aderyn urged. There were four other doors leading out, and she threw herself at the northern one, slapping her hand all up and down the frame. But when she found the override panel, pushing down on it did nothing but cause a red light to flash and a dull buzz to sound. The other doors were the same, though the western door didn't make a sound.

She met Owen halfway around the room, and they ran back to where they'd started. Owen said, "Is there anything else? Some Assessment?"

Aderyn frantically Assessed the panels, but no new information appeared. "Weston, do you know what controls the vents? If we can shut them—"

"Looking now," Weston said, his voice tight with tension. "Livia—"

"I said *let me think!*" Livia shouted. Her eyes were closed and her head thrown back. "I'm not a stupid Windwarden, and I've got a million spells that are useless."

"That's not true—"

"Weston, I love you, but you need to shut up and do your job and let me do mine." Livia laid a hand on the giant Moonlighter's shoulder, a caressing gesture that belied the harshness of her words.

Aderyn joined Owen, who was searching the door for a latch or another override panel or any one of a dozen things she was sure it didn't have. "We need to try something else," she said.

"I know." Owen hurried to the panel beneath the window and began pushing buttons and flipping switches. It wasn't at random, Aderyn realized; he was moving outward from the disc that had sent magical power to the scrying window. But none of it stopped the airflow, or changed the message on the window, or made a new window display more options.

"If we could tell it we don't mean any harm," she began. "It has to know this is a mistake."

"Not according to its programming—damn, I did it again, making assumptions." Owen moved to the array of buttons and poked at them, long strings of letters Aderyn couldn't follow. Her head felt tight, and her lungs strained to get enough air.

"What are you doing?" she asked, to distract herself.

"Trying other commands. Like 'deactivate' or 'override.'" Owen kept poking.

"*Dispel magic*," Livia shouted. "I can stop the device with *dispel magic*."

Weston stopped what he was doing. "Don't you have to be able to see the thing producing magic? I still don't know what's causing this."

"Not with *greater dispel magic*. That will break every magical effect in the area." Livia cracked her neck. "Assuming the spells aren't too high a level, but it's worth trying."

"No, it isn't," Isold said. He'd been quiet, but now he spoke with a force that frightened Aderyn with its intensity. "That spell will negate *every* magical effect, including on the items we possess."

"I think getting out of here is the important thing," Livia said.

"That's the second problem," Isold said. "It will destroy the magic that opens that door. And if the walls and door are as dense as you say, that will mean trapping us in here for a slow death by starvation instead of a slightly faster death by asphyxiation."

Livia stared at him. She swallowed, and said, "I can't do *nothing*."

"If we can find the Spellcrafted item that's evacuating the air, you can use an ordinary *dispel magic* spell to break only that." Isold gripped her shoulder in reassurance. "There's still time."

"Try everything," Owen said curtly. "It doesn't matter what else we find. We're past the time for being cautious."

Aderyn found a panel no one else had looked at and, remembering Weston's first action, turned the only dial she could see. Colored lights glowed, more dimly than the others, and another scrying window lit with a faint gray aura. She moved switches and pressed buttons at random, and was startled when the window displayed a message. She read it avidly. It could be a solution!

Reference access available
Choose one of the following options

She stopped reading and mashed more buttons. Reference might be the map they'd hoped for, but it wouldn't save them now. Dizziness threatened to overwhelm her, and her body felt swollen. She staggered to Owen's side and said, "I don't know what else to try." Her voice sounded like it was coming from a mile away, faint and weak.

"We can't give up," Owen replied. His voice sounded as distant as hers. "Maybe it's time for *air bubble*."

"Livia can't cast both at the same time," Aderyn said.

Her vision tunneled, and she blinked to clear her eyes, but it didn't make a difference. From far away, she heard someone shout something incoherent. Weston was waving his arms and his lips were moving, but there wasn't enough air to carry the sound. He had pulled part of a panel away from the wall, revealing strange boxy shapes and a lot of hair-thin silver wires, and was pointing at something in the mess.

Livia took a few slow steps toward him and fell to her knees. Aderyn gasped, but there was no air to gasp with. She dropped to kneel beside Livia, and the two of them crawled with one another's help to where Weston lay—when had he fallen?

The silence pressed down on Aderyn's ears, hurting them. She barely heard through the oppressive silence Livia's garbled voice. Then Livia slapped her stone hand over something that looked like a giant spiral seashell and spat out two final words.

An enormous thump like being inside a room-sized drum shook Aderyn out of her near-unconsciousness. She drew in a breath and found the air was thin but present. The rushing sound of air currents gradually became louder, and she became conscious of wind blowing over her skin, cold and smelling of violets. Blinking, she sat upright. Everyone else was stirring from where they'd fallen, their hair mussed and their clothes disordered.

You have received [7000 XP] for defeating the [Evacuation Hazard].

Aderyn crawled to where Owen sat and collapsed against him, dragging deep lungful of air into her body. "That was close," she gasped when she finally felt able to speak.

"Closer than I ever want to be," Owen said, and drew her into his arms and kissed her passionately. She returned his kiss, grateful beyond words that she could.

After a few minutes, the air movement stopped, and the room was still and quiet again, though it wasn't the terrible silence of airlessness. Owen said, "I'm not sure we should take any more chances with this place."

"I agree," Isold said. "Let's take what we can from our fallen friends and continue searching for the dragon."

"But I made something work," Aderyn said. "It says 'reference.' That could mean a map."

"And if we trigger another intruder defense system?" Owen demanded. "We shouldn't push our luck."

"There was only one," Weston said. "That's how I found it. Every panel has a connection to that one magic item. I'm willing to bet they all use the same, what did you say? The same intruder defense system, and it's permanently disabled."

"Willing to bet your life?" Livia said.

"You know I don't gamble unless it's a sure thing. So... yes." Weston pushed himself to his feet and helped Livia stand. "Tell you what. You all loot the bodies, and I'll see what I can get this reference system of Aderyn's to disgorge."

Owen sat silent for a moment. Finally, he said, "Okay. You make a good point."

"And you're never using those words again?" Weston joked.

"You and Livia saved our lives. I'll say it as often as it's relevant," Owen said.

They spread out to look at the bodies. Aderyn expected, since the room was airtight as they'd very nearly found out first hand, the dead adventurers would be desiccated rather than skeletal. But she was wrong. The skeletons were clean, with only a few wisps of hair to show what they'd once been. "The evacuation hazard couldn't have lasted forever," she said. "There have to be gaps, or nothing could have gotten in here to, ew, remove their flesh. I can't believe I just said those words."

"They're dead, they don't mind," Livia said. "And they must have been high level, because all of them have at least one magical thing on them. Two are wearing magic armor, Owen."

"I hope one of them fits," Owen said. "I feel so exposed without my brigandine."

Isold walked over to stand by Livia. "The armor doesn't have any special qualities beyond being difficult to damage and providing extra protection against piercing and slashing weapons beyond what their materials convey."

"That's enough for me." Owen joined them. "What about weapons?"

"One has a nonmagical but nice steel-shod staff," Livia said. "The one in chainmail. The other is missing his weapon, since I can't picture a Swifthands or Lone Wolf wearing plate."

"A chainmail shirt, and—I don't know, is plate mail armor really a good idea? Won't it slow me down and make me really noisy?"

"It's half-plate, not a full suit," Aderyn said, "and [Keep Pace] means you and I will always run at the same speed, which is all that matters. Why don't you try it and see what you think?"

Owen nodded, and he and Aderyn began removing the armor from the skeletal remains. "I'm surprised the leather straps are intact after all this time. You'd think rodents would have eaten them, at the very least."

"Father says magic armor is made for longevity," Aderyn said. "The magic the Spellcrafter puts into it covers the whole thing, not just the metal parts. Maybe it makes the leather taste bad."

Owen chuckled. "You know, I can't remember the last time I laughed?"

"It's been a tense time, and we haven't even been in here a full day." Aderyn helped him put on the armor, which covered his shoulders, chest, upper thighs, and shins. "No gauntlets."

"That's all right, I like what I have." He slapped the hardened leather vambraces and then stretched, making the armor chime as the pieces shifted. "This feels all right, actually. Is magic armor lighter, or easier to wear, or something?"

"Well, you have **[Advanced Armor Proficiency]** as of level fourteen, so you won't notice the disadvantages you'd have had if you tried to wear this a level ago. But yes, magic armor is generally lighter than its nonmagical counterparts, though you still won't want to sleep in it if you can help it." Aderyn kissed him lightly. "You're also less fun to put my arms around. It's like hugging a can full of metal scraps."

"Well, *that* is a serious drawback." Owen drew her into his arms and kissed her, a long, lingering kiss that made her forget her objections. "Still, I think it's more important that I remain unharmed so you can continue to put your arms around me."

"I agree."

"Which means we ought to look for better armor for you. What about that chainmail shirt?"

"It's too big. It will probably fit Weston, though."

"Come look at this," Isold called.

Owen took a few awkward steps before **[Advanced Armor Proficiency]** took effect. Aderyn admired his long stride. He looked really good in plate mail, confident and powerful and... was the room hotter now?

As she started to follow him, she kicked something that rolled a short distance from beneath the skeleton's leg, a bumpy, awkward roll that made it turn in a circle. Aderyn picked it up. It looked like a sword hilt, with a grip wrapped in worn red leather, a plain silver marble of a pommel, and an intricate basket guard of tarnished silver. The blade was missing, with a deep hole in the hilt where the tang would fit. Aderyn turned it over in both hands. Whatever had destroyed the blade had done so without damaging the hilt. She briefly imagined rust monsters that fed solely on steel and grinned. It was true, she felt better than she had in a long while.

When she joined Isold, Livia, and Owen near a third body, Isold was saying, "...probably not a good idea to take any potions, and only one scroll remains. It's tattered, too, and doesn't do anything we immediately need. But the other things are interesting. And I found this journal—" He held up a small book bound in disintegrating blue leather. "It could be useful."

"There's a <**Traveler's Aid**> like the one Embrus had, Aderyn," Owen said, "and a <**Laborer's Staff**> that turns into various useful objects, like a shovel or a pick." The staff he held looked like a shepherd's crook, not like anything magical. "Will it fit in the knapsack?"

"I think so. I don't know the knapsack's limits on dimensions, but we can try. Was there more? Isold, what are you wearing?"

Isold's smile was self-conscious, but he drew the odd garment close around him. "It's called a <**Robe of Sprockets and Cogs**>, and while the inner layer is velvet, the outer layer is of, well, sprockets and cogs. They mesh together to act as armor in a fight. Perfect for someone who has no armor proficiency and is rarely in battle."

"I think you should take this one, Aderyn," Livia said. She extended a short length of rigid chain to Aderyn, who took it reflexively and discovered it was actually an ebony rod the length of her forearm carved and painted to look like a chain. "It's a <**Rod of Unfettering**>. It casts *liberation,* which is a more powerful version of a spell I have called *loose bonds.* That spell loosens anything restraining a person or thing, but with the rod, you can literally untie ropes or force a monster to let someone go. It's good to have two of us with that option."

"I like it," Aderyn said.

"And I have this <**Wand of Epic Bounty**>," Livia continued.

"It's only got three uses left, but each use produces—what did you say, Isold?"

"It produces a meal that will sustain six people for twenty-four hours, as well as reduce damage taken from any source," Isold said. "My [**Identify Magic Items**] skill is not high enough level to be more specific about what kind of meal, but 'epic bounty' suggests something marvelous, don't you think?"

"I love the sound of that," Aderyn said.

She looked around herself for a place to put the rod and remembered she was still holding the sword hilt. She tucked it under one arm to free her hand, and Owen said, "What's that?"

"A broken sword. It was under that adventurer you got the armor from." Aderyn found one last loop of fabric on the <**Knapsack of Plenty**> to hang the rod from.

"Can I see it?" Owen's voice was oddly strained.

"Sure." She handed it over.

"Too bad it's broken, because it's magical," Livia said. "Which is strange, because I've never heard of a broken weapon that retained its magic."

"Isold." Owen's voice shook. "What is this?"

Isold shook his head. "I have no idea. It must be extremely powerful. Perhaps if we found someone to replace the blade—"

"No," Owen said. "That won't be necessary. I can guess what it is. Except—no, it can't be. That would be ridiculous."

He walked a few steps away, turning the hilt over in his hands and running his fingers over the leather and the pommel. Then he gripped the hilt so the basket fit securely over his fingers and held the broken sword as if it still had a blade and he was ready to attack.

A sharp chime like a fingernail on crystal sounded. Bright light burst from the gap in the hilt, shooting out like a beam of light to take the shape of a curved, single-edged blade. Aderyn's mouth fell open, and she blinked tears from her eyes at the sudden brightness. "Owen, what *is* that?"

"Holy shit," Owen breathed. "It's a lightsaber."

"I don't know what that is." Aderyn approached hesitantly, not wanting to get too near the blade if it really was made of light.

"It's not—okay, it's not a lightsaber. It doesn't make the noise, and it looks more like a katana than a glowing stick. And it doesn't feel as dangerous as a lightsaber has to be. But—" He swung the sword, testing its balance. "It feels like a regular longsword, and it's not hot, just bright like sunlight. Where's that adventurer's staff? Not the magic one. Here, hold it up horizontally—no, Aderyn take one end, and Isold take the other, just in case the sword is more powerful than I believe."

Aderyn and Isold did as he instructed. Owen took a position in front of the horizontal staff. He brought the sword down on it like chopping wood.

The staff caught the blade for only a second, quivered, and then sheared neatly in two.

"Holy shit," Owen repeated. "Isold, are you sure you don't know anything about it?"

"Nothing. I'm sorry." Isold's brow furrowed. "I don't know how safe it is for you to use it, if we don't know all its abilities."

"I don't know. It feels right. Comfortable." Owen stepped back and made a few passes with the blade, leaving behind trails of light that became dark inverses. "But I've wanted one of these ever since I saw Qui-Gon Jinn face off against Darth Maul. Though Qui-Gon lost, so maybe that's the wrong example." He looked as if he'd found a lost friend he'd given up on meeting ever again. "And it's weird, knowing that *this* is probably where the idea of the lightsaber came from. The echoes of this weapon reaching my world."

"Don't discard the <**Twinsword**>, at least," Isold said. "Maybe Aderyn should try using it. It's more powerful than her current weapon."

"True, but I'm the one whose Warmaster skills substitute for the second sword," Aderyn said. The woman they'd bought the sword from had said when one of the swords wasn't wielded by someone whose friend bore another, a strange and distracting whispering sounded in the ear of the person wielding it alone. Aderyn's partnership with Owen had compensated. "I guess I could try."

Owen grinned. "Yes, let's try them both out."

"Owen, you're three times the swordsman I am."

"It's just practice. Remember, the <Twinsword> doesn't activate unless you spar against a real weapon." He handed Aderyn the sword. "Just a couple of passes."

Aderyn took a fighting stance. The daylight sword was easier to look now that she was used to it. Tentatively, she tapped her blade against it. Owen disengaged and struck, not powerfully. She blocked, and then they were trading blows, just like any sparring match. It felt so strange fighting Owen. She'd never done that before.

Kick him in the balls, a voice whispered.

Aderyn nearly dropped the <Twinsword>.

Fair fights are for losers. Take advantage where you can. He won't hit you because you're a girl. Every statement sounded like a different person whispering. Aderyn shook her head and only barely blocked Owen's next attack. Owen immediately stepped back and lowered the daylight blade.

"Aderyn, I nearly stabbed you," he exclaimed. "Are you okay?"

"The <Twinsword> talked to me. Or something." Aderyn lowered the sword. "I guess that's not going to work. But we should keep it anyway. I know we can't sell it, but if anything happens—"

"Yeah, I agree." He did something with his left hand Aderyn couldn't make out, and the blade of light retracted into the hilt. "Did we find anything else? Because I gotta say, it has to be pretty epic to top the sword."

"Then you're going to love this," Weston said. "Come over here and take a look."

CHAPTER NINETEEN

Weston stood in front of the panel Aderyn's fumbling had activated. The screen still displayed the message:

Reference access available
Choose one of the following options

Below that, in a numbered list, were the words:

1 – Map
2 – Personnel
3 – Physical facility
4 – Inventory
5 – Defense control

Weston pressed one of the numbered buttons. The same invisible hand swept across the window, erasing the letters, and then wrote:

Select floor to display

"It's not perfect," Weston said, pressing the button labeled 2. "See?"

The text was wiped away, and lines began appearing, sketching out the bones of a map. Unlike the handwriting, the lines stuttered and skipped, and there were blank sections like the unseen artist didn't know what to put there. But in less than a minute, the lines stopped appearing, and most of the map was complete.

Isold reached out to touch the window, but hesitated before his fingers brushed the glass. "This matches what my map shows so far. It's a pity this blank section covers much of the south and southeast, where we haven't yet gone."

"It took me a while to figure out how to return to the list." Weston pressed the letters B-A-C-K, and the map vanished, replaced with the message about selecting a floor. "And it only shows floors one through three. I think there are floors higher than that, and it won't display them because it's broken, but that's not important. There's so much here we could spend a day reading it all."

"Is it important enough for us to spend a day doing that?" Owen asked.

"I don't think so." Weston spelled BACK again, and the original list reappeared. "Personnel has a list of the Spellcrafters and laborers who lived here, with detailed information about them all. I doubt any of that matters to us. Inventory lists both the stuff they made for sale and the equipment they used, and none of the item names are familiar. We might benefit by puzzling those out, but that really would take forever."

"What about Physical Facility?" Aderyn asked.

Weston pressed 3. A new list appeared.

Select from the following options:
1 – Lights
2 – Water
3 – Ventilation
4 – Doors
5 – Hydroponics
6 – Communications

"It will let us turn on the lights?" Owen exclaimed.

"Unfortunately, no. This is all reference, remember?" Weston pressed the number 1. "It tells you everything you need to know about how the lights work, but the controls are on another panel. A panel that doesn't respond to anything I tried. So we're stuck with erratic lighting."

"Doors," Livia said. "Something that unlocks them?"

"That one shows a map with all the doors highlighted, and they're all labeled, presumably so you know how to find one that's malfunctioned or that you want to open. The map isn't complete, but in a different way from the other set, so if we wanted to, we could compare them and get a better picture. It also has a diagram of the keys, which look as strange as I predicted." Weston walked to a different panel and messed with the buttons. Another scrying window lit with that pale gray glow.

"Here's where the doors are controlled," Weston said. "It's easy enough. You press the buttons with the code from the other map, and it tells you what things you can do. Lock, Unlock, Override, that sort of thing." With a few more button taps, the control room door they'd entered by slid open. "I wouldn't bet on all of these still being connected, and we're not going to run back here every time we come across a door I can't open, so it's not useful. But it's interesting." Weston had the look of a child in a toy store offered his pick of the merchandise.

Owen was pressing buttons at the reference panel. "Defense control. What's that?"

"I couldn't get a lot out of it," Weston said. "We already know the dragon was their primary defense, but I gather they had other, less powerful options for defending against minor threats." He returned to Owen's side and pointed at the new image Owen's button pressing had created. "Try 'Dragon Operation.'"

Owen pressed another button. New letters appeared:

Authorization required to proceed

"I can see why that would make you reluctant," Owen said.

"I know I said I was confident I'd detached all the panels from the hazard, but I wasn't quite brave enough to mess with this one." Weston grinned. "There are other things that aren't protected by that authorization request. All the labs are equipped with that evacuation thing as a precaution, for one, and some of them contain <**Flaming Lances**>, which they intended for burning any experiment that got out of control. Those, they probably took with them, because we haven't found any."

"It's just as well. Those tend to be unstable," Isold said.

Owen wasn't paying attention. His fingers flew over the button array. Aderyn watched him curiously. "You look like you have an idea."

"Maybe," Owen said. He'd backed all the way up to the first image and now selected 2.

Please select from the following options
1 – Personnel list, main
2 – Personnel list, Scholars
3 – Personnel list, staff

Owen pressed a button. A long, numbered list appeared, filling the screen in three columns. "At least one of these people had access to the dragon. We just need to figure out who."

Aderyn's heart sank. "There are a lot of people on that list, Owen."

"Yeah. But I can't imagine they didn't have a shortcut." Owen spelled out S-E-A-R-C-H on the button array.

The list disappeared, leaving the window blank. Aderyn clutched Owen's arm. "Did you break it?"

"I don't think so." Owen hesitated a moment, then spelled D-R-A-G-O-N.

Three lines appeared on the window.

Alrick, Spellcrafter level 32
Dulcia, Spellcrafter level 37
Stellen, Spellcrafter level 29

"How did you figure that out?" Weston exclaimed.

"My generation was born knowing how to Google," Owen said. "Let's see... okay, that didn't work," he added after spelling out the first name and getting the message *Input not registered*. "I might have to be back at the main list."

Once he returned to the list of Spellcrafters, he pressed buttons again. "Dulcia helped us with the secret door, so let's see what other help she can provide." More writing appeared.

Dulcia
Spellcrafter
Level 37
Select from the following options
1 – Skills
2 – Class skills
3 – Assignments
4 – Registered experiments
5 – Biography

"That's more like it." Owen tapped 3.

Dulcia
Spellcrafter
Level 37
Ranks:
Second Chief, Enchanterium
Commander, Enchanterium Defense Corps
First Chief, Hydroponics
Assigned to:
Defense Drills
Food Preparation
Morale Squad
Weapons Testing, Melee

Weapons Testing, Ranged

Owen whistled. "Looks like we hit the jackpot. Dulcia was important."

"Then we can use her name to gain access to the dragon failsafe information," Weston said.

"Maybe," Owen said. "If it wants a password, it won't be as simple as her name. Or it might be her name plus the password. Let's dig a little deeper first." He was already pressing buttons.

Morale Squad: responsible for organizing entertainment, contests, games, and other activities to keep morale high. Referred to informally as the Sparky Spirits.

Aderyn snorted a laugh. "The Sparky Spirits?"

"I was beginning to think they all lacked a sense of humor, given how serious and stern the messages have been." Owen's speed with pressing buttons was increasing.

The Enchanterium Defense Corps (EDC): protects the compound from attacks by those who would steal its many valuable creations. Subunits: Dragon Defense, Artillery Squad, Select Fours.

"Well, why not?" Owen muttered.

Dragon Defense: general security for the Enchanterium. See also: Flight Control, Ablative Shield, Elemental Volley.

"That sounds good!" Aderyn exclaimed. "More details about the dragon."

But another series of button taps yielded the message *Authorization required to proceed.* Owen stepped back. "I'm sure this is the part we need to hack," he said. "*Not* with an axe, sorry, I'll stop being an otherworlder." He narrowed his eyes at the window. "Maybe..." His fingers flew across the buttons.

Please select from the following options:
1 – Biography, full
2 – Biography, concise
3 – Highlights
4 – Personal remarks

Livia made a face. "We don't have time to read a biography, especially a long one. If Dulcia had that many responsibilities, we could be here a while."

"But the key to her password might be in there," Aderyn said.

Owen pressed 1. White letters appeared, but after a few lines, they became garbled, going from simple misspellings to letters mingled with numbers at random. Owen returned to the list. "It's amazing we haven't seen more mistakes like that. Well, let's see if she left any of her personality behind." Owen pressed 4. The list erased itself, and the invisible hand began writing again.

My instructors at Postern would be horrified to know I have high rank here. They always claimed someone with a lighthearted sense of humor who loved a good joke shouldn't be trusted with important and sometimes dangerous magic. Well, the joke's on them. Again.

"Woman after my own heart," Weston rumbled.

It's a good fit for me, honestly. After years of leading one warlord's army after another, and designing counter-siege tactics for cities that eventually fell, it's been a relief to turn my skills to something positive. The Enchanterium's commitment to bettering the world satisfies me. Ymri is powerful and, yes, dangerous, but that's the point. If you're pointing a wolf at the enemy, that wolf had better have teeth.

"Ymri? Did she name the dragon?" Aderyn said.

"Sounds like," Livia replied. "That's frivolous, giving a name to a tool."

"Frivolous and helpful," Owen said.

"You think Ymri is the password," Weston remarked. "It's a little obvious."

"We had to dig deep to get this far, and it's only obvious if Dulcia was the one who chose her password. It's worth trying." Owen backed all the way to Dragon Operation and, when the authorization message appeared, tapped out Dulcia's name.

Secondary authorization required

Owen spelled out Y-M-R-I. The window went blank. Aderyn and Livia took involuntary steps back from the panel.

White letters unrolled across the screen, a new list.

1 – Overview
2 – Ablative Shield
3 – Elemental Volley
4 – Flight Control

Owen whooped. "This is it!"

"Don't get excited until we know if we can get at the information," Livia said. "It might still be garbled."

"You're so negative sometimes, dearest," Weston said, sweeping her into his arms for a kiss. "I love that about you."

Owen had already selected 1.

The immolation measures for the destruction of the Enchanterium are tied to the autonomous flying construct in dragon form. Destruction of the dragon signals the defeat of the Enchanterium forces, causing the magma reservoir beneath the mountain to rise, fill the Enchanterium, and erupt, destroying the invading forces as well.

"Wait, what?" Owen said.

Aderyn read the words a second time. They still seemed impossible. "Immolation? Really?"

"Total destruction," Weston said, all traces of good humor gone. "Those Spellcrafters weren't messing around."

"That's not the point," Owen said. "That eruption will destroy everything living for miles around, including all those settlements. Killing the dragon is what sets it off."

Aderyn gasped. Her hand gripped his. "Killing the dragon."

"We have to stop those adventurers," Owen said.

CHAPTER TWENTY

"We don't know where they are," Weston said.

"I've met them, so the <**Wayfinder**> should have no trouble tracking them down." Aderyn reached into the <**Purse of Great Capacity**>, but Owen put a hand on her wrist.

"We can't go running off blindly," he said. "There's no way they've reached the dragon yet. We need more information."

"You're right," Aderyn said. "Revelin said the dragon was attacking and burning settlements. That sounds like it's the threat the [**Fire and Ash**] quest referred to."

"If he was telling the truth about the extent of the attacks," Weston pointed out. "More specifically, I don't believe he was lying, but he might be mistaken. We still have no proof that the dragon is the threat."

"But we can't afford to assume it isn't," Owen said. "The dragon is definitely doing damage, and we've seen nothing else that could be called a threat that comes from the Lonely Tor."

Aderyn nodded. "Which means *we* still have to stop it attacking, whatever Revelin's team does, and that could mean killing it."

"Which will destroy everything in the area," Livia said. "Talk about a solution that endangers the communities in a different way."

"That gives us two possible options." Owen held up one finger. "One, we convince the dragon to leave the communities alone."

"And if it's like these minions, with no mind to change?" Livia said.

"We don't know whether or not that's true, but if it can be reasoned with, that would be one solution." Owen held up a second finger. "Two. We kill the dragon in a way that doesn't trigger the self-destruct sequence. Can anyone think of other possibilities?"

"I considered collapsing part of the mountain to block the magma reservoir," Livia said, "but it's beyond my capabilities. I think you've hit on the only two options."

"Then we address those," Owen said. "And then go after Revelin's team. But we need information."

"Let's see what else we can learn from the reference system," Weston said. "Isold? You've been quiet."

"I have been reading this journal," Isold said, his head still bent over the pages. "I believe it holds some of the answers we need."

The others left the panel to gather around the Herald. "Which answers?" Owen asked.

"The name 'Castilus' is written inside the cover of the book, along with a line of numbers I think is a date. If I'm right, these remains have been here for some two hundred years." Isold flipped back to the beginning of the book. "The earliest pages are irrelevant, though amusing. Castilus had a dry wit and a clever mind. He writes his observations of his teammates and occasionally sketches pictures of them."

Aderyn looked over Isold's arm at a page with some lines of script and a clever little stick figure of a man waving a wand, deftly drawn with just a few lines that nevertheless brought the man's arrogant personality to life. Next to it was a more realistic drawing of a half-open rose, beaded with dew. "He was really good. I wonder why he didn't draw his teammates as realistically as he did the flower?"

"Why bother when a few pencil lines convey everything?" Livia gazed at the paper as avidly as Aderyn. "Wish I could draw like that."

"What did Castilus write about the Lonely Tor?" Owen said.

Isold flipped ahead. "Their team came in from the top, not the bottom. He writes that they were after the dragon's treasure, but when they didn't find it immediately, they directed their search downward. The interesting part, though, is that Castilus refers to information they received from one of the last survivors of the Enchanterium. 'Survivor' is the wrong word—'inhabitant' might be more accurate."

"Either way, you mean someone who used to live in the Lonely Tor," Weston said. "Was it someone who knew important facts like how to kill the dragon without destroying everything?"

"I do mean just that, and yes, it was." Isold cleared his throat. "Castilus said the woman they spoke to was very old, but very lucid. They paid her a large sum of money to gain her knowledge—as Castilus puts it, 'her weight in gold, and she wasn't skinny.'"

"Cut to the chase, Isold, you're building too much suspense," Owen said.

"Cut to the..." Isold shook his head, obviously deciding not to press Owen for the meaning of that otherworlder idiom. "The old woman told them how to get inside from the top level, how to bypass the locks—Castilus was a Lightfingers, it seems, and he enjoyed being able to avoid the brute force approach—and some of the remaining traps to avoid, including how to evade the dragon. Which, according to this, does, in fact, lack higher reasoning skills to be communicated with. She also told them details about the Enchanterium's self-destruction systems."

"Systems? More than one?" Owen said.

"There are two. One is for the destruction of the compound in case an experiment got out of control. That one floods the levels with magma, but doesn't make the volcano explode. The second is the one referred to by that device, in which the dragon's destruction presumes an assault by enemies. The explosion is intended to kill them as well as destroy the compound."

"But there's a way around it," Weston pressed.

Isold turned a page. "Yes. She explained that the Scholars of the Enchanterium had a system for stopping the destruction if the dragon was killed when the compound was not actually in danger, and that it worked both ways. That is, engaging the system unlinks the dragon from the compound so it can be killed with impunity."

"In case the dragon goes rogue," Weston said.

"Yes," Isold replied. "Castilus didn't write all the details down, but he did make note of how the decoupling process should be done, one step at a time."

"Fantastic," Owen said. "We stop those adventurers, we follow the steps of the process... and you don't look happy, Isold. What else is there?"

"According to the old woman," Isold said grimly, "the three Spell-crafted devices to be decoupled are in the central control chambers of the lowest three levels."

"But—" Realization struck Aderyn. "Crap."

"The deep delver," Isold said, nodding. "And the process must begin in that lowest chamber. Each device will only disengage if the device on the previous level has been decoupled."

"All right, so we go in with *invisibility*," Livia began.

Aderyn shook her head. "It tracks by vibration, remember? There's no way we can avoid alerting it."

"Of course," Owen said, throwing up his hands. "It couldn't be easy. No, that would be wrong."

"I'd put it down to you being the Fated One, but none of us are in the mood for jokes," Weston said. "Besides, it doesn't matter. Easy or hard, we have to do something. And it seems like the first something is to convince those adventurers to give up on killing the dragon."

"Right," Owen said. "Okay. Can anyone think of anything else we should try to learn from this not-a-computer?"

"I will examine the maps, and see if I can memorize them," Isold said, "or at worst, sketch them in Castilus's book. Ideally, my seeing them will nudge the system to incorporate them into my own map, but I won't count on it."

"I'll have it display them again," Weston said. He and Isold returned to the reference panel.

"I'm sure we've found everything useful these adventurers carried," Livia said. "It's a good thing Aderyn found that sword hilt, or whatever it is you called the weapon, Owen. I'm not high enough level yet to detect hidden magic."

"Yes, this is the best present ever." Owen hugged Aderyn, sending up shrill squeaking protests from the armor. "Now, if we can find some armor for you—"

"I don't have armor proficiency though," Aderyn said. "This light jerkin is about all I can manage without it affecting my sword skill."

"I have a sword made of light, I choose to believe anything is possible," Owen said loftily. "Why don't you see what the <Wayfinder> knows about Revelin's team's location while we're waiting for Isold?"

Aderyn clasped the spiky steel sphere and filled herself with the desire to join Revelin. She pictured his unusual appearance, his bald head and full bushy beard, his blue knit cap, the staff that was probably fire-hardened oak. Was it strong enough to stand against Owen's new weapon, or would Owen cut through it like he had the other staff? Aderyn hoped it wouldn't come to a battle. As annoying as Revelin and Cyanne were, they had taken this quest for the right reasons, and she didn't want to fight people just because they disagreed about which reasons were better.

The **<Wayfinder>** warmed and turned pink immediately, pointing Aderyn at one of the southern doors. She continued to feel grateful that the magic item understood about doors and walls and didn't just point directly at the object of her heart's desire. She walked back and forth in front of the door for lack of anything better to do until Isold said, "That was lucky. My study of the maps has affected my system map, so although it's spotty knowledge, it's more than we had before."

"Let's go," Owen said. He pressed the override panel, and the door slid open in a series of jerks. "Damn. If that hadn't worked, I was going to try the sword on it."

"It's superdense steel," Livia said. "That would be a thundering powerful sword if it could cut through that."

"Yeah, I don't think it's that powerful, but we'll only learn by experimentation." Owen stood aside for Aderyn. "Everybody hope these people are reasonable."

A short hall led to another room with scribbled-on walls labeled **[Testing Chamber B01]**. Isold exclaimed and hurried across the room to a wall-mounted rack containing three pen-size fat brass cylinders that tapered at both ends. "I know how they did it," he said, removing one and brandishing it like a sword. "This is a **<Write-All>**. With one end, you engrave your printing or script on any surface, and with the other, you fill in the engraved marks so the surface is once more pristine." He demonstrated, drawing a long arc over the written conversation, but nothing happened.

"No more magic," Livia said. "Probably why they're still here."

Isold sighed. "I'll take them anyway. If a Spellcrafter can't reimbue them with magic, I can at least donate them to a museum. These are fine examples of the item, and they aren't made anymore."

"Nobody wanted their words to be quite that immortal, I assume?" Owen said.

"Graffiti competitions, actually." Isold dropped the **<Write-**

Alls> into his knapsack. "Property owners grew tired of having their buildings defaced. Some cities banned even the possession of these magic items."

"And that's why we can't have nice things," Owen said.

Aderyn had already lost interest, drawn on by the pull of the <**Wayfinder**>. "Would somebody open this door—oh." Tiny blue lights spiraled up the round walls of the new room. "It's [**Shaft No. 1**]."

The others followed her onto the walkway. This one wasn't as pristine as [**Shaft No. 2**]'s upper level; large segments of the walkway were missing, clearing up the mystery about where the buckled steel slabs on the floor of the shaft had come from. Aderyn stood at the edge of one of those missing segments and stared across the gap at a door on the far side, toward which the <**Wayfinder**> pointed unerringly. "Crap."

"Hang on," Weston said. "I think we can work our way around, if I figure out how to extend the paths to the center."

"We'd still have to jump across the gaps," Livia said. "Don't worry about it. Everyone gather close."

Aderyn slung one arm around Owen's shoulders and the other around Isold's. Livia chanted a long string of nonsense syllables, and with a jerk, they were all huddled near the door. Livia stretched as they all separated. "I had this strange feeling, like *transport* wouldn't work," she said. "It wasn't real—more like a reaction to being unable to teleport out of the control chamber. I need something to fight."

"You'll have the deep delver to fight, soon enough," Weston said. "How are we going to do that, anyway? It's power level eighteen!" He shook his head. "I know, worry about talking to these other adventurers first. Who are they, anyway?"

Owen recited names, classes, and levels as Aderyn led the way to where the long, dimly-lit corridor turned left. "Cyanne struck me as being the kind of insecure that talks big to conceal it," he said, "and

Revelin didn't like that we were higher level *and* younger than him. We didn't talk to them long enough to know whether they really are as committed to justice and honor as they claim. If it was a put-on, we might be in for a fight."

"I felt like they meant it," Aderyn said. Speaking shook her concentration, so she fell silent.

"So did I, but it's not a chance I want to take," Owen said. "Slow down, Aderyn, let Weston get at this door." They were coming up on the end of the hall, where one of the doors with the false wood façade stood.

The <**Wayfinder**> glowed a bright, hot red that dimmed only slightly when Aderyn lowered her hands. "We're close. They might be behind that door."

"Which is why I'll be cautious," Weston said. "Let's see. If I was that Inaya, and my team was holed up for a rest, I'd set an alarm trap at least, for security—and look at that, she did." He hesitated, then carefully removed something small strung across the door at waist height. "I was going to alert them by setting it off, but they'd jump to the wrong conclusions."

"Then let's be extra polite," Owen said, and rapped on the door, firmly but without pounding.

They waited. Weston, tilting his head to listen, said, "That's got them moving. I think they're preparing to attack."

Owen knocked again. "Revelin? It's Owen. Can we come in?"

Aderyn stifled a giggle. He sounded like a child asking a friend to come out and play.

Weston tensed. "They got very quiet all of a sudden. The kind of quiet—"

"Prove it," came Revelin's voice from behind the door.

Owen rolled his eyes. "You think I'm a jumped-up glory hound who only cares about treasure and experience. And I think you're in over your heads. Is that enough for you?"

The door slid open. Revelin said, "I never said that."

"You didn't have to. And I don't hold it against you," Owen replied.

Revelin surveyed Owen, his gaze lingering on the new armor. Then he said, "Come in, and let's talk."

CHAPTER TWENTY-ONE

The dimly-lit room Revelin's team had camped in smelled of dust, probably from the worn carpet whose pattern was too faded to be distinguishable. Aderyn guessed it had originally been a dormitory, based on the many wooden bedframes shoved against the back wall and in front of the room's other door. The impromptu furniture rearrangement left room for bedrolls spread across the carpet. That was going to be uncomfortable for them, breathing in carpet dust, but it wasn't Aderyn's problem.

Embrus and Inaya lowered their weapons as Aderyn followed Owen into the room. Embrus's left arm was bandaged from elbow to shoulder, and Inaya's jaw bore a livid fist-sized bruise. Cyanne, farther back, looked uninjured, but she still had one hand wreathed in flame. Owen ignored her, though [Read Body Language] told Aderyn he was aware of the Flamecrafter's menace. She slipped the <Wayfinder> into her purse during the maneuvering as everyone found places to stand. Better not to draw attention to it.

She would have been more amused at how their teams ended up facing one another in a couple of lines, Owen and Revelin positioned at the head of each group, if she hadn't been tense over the outcome of this meeting. Her earlier thoughts about not wanting to fight felt like wishful thinking now, between Cyanne's flame and Revelin's aggressive stance. She had trouble making out his expression beneath his heavy beard, but it was easy to imagine a scowl.

"These are your missing teammates?" Revelin's gaze flicked from Livia to Isold and settled on Weston, sizing him up. "I'm glad you found them."

"Thanks. This is Weston, Isold, and Livia." Owen gestured, though Revelin would have already Assessed them for their names and classes. "Everything going all right with you?"

Revelin eyed him without speaking for a moment. Finally, he said, "You're not here for polite chitchat. Sorry to be rude, but what do you want with us?"

"I was hoping to get on a less antagonistic footing with you all first," Owen said. "Because you're not going to like what I have to say."

"Just say it and get back to your looting," Cyanne said. "I'm sure whoever you took that armor from didn't care about your diplomacy skills, if you have any."

"Cyanne," Revelin warned. "Owen, we're not interested in being friends. Our teams have the same goals, mostly, and that makes us competitors. If you're here to intimidate us out of pursuing our quest, you're wasting your breath."

"Not exactly." Owen squared his shoulders as if preparing for a fight. "We've learned something you need to know. Killing the dragon will set off a volcanic explosion that will destroy all those settlements you want to protect."

Revelin's eyes widened. "That's funny," he said. "I knew you were in it for yourselves, but I didn't think you were actively dishonorable."

"See, that's what I thought you'd say." Owen sounded as even-tempered as always. "This isn't a lie. How much do you know about this compound? Do you know it has central chambers that contain most of the controls and information about its systems?"

"Sure," Revelin said. To one side, Embrus shifted his weight and glanced at the floor. Inaya looked like she wanted to speak, but she glanced at Cyanne and subsided.

"So you didn't," Owen went on. "We studied the records of the control chamber on this level and learned the dragon is part of the Enchanterium's defenses. If it's killed, that's a signal to the defense system that enemies have overwhelmed the compound. It triggers an eruption that fills the compound with magma and devastates the surrounding country."

"That makes no sense," Embrus said. "Why would the Spell-crafters want to hurt innocent people?"

"I believe in their time, there were no major settlements surrounding the Lonely Tor," Isold said. "And the Spellcrafters were deeply concerned about the possibility of their more dangerous magic items being used for evil. They preferred to sacrifice their own lives rather than see their work stolen."

"We can take you to the location, show you the evidence." Owen took a step forward. "But you need to know that if you don't back off, we're going to have a problem. I'm counting on you being as genuinely honorable as you seem to prevent that."

"Revelin, you're not listening to this poser, are you?" Cyanne said. The flame surrounding her fist burned whiter.

"Cyanne, stop," Inaya said. "If he's telling the truth—"

"He's saying all this to get us to leave so he and his team can get glory and experience." Cyanne's eyes never left Owen's face. "I've known plenty of men like him. He spins a good line about wanting to do what's right, but it's all to manipulate others."

"You don't know him," Aderyn exclaimed. "You have no busi-ness putting the blame for your past bad experiences on Owen. You just want an excuse to ignore his warning. How can you call that noble?"

Cyanne took a step forward. "I'm not going to listen to this. Not from anyone, and certainly not from a useless Warmaster."

Owen's hand twitched like he wanted to reach for the new weapon. "Like I said," he told Revelin, "we can either figure out how to work together, or we can have a problem."

"Fine words, when you outnumber us and are higher level," Revelin said.

"We need to listen to them," Inaya said. "We can't take the chance that they're lying."

"Please." Isold stepped forward. "We are both committed to protecting the villages from destruction. It does not matter what reasons lie behind those commitments."

Revelin swept his staff around to point its steel-shod end at Isold. "Don't try your Herald's tricks on me. I'm immune."

"I am not. Even if I thought that was the way to solve our problem, I wouldn't take the chance of betraying your trust by attempting to manipulate you." Isold faced the Swifthands fearlessly. "I ask only that you give us the opportunity to prove our words."

Revelin lowered his staff, though not by much. "Prove this, then," he said. "Tell us why you aren't leaving now you know the dragon can't be killed. You didn't come here at the request of the citizens, so what *did* bring you here?"

Isold glanced at Owen. Owen hesitated long enough that Cyanne said, "See? He's thinking up a lie!"

"Cyanne, will you shut up already?" Inaya exclaimed. "You need to let go. I don't care who he looks like—and don't think we don't know why you're being so antagonistic to someone we only just met."

Cyanne, to Aderyn's astonishment, reddened, and the fire around her fist dimmed and then went out. She lowered her gaze and said nothing.

"The truth is, I'm the Fated One and we're pursuing a quest to fulfil my destiny." Owen spoke in a rush.

Now Revelin's astonishment was obvious even through the beard. Then he laughed. "You're serious. I thought you were a selfish glory-hound, but I didn't guess the half of it."

"Laugh if you want. It doesn't change facts." Owen's posture was stiff, enough to tell Aderyn he was hovering between embarrassment and anger. "We need to kill the dragon to complete the quest. We have the information for how to do that without triggering the volcano. I want you to help us."

Revelin stopped laughing. "You want what?"

"Owen, are you sure that's a good idea?" Weston murmured.

"Yes, because if we team up with these do-gooders, I can't guarantee I won't take a swing at one or all of them," Livia said, gripping her stone arm with her flesh-and-blood hand.

"That's not going to work," Revelin said. "Let's say you're right, and the dragon's link to this self-destruct system can be severed. Are you counting on us being so altruistic we don't care who kills the dragon? Because we took an oath to protect the people of the Lonely Tor, and this is our quest. We're not abandoning it, certainly not on behalf of some fake Fated One."

"But if the people are protected, does it really matter who kills the dragon?" Aderyn asked.

"Like I said, I'm sure you want to believe that." Revelin shifted his stance, raising his staff to a defensive position. "We don't want experience for its own sake. We want it because it makes us stronger and better able to defend others."

Aderyn remembered what Owen had said about not trusting anyone that altruistic. [Read Body Language] only worked on her partner, but her [Sense Truth] ability worked on everyone, and Aderyn felt sure Revelin wasn't being totally honest with them—that, or he was the kind of person who was good at deceiving himself about his own motives. Either way, the one thing Aderyn believed Revelin was telling the truth about was that he was utterly committed to killing the dragon so his team could benefit.

"This doesn't have to be a fight," Embrus said. "I believe you mean well, whatever your ultimate reason for being here. You have to see the rightness of our position. If you really are the Fated One, there will be other quests. Show us how to disconnect the dragon from the Lonely Tor defenses, and you can go searching for those quests. We'll take care of the rest."

Owen shook his head. "It doesn't work like that. And even if I was willing to go along with that plan, your team would never survive the encounter with the creature downstairs, the one guarding the first part of the quest."

"Then you really are selfish," Inaya said. She sounded disappointed rather than angry.

"No, if I was selfish, I'd steer you toward that encounter and wait for the monster to kill you all." Owen stared down Revelin. "You were right. There will be other quests. You need to go find them."

"You'll have to kill us to stop us," Revelin said. He brought his staff to the ready.

Owen's hand twitched again, but he didn't draw the sword of light. "You know I won't do that."

"Do I?"

Owen shook his head. "There are enough monsters in the world that I don't believe in killing those who are our allies in fighting them. Or should be our allies." He turned his back on Revelin.

"But—" Weston began.

"We did our best. Let's go." Owen opened the door and walked out without waiting for the others. Startled, Aderyn hurried to follow him, and was the last out the door. She heard Revelin say Embrus's name, and then the door slid shut, cutting him off.

"They're going to follow us at a safe distance and steal our kill when we reach the dragon," Weston exclaimed. "What are we supposed to do?"

"Keep them from following us," Owen said. "Aderyn, how do you feel about testing [**Bonded Mind**]?"

IT WAS ONLY about three minutes before the door slid open and Revelin emerged, followed closely by Inaya. He stopped short when he saw Aderyn waiting outside. "Hi," Aderyn said. "Can we talk?"

"There's nothing to talk about," Revelin said. "And I don't believe your husband has changed his mind, or he'd be here himself."

"I told him I wanted a chance to convince you." Aderyn stood up from where she'd been leaning against the wall. "Give me a few minutes, that's all."

"It's a trick," Cyanne said. "She's a Warmaster. What can she possibly say?"

"I'm a level fourteen Warmaster. Ever met one that high a level before?" Aderyn stared coolly at Cyanne. "You have to be at least a little curious."

Revelin nodded. "You're right. I am." He turned to go back into the room, and Aderyn followed him. She controlled a sigh of relief. One hurdle down.

"You didn't need to move your camp," she told the team. "We wouldn't come after you."

"It's standard practice," Revelin said. "You would have done the same."

"I suppose that's true." Aderyn swiftly Assessed the room and got the description tag [**Dormitory B01**]. She saw no other doors than the one they'd entered by and the one behind the pile of bedframes, which was good for their plan. She didn't dwell on how the plan might be impossible. If it failed, Revelin's team wouldn't have any idea what she and her friends had tried.

"I was wondering—it doesn't matter, I guess, but where did you come from before you arrived at the Lonely Tor?" she asked. It was true, she was genuinely curious. The journey past the safe zone and through the jungles covering the peninsula between them and the

Lonely Tor was hazardous enough she was glad her team hadn't needed to make it.

"We've been traveling the southern lands for the last two years," Embrus said. "We were headed for Obsidian by ship, but we wanted to gain another level first, just in case. We've heard Obsidian is dangerous even for higher-level adventurers."

"It is," Aderyn said. She summoned up Owen's face in memory and silently pretended to speak the words *[Dormitory B01]*, *two doors*. **[Bonded Mind]** had turned out to be easy in concept and fiendishly difficult in practice. Full sentences arrived in confused fragments, and Aderyn and Owen had fallen back on speaking single words or short phrases. A moment later, the base of Aderyn's neck tingled like fingers ran lightly across the soft skin there, and the thoughts in her head sounded like Owen's voice saying *yes*. There went the second hurdle.

"So is that why you're so set on killing this dragon? So you can be safer in Obsidian?" she asked.

"We made a commitment, and we honor our promises." Revelin was watching her closely, anticipating a trick. Well, he wouldn't see this trick coming.

"But you're going to have to behave dishonorably to fulfil this one," Aderyn said. "You'll follow us around until we release the dragon, and then you'll swoop in and take advantage of our hard work. Right?"

Inaya shifted uncomfortably. Embrus glared at Revelin. Revelin didn't flinch. "We'd offer to help. All Owen has to do is agree to our terms."

Owen's words sounded faintly in Aderyn's head, part thought, part instinct, as if she were talking to herself using Owen's voice: ... *ready...* Three hurdles down. Time to end the conversation.

"Then we're really at an impasse," she said. "I'm not sure why you think your quest is morally superior to ours. The Fated One will break the level cap—that benefits the world, not just the villages and towns around here."

"Like we believe that," Cyanne said. "It's a myth."

"That's what everyone believes." Aderyn swept a hand down the length of her body. "Just like everyone believes the Warmaster class is useless. But Owen and I proved that wrong. And we're going to succeed at this quest. You might want to consider which side you want to be on." She turned and strode out of the room. Behind her, Embrus and Inaya began speaking over each other, words Aderyn didn't pay attention to because she was telling Owen *do it now*.

She turned around in time to see Revelin's face as the door banged shut between them. A second later, the heavy thump of a bolt slamming home echoed dully in the hallway. Aderyn waited long enough to hear the pounding of fists as the other adventurers realized they were locked in. Then she sprinted for [**Shaft No. 1**].

The others piled in by the far entrance just as she arrived on her side of the shaft. "It worked," she panted. "They're going to be there for a while."

"Unless that Flamecrafter knows *transport*," Livia said. "But I wouldn't count on it. Anyway, it was worth it for even a few minutes of them knowing we got the better of them."

"I'm grateful the control system was still connected to those doors," Weston said. "That wasn't a given either. Shut, bolted, and sealed, every command I could think of."

"We have had tremendous good luck recently," Isold said. "Let's hope it continues."

"That's right," Owen said. "Because next we have to kill the deep delver."

CHAPTER TWENTY-TWO

"We could rest first," Isold said as they descended the steel slab staircase to the floor of the shaft. "We have been active for several hours."

"I've barely expended any resources," Livia said. "Even *dispel magic* didn't take much out of me, and I've replenished my power since creating that earth cave against the waspnettles. Besides, I want to get a head start on Revelin's team. I doubt they'll find a way out of there in less than a day, but I don't like pushing the odds."

"If Livia isn't worried, I'd rather press on," Weston said. "Before I start remembering what that deep delver looked like, rearing up over us, and lose my nerve."

Aderyn shuddered. "I agree. I don't think we should waste time."

"Then we should prepare ourselves," Isold said.

"Yeah," Owen said. He patted the sword hilt. "I want to try this baby out. Aderyn, how do we approach this fight?"

Aderyn recalled the deep delver and her Assessment of it, this time dispassionately. "It's big enough that [Outflank] won't be effective, so we shouldn't count on that. The same with [To the Heart], Weston—most of its vital organs are deep enough your weapons won't reach them. It doesn't have any especially vulnerable parts, which is good news for us because it means we can stab it where we can reach it."

"So, deliver a shit-ton of damage?" Owen said.

"Yes, but we can still maximize that damage delivery." Aderyn turned to Livia. "It's got the same resistance to elemental earth damage as to weapons, but it's vulnerable to light, specifically *sunburst*. We need to start our attack with that."

"And I think it's time to use the Spiritsmith Tirla's gifts," Isold said. "You recall she gave us several potions to increase our abilities? Three of them are intended to be poured over weapons, to poison an enemy, and we have others that increase the user's strength. Both of those seem appropriate to this combat."

"I have some other spells I'll try," Livia said. "*Greater immobilize* may not work, but at the very least I'll learn its limits, and it only takes a couple of seconds to cast, so I won't waste time on a dead end. And I haven't tried *stoneskin* on all of us before—that works like ablative armor, taking damage and gradually being destroyed."

"Isold, it's immune to mind magic, but if you boost our spirits with your song, I think that's more valuable." Aderyn turned to Owen. "And I'm wondering if that new sword will do greater damage, since it's made of light and the deep delver hates light."

"I'm looking forward to finding out." Owen gripped Aderyn's hand. "Let's get to the room and take care of these buffs... that is what you call it, right?"

"Of course it is," Aderyn said. "And I already feel more confident." That was, surprisingly, true. Having a plan made her feel better. Of course, as her mother always said, no plan lasts past the first three seconds of a fight, so it was bad to depend too much on early tactical decisions. But they'd all fled the deep delver before; anything that helped them step back into that room was welcome.

They ended up in **[Laboratory A09]** to make their preparations. Aderyn accepted one of the purple potion vials from Isold and uncorked it. The sweet scent of wisteria wafted from the prism-shaped vial, strong and rich enough she involuntarily plugged her nose with her free hand. Beside her, Owen sneezed at the scent as he opened his own vial. "Is this normal?"

"The scent is supposed to be part of how you identify a potion or tincture," Aderyn replied. "This is an exceptionally strong smell, though. My mother's potions carry a more subtle scent. Watch, I'll show you what to do." She drew her sword and rested its tip on one of the laboratory cabinets to steady the blade, then carefully tipped the vial over the nearer end of the fuller, not touching the glass to the groove.

A thick, gritty paste oozed out like a slime mold filled with glittering sand. The purple mixture hung for a moment, coalescing into a teardrop hanging from the thinnest of threads, and then dropped into the groove. The scent of wisteria grew briefly stronger. Aderyn angled the sword so the potion would run down the fuller, but before it flowed more than an inch, it evaporated, leaving behind a slick, oily sheen of purple and violet shades.

She went on applying the potion the length of the blade, not just filling the groove but coating the edges before flipping the weapon over to repeat the process in reverse, tip to hilt. She ran out of potion an inch and a half before reaching the crossguard, but that was close enough.

Owen had drawn his sword, or whatever he called it when he made the blade appear, but hadn't applied the potion yet. When Aderyn finished, he said, "I'm not sure this is going to work. What happens if I retract the blade after dousing it in this stuff?"

"I don't know." Aderyn eyed the glowing sword speculatively. "Aren't you afraid of burning your fingers when you get near it?"

"No, it's just light." Owen tapped the flat of the blade with his finger and then wiggled the digit at her. "I'm not testing the edge, because that thing is sharp. But I don't want to waste this potion if it won't work."

"Try just the tip," Aderyn suggested.

The tip soaked up the potion as readily as Aderyn's sword had. It also tinted the light purple, making Owen grin and say something about Mace Windu. But when he sheathed the sword and then activated it again, the purple tint was gone. "Well, crap," Owen said. "I guess I'll have to leave the sword running. I hope that doesn't ruin our plan, going in there with a daylight blade and maybe making the deep delver cautious."

"I don't know. We'll have to take the risk." Aderyn took another potion bottle, this one slightly fatter, and handed its twin to Owen. The blue liquid inside swirled with glittering orange currents. "This only lasts for five minutes, so we'll want to wait until just before entering to drink it."

"Yes, and it's time for *stoneskin*," Livia announced. "All of you stand close together—no, not that close, just close enough to clasp hands without touching anywhere else. Yes, like that." She closed her eyes and flexed her stone hand briefly, then chanted a few words that almost made sense and took Weston's free hand in her stone one.

A flood of gray that glittered like mica spread from Livia's hand up Weston's arm and then gained speed, flowing over his body and from there to Isold, who held his other hand. Before Aderyn could exclaim, the gray flood had reached her, washing over her with a cold tingle like plunging naked into a snowdrift. The tingle disappeared almost immediately, making her skin feel tight and dry. She held up her hand and examined it. Her skin now had a light gray sheen to it, and when she curled her fingers into a fist, they resisted, as if they were sheathed in a stiff glove.

"Are we supposed to not be able to move easily?" Weston asked.

"The stiffness passes. That's why we did it first, so you can walk around and stretch it out." Livia chanted more words, and inch-thick slabs of stone surrounded her like constantly moving armor plates. "Just so I'm clear, if the monster isn't there when we enter, I'll cast *thunderstomp* to lure it out, then *sunburst* once it's in the room?"

"Yes, because if it can sense light, it might not take the bait if the room is already bright," Aderyn said. She blew out her breath nervously. "Are we ready? I feel ready. And jittery. If we wait too long, I might lose my nerve."

"Drink up," Owen said, saluting her with the blue potion. Aderyn uncorked hers and swigged it down before the musty scent of old paper could deter her. It tasted like sour apples rather than paper, not so sour as to sicken her, and she drained the vial and put it into her purse. Her mother had taught her to save the vials.

She burped, tasted apples again, and said, "Did it—"

A rush of fire overcame her, sweeping through her body. It wasn't painful, just hot like a campfire on a cold night, like snuggling in a warm blanket by the hearth. All her muscles felt suddenly relaxed, as if she'd been massaged all over by an expert. She lifted her sword from where she'd set it on the counter and marveled at how light it felt thanks to the potion's gift of strength. She was sure she could wield it for hours, feeling this way.

Owen was rapidly pouring purple ooze over the daylight sword, turning the weapon back and forth to keep droplets from falling. "I think that's it," he said. The purple light cast strange shadows over his gray skin, making him look like a distant relative of the deep delver. "Let's do this."

Weston opened the door a crack and peered inside. "Empty." He slid the door open all the way. Again, lights came on here and there across the walls, casting odd shadows across the wrecked floor. Owen's purple sword dragged at Aderyn's vision like a toothache, seeming to cut a hole in reality wherever he went.

Aderyn's heart hammered, sending nervous energy through her. The control chamber was empty, but it smelled like mushrooms now, and the smell made her even more anxious. This was the stupidest thing they'd ever done, going after a power level eighteen monster *on purpose*. Obviously they had to do it, because the alternative was giving up, but even with all their preparations it felt foolish.

Livia flung some chunks of concrete and a metal slab out of the way with *telekinesis* so she was standing on earth. She took a solid stance in preparation for *thunderstomp*, but interrupted herself before uttering more than two syllables. "I feel it coming. It's moving faster than before." She scrambled away from the room's center, putting the wall at her back.

"Spread out, everyone," Aderyn said, making herself speak calmly. "Wait for *sunburst*, then—"

With a titanic roar, the deep delver erupted from the ground, scattering concrete and metal. Its head rose to brush the distant ceiling, and its mouth retracted from its bony jaws. It screamed again.

Livia shouted a string of words Aderyn didn't understand, but she didn't need to. She ducked her head against her chest and covered it with both arms, squeezing her eyes tight shut.

A silent explosion rocked the chamber, and light bled past Aderyn's protections, pink like the <**Wayfinder**> but much, much brighter. The deep delver roared, this time in pain. Aderyn lowered her arms and shouted, "Go! Go!"

Chapter Twenty-Three

In the light from *sunburst*, free from shadows, the chamber looked smaller. The deep delver, though, looked bigger than Aderyn remembered. She told herself that meant its movement was restricted by the room's limitations, and it wouldn't be able to put its full weight behind its slams, but her body hadn't waited for her to mull over tactics and was sprinting for the monster as fast as she could over the broken ground.

The ground rumbled again, and fat tentacles of rich, moist earth rose up to entangle the deep delver. For all they looked as soft as good loam, they held the monster in place better than Aderyn had hoped. Her excitement over Livia's success at *greater immobilize* faded when she realized the tentacles couldn't reach higher than halfway up what was visible of the deep delver—and its head and upper body were free.

The deep delver roared and lunged at Owen, who dodged and thrust with the mystery sword. The blade of light connected solidly with the monster's flesh. It screamed in pain and whipped its body away from Owen, who barely kept his grip on the sword. Then Weston was there, climbing up the immobilized half of the deep delver's body to thrust his sword into the space below its jaw. The deep delver twisted awkwardly trying to get its teeth on Weston, who vaulted away to the far side of the room.

Aderyn reached the monster and searched for an opening, but the earth tentacles were a nearly solid mass at her level. Before she could tell herself how stupid it was, she clambered one-handed over the tentacles, up to where the flesh was visible. She slashed and struck it a glancing blow, raised her sword to hit it again, and heard Livia shouting, "It's breaking free!"

Cursing, Aderyn scrambled back down and ran just as the deep delver shook itself, flexed its lower body, and sent fragments of tentacles flying. One struck Aderyn across the back, knocking her to her knees. She lost her grip on her sword, which bounced a few feet away. Isold's song rose above the din as if he had [**Amplify Voice**], but the jolt of fear that struck her as she cast about for her weapon overrode whatever boost to morale his music provided.

She found her sword and got to her feet. Owen and Weston were taking turns attacking, but their weapons were so small compared to the monster's bulk they seemed irrelevant. The deep delver drew back from Owen, rising higher and opening its terrible maw. Aderyn screamed, "Watch out for the acid slime attack!"

Owen disengaged and balanced on the balls of his feet, waiting. Aderyn screamed again as ripples of convulsions surged across the giant worm body and an enormous gout of pale purple ooze gushed from its mouth just seconds before Owen moved. Splashes of acid sprayed everywhere, and Weston shouted as one of them struck his arm. Whatever *stoneskin* did seemed not to defend perfectly against acid.

The deep delver followed Owen's fleeing form, lunging after him and slamming into the wall just behind him, once, twice. The third time, it hit him a glancing blow, smashing him into the metal panels and making him fall. The monster shook its head as if the blow had stunned it, too. Isold hurried to kneel beside Owen, the <**Healing**

Stone> in his hand. The deep delver reared up as if it was Livia drawing back an arm for *thunder punch*. It gnashed its rows of sharp teeth like a gourmand ready for a delicious meal.

Aderyn groped along her thigh and pulled out the <**Wand of Limited Paralysis**>. She aimed it at the deep delver's head and gestured in the complicated way Isold had taught them all, and ended by thrusting the wand's tip at the monster as if performing a finishing move with her sword.

A spark of light flashed at the tip of the wand, tiny and green like a sick firefly, but nothing else happened. Aderyn's heart sank. The deep delver continued to position itself for an attack, its jaws gaping wide. Then it stilled. It twisted its head back and forth and jerked up and down as if having a seizure. It took Aderyn a moment to realize its jaws were paralyzed, frozen open and immobile. She shrieked in delight and rushed to attack, hoping to keep its attention on her while Isold healed Owen.

This time, her sword bit deep, and she plunged it into the deep delver's body almost to the hilt. She had no idea if the weapon poison was working, but there wasn't anything she could do about it if it wasn't, so she struck again and again. She was barely aware of Weston nearby, doing the same. Someone was shouting at her, but she didn't dare take her attention off the monster to find out who.

The ground rumbled again, and the earth between her and the deep delver surged upward like a wave cresting over her. In the next second, the ghostly image of pale purple slime sloshed over the barrier, followed almost immediately by the real thing. It dripped down the top and sides without touching Aderyn. Belated fear shot through her, and she lowered her sword, catching her breath. If Livia hadn't been watching, she would be a writhing mass of acid burns right now.

The earthworks shuddered, and instinct threw Aderyn into motion, running away from the protective barrier seconds before the deep delver smashed it under its tremendous weight. Aderyn tripped, stumbled to her feet, and kept going until Owen caught her under one arm and hauled her to a stop.

"It's still going strong," he shouted. "Too bad your Assessment doesn't show us its health bar."

"Oh, that would be useful," Aderyn said. "We can't stop now, though!"

"No. Keep at it, partner!" Owen grinned and rushed back into battle.

Aderyn took a moment to assess the situation. Vivid green stippled the monster's purple hide where the poisoned swords had struck it, but she couldn't tell if it was slowing down at all. It really did seem infuriated by Owen's light sword, because whenever its attention wasn't distracted, it focused on Owen with an intensity that rivaled the sword's brilliance. The monster's jaws were still locked open, which looked like it stopped it trying to slam its head against its enemies—that was something, anyway. Isold had picked up his song again, and Livia was taking a stance that meant another *greater immobilize* was on the way.

Once the earth tentacles again dragged the deep delver down, impeding its movement, Aderyn ran to Livia's side. Livia was pulling a wand off a sheath on her knapsack. "I'm going to try putting it to sleep," she said, dropping the knapsack at her feet and aiming the wand at the back of the monster's head.

"Oh! Why didn't we do that first?"

"Because I don't know what kind of effect it is. Sleep might qualify as mind magic. And we couldn't base our initial strategy on the possibility of it falling asleep." Livia waved the wand, but cut the movement off. "And now our people keep getting in the way. I'm running out of ideas. And magical energy."

Aderyn's arms ached despite the boost of strength, and her breathing remained ragged though she was now standing still. "We have to keep hitting it. There's no other way."

The earth tentacles shattered again, and the deep delver's body bulged as it prepared to spew acid vomit again. "I can do *greater immobilize* again," Livia said, "and if you can get the others out of the way, I can try putting it to sleep." She took a stance for casting the spell.

Aderyn nodded and ran toward where Owen and Weston had moved to avoid the acid slime. The deep delver jerked its head toward her like a falcon spying a fleeing mouse. **[See It Coming]** gave her barely enough warning of its body slamming toward her to get her out of its path. She stumbled again over a fallen sheet of steel, this time keeping her grip on her sword as she fell to her knees, but sharp pain shot through her leg as she tried to rise. When **[See It Coming]** showed her the ghostly image of the deep delver's head speeding toward her, she barely got her good leg under her before the monster plowed into her, crushing her against the broken ground.

The next thing she knew, the air was full of screams, and the worst pain she'd ever experienced stabbed through her broken body. Someone carried her at a run across the uneven ground, and every bounce and jolt was white-hot agony that brought her closer to blessed unconsciousness without ever taking her over that line. She hurt too much even to weep.

The person carrying her dropped her, making her black out again. She came to only to find someone shaking her, and then a hand cracking across her cheek like a whip. She hadn't seen the deep delver had human allies. Maybe it was Revelin's team, attacking her in revenge for locking them in that room. She wanted to tell her assailant not to bother, that she was already dying, but her jaw wasn't connected to her face.

The hand slid around the back of her head. Aderyn closed her eyes and prepared for the person to break her neck. Instead, whoever it was lifted her head to rest on his knee. Something cold and smooth that smelled of raspberries touched her lips. "Drink it," Isold said. "Now, Aderyn!"

He tipped the vial so a cool, thin fluid poured into Aderyn's mouth.

Some trickled out the corners of her mouth, but she swallowed most of it, gulping the liquid down. It tasted like raspberries and burned like alcohol. She licked her lips to get the last drops. In the next moment, she convulsed so hard she bit her tongue. A cold rush like icy water flooded her body, chilling her to the bone, but she barely noticed because her body was knitting itself back together. The feeling was indescribable, if only because she had no words for being totally aware of her body's workings. She had never been so completely herself, and at the same time she felt detached from the healing, as if watching it from outside.

With a snap like a whip crack, the dual state ended. Aderyn flexed her fingers. She felt more whole than she'd ever felt in her entire life. Swiftly, she rolled to her feet. "Where's my sword?"

"Shattered," Isold said. His hair and clothes were disordered like he'd rolled around on the filthy floor. "I'm sorry."

"It's fine. I figured it out. Finally." Aderyn surveyed the room. The deep delver had smashed into the wall again, missing Weston, who was running in their direction. Owen was on the monster's far side, slashing it with his sword whose light was only barely purple now. The deep delver reared up, and this time Aderyn was sure it was moving more slowly. Livia stood nearby, drinking a potion that glimmered red in the sunlight. A red glow surrounded her briefly, and she sighed and tossed the empty bottle aside. "That replenished my magical energy, but I'm running through my reserves fast," she said.

Aderyn plucked the <**Wand of Limited Paralysis**> from its sheath and shouted, letting **[Amplify Voice]** carry her words across the chamber. "Weston, Owen, get ready to climb! Livia, cast *immobilize* on my mark!" She twirled the wand through its activation sequence, and as the greenish firefly glow lit its tip, shouted, "*Now!*"

The paralysis struck the deep delver just as its mouth yawned open to vomit slime. Earth tentacles rose up to restrain it as it again went rigid trying to make its jaws close. Owen and Weston clambered up the tentacles and then farther up. Owen stabbed his shining blade into the monster's flesh to haul himself up, while Weston found handholds Aderyn couldn't see.

"Yes, up!" she screamed. "Hurry, the paralysis won't last long!"

The two men reached the deep delver's massive head and prepared to attack. "No!" Aderyn shouted. "Into the mouth, the mouth! Attack through the roof of its mouth!"

Livia gasped. "What?"

Neither Owen nor Weston hesitated. They climbed past the brutal rows of jaggedly sharp teeth, keeping their balance as the deep delver twisted in its attempts to close its jaws on them. Aderyn couldn't see them anymore. Her ragged breathing was loud in her ears. If she'd just sent them both to their deaths—

With an agonized cry, the deep delver threw its head back, and Aderyn screamed in terror at the thought of Owen and Weston tumbling helplessly down its gullet. Black blood spewed from its mouth, and with a ponderous thump, its body sagged and slammed into the ground, where it lay unmoving.

**Congratulations! You have defeated [Deep Delver].
You have earned [40,000 XP]**

Aderyn and Livia ran for the mouth, which was still rigid, but Isold outpaced them and reached into the mouth to help Weston climb out. Owen followed behind him. Both men were covered in black blood that stank of acid and soot. Livia stopped a few feet away and cast *drench* to wash away the worst of the mess.

"Why couldn't we have done that from the outside?" Owen said, shivering from the cold water.

"Because its brain couldn't be reached from there. Too much flesh in the way." Aderyn hugged Owen, heedless of the wet and the remaining blood stink and the hard armor plates. "I realized if its flesh wasn't armored, and I didn't see a vulnerable spot near its brain, that was because the vulnerable spot was inside. That was terrifying, watching you walk into its mouth."

"Pretty terrifying from our perspective, too," Owen said. "Though not as terrifying as you nearly dying." He held her close, his breathing gradually calming.

"You would have died if not for Tirla's other gift," Isold said. "The <Healing Stone> is powerful, but slower than a <Potion of Life>. We owe her a tremendous debt."

"I can't believe we did it," Livia said, clasping Weston's hand.

"Neither can I, and you know I'm terminally optimistic," Weston said. "The thing is—" He stopped and turned, surveying the destruction. "The deep delver smashed a lot of the panels. We might be out of luck."

They all stared at the wrecked instrument panels. "Which one is it, Isold?" Owen asked.

Isold picked his way across the rubble-strewn floor and examined each panel in turn, comparing them with the neat little diagram Castilus had drawn in his journal. He stopped in front of one the deep delver had rammed into, long enough that Aderyn said, "That's not it, is it? Please say it isn't."

"It's either this one, or the one next to it," Isold said. "They're almost identical."

The others joined him and took turns looking at the drawing. Aderyn traced a couple of lines with her fingertip. "We can't stay here dithering. We need to act."

"But if we choose the wrong one, maybe that will lock the device and we really will be out of luck," Livia said.

"We can't worry about 'if,'" Owen said. "We make the best choice we can, and we live with it. Weston?"

Weston had been examining the panels rather than looking at the journal. Now he turned a dial on the undamaged panel, and lights came on all across it, blue and amber and red. "The other one is a total loss, so it doesn't matter if it was the right one or not. This one, however, is definitely connected to the dragon. It—hang on." He thumped the black glass scrying window at the center of the panel. Immediately, it glowed gray, and then words scrolled across it:

Authorization required.

Weston spelled out *Dulcia* on the button array.

Dragon System 1: Ablative Shield

"Ablative shield—that means armor. Can we turn its armor off?" Aderyn said.

"I think so. It's these switches here." Weston flicked each of three switches in a row down, turning their lights from blue to amber.

The message on the scrying window changed.

Deactivating the ablative shield requires decoupling the system from the Enchanterium defenses. Do not attempt except in time of crisis. Please confirm decision.

"Um," Weston said, his hand hovering over the panel as he searched it. Finally, he pressed a big green button.

Decision confirmed. Decoupling in process.

Weston let out a deep breath. "I didn't think—"

Lights flickered across the damaged panel to the left, glowed momentarily, then faded. The letters on the window trembled, then vanished. A new message appeared.

Automatic decoupling failed.

CHAPTER TWENTY-FOUR

Aderyn sagged and leaned heavily on Owen. "No. We're so close!"

"It's not over," Owen said. "Can you stand? I thought you were healed completely."

"That was just despair." Aderyn straightened. "Owen, how is it not over? Look at that message!"

"I did. It says 'automatic.'" Owen nudged Weston away from the button array. "Let's see if we can get this thing on our side." Stabbing each button with slow deliberation, he spelled out H-E-L-P.

The writing vanished, wiped away by the invisible hand. Owen pressed more buttons, muttering, "Just a little more luck, okay? Show me 'manual decoupling.'"

When he finished pressing buttons, a white dot appeared on the left side of the window, pulsing like a drum. Then letters unrolled across the window.

To manually decouple the dragon defense system from the Enchanterium defenses, engage the blue lever beneath the defense panel.

Weston whooped. "Great! Hang on, I'll find it." He dropped to his knees and began feeling along the base of the ruined panel. Aderyn watched, feeling helpless—but that was stupid, because she'd worked out how to kill the deep delver, hadn't she? She couldn't do *everything* her team needed.

Weston slammed one large fist against the corner of the panel, making Aderyn jump at the sudden loud noise. The opposite corner of the panel popped away from the wall, leaving an inch-wide gap. Weston worked his fingers into it and eased that section of panel free in a series of sharp noises like fingers snapping. "This is it," he grunted. He set the sheet of metal aside and took hold of a fat blue lever that reminded Aderyn of a giant version of the stopcock on her mother's distilling apparatus. With another grunt, Weston eased the lever from a horizontal position to a vertical one.

Aderyn expected some loud reaction, a hiss of escaping gas or a clunk from within the damaged panel. But all that happened was the window cleared again to that blank gray luminescence, and then the words

Manual decoupling successful. Enter authorization to deactivate ablative shield

appeared on the surface.

Owen again spelled Dulcia's name. The window cleared again. After several seconds during which Aderyn thought she might scream with tension, more words appeared:

Ablative shield deactivated.

Aderyn sagged in relief. She rested her forehead against Owen's armored back and immediately pulled away when it turned out to still be sticky with monster blood. Then she jerked fully upright as a system message appeared.

You have received a [Perseverance] bonus of [5000 XP] for solving [Element 2] of the Lonely Tor mysteries. Experience bonuses increase with each element solved.

"Perseverance?" Livia exclaimed. "What a way to say 'refused to give up in the face of repeated disappointment'!"

"I'll take it," Weston said, hugging her.

Aderyn looked past Owen and said, "There's more, look!"

The invisible hand had added to the line about the shield another couple of sentences.

This action has been communicated to the commander of the Enchanterium Defense Corps. Send message to Central Control 2?

Owen didn't hesitate. "There's no point, because there's no one there to receive the message," he said as he pressed N. "I'm betting that was related to how the defense system works. They assumed anyone shutting off the first part of the dragon defense would have allies ready to turn off the other parts."

"But it's just us," Weston agreed. "I say we head back upstairs, turn off the second part, and find someplace to hole up for food and rest."

"I love that plan," Owen said. "If the second part gives us as much trouble as the first, we're really going to want a break afterward."

"WELL, THAT WAS ANTICLIMACTIC," Owen said. "Just pressing a couple of switches and buttons in the right order."

A system message appeared.

You have received a [Synergy] bonus of [5500 XP] for solving [Element 3] of the Lonely Tor mysteries. Experience bonuses increase with each element solved.

"I don't feel like we solved anything," Aderyn said. "Certainly not after what we managed on the previous level." She read again the words on the scrying window.

Automatic decoupling complete. Elemental volley deactivated. This action has been communicated to the commander of the Enchanterium Defense Corps. Send message to Central Control 3?

"That could be why it is a synergy bonus," Isold said. "Castilus did write that the different systems built on one another, and we could not have completed this task without having first completed the other."

"I'm not questioning it," Livia said. "As far as I'm concerned, we deserve extra experience for that fight, and for figuring out how to turn off the first system. The Spellcrafters couldn't have believed it would be that difficult." She flexed her stone hand before pushing her short blonde hair out of her eyes. "And I'm exhausted. Even using that **<Potion of Magical Energy>** only replenished my reserves. It didn't restore my sore muscles."

"Time for a rest, definitely. Anybody have a preference as to where? Aderyn?" Owen asked.

"This room is the most easily secured we've been in, but none of us want to sleep near the bodies," Aderyn said, casting a glance at the anonymous adventurer who'd carried Owen's sword. "We should see if the map gives us any guidance. I don't want to backtrack to the first level."

Isold nodded. His eyes focused on the middle distance. "The map is, as I said, incomplete, but most of the visible rooms have many doors we would have to be vigilant in guarding. There is, however, one room in the northeast corner that has a single door. If it's safe, that would be a good place to rest."

"Let's investigate it, then—Weston, what are you doing?"

Weston was tapping buttons at the door control panel. "Just checking to see if those other adventurers are still locked safely away. The doors are still locked and bolted shut. That doesn't mean they didn't figure out another way to escape, but the odds are good."

"We'll have to let them out eventually," Aderyn said. "They're not evil."

"No, just misguided." Owen gazed at the list of door codes Weston had brought up on that scrying window. Unlike the messages, they were in colored text, green, or blue, or gold. The two locking Revelin's team in pulsed red. "I really hope there's no automatic fire suppression system. If the Spellcrafters set it up so no one could be locked in if there was a fire, and Cyanne figures it out... it doesn't matter. Let's go."

Isold led them back the way they'd first come, through the testing chamber and the dining room and to the door mostly concealed by a tapestry on rails. The hall beyond was long and dimly lit, but Aderyn was too tired to feel excitement over her fantasies about what great treasure might lie at the end. The rush of healing power had faded, leaving her surprisingly achy.

Weston unlocked the reinforced door at the end of the hall, which scraped open with a *skree* of metal on metal but otherwise didn't resist. No lights turned on when he entered. Livia's lights illuminated a round space, smaller in diameter than the levitation shafts but with a similarly high ceiling. Aderyn walked forward cautiously, looking for a change in floor surface, but there was nothing but rough-patterned steel panels. Assessment told her this was [**Air Control**].

"This must be where the ventilation is managed," Weston said.

"Good thing it's still working, because we'd be asphyxiated otherwise, in a sealed compound this far underground."

"It seems safe enough," Owen said. "But we should check for secret doors anyway. I don't want us sneaked up on."

Aderyn examined the instrument panels to the right of the door. "Messing with these would be bad, I know, but I am curious about whether we could have deactivated the vacuum chamber trap from here. Not curious enough to go poking around, obviously, but still."

"Yeah, let's not interfere with the system that's keeping us alive." Owen came to stand behind her and put his arms around her waist. "And on that note, when I thought you were dead—" His voice cut off, and when he spoke again, it sounded shaky. "I wish I could make you promise not to do that again. We're in the wrong line of work for that."

"It was stupid of me to get so close when the ground was too uneven to run fast." She leaned into him, not caring about the armor and the smell of monster blood. "But you're right, these are the dangers we signed up for. So unless you want to retire..."

Owen blew out a breath that stirred her hair. "No. And besides, there's no reason we'd be safe if we weren't adventurers anymore. We might get run over by a horse, or die of disease, or eat bad mushrooms."

"So we might as well do what we love." Aderyn turned around in his arms, and they held each other for a while. Memory struck, nothing earthshattering, just a memory of talking to her brother Borrus that led to them swearing they wouldn't be distracted by romance, and Aderyn chuckled. "I can't believe I ever thought love was a distraction."

"I'm glad you didn't feel obligated to stick to your early commitment about no romance," Owen murmured. "Come, help me get out of this armor, and let's sleep for a bit."

They unfastened buckles and loosened straps, though the armor was light enough Aderyn thought Owen could probably take it off or put it on himself if he was desperate. She helped him scrub off the remaining deep delver blood and dry each piece. Then they lay down on their combined bedrolls and snuggled close together. Aderyn was almost asleep when Owen said, "Your sword broke."

"I know."

"It's too bad you can't use the <**Twinsword**>. You shouldn't be unarmed." Owen yawned. "Sleep, and I'll wake you when it's your turn to watch."

Aderyn nodded and drifted off.

Only a few hours passed before Owen woke her, but that short sleep was enough to fully refresh Aderyn. She walked the room's perimeter as a matter of formality, since there was only the one door and Weston had confirmed there were no secret entrances. Then she sat next to the door and settled in to watch. Daydreams kept her occupied, thoughts of how they might reach the next level, curiosity over the dragon's hoard—it had to have one, didn't it? Even if it was Forged instead of flesh and blood. She reviewed the hazards they'd faced already and tried to imagine other possible traps, but her knowledge of the Enchanterium was so spotty she gave up on that.

Somehow, her mind drifted to thoughts of Revelin and his team. They really did mean well, she was convinced, but they still managed to be selfish despite their professed interest in doing right. Or maybe selfish was the wrong word. Self-interested fit better. She wished they hadn't been so antagonistic. Working together would help everyone, except by the system's rules that wasn't true. Only one team could kill the dragon, only one team could complete their quest, and only one team could gain the experience.

Someone shifted in their sleep, scraping a boot across the floor. Aderyn cast her gaze around the room to see who it was. Another scraping sound redirected her gaze and jolted her into full alertness. The sound had come from the wall, not her friends sleeping in the center of the room.

Aderyn quelled her first impulse, which was to scream a warning.

Whatever this was thought itself unnoticed, and if she surprised it, it would flee without giving her the opportunity to Assess what kind of threat it was and whether it was a threat with friends. She held still and fixed her gaze on the spot the sound had come from. It was one of the areas that didn't have instrument panels, just ordinary steel sheets plating the wall.

And one of those sheets moved.

CHAPTER TWENTY-FIVE

Aderyn continued to watch through half-lidded eyes as the corner of the lowest steel sheet, the one meeting the ground, slowly curved up like someone was peeling it away from the wall. It made a dark gap through which something small emerged. Aderyn immediately Assessed it.

Name: Kobold Sneaker [1]

Type: Abomination

Power Level: 2

Attack(s): weapon x1, bite x1

Immune to: none

Resistant to: bludgeoning weapon damage, elemental fire damage

Vulnerable to: sunlight, *daylight, sunburst*

Kobolds are reptilian creatures that lair deep underground in elaborate warrens centered on their matriarch's den. They avoid direct contact with their enemies, preferring to attack from a distance and under the protection of shadows. Kobolds have a reputation among other monsters for craftiness and cunning, and are known for their clever traps.

Kobold sneakers are particularly good at moving silently and hiding. They use their skills to evaluate threats to the warren.

Kobolds are tool-using creatures and have the ability to activate some magic items. A kobold in possession of a <Flaming Lance> is nothing to be trifled with despite its low level.

Aderyn continued to hold still, though she wished she knew if the mention of a <**Flaming Lance**> was coincidental. They'd assumed those devices were missing because the Spellcrafters had removed them, but what if something else had gotten to them first?

The kobold sneaker hesitated just past the panel, tilting its head as if sniffing the air. It was no bigger than a five-year-old child, but there was nothing cute or childlike about it. Its lizard-like head was shaped like a wedge, with large, deep-set dark eyes under heavy brow ridges. It wore no clothes, and in the low light, its rough skin appeared to be a bright blue. Its thin, whippy tail curled and uncurled like it operated independently of its owner, apparently providing balance so the creature could walk upright.

Just as Aderyn noticed that, the kobold dropped to all fours and crept forward like a skittish cat, approaching Livia, who slept closest to where it had entered. Aderyn's hand closed on her belt knife. It wasn't weighted for throwing, but she had [**Improvised Distraction**] at a high enough level it wouldn't matter.

When the kobold sneaker got within five feet of Livia, it slowed its advance, sniffing the ground more like a dog than a cat. Aderyn flung the knife. The swish of the knife flying through the air alerted the kobold, who reared up so the blade took it below the chin, embedding itself in the monster's throat. The kobold staggered back, clutching the knife. Aderyn leaped to her feet and shouted, "Look out! Monster!"

The others came alert immediately, grabbing weapons or magic items. Aderyn darted past Livia and grabbed the kobold, which convulsed once and then sagged in her grip. "It's dead," she told her friends. "But there might be others. Look, that's where it came in."

Weston crouched beside the panel and peered behind it. He let out a pained cry and jerked his hand away from the steel. "It's hot!"

The others joined him. Weston sucked on his finger and gingerly touched its tip to the metal. "Cooling off, but still warm. How did that thing manage it?"

"If it had a way to heat steel to the bending point, we should be worried," Owen said. "Aderyn, did you Assess it?"

"It's a kobold. **[Improved Assess 3]** says they can use tools and some magic items." Aderyn knelt beside the kobold's body. "It wasn't carrying anything."

Weston pulled the panel wider with some effort and the creak of tortured metal. "There's a hole—no, a tunnel. This must be it. Is it a **<Flaming Lance>**, Isold?" He dragged an object out from behind the panel.

Livia made more lights, and Isold picked the thing up. "It is. But it's barely functional. Most of the magical energy is gone." He ran a hand through the tangle of webbing that Aderyn guessed was a harness. "This was sized for a human to carry the item on their back, but the kobold altered it to fit itself. The lance's body is steel with a silver lining to trap the magical energy inside, and this part here transforms the energy into an inflammable gas that flows down the hose and out the nozzle, where it ignites. They are not only powerful, but dangerous."

"Because you're carrying a canister of explosive gas on your back?" Owen exclaimed. "Damn right that's dangerous."

"They very rarely explode," Isold said. "And this one is depleted enough its flame would be weak. The kobold must have spent an hour heating the metal to where it could be bent." Isold carried the **<Flaming Lance>** across the room, set the metal canister on the floor, and held the inch-thick hose in his left hand. With the hose fully extended away from his body, he twisted a dial on the side of the canister. There was a hiss, a pop, and then a thin tongue of yellow flame burned at the mouth of the nozzle. Isold waved the hose a few times, making the flame flicker, then turned the dial again, extinguishing the fire.

"I see," Owen said. "So it's not really a weapon anymore."

"No." Isold set the hose down as the others gathered around him. "But as a tool for manipulating metal... well, it's slow and awkward. I imagine a monstrous race incapable of building their own magic items would think it was useful."

"I have a spell for heating metal," Livia said, "a low-level spell. It takes forever for the heat to build up to a point where it can do damage, or warp metal. This looks like it's about as effective."

"You've never used it," Aderyn said.

"Not much point. Early on, I always took a spell or two, when I leveled, that I didn't have an immediate use for. It was like offering the system the chance to give me a challenge the spells will be good for. But that one, I've never needed." Livia looked at the panel across the room. She stiffened and glanced around. "Where did it go?"

"What?" Owen asked, then added, "Crap. The kobold." The small monster was gone, leaving only a trail of blood drops and smears leading to the hole behind the panel.

"Of course!" Aderyn said. "We didn't get a system defeat notice. I was so distracted by the bent panel and the magic item I didn't realize. We need to get out of here."

"What, in case it comes back?" Weston said. "It didn't seem like much of a threat."

Aderyn explained what she'd learned from her Assessment, about kobolds being pack creatures living in a warren. "That one will take information about us back to its people," she said, "and a lot of low-level creatures working together can be dangerous even to higher-level adventurers. Remember the gopheroons?"

"Let's find somewhere else to hole up, then," Owen said,

"though frankly after waking up that abruptly, I'm not tired anymore."

"I was going to wake Weston in half an hour for the final watch." Aderyn busied herself with packing her bedroll.

"Well, if we're done sleeping, I have an idea," Livia said. "I think we should see what kind of meal the <**Wand of Epic Bounty**> produces."

"Ohhh," Aderyn moaned. "A real meal. I was resigned to rations and grapes and beef jerky, but now—"

"We still have to find a safe location, if we're going to eat," Owen said. "Isold, what do you see on your map?"

"There's a room west of here down a couple of corridors, but I don't know what lies beyond it," Isold said. "It has many doors to secure, but it will get us away from this room."

"Let's try it," Owen said.

The room turned out to be storage—[**Storage B01**], specifically —and while it did have four doors, two of them were jammed shut and the third was locked. Everyone laid down their gear and settled in a circle between the empty, abandoned shelves. Livia stood outside the circle. "Let's hope this is enough space."

She waved the wand, and with the last flick of her wrist, pink and purple stars of light flashed over the center of their circle like a rain of glitter. They cascaded down in a colorful rush that struck the metal floor and spread out, more like water flowing than anything solid. The mass of sparkling light bubbled like a pot boiling, then abruptly shrank in on itself and flashed brightly one last time.

The circle was empty except for something not very large at its center. Aderyn leaned forward. "Is that a jar?"

"It's a glass jar," Owen said. He knelt forward and picked it up, turning it around. "There's a label. It says 'Bricen's Miracle Meals. Take one with water. Guaranteed complete nutrition and hunger control for 24 hours. Guaranteed damage reduction from all sources for 18 hours. Do not consume more than one Miracle Meal in a 24-

hour period. Keep out of reach of domesticated animals.' What the hell?"

"What happened to 'epic bounty'?" Weston said. "I was hoping for bacon!"

"If it does what the label says, it's true," Isold said. "Just not what we assumed."

Owen sighed. "I suppose we ought to take advantage of it. Damage reduction is worth the loss of a feast." He opened the jar and shook its contents into his hand. "Six pills, enough for a full adventuring team. I wonder if the sixth pill disappears after twenty-four hours?"

Aderyn accepted her pill and held it close to her eyes. The capsule's surface swirled a nauseating purple-green. Her stomach chose that moment to beg for real food. With a silent apology to her digestive system, she swallowed the capsule and washed it down with several gulps of water. She waited. "Nothing's happening."

"It takes a while for pills to dissolve," Owen said. "I—" He paused, and a peculiar, inward-turned look crossed his face. "That feels strange."

A funny little ripple passed through Aderyn's stomach. She put a hand to her belly, but felt no more movement. Gradually, a feeling of fullness suffused her, as if she were eating a good meal. Just before the feeling became the painful one of having overeaten, it turned into a nice, comfortable sense of satiation, the point where she felt so satisfied she didn't want to eat ever again. Her muscles warmed and loosened like she'd had her meal in front of a warm fire on a freezing night. She let out a long, happy breath. "All right, maybe it's not so bad."

"I conditionally withdraw my objections," Weston said. "If it turns out to really decrease the damage we take, I'll eat one of these every day for a year with pleasure. Well, maybe not with pleasure. But with resignation, at least."

"We've only got two more charges of this," Livia warned him. "We should use them with caution."

"No fear of that," Weston said. "Anything that kills my appetite this thoroughly is powerful magic, not to be trifled with." He frowned. "And mentioning 'trifle' doesn't even get me salivating. Let's move out. I need a distraction."

"We have to find a way to the third floor, which means exploring all the blank places on Isold's map." Owen picked up his knapsack and settled it in place. "And we have to do it before Revelin's team gets free. I'm not confident they won't be gunning for us—coming for revenge," he said before Aderyn could chastise him for using an otherworlder metaphor.

"I'm starting to feel bad about locking them up," Aderyn said. "I know, it's inappropriate guilt. Don't take it seriously. I'm too good at thinking myself into other people's heads, I know that, too."

"They'd have done it to us, so we're hardly villains," Weston said. "And based on that, I'm guessing they won't take it too hard that we got the drop on them. Isold, which way?"

"West, generally speaking. I have no map of that area." Isold nodded at the western door. "And, coincidentally, that is the only other door out of here that isn't jammed shut."

"Then let's see where it goes," Weston said.

CHAPTER TWENTY-SIX

The door opened on a short corridor, dimly lit by bulbs in steel cages glowing warm gold, which ended at a T-junction. Owen hesitated only a moment before saying, "Go right. North. Away from the control chamber. It occurs to me that the shafts we've found so far have been at the outer edges of the level, and maybe that's not a given here, but we have to base our decision on something."

"Maybe I could try the <**Wayfinder**>," Aderyn said. "The other two shafts were almost identical, or used to be before the walkway collapsed. I know them well enough the magic should direct me."

"Good idea, but don't walk ahead," Owen replied. "If there are nonmagical hazards, Weston needs to be able to detect them."

Aderyn was already digging the <**Wayfinder**> out of her purse. The spike warmed immediately, with the glow increasing as she faced right. "Good guess."

"Then everyone follow me," Weston said.

They proceeded through the halls, which continued to have many abrupt turns. Despite this, the <**Wayfinder**> never wavered in its direction. After a few minutes, Isold said, "This is filling in my map nicely. We are moving steadily west and a little south."

"But it's strange that we haven't found any more rooms," Aderyn said.

"This is worse than the endless long halls as far as dungeon design goes," Livia said. "I see no point to it."

"Unless someone wanted to protect a thing by confusing strangers," Weston said. He stopped suddenly, making Aderyn bump into him. "Sorry. There's something wrong ahead."

"A hazard?" Owen asked.

"No." Weston waved at the others to stay back and stepped forward, slowly, placing his feet with deliberation like he was feeling for unsteady ground underfoot. He stopped again and crouched to peer at something invisible on the wall below waist height, then backed up a step and tilted his head, turning it as if following a line drawn on the walls and ceiling. Finally, he crouched again and did something with his hands to the invisible thing he'd first examined.

"Interesting," he said, returning to the others. "It's an alarm trip-wire. Connected to something I couldn't see, which is to say the bell it rings is somewhere far from here."

"Kobolds," Aderyn said. "This must be the edge of their territory. Their warren."

"It's definitely a warning." Weston rubbed one hand on his trousers. "And will act as a warning to us that we're in hostile territory. Didn't you say kobolds are known for being trap-setters, Aderyn?"

"Yes, and for being cunning. I think we should assume there will be other, more dangerous traps as we go." Aderyn looked down the corridor, which was about twenty feet long and one of the longer halls they'd found since setting out. "Because the <**Wayfinder**> still points that way."

"Extra caution, then," Owen said.

They moved less rapidly now, though they hadn't been running before. Aderyn focused on giving Weston directions and didn't pay attention to their surroundings until Weston stopped again, this time giving warning so she didn't bump into him.

"Trap," Weston said. He pointed at the hall ahead. "Not a subtle one."

Spikes protruded from between two floor panels about ten feet away. A second look told Aderyn they were javelin heads, old and rusting and probably not sharp, which meant stepping on them would be painful but not fatal unless you got tetanus from the wound. Weston was right; it wasn't a subtle trap or even really a trap at all.

Weston pointed at the floor panel just next to where they stood. "It's a pressure plate. Step on it, and the javelins launch."

"That's more subtle than I thought from looking at it," Owen said. "So we just walk around?"

Weston grinned. "You know," he said, "I never realized monsters could be clever. The real trap is here." He gestured with his foot at the floor panels to either side of the pressure plate. "See, if you step on either of *those*, well…" He removed his sword in its scabbard from his belt, reversed it, and gingerly prodded one of the indicated panels with the pommel.

Both panels to the side of the pressure plate tilted vertical so anything standing on them would be pushed onto the pressure plate. Weston lifted his sword away before it touched the plate. "Devious."

"I'll say." Owen regarded the trap with what to Aderyn's [**Read Body Language**] was grudging admiration. "Can we get around once the second trap is triggered?"

"Sure." Weston demonstrated by walking on the earth revealed when the trap plates lifted. "They're persistent little critters, too. This should all be concrete subfloor."

Aderyn followed Weston past the trap and glanced back at it when she was on the far side. Something about the trap resonated with her Warmaster's vision, something she felt she ought to understand, but Assessing it gave her no extra information. She put the feeling aside for later consideration and focused on the <**Wayfinder**> again.

They began finding small rooms, all of which were either laboratories or testing chambers, about ten minutes after passing the javelin trap. Most of their doors were jammed open. Weston identified and bypassed several other traps, none of them deadly. "Not deadly to us at our level, anyway," he said. "But it's interesting. They're not randomly set. There's a pattern."

"What pattern?" Owen asked.

"It's hard to explain in detail, but in general the traps steer intruders away from a location." Weston gestured broadly with one hand. "Like, if we'd found the traps and been deterred by them, we'd be circling the northwest corner of this level. We've been following the <**Wayfinder**>, which means we've plowed past some of the traps that blocked the way it leads."

"So we're getting a sense for where the heart of the warren is?" Owen's eyes narrowed. "That would be useful if we meant to exterminate these creatures."

"Maybe we should," Livia said. "If they're left unchecked, they might overflow the Lonely Tor and attack the nearby settlements. That could be what the quest meant about danger from another source, or part of what it meant, anyway."

"That's true, and it's a possibility, but it will have to wait on killing the dragon," Owen said. "Fighting a warren of kobolds, even if they're all low-level monsters, means using up our resources rapidly. We should consider it for later."

"Castilus wrote about the other defense mechanism, the one for if an experiment got out of hand," Isold said. "It floods the compound with magma without making the volcano erupt. That would be an easier solution than killing monsters one at a time. And it is a solution we can't implement before destroying the dragon."

"I like the sound of that," Livia said.

The <**Wayfinder**> gradually grew warmer and brighter until they reached one of the more secure doors and Weston worked his unlocking magic on it. The door slid open silently, revealing a dark space beyond that didn't light up when he stepped inside. But by the way her magic item cooled and darkened, Aderyn knew what it was. "It's another shaft," she said in a low voice. "The tag says **[Shaft No. 4]**."

"Why are you whispering?" Livia said in a normal voice.

Aderyn shrugged. "It's just creepy, all that dark, empty space."

"Not for long." Livia conjured a dozen *orbs of light* and flung them by the handful into the shaft. It illuminated steel-panel walls, some of them with levers and buttons, and a circle of light-gray rubbery stuff defining the extent of the levitation pad.

It also illuminated a dozen or more kobolds who stared back at them, frozen in surprise.

For a moment, no one moved. Then the kobolds let out loud cries and scattered. Owen rushed ahead of Aderyn, daylight sword shining, with Weston only a step behind. Aderyn ran after Owen before remembering she was unarmed except for her knife. She Assessed the kobolds instead.

Name: Kobold Sneaker [3]

Type: Abomination

Power Level: 2

Attack(s): weapon, bite

Immune to: none

Resistant to: bludgeoning weapon damage, elemental fire damage

Vulnerable to: sunlight, *daylight*, *sunburst*

You haven't fallen prey to their traps yet. Is that because you're good, or because you're lucky?

NAME: Kobold Stabber [5]

Type: Abomination
Power Level: 5
Attack(s): weapon, bite, claw x2
Immune to: none
Resistant to: bludgeoning weapon damage, elemental fire damage
Vulnerable to: sunlight, *daylight, sunburst*
Keep in mind kobolds prefer to fight from the shadows and at a distance. They're also fast, almost certainly faster than you and your friends. A fleeing kobold is likely to lead you into an ambush.

NAME: Kobold Watcher [3]
Type: Abomination
Power Level: 3
Attack: bite
Immune to: none
Resistant to: bludgeoning weapon damage, elemental fire damage
Vulnerable to: sunlight, *daylight, sunburst*
Kobold watchers maintain the boundaries of the warren. They also serve as lookouts when a warband is on the move. Makes you wonder what they're doing here, doesn't it?

It took only seconds for Aderyn to read the system messages, but that was time enough for the kobolds to spread out throughout the shaft. Aderyn drew in a breath and shouted, "Don't chase them if they run, it will be an ambush!"

"It doesn't matter, they're gone," Owen said, lowering his sword. He pointed with the tip of the blade at a patch of earth where a wall panel was missing. A hole crusted around the edges with something that gleamed showed where at least one kobold had made an escape. "They must be smart if they knew not to stay and be slaughtered."

"And that wasn't even *daylight* or *sunburst*," Livia said. She made more orbs and sent them spinning after the first ones until the room was free of shadows. "We scared them off."

"They clearly weren't expecting us," Weston said. He knelt beside the hole where Owen stood and touched the rim. "This is lined with scraped-off kobold hide. They must have lived here a while for it to build up like this."

Aderyn joined him to see for herself. The rim looked like a dull oil slick, gleaming with iridescent blue and brown and green streaks. "I thought their hide was pebbly, but these look like scales."

"They might be closer to dragons than lizards," Isold suggested. "If they're resistant to elemental fire damage, that would make sense, given that most lizards and lizard-like monsters lack that trait."

"Interesting, but we should be more concerned about when they're coming back." Owen turned off his sword blade and tilted his head back to look far up at where the lights orbited the ceiling. Another walkway missing large sections of itself circled the room high above. "If they've occupied this place long enough to leave marks, they're not going to leave it to us just because we're bigger and stronger. They'll return in force and attack when we're not expecting them."

"That doesn't give us time to figure out how to extend the emergency stair," Weston said, "at least if it's not obvious. And I'm guessing there isn't a way from down here. But we should look, just in case."

Aderyn cautiously approached the levitation pad, but remembered she'd seen kobolds race across it in their flight without being tossed into the air. She avoided stepping on it anyway. "Funny thing, though. [Improved Assess 3] said something about the kobold watchers—that was one of the types of kobolds here—about them playing lookout for a warband on the move. But this wasn't a warband, because they clearly held this territory. So what was their role here?"

"I see," Owen said. "Watching, but for what?"

"The only reason I can think of is that they were afraid of being attacked." Aderyn walked over to join Owen near the first set of instrument panels. "But if it was us they were afraid of, they'd have been on alert, because we're not that far from where Weston started disabling traps. So it must be some other threat."

"Revelin's team?"

"Maybe. We don't know how much of this area they explored before we met them at their camp, and they were fairly banged-up, like they'd been in more than one fight." Aderyn chewed her lower lip in thought. "It could be the waspnettles. In fact, the more I think about it, the more likely that seems. The waspnettles are on the move, and you said it was likely they were searching for a new home. Hive. They'd be in conflict with the kobolds over territory."

"That's good for us." Owen turned his attention on the instrument panel. "Let the kobolds and the waspnettles wipe each other out, or at least decimate each other so they're easy for us to kill."

His words sent an unexpected pang through Aderyn. "I sort of sympathize with the kobolds, though. Maybe it's that the waspnettles are vicious and frightening-looking, or maybe it's just that the kobolds were here first and the waspnettles are encroaching—" She laughed. "And there I go being inappropriately sympathetic again."

"Kobolds are vicious too. Remember that when you start inventing stories about their noble savage natures." Owen's smile took the sting out of his words. "I understand. One of my college professors used to say it was part of human nature to want to take sides in any conflict. We're happier when we can divide the world into Us versus Them. You're just good at thinking yourself into other people's conflicts."

Aderyn laughed again. "I hope it's not a terrible flaw that will get people I love hurt."

"Unlikely. You're fierce in defense of your friends." Owen stopped what he was doing and kissed her. "I don't think we're going to find anything useful down here. Too bad Livia doesn't know *levitation.*"

"Because there's no thundering way I'm learning a spell that lifts things off the solid, wonderful ground where we all naturally belong," Livia said from across the room. "We just have to find stairs, that's all."

"I can't use the <**Wayfinder**> for that. Stairs are too generic. I'd have to know the specific stair." Aderyn dropped the item back into the <**Purse of Great Capacity**>.

"Then it's back to covering ground and filling in Isold's map," Owen said. "And since there's only one other door out of this place, it's either that or backtrack. Any preferences?"

"Move forward, though we're undoubtedly going deeper into kobold territory," Livia said, flexing her stone hand. "That could be a benefit. We could make a start on killing them as we go."

"A series of fights that wears us down might be a bad idea," Weston said. "On the other hand, we have no idea where the stairs are. We can't afford to bypass territory where they might be."

"Good points," Owen said. "Through door number two it is."

Weston struggled with the door briefly before hauling it open. "The lock was disabled, but the door was jammed, probably by a kobold sneaker. But the hall is clear." This one was long and poorly lit, reminding Aderyn of the hall Owen had said felt like something out of a movie with monsters in the ceiling. He'd explained movies as best he could, but Aderyn still wasn't clear on why anyone would want to experience a movie that scared them.

They had only gone a few steps when Weston halted. "Trap?" Owen asked.

"No. Something's coming." Weston tilted his head back. "Several creatures. A buzzing—it's waspnettles. And there's a fight."

"Coming closer?"

Weston nodded.

"Then let's not wait for it come to us," Owen said. "Go! Go!"

CHAPTER TWENTY-SEVEN

As they raced down the hall and around corners, the sounds of battle grew and faded and then gained in volume again, always gradually increasing. Aderyn ran beside Owen, [Keep Pace] tugging her along. She ran over possibilities in her mind, evaluating plans. Buzzing meant waspnettles. If they were fighting kobolds, the sensible thing was to wait until one side eliminated the other and then attack the winner. But if it was Revelin's team fighting the waspnettles, then, rivals or not, they had to help them. That meant diving right in. Either way, they needed the advantage of surprise.

"Owen, slow down," she said. "We can't go bursting in. We need to Assess the situation."

"Good point." Owen slowed. "You go first, then."

The sounds of fighting and buzzing and cries of pain or anger now filled the corridor. Aderyn slowed and peeked around the next corner. It was another one of those rooms with the door permanently wedged open. Small lizard-like bodies lay sprawled in death, with a few brown-carapaced waspnettle corpses lying here and there. The room was a flurry of movement, waspnettles wielding swords and javelins against smaller kobolds bearing an assortment of weapons, as well as random implements being used as improvised bludgeons or knives. As Aderyn took this in, one of the waspnettles impaled a green kobold against the wall and dropped its javelin rather than try to retrieve it from the corpse.

She said, "The kobolds are losing. We take the waspnettles by surprise after they've won the battle and believe they're safe."

"That feels dishonorable," Weston said. "But—all right, I know, we take the advantages given us."

"That's right." Aderyn felt dishonorable about it herself. But they were monsters, and there was no sense in piling in there and fighting two battles at once.

She watched, Assessing the waspnettles in preparation for the attack.

Name: Waspnettle Warrior [5]
Type: Magical beast, intelligent
Power Level: 9
Attack(s): weapon or claw x2; special
Immune to: none
Resistant to: bludgeoning damage, mind control
Vulnerable to: trip attacks, *daylight, sunburst*
Special attacks: stinger (poison)
Don't get stung. I know, you're tired of hearing it, but I guarantee you this is a warning worth repeating.

Again, the oddity of the Assessment struck her. Who was the "I" talking to her? She'd always assumed her Assessments came from the system, but the system wasn't a person. Aderyn could believe dungeons might have personality, because those arose from the system and their development was strange. But it wasn't possible for the system itself to have an identity, because with dungeons being part of it, that would mean two separate entities that were one creature. Or—was that wrong? Dungeons' personalities were different—compare Gamboling Coil with Sorrowvale, for example—so the system already technically had several identities. Aderyn squeezed her eyes shut against the crazy thoughts. Now was not the time to analyze.

When she opened her eyes, the noises had faded out of hearing. She waved her arms wildly and mouthed the word *Go* at the others. Then she stood back for Weston, Owen, and Livia to pass her.

With no weapon, there was nothing she could do past providing tactical support. She hated being helpless. It didn't matter that her tactical support was more important than anything she could do with a sword; she still felt she wasn't pulling her weight.

They'd taken the waspnettles by surprise, just as she'd planned, and after only a few seconds, the system defeat notices began appearing. Aderyn watched Owen's opponents out of habit before remembering he wasn't wielding the <**Twinsword**> anymore and wouldn't hear her tactical advice unless she yelled it, which was a bad idea because it meant the opponent heard it too and could defend against it.

In less than a minute, the fight was over. Owen stretched his left arm and winced. "I can tell this wound isn't as bad as it looks," he told Aderyn while Isold ran the <**Wand of Healing**> over it, "but reduced damage isn't no damage as far as pain goes. Not that I'm complaining. Except I guess I am."

"Nobody likes pain, so you're all right complaining a bit." Aderyn cast her gaze over the room, counting. There were thirteen dead kobolds and seven waspnettle warrior bodies. "I wonder if any of the kobolds fled."

"More inappropriate sympathy, sweetheart?" Owen asked.

"No. Just considering whether they might have gone for reinforcements." There were two other doors, one open, one closed. Through the open door she saw a few dim lights, not enough to clearly illuminate the hall past the first few feet. "That will influence which way we go next. I'd rather not run into a kobold trap."

"This other door is jammed shut," Weston said. "I think—" He took out his diary and a stub of charcoal pencil. "Isold, can you sketch the map of where we've been, starting at Shaft Number 4?"

Isold made several deft lines and squares on the pages and handed the book back to Weston. "Did you think of something?"

Weston started drawing tiny circles and X's over Isold's tidy map. "This is what I recall of the doors we passed. Look at the pattern. You know I said the traps were meant to herd someone away from something? The doors do the same thing." He finished drawing and held the book open to display the marked-up map. "This part over here is almost certainly the heart of the kobold warren."

"Meaning that's where we should go?" Owen asked.

"No. It's what we should steer clear of." Weston closed the book on his finger to mark his place. "Kobolds use tunnels, not stairs. Stairs are an advantage to invaders. They wouldn't build their lair around something that would give an enemy a direct line to its center. Especially not if all the stairs in this place look like the ones we found, broad and easy to climb."

"You mean, don't waste our time searching that area," Aderyn said.

"Right. We should move south from here, see if we can find the southern boundary. If this is near the westernmost edge of the compound, which I think it is—"

"That's my guess as well," Isold said.

"Well, the other stairs were also far out to one side. It makes sense to circle the place if we can, staying close to the outer edges." Weston glanced at his hand as if he'd forgotten he held his diary and put it away.

"I like this idea," Aderyn said. "It makes sense. As much as anything about this place does."

"And south leads through the jammed door," Owen said. "The open one goes west, back toward the lair. It's sound reasoning."

Weston turned to Livia and said, "Well?"

"I said I wasn't going to use those words again," Livia said primly.

"What I will say is you're never more attractive than when you're logical."

Weston's eyebrows raised. "You want to save that compliment for when I can do something about it?"

Livia took his face in both her hands and kissed him soundly. "Lead the way, dearest."

It took all of them to get the door open when it turned out Weston's skills couldn't do anything about the wreck the kobolds had made of the lock. Eventually, Livia used her *pass through walls* spell to force the door to slide a few inches open, and with all of them shoving, the door finally gave in. Lights flickered on in the hall, brighter than in the other passages.

"That's another clue," Aderyn said as they continued south. "The places the kobolds occupy are either dimly lit or totally dark. They can see in the dark, after all."

"You're right, though with how erratic the lighting here is, we unfortunately can't depend on that fact," Owen said. "Do you smell that?"

Aderyn sniffed. "It smells damp, and earthy. Like a forest after a light rain."

Weston signaled a halt. "We're coming up on another closed door. I don't like it. There's nothing here that could cause that smell, and the door is one of the heavy ones. It ought to block smell, too."

"We could go back. There was a side corridor we passed," Aderyn offered.

"That led back east. We need to keep moving south and west, or just south, if we want to cover all the territory." Weston examined the door. "Locked."

"Locked? Not trapped?" Owen said.

"Well, I—*hey!*" Weston took a step back as the door abruptly slid open, fast like a snake catching prey. "That was unexpected," he added, sucking his fingers. "I think I lost some skin."

Aderyn peered past him at the open room. "Lights. But the room looks empty. It says [**Testing Chamber B32**]."

"Be cautious anyway." Owen gently moved her aside so he could enter. Aderyn followed him.

The air in this room was damp and warm, almost muggy, and the smell of wet earth overpowered any other smells. Unlike the other testing chambers they'd found, this one's walls were unmarked by writing. A sheen of moisture coated all the walls, condensation beading and running in thin channels to pool on the floor, which was almost as torn up as the deep delver's lair. Both floor and ceiling looked like someone hurling boulders had made enormous dents in all the steel panels.

Aderyn moved cautiously to avoid tripping over the exposed edges. "The concrete is gone in places here, too, just like in that first trap Weston found."

"This is where the smell comes from," Livia said. She crouched beside one of the damaged panels and dug two fingers deep into the exposed earth. They came away covered in rich, black soil that clung to her skin. "What did I tell you about fertile soil? I bet if you planted a fork in this stuff you'd grow a silverware tree in three months."

"No wonder the kobolds found this place attractive. That looks easy to dig through," Isold said. "This wreckage makes me think they might have been here and chose not to stay."

Weston was already checking out the room's three other doors. "I have so many questions I wish I could ask the Enchanterium builders. At the top of the list is 'why did you love doors so much?' Because I do not understand—" He grunted and took a step back. "The door just sealed itself."

Aderyn froze. "Sealed itself?"

"Gave me a little zap, too." Weston hurried to the door they'd entered by. "Locked again. It's a trap."

"What about—" Owen began.

Two loud crackling sounds and a whiff of ozone drew Aderyn's attention to another door, which had flashed with an electrical discharge. She ran to it and tugged, then felt all over for the override. Her relief at finding it died when she pressed down and met no resistance.

Owen drew his sword. Even in the well-lit room, the glowing blade's brightness was dramatic. "Be ready for an attack. Aderyn, over here."

Aderyn took two steps across the jagged floor. A shrill screech filled the air. Ceiling panels tilted and shifted, and kobolds poured through the gaps, shrieking and brandishing weapons. Aderyn resisted the urge to cover her head and Assessed rapidly, not paying attention to anything but names and numbers. Twenty-nine kobold stabbers. Fifteen kobold sneakers. The numbers kept rising. Thirty-two. Thirty-six. Forty-one.

A system defeat notice appeared, followed by another identical one, but Aderyn was too busy staying out of range of the kobold weapons to read them. She drew her belt knife and slashed wildly, not trying to kill anything, wanting only to give herself time to find a better weapon. Her other hand fell on the <**Rod of Unfettering**>; not useful now. The <**Wand of Limited Paralysis**>? Too specific, and only two charges left. She stabbed a kobold threatening her whose knife was larger than her own, making it squeal and retreat.

She backed into the wall to give herself some cover and risked a glance around. Owen and Weston were fighting back to back. Livia was laying about with *stone fist,* the spell cast on her right hand paired with the actual stone fist of her left. Isold had just compelled a kobold to attack its friends. She was the only useless one, if she couldn't come up with something.

She reached into the <**Knapsack of Plenty**>, and her hand fell on a length of polished wood that curved. She drew it out. It was the <**Laborer's Staff**>, the one that turned into useful items. At the moment, the most useful item it could be was a hardened oak staff.

She swung the staff awkwardly, hitting a kobold who staggered but didn't fall. It snarled and turned on her, raising its knife that was to it as big as a sword. She brought the staff up to block the blow and, with both hands gripping the staff, shoved the kobold back into the knife wielded by one of its friends. Its slit-pupiled eyes widened, and blood trickled down its brown hide where the knife ran him clean through.

Congratulations! You have defeated [Kobold Stabber]. You have earned [650 XP]

Aderyn sidled away, searching for a new target. Her foot found a sharp floor panel edge, and she glanced down to find more secure footing. When she looked up, a bronze kobold was two feet away and flinging itself at her face.

She screamed in mingled surprise and anger and raised the staff. The kobold bounded over it and slashed with its weapon, scoring her armor with a downward slice and continuing diagonally to her opposite hip, where the blade found flesh. It wasn't a deep wound, but the knife wasn't sharp and it tore rather than cut, making her scream again, this time in pain. She struck the kobold with the heavy crook of the staff, catching it in the belly and propelling it a few feet away. It caught itself and made a leap toward her.

[See It Coming] showed her the blast of flames from the kobold's mouth in time to barely dodge out of the way. Panting, Aderyn swung the staff again. Her damp palms slid and caught on the smoothly polished staff, and she gripped it harder to dispel visions of it slipping out of her hands and flying out of reach. The system defeat notices were coming faster now, but didn't occlude her vision.

Her second blow slammed into the kobold's shoulder. The kobold shrugged it off like her attacks were nothing. Flame breath, unusual resilience—this was no ordinary kobold. She took a defensive position and rapidly Assessed the creature.

Name: Kobold Bushwhacker
Type: Abomination
Power Level: 6
Attack(s): weapon x2, bite, special
Immune to: none
Resistant to: bludgeoning weapon damage, elemental fire damage
Vulnerable to: sunlight, *daylight, sunburst*
Special attack: flame breath

The elite warriors of the kobold tribes, kobold bushwhackers are known for their persistence in attacking and destroying threats to the warren and to the matriarch. A kobold's native cunning pairs with unusual strength to make bushwhackers formidable foes even to higher-level adventurers. Kobold bushwhackers have enough of their draconic ancestors' blood to be capable of breathing fire. It's not a very hot fire, not something that can melt steel, but I guarantee that's small comfort when it's your face being burned off.

Aderyn blocked the next swing of its knife and edged sideways. She heard her friends shouting to one another, and once Owen called her name, but she couldn't take her eyes off the kobold bushwhacker. Any time she did, it scored another hit, mostly glancing blows, but blood flowed from wounds in her shoulder and the place where the first slash had hit her hip.

She smacked it again, this time forcing it back a step. Anger filled her. This was a… a *damn* power level six monster, and she was letting it beat her down! Roaring a challenge, she leaped at the creature before it could recover from the blow.

The ground tilted beneath her foot. She flailed around with her other foot, searching for a floor panel that wasn't off-kilter, but her foot slid and kept sliding. She screamed Owen's name and flung herself backward, hit her head against the floor that had become a wall, and bit her tongue hard enough to make blood flow. The sound of her own name shouted in response was dim and far away. Then she was tumbling down a metal-lined shaft, rolling and bouncing painfully against the walls, dizzied by movement and the continuing flashes of system defeat messages.

After an eternity, she shot out of the shaft and came to a stop on rocky ground. She lay there panting, willing herself to stay conscious. Gradually, her breathing slowed, and she opened her eyes.

Dim light barely illuminated the space around her, but it was enough to see she was in one of the Enchanterium's many rooms, though one that was long abandoned based on the heaps of dirt, the missing floor panels, and how several of the lights had been torn from the walls. The hole she'd fallen through was high on one wall, not in the ceiling, and as she watched, its top and sides crumbled, narrowing it.

She was about to Assess the room—at least she could find out what its tag said—when she realized her breathing had an echo. Carefully, trying to lessen the pain that flashed through her skull, she turned her head.

Across the room, lying in another pile of rubble, the kobold bushwhacker glared back at her.

CHAPTER TWENTY-EIGHT

Surprise and fear struck Aderyn like the sharp rap of a staff across her knuckles. The feeling reminded her of her only weapon, which she wasn't holding anymore. She cast about frantically for it, and another pulse jolted her when she saw it some five feet away, tilted at an angle near one corner of the room.

The kobold shifted. The small sound of its body dragging across dirt and stones echoed in the stillness. Aderyn lunged for the staff. Agony lanced down her right leg, and she collapsed, breathing heavily in another effort not to black out from the pain. When her vision steadied, she gingerly felt along her shin and was rewarded with another stab, not as bad as when she'd put her whole weight on it, but enough to tell her she'd broken her leg.

The rattling of stones moving drew her attention back to the kobold. It was on its knees now, cradling one bloody arm in the other and weaving slightly. Slowly, it got one foot beneath it. Aderyn's breathing sped up. She dragged herself to the staff, clawing the wrecked floor panels for leverage, shoving with her good leg and ignoring the terrible pain that made her vision blur every time she jarred the bad one. She didn't dare look back to see if the kobold had retrieved its weapon and was coming after her.

After what felt like forever, Aderyn wrapped her hand around the staff's crook. She fumbled the weapon into a fighting position and with her last surge of energy turned herself around and put her back to the wall. "Come on!" she shouted. It came out as a wheezing gasp with no power to it, but she brandished the staff at the kobold. "Come on and try to take me!"

The kobold hadn't advanced more than a few steps. Now it stood, still holding one arm close to its chest, staring at her with that malevolent gaze. It coughed once, a horrible dry rasping noise. Then it folded at the knees and collapsed.

Aderyn didn't relax. She remembered the kobold sneaker she'd stabbed back in the **[Air Control]** room, how she'd believed it dead. This could be a ruse, too. She used the staff to push herself more upright and watched the kobold closely. Its sides moved rapidly in heavy breathing, and it lay on its side so the uninjured arm was beneath it. She didn't see its knife anywhere, but suppose it was concealing it so it could stab her when she got close?

After a minute or two in which neither of them moved, Aderyn decided to take a chance. She hitched herself to one knee with the staff's help and hobbled, dragging her broken leg behind her. The pain was less now, or maybe she was just used to it. Or maybe she was dying and losing contact with her body. She deliberately refused to look at her health indicator. She couldn't do anything about it if she was dying.

She stopped a foot away from the kobold. It didn't react as if it knew she was there. Awkwardly, she maneuvered the staff into a striking position, gripping it closer to the crook than usual to compensate for kneeling. Dizziness made the room swim, but she blinked and clenched her hands tightly on the staff.

When her vision cleared, the kobold was looking up at her. Its large, deep-set dark eyes beneath heavy brow ridges had barely any whites, and the slits of its pupils had a purple hue that made its eyes look shallow and blind. But it clearly saw her. Its gaze flicked to the staff Aderyn held, then back to her face. Aderyn raised the staff higher. It didn't look away. It coughed again, a sound like gravel rattling in a tin cup. Then it bared its teeth, not in an attempted attack, but in what Aderyn would swear was defiance.

Aderyn hesitated. She told herself not to be stupid. This creature would kill her without a second thought if their positions were reversed. It wanted her and all her friends dead because they were a threat to its people. It might someday lead raids against the defenseless settlers surrounding the Lonely Tor.

She lowered the staff.

The kobold's mouth closed. The heavy brows twitched, surprising Aderyn with their mobility. Aderyn sighed. "I'm probably going to regret sparing you. Maybe that makes me stupid and soft. But I can't do it. Not in cold blood. Not when I'm sure you were only attacking because you were afraid of what my friends and I might do to your warren."

She sat, and hissed as the move jarred her broken leg. The kobold twitched at the sudden sound. It loosened its grip on its wounded arm and then propped itself on its good elbow, examining Aderyn. Its breathing was still rapid, and it trembled as if holding that position weakened it.

Something tickled the back of her neck. In her mind, Owen whispered, ...*where*...

She covered her mouth to hold in a shriek. In her pain and disorientation and the encounter with the kobold, she hadn't remembered she wasn't truly alone. Focusing her thoughts for **[Bonded Mind]** proved difficult through her pain, but she squeezed her eyes shut, pictured Owen's face, and thought *Safe. Go down.*

Nothing happened at first. Then the tickling sensation returned, like gentle fingers brushing her skin. ...*find you?*...

Aderyn considered that. Under normal conditions, she would

tell Owen and the others to stay put and let her come to them, just as she and Owen had done when they were separated before. But she was wounded, and probably trapped, and while this wasn't the ideal move, it was the best of a lot of bad options. *Find me on first level.*

...coming now... ...love...

That brought tears to her eyes. *I love you, too,* she thought, hoping it was a short enough phrase to be passed along in its entirety. The tickling sensation vanished, leaving her feeling bereft.

To distract herself, she pulled the <**Knapsack of Plenty**> off her shoulders. "Good thing this is magical, or my belongings would be crushed," she murmured, half to herself and half to the kobold. It twitched again, its eyes blinking rapidly as it looked at her more closely. Aderyn felt around in the knapsack for her waterskin. It was half full, which was better than half empty, or so her father always said. As a child, Aderyn had thought he said it to mess with her, but she'd come to see the wisdom of his position later: dwell on what you have and not on what you don't. That seemed an ideal attitude for her current situation.

She drank and felt better, though she deliberately took no more than a swallow or two. Conserving rations was important. Lowering the waterskin, she caught the kobold's eye. The creature had followed her movements, watching her in silence. It occurred to her she hadn't heard a sound out of it since they'd both landed here. She considered for a moment, then offered the waterskin to the kobold.

It stared at the leather sack like it didn't know what a waterskin was. Aderyn tilted it and shook a few drops onto her hand. "You must need some of this," she said, and felt stupid for talking to a monster like it was a person who could understand her.

The kobold looked at her, then at the waterskin again. Its body trembled visibly. In the next moment, its arm gave out from beneath it, and it collapsed.

"Oh!" Aderyn exclaimed. She reached for the kobold. It drew back its lips again, or what would have been lips if it had any, and hissed a warning. Aderyn raised both hands to show she was unarmed. "You don't want me touching you. I get it." She opened her mouth, tilted her head back, and mimed pouring water into her mouth from the waterskin held where it didn't touch her face.

The kobold stared at her again with that slit-pupiled, unreadable expression. Then it tilted its head back and opened its mouth.

Aderyn poured a thin stream of water into the kobold's mouth, not too much, and watched to make sure it didn't choke. Then she capped the waterskin and put it away. "I don't know what I can do for either of us," she said. "Your arm is in bad shape, and my leg is broken. I guess we're stuck here for a while. My team will find me, I know."

As she said this, a tremor ran through the room, building until the whole place shook. Earth and stones rained from the wrecked ceiling, enough that Aderyn involuntarily shrieked and covered her head with her arms. The kobold writhed, trying to protect itself with one arm. Without thinking, Aderyn leaned forward so her upper body loomed over the creature. Pebbles bounced off her back and skull, not hard enough to do more than sting, but when the tremors didn't immediately stop, the pebbles were soon joined by larger stones, one of which cracked against her interlaced fingers protecting the back of her head and numbed them for a few seconds.

Desperately, she sent out a mental call: *Stop, stop!* They hadn't felt any earth movement the whole time they'd been in the Lonely Tor, so the earthquake was likely Livia moving the earth, trying to reach her. She distilled the long plea she wanted to send into *Will crush us, stop!*

The tremors stopped. Aderyn sat up. The first thing she saw was that the hole she and the kobold had fallen through had fully collapsed. Well, it wasn't as if she could have gotten out that way. She peered up at the ceiling. She hadn't paid much attention to it in her fear for her life, but surely it was lower than it had been?

Moments later, Owen said *...sorry, you all right?*

She sent back *Yes* and followed it with *No more, will collapse.*

Owen replied with *...who us?*

That, Aderyn didn't know how to answer. *Later*, she thought. The sensation of being spoken to vanished.

She controlled her fear about the sagging ceiling and said, more for comfort than communication, "I told them to stop trying to get at us that way. I guess this place isn't all that stable."

The kobold stared at her without comprehension.

"I know you don't understand me," Aderyn went on. "But I have to talk or I'll go crazy. I bet kobolds don't have claustrophobia, not living in tunnels the way you do. I can't look up or I'll start thinking about being—" She shut up before she could say *buried alive*. "Anyway, I wish you could talk, but monsters generally don't."

The kobold managed to sit up. Aderyn didn't offer to help. Its tail curled around its body, the tip twitching. Then it let out a series of rasping, guttural noises that rose and fell rhythmically.

Aderyn jumped. "Was that—you *do* speak!"

The kobold made more noises.

"You'd have to be able to communicate with other kobolds, if you live in a warren and use tools and all that." Aderyn watched it for signs of comprehension, but it didn't react to her words. "I'm glad you don't speak the human language, because that would be too unbelievable. Even if it would make things easier for the two of us."

The kobold remained silent. Then it muttered something less intelligible even than the previous sounds, almost like it was grumbling to itself about stupid humans who couldn't speak Kobold. Aderyn smiled. Her face felt stiff, like she hadn't smiled in years instead of the hour or so she'd been down here.

"I hope everyone else is all right," she murmured to herself. "I mean, not severely injured. Owen couldn't have spoken to me if he was unconscious." Finally, she turned her attention to the heads-up display, as Owen called it. Each of her friends was still on it, calming her most extreme fear that someone had died in the trap. None of the fat blue lines indicating their current health were at full, but they were close enough to maximum she could relax.

Her own health indicator, a blue line along the bottom of the team roster, was at about half. That seemed high for having tumbled down a fifty-foot shaft and broken a leg. "That miracle meal saved my life," she told the kobold. It was patting itself down and ignored her.

"Well, that's enough sitting and waiting," she said. "I'm the one with the <Wayfinder>, so them finding me is going to take a while. And something you should know about me, friend kobold, is that I'm not good at waiting for things, not if I can make them happen faster. So if you don't mind, I'm going to see about getting out of here."

She picked up the <Laborer's Staff> and used it to get to her feet, leaning on it to compensate for her broken leg. Immediately, she discovered there was no way to avoid putting *some* weight on both legs. The pain spiked again, and she collapsed. The kobold looked her way and made some chittering noises, followed by a couple of grunts. "Yes, fine, I should have known better," she told it. "I don't see you getting up to race out of here."

As if it understood, the kobold picked up a fist-sized stone and slowly got to its feet. It teetered for a moment with its good arm flung out for balance, and then it took a tentative step, and another. It made its way to the wall before collapsing, falling into the wall and flinging its arm out to keep from sliding to its base.

"Nice work," Aderyn said. "How does it help?"

The kobold passed the stone to its other hand and sidled along the wall, pressing its good arm against the steel to keep itself upright as its feet felt for purchase on the irregular floor. Aderyn realized there was a door, half buried in rubble, toward which the kobold headed. She shot upright, nearly fainted from pain, and ended by sagging against the staff whose end she'd wedged between two bent floor panels for added support.

The kobold heaved itself over a pile of loose stones to lie flat against the closed door. Its heavy breathing shook its small frame, and its head sagged briefly against the door as if its neck was too weak to support it for the moment. Then, with a deep sigh, it passed the stone back to its other hand and slammed it against the door. A deep ringing like the toll of a bell underwater filled the room, followed by a faint tremor Aderyn felt through the metal floor panels. The kobold knocked, and knocked, and knocked again until the whole room trembled and sang with a metallic chorus that turned Aderyn's mild headache into a skull-throbbing nightmare.

"Stop!" she shouted, putting her hands over her ears. That dimmed the ringing, but the vibrations got worse. "Stop! I can't bear it!"

The kobold glanced her way. It lowered the stone and grunted something. Then it sank to a sitting position and tossed the stone away, a gesture that looked like dismissal, as if its work was finished.

"That was a signal, wasn't it," Aderyn said. "Your people will come for you." She was too tired, and hurt too much, to be afraid of what would happen to her when they did. For all she knew, this kobold didn't care that she'd helped it and was waiting for its moment to attack. She didn't have the strength to care about that, either.

The kobold ran stubby fingers lightly over its injured, bloody arm. It spoke again, a few sharp guttural syllables. Then it hitched itself one-handed away from the door a few paces before its arm gave out and it sagged again. This time, its tail twitched, in a rhythm more lively than its halting pace. It stared at Aderyn. Aderyn stared back. Finally, it pushed itself into a sitting position with its tail wrapped around its legs and let out a couple of sharp yips and a grunt.

"We can't talk to each other," Aderyn pointed out. "Though it's nice that you're trying. If that's what you're doing."

The creature bared its teeth. Then it spoke again. It took Aderyn a few seconds to realize it was repeating the same three syllables. "You —what was that?"

The kobold slapped its chest twice and spoke a third time, slowly enough Aderyn got the message. "It's your name. You have a name— oh, it's stupid to be amazed at that. Ak tuk something. Wait!" She Assessed the kobold, willing her hunch to be right.

Name: Akdukhur

Type: Anomaly

Power Level: 6

Attack(s): weapon x2, bite, special

Immune to: none

Resistant to: bludgeoning weapon damage, elemental fire damage

Vulnerable to: sunlight, *daylight*, *sunburst*

Special attack: flame breath

Akdukhur is a kobold bushwhacker in service to the warren's matriarch. He is fearless in defense of his people, but not stupid. You forgot about the flame breath, didn't you? He didn't. You were luckier than you realize.

As she neared the end of the Assessment, another two lines appeared below it.

There's a thin line between daring and foolhardy. I applaud you for continuing to walk it.

CHAPTER TWENTY-NINE

Aderyn gazed in stunned silence at the letters until they vanished. "Akdukhur," she said, though her pronunciation didn't match his very well. Then another fact penetrated her bewilderment. "Anomaly. **[Improved Assess 3]** says you're an anomaly type. Before, all you kobolds were abominations." After all this time Assessing and killing monsters, Aderyn knew "abomination" was a hostile monster that didn't fit into other categories, and "anomaly" was the same but non-hostile. She'd never seen an Assessment change its mind before.

Akdukhur slapped his chest more forcefully and repeated his name, then jabbed a finger at Aderyn. She noted in passing his hands only had four fingers before realizing what he wanted. "Oh! Aderyn." She pointed at herself. "Uh. Dare. In."

Akdukhur hesitated, then said, "Ehdern."

"Close enough." Aderyn relaxed her grip on the staff, which promptly fell over, startling both of them with the sharp clang it made on what was left of the flooring. "Sorry." She dragged the staff to lie across her lap.

The kobold shifted his position and let out a hiss when the movement jogged his arm. "That looks pretty bad," Aderyn said. "Can I see? I could at least clean—"

She reached for Akdukhur, who recoiled and bared his teeth at her. Aderyn backed down. "I guess that's a no."

Just then, the back of her neck tingled, and Aderyn let out a gasp of excitement. "Maybe he's found a way here," she exclaimed.

Owen's thoughts sounded in her head. *...still well?*

Yes. Where are you?

...library... ...down...

It was a good start. *Waiting*, she replied.

...patience... ...I will find you...

Emotion and tone didn't come through the **[Bonded Mind]** connection, but Aderyn could picture the determined set of Owen's jaw and the intensity of his speech. She shivered with happiness. *I know*, she replied.

She grabbed the <**Knapsack of Plenty**> and pulled it onto her lap. "Let's see what's in here. Probably nothing that will magically transport me away or bring Owen and the others here, but we've been tossing things in here without paying attention ever since we left Finion's Gate, so it's worth looking."

Akdukhur watched with interest as she pulled objects out of the apparently empty bag. "Mess kit... spare blanket... bedroll... Owen's bedroll—" A pang of loneliness struck, longing for her husband and the comfort of his embrace, and she bit her lip and turned her head away from Akdukhur, though he likely didn't have any idea what her sudden tears meant. When she got herself under control, she continued in a shaky voice, "The <**Traveler's Aid**>, which I really should have given to one of the others. There's no point in me having both the direction finding items. Rations—they aren't terribly appetizing in normal times, and I still feel like I ate the best meal of my life only two minutes ago."

She glanced at Akdukhur, who continued to watch her—no, he was staring at the wrapped packet containing hard biscuit. "Do you want some?" she asked. When he didn't answer, she broke off a hunk of the dry stuff and showed it to him. "Food?"

Akdukhur made some guttural noises and patted his chest. Aderyn tossed the biscuit, and he caught it neatly. "It's dry," she warned, but the kobold ignored her and gnawed on the hard lump. Aderyn shrugged and continued searching.

When the knapsack was actually empty, she surveyed its contents and sighed. "I really do wonder what you did when you worked," she said, prodding the pieces of the bronze laboratory minion. "The Assessment said menial or repetitive labor, but maybe you could deliver a message. Though I don't see how to attach a message to you or how to get you out of this room if I did."

She wearily loaded items back into the knapsack and started to put it on, just in case her leg miraculously healed and she needed to flee. Her hand brushed something smooth fastened to the bag's side. "The wand—oh, the <**Wand of Limited Paralysis**>. I forgot about it because it wasn't useful in that fight." She slid it out of its sheath and examined it. "It worked really well on the deep delver, for something used to treat—"

With a gasp, she fumbled the wand in suddenly numb fingers. "Isold said it was used for treating broken bones! Akdukhur, this could do it!" She set the wand down carefully and with both hands rearranged her broken leg so it was stretched straight in front of her. "I don't know how to set a broken bone, but hopefully it won't matter." She clasped the wand in newly-steady fingers and wove the complicated activation pattern, ending by flicking the tip at her shin.

The sickly green light gleamed briefly. A powerful force grabbed Aderyn's leg, sending pain shooting through her shin. She screamed, but the pain vanished before the sound did—vanished entirely, as if her leg were whole again. Aderyn got to her feet, carefully not putting her full weight on her broken leg. When she was finally standing, she leaned on the <**Laborer's Staff**> and gingerly bore down on her right leg. Pain throbbed again, but not as bad as before, and it stopped when she eased up.

"All right," she panted, "all right. It's not set properly, so it still hurts, but the bones don't shift, so I think I can hobble." She made her halting way to the door and felt along the frame for an override. Akdukhur gabbled something. "It's—crap. Either there isn't one, or it's broken." She tugged on the door handle. "Locked." She hopped back a couple of steps and nearly tripped over a bent floor panel. Lowering herself to sit beside it, she said, "I'm out of ideas."

Akdukhur gripped the edge of a broken wall panel that lay near him. The steel of the walls was thinner than the floor, and more of the walls were damaged than the floor panels. The one Akdukhur selected had a sharp edge where it had been torn into two unequal pieces and was curved like a shallow bowl. The kobold weighed it in his hand. Despite its size—it was easily as wide as his chest—he handled it easily, even one-handed.

Aderyn eyed him skeptically. "What are you doing?"

With a groan, Akdukhur threw the panel at the wall across from him. It clanged as metal struck metal, though it didn't send up that awful racket Aderyn hated. The kobold crawled after it. Food seemed to have revitalized him, because he moved less stiffly and painfully than before. When he reached the panel, he picked it up again, examining it. Then he turned his attention to the wall. It had been a lucky fluke that the panel had struck metal, because about half this wall was bare of paneling, and most of the exposed, compacted dirt behind the paneling was coming down. Aderyn looked up and froze. The ceiling sagged there more than anywhere else, with the heavy earth bearing down, falling—

She closed her eyes and shuddered, telling herself it was an illusion. When she looked again, Akdukhur was scooping dirt from the wall, using the bent panel as a shovel.

"No!" Aderyn exclaimed. "You'll bring it down on us! We'll be buried—"

Akdukhur laid the makeshift shovel down and turned to face Aderyn. He spoke at length, words she didn't understand but whose meaning she could grasp: *I am an expert digger; leave this to me.* Then he picked up his tool and attacked the wall again.

Aderyn peeled first one hand, then the other, off the <**Laborer's Staff**> and ran her gaze up and down its length. "Akdukhur, wait," she said. Her heart pounded. Giving food and water to a helpless enemy was different from giving up her best weapon. But if the kobold knew how to escape...

With a sigh, she spoke the command words Isold had said would activate the staff. "Staff, I have need. Make for me a shovel."

The staff shivered. Its polished shaft narrowed, and the crook end curled in on itself to make a knot of wood the size of Aderyn's head. Akdukhur pressed against the wall and began shouting, but Aderyn ignored him. The staff shivered again, and suddenly Aderyn was holding a shovel finer than any she'd seen in her life, with a shining silver blade and a smoothly polished oak shaft.

Akdukhur's voice cut off. Then he said something that sounded like a question. Aderyn wasn't sure if it was, because why would kobolds and humans share any similarities between their languages? Or maybe she was wrong. She pretended he'd asked the most obvious question and said, "It's a magic shovel. Will it work?"

She scooted closer and extended the shovel to the kobold, who wrapped his fingers around the shaft tentatively. When Aderyn let go, Akdukhur's arm dropped, and the shovel struck the floor with a thud. "It's too heavy," Aderyn said. "If your arm was healed, maybe—"

Akdukhur hefted the shovel one-handed and dug into the wall. The blade penetrated only a few inches, but the kobold lifted it away and dumped a few ounces of earth in a pile nearby. When he lifted the shovel to try again, his arm quivered with effort.

"It's not going to work," Aderyn said. "Don't hurt yourself. We'll think of something else."

Akdukhur let the shovel fall again and sat heavily beside it, his tail curling around him again like it had a mind of its own. Maybe it did. **[Improved Assess 3]** helped when it came to a fight, but Aderyn was becoming aware that there was still a lot she didn't know about monsters. Or about creatures that might not be as monstrous as everyone assumed.

She ran through the list of things the <**Laborer's Staff**> could turn into: shovel, axe, pickaxe, coil of rope, pitchfork, scythe. How funny that most of those could be weapons in the right hands. Her father always said never to underestimate the non-classed just because they didn't have weapon skills. "You tell me that matters when you're facing a heavily-muscled farmer pointing a pitchfork at your belly," he'd told his children, and Aderyn had remembered the lesson.

"Maybe we could pry the door open with the shovel blade," she told Akdukhur. "Or—no, the axe wouldn't make a difference to a steel door."

Akdukhur closed his eyes and said something curt. He followed it with a longer string of guttural syllables.

"Fine. You want to give up? Give up." Aderyn's leg twinged. "Actually, I don't blame you. Let's both give up." She propped one elbow on her left knee and lowered her chin to rest on her palm. "I really don't know what else to do."

A grunt from Akdukhur drew her attention. The kobold was sitting up alertly, his gaze fixed on the door. Slowly, he got to his feet. Then Aderyn heard it—the sound of feet reverberating on a metal floor, headed their way.

She lurched to her feet and let out a choked scream when she discovered the paralysis had worn off. She collapsed, breathing heavily—the pain was so much worse than she remembered. The footsteps grew louder, faster. It sounded like dozens of people. Chill fear struck Aderyn. Dozens meant kobolds. No matter the accord they'd found, she had no illusions about where Akdukhur's true loyalties lay.

"Give me the shovel. The shovel!" she hissed.

Akdukhur stared at her. She pointed at the shovel and waved her hands. Akdukhur slowly picked the magic item up and weighed it in one hand. Aderyn could practically hear him considering his options. Then he set the shovel down and prodded it with his foot, kicking it toward her. Aderyn leaned far forward and got her fingers on the blade.

Something scratched at the door, the sound of long, sharp fingernails on metal. Aderyn couldn't help looking at the horny nails on Akdukhur's four-fingered hands. Desperately, she dragged the shovel closer until she could grip the shaft. She gabbled out, "Shovel, my need is done, be staff once more!"

The shovel quivered. The door rattled, then shook with pounding. Aderyn gripped the magic item so tightly she felt its transformation in her bones. As it became a staff again, the door latch snapped, and the door slammed sideways, too rapidly to be anything but intentional. Piles of dirt and rocks cascaded down from where they'd lain against the door. Aderyn raised the staff, her heart hammering, and prepared to meet her death.

Four figures tumbled through the doorway and stopped just feet from her. "What in thunder are you doing here?" Revelin demanded.

Chapter Thirty

Aderyn gaped. "It's you! How did you find me?"

"We weren't looking for you. We were searching for a way up you bastards wouldn't interfere with." Revelin's epic scowl was visible even through the beard. "I suppose you thought it was funny, locking us in?"

"I—" Aderyn searched their faces. Cyanne looked furious. Inaya and Embrus were watching Revelin. "We wanted to slow you down, since you clearly didn't believe us about the danger the dragon poses to everything and everyone in the area. It wasn't a prank."

"Sure it wasn't," Cyanne said. Both her fists were on fire. "Didn't you care that we might not find a way out?"

"We would have come back for you." Aderyn hoped she sounded more assertive than she felt. Of all the possible outcomes this farce could have, she hadn't imagined this one. "We're not heartless. And we were sure you'd figure something out. You're not stupid."

"Stupid enough to have listened to you when you lied to us." Revelin shifted his grip on his staff like he meant to attack her. "You have the nerve to talk about honor and then pull that trick?"

"Like you meant to be honorable, either," Aderyn shot back.

"We haven't lied to you. Killing the dragon without disconnecting it from the Enchanterium will make the volcano explode. You can't possibly want that."

"You just said that so you could get the experience for killing it," Cyanne said.

Aderyn rolled her eyes. "Your lack of trust in everything is going to kick you in the teeth someday, you know that?"

Embrus stirred. "If you're not lying, you should be able to prove it. You learned the information from somewhere—show us."

"It's not on me. My team has it. And *don't* say anything about how convenient that is," she warned Cyanne, who to her surprise shut her mouth. "If you help me, maybe I can walk, and I'll take you to my team."

"Yes, why are you alone in here?" Inaya asked. She was the only one who didn't sound hostile, which would have raised Aderyn's spirits if she'd believed that would influence the others.

Revelin scanned the room. "This is—" He stiffened. With a shout of "Monster!" he lunged forward.

"No, don't!" Aderyn shrieked. She whipped the **<Laborer's Staff>** around and hooked Revelin's ankle, bringing him down. Without reflecting on how lucky a strike that had been, she dragged herself to where Akdukhur was half-hidden behind the pile of dirt from the collapsing wall and ceiling. Putting her body between him and the others, she panted, "He's not—this isn't what you think. Assess him."

Embrus stepped forward, his eyes narrowed. "Assess for what? He's a kobold. We've fought enough of their kind to know he's a monster."

Aderyn knew nobody but a Warmaster saw much information about monsters, but she'd hoped these adventurers could see at least the fact that Akdukhur was an anomaly rather than an abomination. Despairing, she said, "They fight us because we're a threat to their lair, they believe. I think they just want to be left alone. He didn't attack me when we both fell down here, and he tried to get us out. Please. Don't kill him."

Revelin got up from sprawling full length on the floor. "You protect evil," he snarled. "You're more deviant than I believed. Get out of the way."

"No." Aderyn glared up at him. Behind her, Akdukhur stayed perfectly still. With her back pressed against his arm, she could feel his muscles were rock hard with readiness to defend himself.

Revelin raised his staff. "If I have to kill you, too—"

"Revelin, no!" Embrus exclaimed. "We don't kill our own. She's no Bandit or Assassin."

"Unless she is, and she's disguised herself," Revelin said. His eyes never left Aderyn's.

In desperation, Aderyn Assessed him, swiftly looking over skills she'd only glanced at once before. "Name, Revelin. Class, Swifthands. Level thirteen. Your skill rankings are high for your level —seventeen ranks in **[Unarmed Combat]**, twelve ranks in **[Hand and Foot]**. I don't know anything about **[Heron Style]**—wait." She held up a hand to his astonished face as she Assessed the skill. "Oh, that's interesting, it modifies your **[Unarmed Combat]** with specialty kicks and maneuvers. And you have five ranks in that even though you only got it three levels ago."

"What the blistering thunder are you doing? How do you know all that?" Revelin shouted.

"I'm a Warmaster. This is what Warmasters do if they find a partner to team with." Aderyn's leg was throbbing, and her back hurt from staying upright without jogging her leg further, but she continued to face Revelin down. "And Assessing monsters to learn their weaknesses and abilities is another thing we do. I know the kobolds attack us. I also know they don't have to be our enemies."

Revelin's gaze flicked past her. Akdukhur tensed further, and a low growl issued from his throat. "Shut up," Aderyn hissed. "That's not helping." She knew he didn't understand her words, but her tone might have worked, because he stopped growling.

"It looks vicious," Revelin said.

"It hasn't attacked Aderyn," Inaya said. "It's in a position to easily rip her throat out with those teeth, and it hasn't done that either. Revelin, what does it mean?"

Revelin's gaze moved back to Aderyn, then to Akdukhur again. He lowered his staff. "It means we don't know everything," he said. "Stand down."

Aderyn let out her breath in a great whoosh. Akdukhur didn't relax. That seemed wise, given that he only barely understood what was going on. "It's all right," she told him, but stopped short of saying *You're safe* because it wasn't a good idea for a kobold to go around trusting humans who might not have Aderyn's understanding. "He's not going to hurt you." To Revelin, she said, "We should get out of here. Akdukhur summoned help from his people, and they won't know we don't mean their warren any harm."

"We've already killed some kobolds. We *did* mean them harm," Embrus said.

"Nonaggressive or not, we'll defend ourselves," Cyanne said.

"Which is why I don't want us to stay where it will be an issue." Aderyn pulled herself up using the staff's support. As long as she didn't put any weight on her broken leg, it hurt with only a throbbing ache she could live with.

Inaya regarded her curiously. "Do you need healing?"

"I didn't want to ask to use up your resources," Aderyn replied.

"That's not how we think," Revelin said. "Cyanne will set your leg and use the <**Wand of Minor Healing**> on it."

"*Cyanne* will?"

Aderyn instantly regretted how surprised she'd sounded. Cyanne's scowl deepened into anger. "What, I can't know doctoring because I'm a Flamecrafter?" she snarled. "Because we're all erratic and quick to anger?"

"Um," Aderyn said.

Inaya laughed. "You mean, quick to anger like you are right now?"

Cyanne blushed. The flames surrounding her fists died and went out. "So I have a temper. There's nothing wrong with that."

Aderyn was sure that wasn't true, but she felt she'd antagonized the woman enough already. "I'm sorry I sounded so disbelieving. I just didn't think any spellslingers but Bonemenders learned medicine."

Cyanne knelt beside Aderyn and gently felt along the broken leg. "I wanted to be doubly useful to a team. Most Bonemenders don't join adventuring teams for long because there's more use for their abilities in cities. Hold onto something, this will hurt."

Aderyn gripped the staff hard and ground her teeth on an involuntary moan as Cyanne realigned the bone. "It's a bad break, so it will take several passes with the healing wand."

"I really shouldn't deprive you—"

"Revelin's right. We use what we have to help others, not just ourselves." Cyanne withdrew a slim wand of ash wood wound about with a copper coil of wire, aimed it at Aderyn's leg, and activated it. Warmth and comfort flooded through Aderyn, focused on her broken leg, dulling the throbbing pain. Cyanne repeated the motions three more times before saying, "That does it."

Aderyn got her leg beneath her and inwardly rejoiced when it took her weight without complaining. She'd never appreciated being whole before. "Thank you. And now we really should get out of here."

Akdukhur suddenly got to his feet. He definitely looked better now that he'd had food and water and some rest. Now, however, he looked agitated, shifting back and forth on his feet and clutching his wounded arm closer. He made a series of chittering, gulping noises.

"We have to go, Akdukhur," Aderyn said. "Your people will come for you, and if we're here, there will be a fight." She gestured with her staff, pretending to fight an invisible opponent. "Fight? Yes?"

The kobold stopped his restless movement and gave Aderyn a look that clearly showed his impatience with her ignorance. He raised his good arm and bared his teeth, then pretended to swing a sword that "connected" with Aderyn's midsection. Then he clutched his own stomach and bent as if in pain.

"Oh," Aderyn said. "You get it. All right, we'll go. I—um. Thank you. I don't know how to say it in your language. Thank you." She enunciated the words clearly and bowed. Maybe that was a gesture kobolds understood.

Akdukhur stared. Then he said, "Ankoo," and repeated her bow.

Stunned, Aderyn backed away, tripped on the edge of a floor panel, and caught herself with the staff. "They're coming now, I think. We should hurry."

They ran down long, winding corridors that were typical of what Aderyn remembered of the first level of the Enchanterium, passing through areas of light and darkness, until they rounded a corner and Aderyn exclaimed, "Oh! Shaft Number 2!"

"Let's rest a moment," Revelin said.

Aderyn leaned against a wall and tilted her head back. The tiny blue lights were dimmer now that the main lights on the upper level were lit, but they still gave the impression of a night sky with only a few large stars shining. Her encounter with Akdukhur wasn't fading with time; if anything, it felt more immediate, more real even than the shaft and Revelin's team and the bliss of being free of pain. She hoped the kobold's fellows would come for him soon. She'd considered asking Cyanne to heal Akdukhur's arm, but with time pressure and the likelihood that Akdukhur would refuse to let a human touch him, she'd decided against it.

With her eyes closed, she focused on Owen and thought, *Safe in* **[Shaft No. 2]**.

Immediately Owen responded with *...in shaft one...*

Aderyn chuckled. *Wrong shaft.*

...coming now... ...stay there...

"So," Inaya said from close beside her. Aderyn jumped. "Sorry," Inaya said with a chuckle. "I can't not move silently. I've tried."

"My friend Weston says the same." Aderyn stood upright. "I really am sorry we had to trick you."

Inaya waved that away. "It's fine. We'd have done the same to you if we could. Winning matters, right? And there's only so much experience to go around when it's a matter of killing a monster."

"We're not in it for the experience, not really. Just the quest."

"Sure," Inaya said, sounding sincere though Aderyn was sure she didn't believe it. "How did you get separated from your team a second time? Does this happen to you often?"

"No, not—" Aderyn thought back on some of their earlier adventures. "Well, sometimes. More than usual since we arrived here."

"And you have a way to find them. Or is that with your team, too?" Inaya smiled to show it was a joke.

"Actually, I have both of them." Aderyn found the <**Traveler's Aid**> where she'd stowed it in the <**Purse of Great Capacity**> for easier access and displayed it. "We found this after we talked to you."

"Where? Not to accuse you of anything, but we haven't found a single thing worth keeping."

"Meaning, did we beat you to it? Some. The central control chamber on the second level had a nasty trap that killed a team of adventurers a hundred or more years ago. There's nothing wrong with taking what they can no longer use." Aderyn hoped she didn't sound defensive.

"I see. No, that's fair. I take it you avoided the trap? What was it?" Inaya spoke with professional interest. Aderyn explained the evacuation hazard, and Inaya whistled. "Not exactly a trap. I get it. We ran into something like that—there was a room that had a slow leak from somewhere and a radiant heating device that turned the whole thing into a steam bath."

"Did it burn you?"

"No. It was uncomfortable, nothing more. But the giant fungus living in it thought we looked tasty." Inaya grinned. "Never saw anything like it before. Put me off mushrooms for life."

Aderyn laughed with her. "Anyway," she went on, "what I use to find my friends is this." She took the <**Wayfinder**> out of the purse and displayed it.

Inaya's eyes widened. "By thunder, you've got a <**Wayfinder**>. No wonder you've been five steps ahead of us this whole time. What are you, heir to a fortune?"

Aderyn smiled. "No, just the granddaughter of a talented and generous high-level Spellcrafter."

"That thing is worth its weight in gold, silver, and platinum. Wish I had one. Someday." Inaya extended a hand. "Can I hold it?"

With only a moment's hesitation, Aderyn handed it over. Inaya ran her fingers over the rows of dull spikes and examined the rotating rings within, then gave it back. "It's beautiful. I've never stopped wishing the system had made me a Spellcrafter."

"Really? You seem so comfortable with your class."

"I like being a Moonlighter. But magic items have always fascinated me." Inaya glanced around. "And this place... it's sad to think it was abandoned. Do you know why they left?"

"It happened after the level cap. The old Spellcrafters died off, and the new Spellcrafters weren't able to reach high enough levels to maintain it. I agree, it's sad." Aderyn thought of the [**Library**] and [**Scriptorium**], of the hydroponics laboratories, of the broken minion in her knapsack, and imagined what the Enchanterium had been like when those places were active and vibrant.

A crack of thunder shook the room, making Aderyn and Inaya stagger and clutch one another to stay upright. A great wind blew out of nowhere, buffeting them. Between one blink and the next, four figures appeared in the center of the deactivated levitation pad, huddled close together.

"Wow," Inaya said. "That was dramatic."

Aderyn wasn't listening. Owen straightened and turned, searching the room, but Aderyn was already in motion. She crossed the space between them in a few swift strides, and as he said her name, she threw herself into his arms.

CHAPTER THIRTY-ONE

"Aderyn," Owen said again. His voice shook. "I—"

"It's all right," she whispered. "It really is." She buried her face in his shoulder and drew in a deep breath, letting his familiar scent and the feel of his armored body against hers calm her.

"[**Bonded Mind**] kept me from going crazy with worry," Owen murmured. "All we knew was that you were lost and wounded, with —" He raised his head. "Is this who you were with?"

"Um, no." Aderyn hugged him one last time and stepped away, but kept hold of his hand. "But they did rescue me."

Owen and Revelin stared at one another. Revelin was back to looking hairy and impassive. Behind him, his teammates watched Owen warily. Owen let out a deep breath. "I won't apologize," he said, "because I believe we made the right decision. But I owe you everything, and I can't tell you how grateful I am. Thank you."

Revelin glanced at Aderyn. "You should know we happened on Aderyn by accident. In case that affects your gratitude."

"It doesn't." Owen's hand closed more tightly over Aderyn's. "I was afraid we would wander this place forever without finding her. So however it happened, thanks."

"You're welcome." Revelin leaned his staff against the wall and folded his arms over his chest. "But we're back at an impasse. We want to protect this land by killing the dragon. You insist that's impossible. Convince me."

"I told you we have evidence," Aderyn said. "The record of an adventurer from long ago who came here to destroy the dragon." She turned to Isold. "Will you show him?"

Isold removed his knapsack and reached inside. "His name was Castilus. We found his journal with his remains." He flipped through the pages of the small book until he found the one he wanted. Extending the open book to Revelin, he continued, "The same information is in a device used by the Spellcrafters to store knowledge about the Enchanterium—this compound. If the book doesn't convince you, we can take you there to see for yourselves."

Revelin accepted the book and read with one finger trailing down the page. He was a slow reader, Aderyn judged by the speed of that finger. "This says there was another method of destruction. One that doesn't make the compound explode."

"That's right," Weston said. "That one is for if one of their Spellcrafted devices got out of control. It floods the compound, but it doesn't kill the dragon."

"I've been wondering why the old Spellcrafters didn't destroy the dragon themselves before they left," Inaya said. "If they had access to this method you're after, wouldn't it have been safer to get rid of it?"

"I have no answer for that," Isold said. "Just many speculations. They might have had sentimental reasons not to want this place destroyed. They might have hoped to return someday. Or they might not have been powerful enough to kill the dragon even after it was decoupled from the compound—the path we pursue now doesn't destroy the dragon, it only makes it possible to kill the creature with impunity. For us, all of us, their reasons are irrelevant. What matters is stopping the dragon. We know how to do that."

Revelin finished his reading and handed the journal back to Isold. "All right, I believe that the writer of that journal believed what he was told," he said. He held up a hand to forestall Owen's objection. "And since you say you have corroborating evidence, that's good enough for me. But we're not going to turn around and leave before the dragon is dead."

"We told you, we have to kill the dragon to fulfil our quest," Aderyn said.

"So do we," said Embrus. "And your quest isn't any nobler than ours."

"Stop," Livia said, walking between the two groups with her hands outstretched to either side as if pushing them apart. "The only consequence of arguing over who gets to kill the dragon is that the dragon stays alive to go on attacking the settlements. How about we focus on making it possible to kill it, and worry about who gets the prize after?"

"We?" Revelin said.

"Yes, we. You said you're not giving up and leaving the task to us. Well, we're not standing aside for you. So we might as well team up." Livia sounded as logical as ever, but her scowl said she thought it was stupid that she had to lay out this obvious solution.

Revelin's gaze grew thoughtful. Embrus and Inaya stared in fascination at Livia's stone arm. Cyanne was watching Owen with a look equal parts anger and indecision. Aderyn decided she was going to learn why Cyanne hated Owen on sight. But not right then. "Livia is right," she said. "We both want the same thing. We should work together to get it."

"And when the dragon is free?" Revelin asked. "Are you going to attack us to stop us usurping your quest?"

"Are you?" Owen said. "Look, Revelin. I don't have a solution for that. But this place can be deadly, and if we're working together, we have a better chance of all of us getting out alive. Which to me is frankly the most important thing." He extended his hand. "I promise to deal fairly with you, now and when the time comes to kill the dragon. What do you say?"

Revelin didn't hesitate to clasp Owen's hand. "I say that's fair. We'll work together."

"Good," Weston said. "Now we come to the bad news."

Aderyn startled. "Bad news?"

"We had to skirt a lot of kobold territory to reach the stairs," Weston replied. "And then avoid waspnettles. And waspnettles fighting kobolds. We didn't want to waste time and energy getting involved, not while we had to reach you. But that means the conflict between the waspnettles and the kobolds is heating up, and if it's as bad as that on the first two floors, it won't be any better on the upper floors."

"Might be worse, if the waspnettles decided to make their new hive somewhere up there," Livia added.

"Then why not use that other destruction method, the one that floods the compound with magma?" Embrus said. "No. Wait. That would make it impossible to deactivate the third control, or whatever you call it."

"That's true," Isold said. "We will have to fight our way to the third control chamber. But after that, we believe activating that means of destruction to flood the Enchanterium will make it easier for us to reach the dragon by eliminating both sets of foes."

"And it will rid the area of two potential dangers to the settlements," Owen said.

"You can't!" Aderyn exclaimed. "What about the kobolds?"

Owen gave her a puzzled look. "It would take care of them. Aderyn, please tell me you're not sympathizing with vicious monsters again. They nearly killed Livia in that last battle. They are clearly dangerous."

Aderyn shook her head. "No. They—" She reddened. "I know it

will sound like I'm doing it again, but I'm serious, Owen, they really aren't what you think."

"She's right," Revelin said. "She protected one that didn't try to kill her, or us. I want to know the details now that we're relatively safe."

"You what?" Owen gripped Aderyn's shoulder. "Aderyn, this is a little much!"

"I know. Please, just listen! I promise it will make sense. Owen, when have I ever let my sympathies endanger us?" She glared at him. "And last time this happened, it was you, arguing on behalf of Clapperclaw, who was a lot more dangerous than a kobold tribe."

Owen's hand relaxed. "You have a point. All right. Tell us about how the kobolds are secretly good warriors who fight a noble battle against prejudice and hatred."

"Don't make fun. That's not how the story goes."

They sat together while Revelin's team ate, and Aderyn told what happened when she fell down the shaft with Akdukhur. Leaning against Owen's shoulder as she was, she couldn't see his expression, but the tensing and relaxing of his arm around her waist was good enough for [Read Body Language]. It tensed when she mentioned sparing Akdukhur's life, before she knew he wasn't going to kill her; relaxed as she related speaking to Owen via [Bonded Mind]; tensed again when she wrapped up her story with the words, "Akdukhur warned us that his people were coming in time for us to avoid them. You see, Owen? I'm sure the kobolds only attacked us because they thought we meant to destroy the warren."

"So you think they're actually peaceful?" Inaya said.

"No. I think they are dangerous in defense of their home, just like anyone. But since we can't communicate with each other, they have to assume anyone who isn't a kobold is hostile. So they might as well be enemies."

"*Are* enemies," Revelin said. "And don't give me that look. You were lucky to find one who saw the virtue of not aggressing on you when you had the upper hand. You said you gave it—"

"Him," Aderyn said. "He has a name. Does that sound like a mindless killer to you? I bet the waspnettles don't have names."

"Fine. You gave *him* food and water, and you didn't kill him when he was helpless. Even with a broken leg, you had the power in that situation. I don't think we should count on all the kobolds being that willing to compromise."

"I'm not saying that!" Aderyn drew in a breath to calm herself. "I don't want us to make friends with them. I agree with you that that would be dangerous and it would also assume too much from one interaction. I'm just saying this is their home, and I want us to do what we can to avoid threatening it."

Owen gave her a squeeze. "Spoken like the woman I love."

"Noble, but how possible is it to avoid *all* conflict with the kobolds?" Embrus said. "Weston told us the place is crawling with them, fighting the waspnettles. We might not have a choice."

"We have one option we should try first," Isold said. "My map of this level is nearly complete, and I have a good sense of the different territories on the second level. Where we are now, **[Shaft No. 2]**, is uncontested space, held by neither the kobolds nor the waspnettles and not currently being fought over. They have also not taken over the corresponding space above. Since my map of that part of the second level is incomplete, I suggest we explore it fully for ways to access the third floor before entering hostile territory."

"That's smart," Embrus said. "All right. I think we need another hour of rest. My arm is still bothering me."

Aderyn turned on him. "You're still injured? But why didn't Cyanne heal you?"

"We save the healing for the direst wounds," Revelin said. "We can endure a few minor injuries."

"Yes, but you spent healing resources on me!"

"Direst wounds, remember?" Revelin smiled for the first time

Aderyn could remember. "If it makes you feel better, you'd have slowed our retreat down with that broken leg. Healing you was pragmatic."

"Not to throw your generosity back in your face," Isold said, pulling out a wand, "but we have rather more resources than you do." He waved the <**Wand of Minor Healing**> across Embrus's bandaged arm, making green light bubble up from the wand's tip and flow over the Pathseer's arm from shoulder to elbow. Aderyn watched him relax, as if he'd been tense with pain this whole time. "Anyone else?" Isold said.

"Thanks," Embrus said. "I guess it hurt worse than I realized."

Isold nodded. "Which of you does the healing? Cyanne?" He presented her with the wand. "It has another nine charges, and it will be better, if we are working together, to make sure more than one person has healing capabilities."

Cyanne hesitated. Then she took the wand, surprising Aderyn again by smiling. "This is a fine loan. Thank you."

"It's a gift," Owen said. "Call it reparations for locking you up. How did you get out, by the way?"

Cyanne's smile turned impish. "I guessed the Spellcrafters might not have wanted people to burn to death in locked rooms, so I waved fire over the door and it sprang open."

Owen groaned in a comically exaggerated fashion. "I knew it! Sometimes I hate being right." He held out a hand to Cyanne. "We got off on the wrong foot, you and I. Can we call a truce?"

With a nod, Cyanne clasped Owen's hand. "I let my past get in the way of the present. I'm sorry."

"I admit I'd rather work together than oppose you all," Revelin said. "Even if you are one of those deluded Fated Ones."

Aderyn was about to protest when she realized he was smiling behind all that hair.

Owen said, "So you believe us?"

"I don't know that I believe in the Fated One, period," Revelin said, "but I certainly believe, if there was such a thing, you would be a good candidate. You're married, for one, and you wouldn't do that if you were faking, not when all the supposed Fated Ones tend to be in it for bed-hopping privileges. So let's just say I'm keeping an open mind."

"I can live with that," Owen said. "Let's get moving. We still have a long way to go."

CHAPTER THIRTY-TWO

The spiral staircase of steel slabs felt more secure than it looked, though the "steps" weren't more than two feet wide and they had to climb single file. Aderyn rested her fingertips on the wall, trailing them after her as she ascended step after step. She deliberately didn't look down. With no handrail, the drop was unimpeded, and she didn't like thinking about the hard ground that lay at the bottom of that drop. Afraid of heights, afraid of small spaces... she wasn't much of an adventurer if she let those fears influence her. Which she wasn't going to do. After all, she hadn't refused to climb the steps, and she hadn't freaked out when she was trapped with Akdukhur. She was tougher than that.

The memory of Akdukhur started her thinking about what had happened to him. His people would have rescued him by now, and suppose he'd told them about her? Suppose they were coming after the human adventurers next? No, Aderyn was convinced the kobold bushwhacker wouldn't betray them. At least not now. He might change his mind after some time had passed and the memory of being helped had faded. She couldn't assume he was a friend even if she had spared his life and then given him food and water.

The possibility that they might have to fight more kobolds worried her. Of course they weren't going to let the kobolds attack them without fighting back, and it wasn't as if the kobolds knew they weren't a danger. It just felt wrong, as if Aderyn's accord with Akdukhur was tainted if they couldn't find a peaceful solution. She was getting soft.

She stepped onto the walkway with a sigh of relief and took a few more steps to carry her away from the edge. Not letting fear control her didn't mean taking unnecessary risks. "Where to next?"

"The control chamber," Isold said, "or at least the rooms in that direction. We did not explore south of [Testing Chamber B05], and that should put us close to the edge of the disputed territory. We can move south and east from there."

"We haven't been in this part of the second level," Revelin said. "I wouldn't mind seeing that control chamber, though we shouldn't spend much time there."

"It's not far," Owen said.

Inaya marveled at the colored writing on the walls of [Testing Chamber B05] and made excited noises when Isold showed her a <Write-All>. "I always wanted one of these," she said. "I used to scribble on the walls of my bedroom with charcoal pencils when I was little, writing my name and drawing pictures. It drove my parents crazy. This would have been amazing!"

Revelin had already moved on to the doorway of the control chamber and now stood looking in without entering. "It's sad that their bodies were left here all this time without a proper memorial. Though you made good use of their equipment."

"I won't apologize for that," Owen said.

"They're past caring," Livia said with a shrug.

"True. It wasn't a criticism, just thinking that that's a memorial of sorts. Passing on gear to others." Revelin circled the room in the opposite direction from Embrus, who was examining the scrying windows.

Aderyn wandered away to look at the northern door. "You said these weren't as reinforced, right, Weston?"

"Right, though that one is jammed shut." Weston crouched at the southern door, messing with the lock. "This one is just locked—or was." He slid the door open. "You want to take a look—" He fell silent.

Aderyn said, "What?"

"We got lucky," Weston said. "It's another shaft. Going up."

Aderyn hurried across the room. "Up?"

Weston gestured to her to look inside. **[Improved Assess 3]** told her this was **[Shaft No. 5]**. It was narrower than the other shafts they'd found, but dark enough to obscure the interior and make it feel larger than it was. She crossed to the levitation pad at its center and felt around her for something to test the field.

An apple sailed past her and hit the rubbery floor, bouncing once and then rolling away. "Not active," Cyanne said. She walked over to retrieve her apple and buffed its surface on her trousers. "Did you find **[Shaft No. 1]**?"

"Yes." Aderyn chose not to reveal that she'd been caught in the still-active field. "How did you get out of there without us knowing?"

"I cast *fly* and found the lever to extend the stairs." Cyanne moved to Weston's side. "There's no point activating the levitation fields. *Flying* is more efficient."

"I agree. I was looking for the lights." Weston scanned the instrument panels, then poked a couple of buttons and flicked a switch. Lights came on, glowing wanly, but providing enough illumination to show the walkways high above as dim shapes circling the shaft.

"That helps. I'll *fly* up there—"

"Wait a moment, Cyanne," Owen said from the doorway. "Let Aderyn Assess the area. If there are monsters concealed up there, or a trap, she will see them."

"Is that a Warmaster ability?"

"Yes. It's called [**Improved Assess 3**]." Aderyn watched Cyanne closely, but the woman didn't show any of the anger or hostility she'd displayed to Owen previously. Aderyn wanted to believe in Cyanne's change of heart, but it was hard to accept, given how irrational she'd been before. She was still resolved to find out what Cyanne's problem was.

She tilted her head back and Assessed the distant platforms. "There isn't anything alive up there, and I don't see any magical traps."

"I'll take a closer look." Cyanne chanted a few nonsense words, and heat haze enveloped her, warming the air so Aderyn felt like she sat beside a dwindling bonfire. Then Cyanne leaped into the air and flew upward, trailing pale, almost imperceptible rose-pink fire the same color as the <**Wayfinder**>. As she neared the walkways, she was visible only as a pink haze that then disappeared over the edge.

"Everything all right?" Owen called out.

"It's fine." A distant clunk sounded, and then the rattling metallic noise of the emergency stairs extending filled the air. The rosy haze descended, and Cyanne's form came into focus. She hovered a few inches above the floor, watching the stairs appear. "I'd rather fly, honestly, but those stairs are good for an emergency."

"I'll gather the others," Owen said. "You all go ahead."

"I need to check these other doors first," Weston said. "I want to be sure we're not leaving anything open behind us for an ambush."

Aderyn waited for the final steel slab to extend, then immediately headed up. She wasn't a coward, and she wouldn't let her discomfort with heights stop her. She kept her hand on the wall anyway.

Cyanne kept pace with her, flying instead of walking. "You don't look like you love heights."

"I don't, but it doesn't matter." Aderyn kept her gaze fixed on the steps in front of her.

"I always wanted to be a Windwarden," Cyanne said. She did a slow midair backflip Aderyn saw out of the corner of her eye. "I wasn't happy about being made a Flamecrafter instead, not at first. But there are compensations."

"I guess the system doesn't restrict you to only taking spells relating to your element. Livia uses *drench* all the time." The stairs just went on and on, didn't they?

"*Fly* is my favorite spell. It's wonderful." Cyanne went back to hovering. "So, what can a Warmaster do at higher levels? I thought the class was useless—no offense."

"It's what everyone thinks." Talking was a good distraction. "I provide tactical analysis for my partner and my team. Monster Assessments, dungeon Assessments, city Assessments. And I have skills that make me effective in combat even though I don't have strong weapons abilities. Then there are paired skills Owen and I share that make him a more powerful Swordsworn."

"Owen. Yes." Cyanne flew higher for a moment, then hovered until Aderyn was level with her again. "I know I was irrational when we met your team the first time. He reminds me of someone, that's all, and... you probably noticed I have a temper."

Aderyn bit back a sharp reply. "It sounded like someone you have a history with."

"It's not important. I'd rather not discuss it." Cyanne didn't sound as if she felt Aderyn had been prying, which she had. "I was stupid, and I don't want to think about it."

"It's none of my business."

"How long have you been married?"

"Oh, since—" Aderyn counted. "I guess it's only been ten days."

Cyanne whistled. "That newly married? Congratulations."

"Thanks. It feels like longer. And like no time at all." Aderyn stepped off the last metal slab and hurried to the closed door across the walkway. "Let me see if I can find the override."

Cyanne drifted down to join her. "And you're sure Owen is the Fated One?"

Aderyn patted around the door frame, pressing each section of panel. She found nothing. "Positive. It's all right if you don't agree."

"It's more that I don't really see the point," Cyanne said. "Everything people claim about the Fated One is fantasy. Level twenty is hard to reach already, so why daydream about unlimited leveling? Be satisfied with what you have, that's how I feel."

"That's not unreasonable." Aderyn dusted off her hands and leaned against the wall next to the emergency stairs lever. "But then I look at this place and think, how much more were people capable of before the level cap? Those Spellcrafters did amazing things here, and none of it is available to us anymore. I want it to be possible again, even if most people never take advantage of it."

Cyanne shrugged. "That makes sense."

Clanging footsteps drew nearer, and soon Livia came into view, followed by Weston and Isold. Livia set each foot down as if she meant to drive her boot through the steel slab. "Sorry, that's noisy," she said as she stumped off the steps. "The contact with steel keeps me from dwelling on how far off the earth I am."

"And once more the shaft doesn't reach higher than this level," Weston said, craning his neck to look up. "I'm starting to feel like I understand how these Spellcrafters thought. I hope that doesn't mean insanity lurks around the corner, given how strange this place is." He tested the door latch, then pulled out his brass door-opening contraption.

More footsteps rang out, and soon Owen and Revelin joined them, with Inaya trailing behind. Inaya moved as quietly as Weston even on the steel slabs, and she appeared to be examining the walls as she ascended. "These lights," she said, brushing a fingertip across one of the little blue glows. "I wonder why they're always lit when no other lights are?"

"In my—" Owen coughed. "Sorry. I mean, everything we've encountered has been on its own system. The panels in the control rooms, the emergency stairs. I think the Spellcrafters set things up so the magical energy that powers the Enchanterium is isolated by system, and some of them have run out of energy and others haven't."

"It's too bad we don't have time to work out the details," Aderyn said, glaring at Owen. She knew by now what it sounded like when he stopped himself saying something that would reveal his other-worldly origin. She only barely trusted Revelin's team not to betray them; there was no way she wanted them to know Owen wasn't from their world. Revelin in particular seemed the sort to leap from that straight to "demon."

The door hissed open. "I was thinking," Weston said, "it might be time to try the <**Wayfinder**>. The control chambers have been as similar as the shafts, and maybe that's good enough."

"I really want to see it in action," Inaya exclaimed.

"It's worth trying." Aderyn cupped the <**Wayfinder**> in both hands and held it in front of her. With a deep sigh, she relaxed her shoulders and neck and bowed her head, filling her mind with memories of the other control chambers. Immediately she saw her mistake: all those memories were of danger and fear, of fighting the deep delver and gasping for breath. She cleared her mind and focused on smaller memories, images of the scrying windows and the instrument panels. The <**Wayfinder**> pulsed briefly, the spike glowed rosy pink, and then the glow brightened and warmed so her fingers tingled with heat.

"It's working. It's caught on to something, anyway," she said. She walked into the corridor, which was long and straight and lit dimly by red-tinged lights in steel cages. "Though we shouldn't get excited. There's only one way to go for now."

"Let's see what's possible," Revelin said.

Aderyn caught Owen's eye. Owen looked amused. "We usually have Weston scout ahead, if you're all right with that," he said.

Revelin's impassive face turned pink. "I suppose we ought to work out how this partnership will go. I'm used to leading."

"So am I." Owen's smile widened. "How about our team takes the lead as long as Aderyn is finding our way? No confusion over leadership."

"That's fair." Revelin inclined his head in agreement.

Owen joined Aderyn and rested his hand on her shoulder briefly. "We form up around Aderyn, with Weston in the lead. You know your strengths best, but if Inaya wants to take the rear, watch for threats—"

"I'll join her. Good idea." Revelin nodded at Inaya, who looked disappointed but said nothing. If she'd wanted a close look at the <Wayfinder> in action, no wonder.

"We shouldn't stay too far apart/*Is this going to be a problem?*" Aderyn addressed her [Secret Message] to Owen.

"I think we'll be fine spaced this way," Owen said, fixing Aderyn with his gaze. "It shouldn't be a problem. Let's head out."

Aderyn wished she had him alone to talk more specifically. She still didn't feel confident about partnering with Revelin's team. She was sure they hadn't lied when they said they were willing to work together, and she didn't think they were biding their time to attack— after all, they shared the same goal, and what was the benefit of inter- fering with the team that knew how to make that goal possible? But she couldn't forget the way Revelin had looked when he'd talked about his devotion to his quest. Maybe she didn't have to worry about a knife in the back, but that didn't mean she wouldn't stay diligent.

She noticed the <Wayfinder> had dimmed as her concentration lapsed. Focusing on the item once more, she set off down the corridor behind Weston.

Chapter Thirty-Three

The dimly-lit corridor extended out of sight and grew even darker when they left the well-lit shaft behind. Aderyn didn't bother watching the <**Wayfinder**> closely, though she did keep an eye on it in case it indicated a secret door that was their path to the control chamber. Moving as slowly as they did for Weston to check for traps, she had plenty of time to look around. If the corridor had been narrower with a lower ceiling, the dim, reddish lights and their echoing footsteps might have been frightening. Surrounded by friends, with a goal ahead, it was just another hallway.

After about a minute of walking, the path turned left onto a short hallway with a couple of doors. The <**Wayfinder**> ignored the doors, so Aderyn did too. More turns came almost immediately, and soon the hall began doubling back on itself like a maze, something Isold commented on as he examined his map. "We are still making progress south and west, but not much."

"Leaving these doors unexplored might be a mistake," Revelin said. "If there's anything living in them, we'll have an enemy at our backs."

"Stopping to examine each one will slow us down," Owen

replied. "We are in a hurry, aren't we? And if we do encounter monsters or hazards, they'll interfere with our quest. It's a risk, yes, but it's a calculated one."

"Fair enough," Revelin said.

Weston turned another corner and froze, grabbing Aderyn's shoulder to stop her. "Waspnettle territory."

The corridor ahead was even less well lit than the others thanks to half the lights being obscured by waxy growths covering most of the walls. The roughly hexagonal shapes fit together like a honeycomb, half the height of a man and deep enough to sit inside. Aderyn couldn't imagine wanting to do that. The smell coming off the growths was powerful and pungent like old cheese and rancid fat, and the substance was a pallid gray in the dim light and looked unstable, crumbling at the edges of the cells.

"That means they've claimed this area," Weston whispered to Aderyn. "Don't look too hard at the cells. Sometimes they stuff dead kobolds into them. We don't know why, but none of my guesses are pleasant."

"It seems the <**Wayfinder**> doesn't know the safe route," Aderyn whispered back. "What now? We can't walk away just because there are monsters ahead."

"Stay behind me," Weston said. "They don't trap the places they've turned into their hive, but no sense taking chances when we don't have to."

He took a few steps into the corridor. Aderyn followed. Ahead, a door half covered in lumpy growths that shone gray in the reddish light marked the end of the corridor. Despite Weston's warning, she couldn't stop herself peeking into the cells near floor level. Most of them were empty. A few were filled with a thick, translucent liquid that clung to the waxy sides, but otherwise appeared unoccupied. The liquid was the source of the stench, and Aderyn breathed through her mouth and walked a little faster.

"Door's unlocked," Weston said when they reached it.

"That means we're solidly in waspnettle territory, based on our earlier experiences," Owen told Revelin. "We should start seeing open doors, too."

Revelin shifted his grip on his staff. "We will fight our way through, then."

The door slid sideways in a series of jerks and halts, finally stopping with a few inches of metal still protruding. Weston slipped through the gap, and Aderyn followed him, turning sideways so none of her touched the slick gray substance caking the door frame. She caught sight of Owen, directly behind her. He gave her a reassuring smile, but the red light cast ghastly shadows over his face that distorted the smile into something sickly. Aderyn smiled back anyway.

The short hallway beyond was even more coated with waspnettle wax than the last. All the doors lining it stood open, most of them obscured by the hexagonal cells that crowded the walls. The stench was so bad Aderyn gagged and swallowed repeatedly to prevent vomiting. A low, buzzing hum filled the air. It wasn't loud, but the metal floor panels vibrated with it. The vibration made Aderyn's teeth ache.

Then she heard the louder sound of scraping claws against metal, coming from one of the rooms on the right. Weston stopped and waved them all to follow suit. He bent to whisper in Aderyn's ear. "At least three of them. How well do you wield that staff?"

Aderyn shrugged. "It's better than nothing."

Weston grimaced. "They aren't fooled by the **<Cloak of Mists>**, or you could sneak up there unnoticed. I think we have to take a chance and make the first move."

Aderyn turned and gestured to the others to huddle up. "We can't sneak past. Be prepared for more of them to come from behind. Cyanne, you stay back and make a defensive fire barrier for crowd control. I'll watch with you. Remember they're resistant to bludgeoning attacks, Revelin—"

"How do you know all this?" Revelin asked. Cyanne looked like she wanted to know why she should obey Aderyn's instructions.

"Warmaster," Owen said. "We can discuss it when we've killed these monsters. For now, listen to Aderyn."

Revelin's eyes narrowed, but he said nothing more.

"And if there are warriors or elites, absolutely do not let yourself be stung," Aderyn concluded. "I don't know what all the poison does and I don't want to find out the hard way."

"You heard her," Owen said. "Form up, and let's go in fast."

To Aderyn, the sound of all of them shuffling into position was as loud as a stampeding herd of waspnettle drones, but nothing came to investigate. She wiped her sweaty palms on her trousers one at a time and gripped the <Laborer's Staff> in a ready position. That warning she had given Revelin applied to her as well, but with luck, she wouldn't need her weapon.

Beside her, Cyanne's fists burst into flame. The woman watched the hall ahead intently, and Aderyn turned to face the direction they'd come from. She heard movement, boots on metal, and then the sounds of weapons striking chitin and the weird high-pitched chittering sound that was a waspnettle scream. Not turning around to join the others took all Aderyn's willpower. She kept an eye on the team roster, though there wasn't anything she could do if someone was wounded. It kept her anxieties from overwhelming her.

Congratulations! You have defeated [Waspnettle Drone].
You have earned [450 XP]

As if the first had been inspiration, the system defeat notices began appearing, drones and warriors falling fast enough to be dizzying if Aderyn paid attention to them. As it was, she feared missing a new attack if she was distracted, so she looked past the words as she'd learned to do after months of fighting and continued to watch the rear.

Cyanne suddenly chanted a short string of syllables, and fire burst from her right hand to strike a waspnettle drone that had emerged from a doorway down the hall. It squealed and fell back, but more took its place, not just drones but a couple of warriors as well. Aderyn Assessed them to get a quick count: three warriors, seven drones. "We're under attack from the rear!" she shouted, controlling herself so **[Amplify Voice]** didn't draw more attention than the sound of the fight already did.

Cyanne chanted again, and a wall of fire sprang up across the hallway, far enough from her and Aderyn not to burn them. The waspnettle drones shied away from the flame, backed up, and ran into the warriors, who prodded them forward with their javelins. Aderyn made herself stop staring at the confrontation and kept her attention on their rear. That attention was all that saved her when a waspnettle warrior surged through the gap where Weston had wedged the door open. "Cyanne!" Aderyn shouted.

"I'm spread too thin!" Cyanne replied. The wall of fire did seem lower now.

"More attackers!" Aderyn cried out, and then the warrior was upon her and she blocked the stinger's attack with her staff. Time seemed to slow as she swung the staff's crook to impact against the hard black carapace. The warrior shrugged the blow off and thrust its javelin at her chest. Aderyn dodged back, and the warrior pressed the attack. Desperate, Aderyn slammed the staff into the warrior's head. It paused as if stunned. Aderyn took the precious two seconds to gabble out, "Staff, I have need. Make for me a scythe!" She'd never used one, but it was the biggest tool the staff could turn into, and with the waspnettle warrior looming over her, she wanted something big.

The <Laborer's Staff> quivered in her hands. The shaft thickened and grew rough, the weight changed, and the crook straightened to a shallow curve and turned bright as silver. Aderyn swiped at the warrior with the scythe and nearly overbalanced as the weight distribution changed. In the next moment, the warrior recovered and stabbed at her again. Aderyn grabbed the short handle attached to the shaft and awkwardly blocked the blow. The warrior was too close for a good sweep of the scythe, and Aderyn backed up only to bump into Cyanne, who shrieked a wordless protest. "Sorry!" Aderyn exclaimed, but the warrior kept advancing and Aderyn had to swing again.

This time, the blade caught the warrior across the shoulder. Whitish ichor flowed from the deep wound, and the waspnettle staggered. Aderyn pressed the attack, bringing the scythe back around and aiming for the monster's legs. The strike hit with the blunt side of the blade, and Aderyn's heart sank. She should have gone with the axe. This was a stupid, useless weapon that was going to get her killed.

To her surprise, the waspnettle stumbled and then fell, kicking its legs in the air. Of course. Vulnerable to trip attacks. Aderyn fumbled the scythe into a better position and struck at the monster's waist. The scythe's tip clanged against the floor, but the sharp curve of the blade didn't reach the waspnettle's body. Cursing, Aderyn dropped the scythe and drew her belt knife. [See It Coming] showed her the stinger lashing out before it struck. She dodged, flung herself forward, and plunged the dagger into the blue spot at its waist, the weakest point in its anatomy revealed by [Discern Weakness].

The waspnettle warrior let out an awful chittering noise and curled in on the wound that pumped whitish liquid from its body. Aderyn dodged another strike of its stinger and struck again, this time at the base of its throat. With a shudder, it fell limp, and a system message appeared.

Congratulations! You have defeated [Waspnettle Warrior]. You have earned [4000 XP]

Panting, Aderyn retrieved the scythe and turned it back into a staff. No other waspnettles followed her victim, but she held her position regardless. The other system messages weren't coming as frequently now. She risked a glance at Cyanne, whose wall of fire had diminished to a warning line of flames blocking the far end of the hall. Cyanne didn't look at all tired even though more than a few charred waspnettle bodies filled the hall at her end. The air stank of smoke and burned fat and a more bitter smell Aderyn imagined was waspnettle flesh. "Are there more?" she asked.

Cyanne shook her head. "Unless there are some hiding in those rooms, I think that's it."

Aderyn checked her team roster again. Weston's health indicator was about three-quarters full, but as she watched, the blue bar grew to full. Then Owen came out of the room, and the last of Aderyn's anxieties vanished. "What happened out here?" he said, swiftly crossing to Aderyn's side.

"Cyanne killed the ones from the other rooms. I killed one that came from behind." Aderyn gripped Owen's hand briefly in reassurance. "We need to move on. There's no guarantee more waspnettles won't come to investigate."

"Where does the <**Wayfinder**> point?"

Aderyn pulled out the metal orb and tucked the staff under one arm. "Down that hall still. Is everyone all right?"

"It's a good thing we're together," Owen said, "because our team alone would have been able to defeat that bunch, but not without casualties. And we'd have been overwhelmed from behind. As it is, it was a tough fight, but not an impossible one."

The others had emerged from the room and gathered around Aderyn and the <**Wayfinder**>. Embrus put an arm around Cyanne, supporting her. "How are you doing?" he asked.

"I'm fine, but that took a lot out of me," Cyanne said.

"Let's move quickly then," Revelin said. "Straight ahead?"

Aderyn kept from looking at Owen to see what he thought of Revelin's assumption of authority. Well, that was where they were going, so what did it matter who asserted authority? "Form up behind me again," she said.

"He's confident," Weston murmured to Aderyn as he passed her. Aderyn shrugged and turned her attention to the <**Wayfinder**>.

They picked their way across the bodies of the waspnettles to the door at the end of the hall, which also stood open. Weston set a quick pace, and they hurried through a series of passages clogged with wax-coated cells. Some of them, Aderyn noticed in passing, held shadowy forms too small to be either waspnettles or kobolds. She felt sick at the thought of more waspnettles being bred, monsters that would overflow the Lonely Tor and attack the human settlements nearby. The thought of flooding the Enchanterium with magma, destroying every trace of the waspnettle hive, comforted her.

Except that was impossible, wasn't it, if they didn't want to destroy the kobolds too? Aderyn reminded herself that kobolds were monsters, and maybe they weren't aggressive except in defense of their homes, but suppose they decided the human settlements were a threat and went to war proactively? She should put the needs of her own kind first. But she couldn't help remembering Akdukhur and his determination not to let her linger to be caught by *his* kind. There had to be a better solution. Too bad she was the only one who wanted to find it.

CHAPTER THIRTY-FOUR

The halls grew more crowded with waspnettle cells as they proceeded deeper into conquered territory, but the two teams encountered no monsters. Aderyn was just about to comment on this when Weston shouted, "Watch out!" and swung his sword at a black-carapaced waspnettle warrior who lunged at him from one of the open doors.

Aderyn let the other fighters rush past her and turned to watch the rear, her staff held at the ready. She was so tired of not having a weapon she was skilled with. The noise of the skirmish grew, and then the first system defeat notice appeared:

**Congratulations! You have defeated [Waspnettle Warrior].
You have earned [4000 XP]**

Then another.

And another.

Someone grabbed her shoulder, and she let out a tiny shriek. "Lead the way," Owen said in her ear. "We have to move. Damn it, I wish the <**Wayfinder**> knew a safer path."

"This may be the only path," Aderyn reminded him. She readied the <Wayfinder> and hurried away from the battle site.

Only seconds later, they encountered more waspnettles, drones that sent up a warning cry that drew two warriors to them. This time, Aderyn stayed where she was, her heart hammering as the fight surged around her, focusing on the orb with its steadily-glowing spike pointing the way. It was Isold who grabbed her next, propelling her forward even as Owen and Revelin, Weston and Embrus fought an increasing horde of enemies. The walls buckled as Livia shifted the earth behind them and tore the panels free to crush a waspnettle or cut its head off.

It felt like a dream to Aderyn after a while, a horrible dream in which the faint sounds of waspnettle screams clashed with grunts of effort and the clatter of weapons against chitin. She could do nothing but move forward, surrounded by her friends and trusting none of them would drop their guard and let a waspnettle—

She shouted and dodged the vicious stinger of one of the attackers. Immediately, Isold let out a pained cry, and to her horror Aderyn saw the stinger she'd avoided embed itself in Isold's thigh. Isold grabbed his leg and then stiffened and fell, locked in that position.

Panicked, Aderyn swung the <Laborer's Staff> and hit the waspnettle a glancing blow that knocked it away from Isold. Before it could recover, she slammed the crook of the staff against the side of its head, crushing its skull.

**Congratulations! You have defeated [Waspnettle Warrior].
You have earned [4000 XP]**

Welcome to Level Fifteen

Aderyn clutched the <Wayfinder> in one hand and dropped to kneel at her friend's side. Isold's face was contorted in a terrible paralyzed rictus, his lips drawn back, his eyes wide open, the cords along his throat tense enough they were visible.

Aderyn pressed her cheek to his mouth, and her immediate terror eased slightly when she discovered he was still breathing. After the system's warnings about not being stung, she'd expected his lungs and heart to be paralyzed as well. But—no, it had said the paralysis lasted only long enough for a waspnettle to eviscerate its victim. That wasn't reassuring.

Then Weston was beside her, lifting Isold's awkwardly twisted body in his arms. "Go, Aderyn, go! We can't stop!"

Aderyn cradled the <**Wayfinder**> again, took two steps, and ran into Revelin. "We should go back," the Swifthands said. "What if that happens to more of us?"

He was facing Aderyn, but it was Owen who replied. "This isn't going to get any easier if we have to retreat. It might even be worse if they are smart enough to reinforce this path. We have to keep going."

"I'm running through magical energy fast," Cyanne said. "If we don't find the control chamber soon, I'll be useless."

"I'm sorry to admit I'm in the same position," Livia said.

"How close are we?" Owen asked.

Aderyn focused on the <**Wayfinder**>. "I'm not sure about distances. We could be a hundred feet from it in a straight line, but the halls turn enough that's not helpful. The <**Wayfinder**> thinks it's close."

"Then we go on, and reevaluate when our spellslingers are close to their limits," Owen said. He fixed Revelin with a steady gaze. "Are we agreed?"

Revelin's lips pinched tight for a moment. Then he nodded. "Agreed."

Owen cast a glance at Isold. "Is he in pain?"

"I don't think so," Aderyn said. "It will wear off." Silently, she hoped it would wear off soon. Between one thing and another, they were losing fighters—she was out of action, Isold was paralyzed, Weston had to carry him and couldn't fight...

She no longer noticed the horrible gray waxy cells with their disgusting contents. If there were dead kobolds in some of them, there was nothing she could do about it. Instead, she filled her awareness with the <**Wayfinder's**> guidance as it glowed steadily brighter and warmed her hands with its heat. When it finally pulsed once and dimmed to cool steel, she put it in her <**Purse of Great Capacity**> with reluctance. She didn't fear what came next, but the simplicity of following a path soothed her. She reminded herself she didn't need to be soothed, not when there were enemies to kill.

Crumbling gray wax covered the walls of this corridor completely, making it seem more like the innards of a horrible beast than the clean metal panels of the Enchanterium. To Aderyn, it felt like corruption, as if some disease had overtaken the compound. She already hated the waspnettles, but the sense that this beautiful place that had been loved by so many people was dying angered her.

Ahead, a doorway crusted over and narrowed by the waspnettles' secretions revealed a large, dimly-lit space. Owen gripped Aderyn's arm and guided her forward. "What is it?"

Aderyn Assessed the room. "It's the central control chamber for this level," she whispered. "There are twenty drones, seven warriors, and two elites. They haven't noticed us yet."

Owen turned to Revelin. "Well?"

Revelin glanced at Embrus and Inaya, who nodded. "We've dealt with more than that before," he said. "But let's move quickly before reinforcements arrive."

His words triggered the ghost of a memory in Aderyn, the feeling that she'd forgotten something important. Something to do with reinforcements. As she searched her memory for more details, Owen said, "Then we go now. Isold?"

Isold waved a hand and pointed at his throat. His posture was lopsided, as if parts of him were still paralyzed. "Crap," Aderyn said. "If you can't sing—"

"We can't afford to wait because we don't know how long his full recovery will take," Owen said. "Everyone ready? Then let's take them by surprise." Without waiting for acknowledgment, he squeezed through the doorway. The light of the mystery blade illuminated the space beyond like a tiny sun.

"Go, go!" Revelin said, darting lithely after him.

One by one, they forced their way through the doorway, with Aderyn behind Revelin. The cavernous chamber looked the way the hall did, with every surface coated with waspnettle wax. The only light came from Owen's sword, which lit just the area about ten feet around him, but Aderyn was aware of movement ahead, on the walls, on the ceiling.

She halted just inside and Assessed the room. A wall of silver letters loomed before her vision, and rather than read the Assessment, she looked for numbers and found more than her initial glance had revealed: twenty-three drones, ten warriors, three elites, none of them reacting to the human intruders' presence yet.

Livia chanted, and brilliant daylight filled the chamber. Dozens of insectoid bodies clung to the walls and ceiling, crawling across the waxy growth and the cells it formed. All the waspnettles cringed away from the light, and some of the drones lost their grip on the ceiling and fell, hitting the floor and not rising immediately.

Owen was already in motion, with Revelin and Weston close behind. Cyanne set fire to the wax coating the ceiling, causing more drones to fall. Aderyn ran forward, examining the room for a tactical advantage and finding nothing in that big, open space. She readied the **<Laborer's Staff>**, though she didn't know how useful she could be.

Ahead, a waspnettle larger than the others scuttled over the uneven ground made by the secretions, heading for Revelin. It was pure white and moved like the wind. Revelin met its attack with a whirling attack of his own. He was as fluid and agile as the white waspnettle elite, and Aderyn watched in fascination as he drove the creature back.

Her only warning was the sound of clawed feet scrabbling toward her from behind. Before she could turn to meet the threat, agonizing pain shot through her as something stabbed her, running her clean through.

She screamed and clutched at the vicious stinger protruding from her belly. For several eternal seconds she hung there, spitted like a butterfly on a thorn, until the stinger withdrew and she collapsed without its horrible support. Stiffness spread outward from the wound, which bled little, and her limbs grew heavy. With her last strength, she rolled to face her attacker.

The waspnettle elite towered over her, though it wasn't really much taller than she. Its upper limbs flexed, bringing its terrible claws closer to Aderyn's chest. Paralyzed, Aderyn could only watch as it slit her jerkin open from top to bottom in a move terrifying in how deliberate it was. She tried to scream again, but her throat wouldn't respond. The elite clashed its claws and then bent its head, bringing its fanged jaws close to her abdomen.

Something struck the elite from the side, knocking it away. Aderyn couldn't move to see what had saved her, but an instant later Livia knelt beside her, surrounded by shifting, hovering plates of stone. "It will pass," she said. She looked up, gestured, and chanted. A slab of steel flew past Aderyn's limited field of vision, spinning like a discus, and shortly after the squeal of a dying waspnettle preceded a system defeat notice.

From where she lay, Aderyn could see the top of the doorway and the wall above it, arching to the ceiling. Straining to move did nothing. She told herself to be grateful breathing was still easy, but there wasn't anything else to be grateful for.

A waspnettle warrior came through the doorway, clinging to the wall and climbing up. Then two more. Then a surge of black waspnettles intermingled with a few white ones poured through the doorway and covered the wall. Livia was watching the combat in the center of the room. Aderyn couldn't even grunt to get her attention. All she could do was watch, and Assess.

Name: Waspnettle Warrior [32]
Type: Magical beast, intelligent
Power Level: 9
Attack(s): weapon or claw x2; special
Immune to: none
Resistant to: bludgeoning damage, mind control
Vulnerable to: trip attacks, *daylight*, *sunburst*
Special attacks: stinger (poison)
I warned you about the stinger.

NAME: Waspnettle Elite [7]
Type: Magical beast, intelligent
Power Level: 14
Attacks: weapon, claw x2, bite, special
Immune to: none
Resistant to: bludgeoning damage, mind control
Vulnerable to: *daylight*, *sunburst*
Special attacks: trample, [Overrun], stinger (poison)
Do you remember yet why the waspnettles are dangerous? It's not the stinger—never mind what I said. Waspnettles have a low-level connection to one another through their queen. You walked into an ambush of your own making.

Aderyn's heart sank. She had forgotten **[Bonded Mind]** and what it meant. Now they were all likely to die.

The first waspnettle warrior leaped, whipping its body around so its stinger slammed into the stone armor protecting Livia's back. Livia shouted and spun, and the stinger scraped across the stone rather than impaling her flesh. With another shout, her right arm glittered like mica, and she punched the waspnettle so hard there was a crunch of chitin and the thing flew backward several feet, knocking two of its fellows over.

Aderyn watched helplessly as more waspnettles scuttled toward them, warily now that they'd seen what Livia's *stone fist* could do. Livia took a solid stance over Aderyn's body and screamed, "We have to retreat! Somebody help me!" She punched another waspnettle and lifted a second with *telekinesis* to fling it into its neighbor. Aderyn could only see some of her back, obscured by the shifting slabs of stone, but Livia was moving slower than usual, and Aderyn was sure she was tiring.

She heard running footsteps, and then Owen came into view, driving the waspnettles back so Weston could pick her up. His hands on her shoulders, his arm beneath her knees to lift her, sent agonizing pain shooting through her body, but she couldn't even weep or keen out her suffering. It didn't matter. She had to endure—she didn't have any choice. And so long as the waspnettles didn't kill them all first, it would pass.

Weston held her close to his body as they squeezed through the door. Every touch felt like fire turning her nerves to long lines of pain; every jogging footstep he took as they ran from the control chamber sent flashes of black-rimmed light through her skull until she wished she could fall unconscious.

From her position in Weston's arms, she could see over his shoulder, which gave her a perfect view of the others stretched out in a line behind them and the waspnettle elites pursuing them. The pain didn't stop her feverishly plotting a defense. If they could make it out of the waspnettle-controlled territory, find a bottleneck or a door they could lock... Isold's map of this part of level three should be complete enough for that... Cyanne could immolate their pursuers if they led them to a small enough chamber, unless Cyanne was as exhausted as Livia...

After a while, the waspnettles stopped following them, and

Aderyn became aware that they had left the wax-clogged hallways behind and were running through passages whose dim red light was still brighter than it had been in waspnettle territory. In the next moment, Weston carried her through a door and into an open space whose walls were randomly illuminated with wan lights. **[Shaft No. 5]**.

Weston, breathing heavily, passed her to someone who crushed her to him, his hand cradling her head. It hurt so badly she quivered with the need to scream. Owen had his forehead pressed against hers and was murmuring things she couldn't understand through the pain. Then he laid her on the floor of the walkway and crouched beside her, controlling his own breathing.

Aderyn heard the shuffling movement of many people finding seats on the ground, the metallic scrape of boots against steel flooring, the miscellaneous tapping and shifting of equipment. Then Revelin said, "Well, that was a rout."

"We were overwhelmed," Owen said. "I underestimated their numbers."

By the sound of his voice, Owen was waiting for Revelin to criticize. Instead, the Swifthands said, "We took a chance, and it didn't pay off. It happens. The question is, what do we intend to do next?"

"I'm at my limit," Livia said. "I need to rest."

"So do I," Cyanne said. "And I think most of us need healing."

"And Aderyn needs to recover," Owen said. "I say we heal up, get some sleep, deal with leveling, and figure out a different plan of attack after that."

"Did you level? So did we," Embrus said.

Owen nodded. "So we'll all want to evaluate our new abilities. Isold, how complete is your map now?"

"Very complete, for the areas we've visited," Isold said. His voice sounded raw and scratchy, but at least he was audible. "Perhaps we could circle around, explore more territory. The <Wayfinder> led us the most direct way, but there are likely other approaches, since I saw at least two other doors opening off that central room."

"It's a start." Owen gently lifted Aderyn so her head rested in his lap and clasped her hand. She wished she could tell him how badly his touch hurt. "Revelin, what sort of watches do you usually set?"

Aderyn's pain-addled brain made no sense of the discussion that followed. Every second felt like an eternity, so she didn't know how much time passed before the pain of being touched subsided enough that she could appreciate Owen holding her hand and the fact that she was now lying on her bedroll instead of the bare floor. She closed her fingers on his, not tightly, and grunted as his twitch of surprise jogged her still-aching head.

Owen clasped her hand in both of his. "Are you coming out of it?"

Aderyn nodded.

Owen closed his eyes and let out a long, relieved breath. "I thought—Aderyn, that was a close one. I'm sorry. I shouldn't have pushed on—"

Aderyn grunted again and twitched her fingers.

"Okay, you're right. It's the waspnettles' fault you were stung, not mine. I just—damn it, I don't know what we should have done differently."

His despair made her own guilt at not remembering the waspnettles' mental connection worse. She strained to move her jaw, which responded after a few tries. "My fault," she whispered through a throat that felt like it might never move again. "They are connected. Like **[Bonded Mind]**. I forgot."

"Oh, great," Owen said with feeling, loudly enough that Embrus and Livia, who were closest, looked over at the two of them. "That means we can never really sneak up on them. *Shit.* How screwed are we?"

Aderyn clutched his hand tighter, but no reassuring words came to mind. Eventually, she said, "We'll think of something."

"Like what?" Owen's voice rose. "We all nearly died because I was overconfident. What else is there?"

"Let this go for now," Isold said. He twirled his newest instrument, a silver flute, in his left hand like a baton. Then he brought it to his lips and played a sweet, simple melody, just five notes in a varied pattern that nevertheless brought tears to Aderyn's eyes with how beautiful it was. She had been wary of his level fourteen Performance choice, given how a Beguiler with a flute had nearly destroyed them and gotten Owen killed, but Isold had said, before they left Finion's Gate, "I choose to embrace the future, and it's not the flute's fault its brother was misused."

Now she listened to him play, and the ache in her heart subsided as the paralysis left her muscles. They were in a terrible position, true, but giving up was unthinkable even if it hadn't been a matter of the **[Fated One's Destiny]** quest. People, strangers they had never met, were counting on them to stop the dragon. And as long as they couldn't give up, they might as well find a way to defeat the waspnettles. Isold's music filled her with a reassuring confidence.

Owen's head was bowed, his face hidden. When Isold finished, he said, "Everyone, I'm sorry. We should have evaluated the situation better, and it's just good luck no one was seriously injured or even killed. I won't make that mistake again."

"We'll talk about it after we've rested," Revelin said. "You, too, Owen."

"Thanks," Owen said. He lay down next to Aderyn, still holding her hand. Aderyn closed her eyes and let the memory of Isold's music carry her off to sleep.

CHAPTER THIRTY-FIVE

When she woke, the paralysis was gone, and she felt fully rested, better than sleeping on the ground ought to make her. She blinked up at the ceiling, which seemed unnaturally far away, then checked her team roster, irrationally afraid someone had gotten hurt while she was asleep. Everyone's health indicators were close to full, though, and she relaxed.

Looking at the display reminded her of something else. She whispered, "Advancement."

Name: Aderyn

∞ Jacob Owen Lindberg

Level: 15

Class: Warmaster

Skills: **Bluff** (14), **Climb** (12), **Conversation** (14), **Intimidate** (10), **Sense Truth** (15), **Survival** (8), **Swim** (1), **Knowledge: Monsters** (12), **Knowledge: World Lore** (6), **Knowledge: Demons** (1), **Unite**

Class Skills: **Improved Assess** 3 (25), **Awareness** (18), **Knowledge: Geography** (12), **Spot** (15), **Discern Weakness** (25), **Dodge** (15), **Improvised Distraction** (14), **Outflank** (18), **Draw**

Fire (11), Keep Pace (18), Amplify Voice (14), See It Coming (20), Basic Weapon Proficiency (Swords) (13), Read Body Language (12), Basic Map Access (5), Compel (8), Spot Weakness (4), Secret Message (3), Bonded Mind (1), Sense Ambush (0)

[Sense Ambush], huh? Every new skill seemed increasingly useful. It was fun to imagine what that skill would feel like—a tingling on her skin, or seeing shadowy outlines, or hearing noises no one else did?

She stretched and sat up. Livia had mended her leather jerkin while she slept, and its snug fit reassured her that she really was restored. Most of the others were still asleep, including Owen, but Embrus sat with his back to the wall where both the door and the top of the emergency staircase were in view. He saluted her with a nod. "You look better."

"I can't recommend being stung by a waspnettle," Aderyn replied, smiling. "What time is it? As if time means anything underground."

"I haven't paid much attention to my timepiece since we arrived, no." Embrus pulled a small silver disc from within his heavy leather jerkin and examined it. "Technically, it's either two in the morning or two in the afternoon, but it's been seven hours since you fell asleep."

"Seven—! Why didn't anyone... no, forget I said that. I'm sure I needed the recovery time." Aderyn got to her feet and joined him. "Were you injured?"

"Fortunately, no. It was a close call a couple of times. You all are powerful fighters, especially Owen. I didn't realize one level could make so much difference."

Aderyn considered her options for a moment and decided to be open. "Some of that is my partnership with Owen. It boosts our skills, plus we have paired skills that are also higher than usual. And some of it is that the Fated One encounters quests and monsters that are more of a challenge than most adventurers get."

"I admit I was skeptical, but after seeing Owen fight, I'm inclined to take his word that he's the Fated One." Embrus stretched both legs straight in front of him. "That's not a destiny I'd want. Too great a demand for me. I've got other plans."

"Your team was going to Obsidian, right?"

"After this quest, yes. But I was going on to Alcester after that. I'm done adventuring. This is my last hurrah before I settle down with my sweetheart Haidie." Embrus held his watch out at arm's length, examining its silver case. "She's a level ten Spiritsmith, retired about a year ago. We'd both been through Alcester a while back, separately, and when we started talking seriously about marriage, we decided that's where we wanted to settle. So I'll join her as soon as this is over."

"That's beautiful! And has potential for heartbreak. Aren't you the least bit superstitious that something terrible will happen just as you're prepared to retire?"

Embrus chuckled. "I don't think that way. It's not like the system is aware of our plans to interfere with them just to make our lives tragic. Besides, the payoff from this dragon's hoard should be substantial. Make a nice little nest egg for our nest."

That made Aderyn uncomfortable. "I hope nobody feels cheated. This ends with only one of us killing the dragon."

"Sure, but there's nothing that says we can't divide the fortune however we like. I think we should share it out equally if we all work together to reach that goal, don't you?"

"I agree." Aderyn settled beside Embrus to join him in watching. She'd never appreciated how nice it was to have a body that moved the way you wanted it to. She stretched her toes and calves, then raised both arms and stretched out her back. "I'm starting to feel hungry finally. That <**Wand of Epic Bounty**> sure does what it promises."

"Owen mentioned that you had some unusual items. That one feeds you for a day, right?"

"And reduces damage. It saved my life when I fell down that hole."

"Amazing." Embrus lifted a hand in greeting as Revelin came to join them. "Sleep well, Rev?"

"Well enough." Revelin rubbed his bearded chin and then ran his hand over his face and bald head before putting his cap back on. "You're recovered, Aderyn?"

"Completely. Though I can't stop kicking myself for not remembering the waspnettles could communicate mind to mind." Aderyn blushed just thinking about it.

"It doesn't matter now. We'll solve the problem another way." Revelin walked away, bending to shake Inaya awake.

"I guess it's time to get up," Aderyn said. Her heart lifted as Owen rolled over and sat up. His gaze fell on her, and he looked so relieved it filled her with an ache that was part sorrow and part joy. Scrambling to her feet, she ran to where he could hold her close, pressed her face against his shoulder, and murmured, "That was a closer call than I ever want to have again."

"I guess [See It Coming] doesn't work if you can't see the threat," Owen replied. "It's fine. We all survived." He kissed her sweetly, and she returned his kiss, feeling as thrilled as if it was the first time.

After a few more moments, they separated, though Owen kept hold of Aderyn's hand. "Did you check your advancement?" he asked.

"I did. What about you?"

Owen lifted the hilt of the mystery sword and turned it so it caught the light. "I have [Weapon Mastery] now, and it seems this is the weapon it applies to."

"[Weapon Mastery] actually applies to a class of weapons, like longswords or staffs," Aderyn said. "It's just coincidence this is the weapon you're wielding now."

"Well, it sure feels specific to this one. It means I know everything about the sword—it's so weird, Aderyn, it's like the knowledge was there in my mind, waiting to be unlocked. I wonder if that's how Isold feels all the time."

Aderyn laid her hand over his. "So, what is it?"

"It's called a <**Sunsword**>. The blade is made of sharpened light —I know that's strange, but that's what the system calls it. It will cut through almost anything, except that superdense material the control chamber walls are made of, and never break. Which makes sense, because how can you break light?" Owen stared at the hilt, or at their joined hands, Aderyn wasn't sure. "And I feel connected to it. Like, if I dropped it in a dark room, I'd put my hand on it immediately."

"Well, yes, because it glows, Owen."

"You know what I mean." Owen blew out his breath. "Let's eat. We need to plan a new attack."

The two teams sat near the door, where the walkway was widest, and shared out rations. Revelin's team marveled at seedless grapes and dried meat that wasn't hard and tasteless, and Aderyn and Isold eagerly accepted the bag of shelled cashews Inaya shared. They ate mostly in silence, and when they were finished, no one spoke for a while. Aderyn tilted her head back and traced patterns she imagined the blue lights made. Possibilities whirled through her head, different attack plans, but all of them eventually came up against the problem of the waspnettles' mental connection. There, she was stumped.

"Aderyn," Owen said, startling her. "Tell us about how the wasp-nettles communicate mind to mind. All I remember is you said it was the reverse of [**Bonded Mind**], that they had to be close to one another."

"They share perceptions with each other and with their queen when they're within one hundred feet. Perceptions, not thoughts, but if a waspnettle sees us and shares that sight with a nearby friend, it hardly matters that it can't also send a spoken message about intruders." Aderyn strained to recall what else [**Improved Assess 3**] had told her. "I wonder about the queen. I don't know anything about her, whether she has extra abilities, but I assume that's so."

"So would killing the queen cripple the others?" Revelin asked.

"I don't know. It might. But I don't know where the queen is so I can Assess her."

"I looked at the map Isold drew of this level," Embrus said. "I see patterns to how the waspnettles have settled. I have a good guess as to where the queen is, if the area they're protecting is her home."

"But we don't know if going after the queen is the right approach," Livia said. "She'd be heavily guarded, probably, and we already got our asses handed to us in the control chamber. I don't want to be overly pessimistic, but we should decide on a goal before we make plans."

"Good point," Revelin said. "Our goal is still the central chamber, right? So we need more information. We need to know how to get around the waspnettles' communication, and we need to know how to weaken them."

"*Daylight* weakened them," Owen said. "It's what got us out of that room alive. Between Livia's spell and my <**Sunsword**>, we have some advantage so long as their numbers don't overwhelm us."

"Weston and I were thinking we can jam the door locks," Inaya said, "but I don't know if we can get the doors closed, given all that yuk covering everything. But if we could do that, we could funnel them down to just one entrance."

"It would also be our only exit, so it's a dangerous tactic," Weston added.

"No," Aderyn said. Everything she'd considered was slotting into place in her mind. "No. That's the short-term solution. It's not just that we have to reach the central chamber. The point of doing that is to disconnect the dragon from the defense system. And that chamber is so overgrown with waspnettle secretions we don't have any idea where the panel is, and we can't reach it if we did. We can't just reach the chamber. We have to control it. And we can't do that unless we eliminate enough of the waspnettles that they stop coming after us there."

No one said anything. Owen's head was bowed, and he seemed deep in thought. Revelin's brow was so deeply furrowed his cap nearly met his eyebrows. Weston opened his mouth and then subsided. Cyanne was playing with a walnut-sized orb of fire, tossing it between her hands without watching it. Finally, Inaya said, "It can't be impossible. We need more information. Weston and Embrus and I can scout the area—"

"You can't go alone," Revelin said. "There are too many of those monsters prowling this place."

"We can't be stealthy if we have the rest of you tagging along," Weston said. "This only works if we're undetected."

"But for my map to be updated, I must be present," Isold said. "And as good as you are, you can't keep a map of this place in your heads. It's far too complex."

"We can at least find out where the queen is," Embrus said. "I really think killing her will affect their morale, if not actually make them flee."

"If I could Assess the queen, I'd know if that was true," Aderyn said.

"Which comes back to more people on the scouting expedition," Revelin said. "If Aderyn and Isold go, we might as well all go. Fight our way through."

"Pardon me, but that could be suicide," Isold said.

"Enough," Owen said, with enough force that even Revelin subsided. "We have to establish our priorities. Our goal is to disconnect the dragon defense system without getting any of us hurt or killed. Everything else is secondary to that. Aderyn made the point that we have to defeat the waspnettles, either by killing them or demoralizing them, in order to accomplish our goal. That means we need to focus on the waspnettles. Aderyn, do you agree with Embrus that finding the queen would be valuable?"

"I do. We shouldn't make guesses based on how similar the wasp-nettles are to insects, but this is a guess we can prove. That the queen has a strong influence, I mean. And whatever that influence is, eliminating her will affect the others. It has to give us an advantage."

"Embrus, where is the map I drew?" Isold interrupted.

Embrus unfolded a sheet of paper with one torn edge, covered with circles, squares, and lines, and handed it to Isold. Isold spread it out so everyone could see. "This is as much as my system map shows," he said, tapping the paper with his forefinger. "Embrus identified the pattern that suggests the waspnettle forces radiate out from this point, or roughly so—you can see it's in an area we haven't visited. If the queen is anywhere, she is there."

"Which is good to know, but we can't reach that point without battling our way through increasing numbers of warriors and elites," Revelin said. "A frontal assault would be fatal to at least a few of us, and if we managed to get through unscathed, we'd be weakened just when we're facing the greatest threat."

"I agree," Owen said. "We need an alternate way to reach the queen. Livia, what about *transport*?"

"If I use *scry*, I can see where I'm going for *transport*," Livia replied, "but I can only *transport* five people at a time. Half of us would be left behind, and I'd use up magical energy in getting us all there, energy I might need to fight the waspnettles. And if the worst happened and we had to retreat, we'd end up fighting our way through regardless. It's not impossible, but I think it should be our last resort."

"It's still a possibility." Owen stared at the penciled map. "What if we established the route with the fewest waspnettles? Scouting could discover that."

"If they're all the same, though," Revelin began.

The back of Aderyn's neck suddenly crawled with gooseflesh, sending a shudder through her. She had the unexpected sensation of someone watching her. At that moment, Weston and Inaya tilted their heads alertly. In unison, they said, "Something's coming."

Everyone froze, listening. At first, Aderyn heard nothing but the sound of nine people breathing. Then, distantly, claws scrabbled on metal far below at the bottom of the shaft.

Everyone sprang to their feet. The claws sounded again, louder, and the weird crawling sensation increased, spreading up Aderyn's scalp and over her shoulders. Something was climbing the stairs—more than one something, she realized, as the noise grew louder and changed so it sounded like the skittering of a dozen metal-clawed mice scrambling to reach them.

"Gather your things," Revelin said. "Quickly."

"We can fight them from here," Aderyn said. "We have the high ground."

"Waspnettles can climb walls," Owen pointed out. "We wouldn't have the advantage long. Let's—"

He hauled the door open and froze again. The corridor beyond was full of kobolds, their blue and green and brown hides turned strange colors by the reddish light. None of them moved, but all of them were armed, and all of them were poised to attack.

Owen activated the <**Sunsword**>. The kobolds drew closer together, but none of them fled from the glowing blade. Owen took a step forward, and the first rank of kobolds brought their weapons up, warning him.

"Aderyn," Owen said in a dangerously calm voice, "what was that you said about them just defending their home?"

"We can't not fight them, not if it means saving our lives," Aderyn said, though her heart ached at the stupidity of it all. If only they could communicate!

"We'll fight our way past," Revelin said from behind Aderyn. "Move aside, Aderyn, and Owen and I will—"

"It's not waspnettles," Isold said from the stairs. "It's more kobolds. They have us surrounded."

Aderyn Assessed the group in the hallway. Muttering to herself, "Thirteen stabbers, seven bushwhackers," she backed away and hurried to where she could see the stairs. More kobolds scurried up the steel slabs, leaping between them as agilely as dancers. They seemed not to care that they were in a perfect position to be picked off by ranged attacks, or maybe they knew that the humans had almost no ranged attacks and they were safe. "Seventeen stabbers, ten bushwhackers," she reported. "Livia and Cyanne, keep the stairs clear. Maybe if we knock enough of them off, they'll retreat. Owen, Revelin, don't back down. We can't let them get past the bottleneck. Isold, how many of them can you subdue?"

"Many," Isold said. "But—look. They aren't approaching closer."

The two kobolds in the lead, a couple of bronze-scaled bush-whackers, had stopped five steps from the top and stood with their long knives bared, their large black eyes fixed on the humans. More kobolds coming up behind them paused as well. Aderyn looked past them to the base of the shaft. "They keep coming," she said, despairing. She hadn't come all this way, faced all these dangers, to be torn apart by a bunch of low power level monsters.

She heard movement and spun around to face the door. The kobolds massed beyond it were shifting to make way for another kobold bushwhacker. This one was unarmed, but Aderyn had barely recognized this when she saw the newcomer's arm was tightly wrapped in a length of dingy blue cloth like a bandage. She took in his dark eyes, his gaze fixed on her, and exclaimed, "Akdukhur!"

Akdukhur pushed his way past the kobolds at the head of the pack and stopped mere feet from Owen and Revelin. He showed no sign that he feared their weapons. Instead, he nodded and said, "Ehdern. Ankoo."

"Stand down," Aderyn hissed. Owen lowered the <Sunsword>, but didn't deactivate it. Revelin was slower to respond, but after a few seconds, he stepped back, making way for Aderyn. The kobolds behind Akdukhur shifted warily, but none attacked.

Akdukhur took another step forward and raised his hand. In it, he held, not a weapon, but a brass cylinder tapered at both ends. A <Write-All>. He knelt before Aderyn and pressed the tip of the cylinder to the floor. With some effort, he dragged the <Write-All> across the steel, scoring it lightly. As he drew, ink pooled in the grooves left behind by the magic item until a picture formed. Aderyn, marveling, stepped closer, ignoring Owen's wordless protest.

It was a rough but intelligible picture of a waspnettle with an oversized stinger. Akdukhur glanced at Aderyn and pointed at the drawing as if asking for comprehension. "Yes, a waspnettle," Aderyn said, then felt stupid, because it wasn't as if he understood her language.

But Akdukhur seemed satisfied, because he went back to drawing. He added the figure of a kobold stabbed through by the stinger, and then an outline of what was clearly meant to be a human, impaled the same way. "I understand. The waspnettles kill kobolds and they kill us, too, or will if they can," Aderyn said.

Akdukhur pointed at the three figures. Then he flipped the <Write-All> over and used the other end to remove the ink and the grooves. Aderyn hadn't fully grasped how powerful that tool was, but watching it erase grooves from solid steel impressed her.

Now Akdukhur drew more figures, one on either side of the waspnettle. In front, a kobold wielding a spear, and behind—

Aderyn grabbed Owen's arm. "That's you! See, he's drawn the <Sunsword>!"

Akdukhur sat back on his haunches and looked up at Aderyn. He spoke a series of barking yips and a growl that ended in what Aderyn thought was an interrogative. Light dawned. "I get it," she said. "You want us to fight the waspnettles together." She pointed at herself, then at Akdukhur, then at the picture of the waspnettle. "Together."

Akdukhur yipped once. Then he stood, his thin tail lashing idly around his legs, and spat on the ground at Owen's feet. Owen recoiled. "What the hell?"

Aderyn studied Akdukhur's face. She couldn't read kobold expressions, but in her heart, she guessed the truth. "I think that's how they seal a promise," she said. "Spit."

"What?"

"Just do it!" If she was wrong, and spitting was a mortal insult, they might all die here. At this point, they didn't have much choice.

Owen sighed. Then he spat a gobbet of spittle that overlapped Akdukhur's.

Akdukhur let out a wild cry that was taken up by the kobolds, a cry that echoed through the shaft. The kobolds lowered their weapons, though they didn't advance. Aderyn, on a whim, offered her hand to Akdukhur. The bushwhacker studied it curiously. Then he laid his palm flat against hers. His hand was dry and hot and rough, but not unpleasantly so, and the sensation thrilled Aderyn. A truce with kobolds! What else might be possible?

CHAPTER THIRTY-SIX

Following a crowd of kobolds through the dimly-lit halls was so surreal Aderyn's imagination ran wild. She didn't believe Akdukhur would betray them, but images of secret kobold tunnels within the walls filled her mind, along with visions of long-abandoned rooms converted to kobold use. She hoped she was wrong, because the thought of crawling through narrow passages carved out of stone and earth started her anxieties shrieking again. She told herself to stop borrowing trouble. If that was what Akdukhur had in mind, she would endure.

But the kobold bushwhacker led their group to a door his comrades shoved open and barked orders that got all the kobolds moving through the doorway. He gestured at Aderyn to follow.

Owen put a hand on her elbow to stop her. "I should go first."

"Akdukhur clearly trusts me over all of you," Aderyn murmured. "It's not any more dangerous for me to go first."

Owen scowled, but stood aside.

The room they entered had been stripped of most of its steel paneling, revealing bare earthen walls and—*shudder*—small holes rimmed with glimmering kobold scales scraped off along the edges.

Aderyn swallowed. Then she walked toward the hole all the kobolds were entering. It would be barely big enough for her to crawl through, and she would rub up against the walls that pressed in on her—

Akdukhur grunted and stepped in front of her, shaking his head. He held up one hand in a stopping gesture. Relieved, Aderyn stepped back. Akdukhur raised the <**Write-All**> and drew on the loose earth of the exposed wall. The magic writing tool didn't disturb the dirt, but white lines followed where it wrote, visible clearly despite the gloom. Aderyn briefly wondered why the ink was white now instead of black before she focused on what the kobold drew.

Akdukhur was as good an artist as Castilus, capturing images with just a few strokes of the <**Write-All**>. "Lots of kobolds," Aderyn muttered. "One kobold—your leader, maybe? Or you? A kobold giving orders, at least. Kobolds fighting waspnettles, small, large, very large." One waspnettle was bigger than the others. "The queen?" Aderyn asked, tapping the picture. Her finger did brush dirt from the wall.

Akdukhur didn't respond to the words he didn't understand. He moved to another section of wall. By now, he and the humans were the only ones remaining in the room. Sketching rapidly, he drew a large room covered in rough hexagonal shapes, with a single large waspnettle at its center. "All right, that must be the queen," Aderyn said.

Akdukhur held up a finger. Then he drew many more waspnettles surrounding the room. "Lots of warriors," Aderyn said.

"We already know this," Revelin said. "The queen is surrounded by too many waspnettle warriors for us to fight our way through."

Aderyn shushed him, her attention still focused on Akdukhur. The kobold drew a white circle on one of the walls of his sketched rooms and pointed at Aderyn, then back at the circle, three times.

"I see," Weston said. "There's an entrance for us. But that still makes no sense. Getting in past the defenses, if that's what he means, doesn't do anything about the waspnettles in the room with the queen."

Aderyn pointed at herself and then each of her companions. Then she pointed at the circle and shook her head. "Too many," she said, indicating the warriors Akdukhur had drawn.

Akdukhur shook his head. He pointed at the circle and then at Aderyn again. Then he muttered something and set to drawing. Images of kobolds filled the scene, kobolds attacking waspnettles. Akdukhur pointed at them, then repeated his gestures including Aderyn and the circle-door. He laid down the <**Write-All**> and with exaggerated movements mimed sneaking up on Aderyn, drawing an imaginary sword. Then he pretended to stab her in the back.

"What?" Aderyn exclaimed. "Oh. *Oh.* You mean the kobolds will keep the warriors and the queen distracted while we sneak up on her." She pointed at the large waspnettle figure and took a few steps in a broadly sneaky manner, then repeated Akdukhur's gesture of stabbing the figure in the back.

Akdukhur let out a grunt and nodded. He again pointed at all of them. Then he moved to a third section of wall and drew a series of lines that made no sense to Aderyn. When he turned to her expectantly, she said, "I'm sorry, I don't understand. What is this?"

With another low grunt, this one sounding exasperated, Akdukhur pointed at the ground, the corridor they'd entered from, and the lines on the wall. He then drew over some of the lines as if for emphasis. "I still don't get it," Aderyn said.

"I think I do," Livia said. She stepped up to the wall, searching the drawing for something, and finally put her finger on the intersection of two lines. Then she pointed at the doorway and touched the intersection again. Akdukhur yipped loudly and nodded. He drew over a few more lines and looked at Livia expectantly.

"It's a map," Livia said. "But not the way we draw it. That makes sense, given that they're tunnelers and probably don't see the world the way we do. This map shows densities of earth and stone. I think he's showing us how to get to where the queen is if we were kobolds. A back route."

Aderyn's skin crawled. "You mean, through tunnels?"

"Yes. I don't know if he realizes I can use *burrow* to make new tunnels, but I don't think I'd dare to because it might damage their digging. But if I understand this, they already have tunnels that lead to the hive center." Livia rubbed the dirt from the wall between the fingers of her flesh-and-blood hand. "This could work."

"It will take careful timing," Owen said. He got Akdukhur's attention, pointed at himself and at the kobold, and held up three fingers. Folding one finger after another, he counted, "Three... two... one... *attack.*" On "attack," he swooped both hands together on the figure of the queen waspnettle, striking it simultaneously.

Akdukhur nodded again. He gestured at the hole in the wall the other kobolds had disappeared into, then at the humans. Owen nodded. "It's going to be a tight fit for some of us, but if this is what we have to do, I guess we start crawling." He ducked his head into the tunnel and crawled inside, scattering earth where the back of his armor rubbed against the tunnel wall.

"Are you going to be all right?" Isold asked Aderyn.

Aderyn clenched her hands to stop their shaking. "I'll be fine," she asserted, and before she could lose her nerve, she followed Owen.

Immediately, she wished she hadn't been so cavalier. There were no lights in the tunnel, and in the darkness, surrounded by the weight of the earth pressing in on all sides, all she had to orient herself was the shuffling movements Owen made ahead of her. She bit back a keening moan of fear and followed him as closely as she could, ducking her head to avoid rubbing it on the tunnel roof.

How long they crawled, she had no idea. Her mind gibbered terrified thoughts at her, fears of being crushed or suffocated or trapped forever in this nightmare. Then she heard Owen say, "Who's behind me?"

"It's me," she managed.

"Aderyn. We're coming up on a lighted space. It's almost over. Just a little farther, okay? I promise we'll be out soon."

Aderyn didn't answer. She knew Owen wouldn't lie to her, but he could be mistaken. Surely this tunnel went on forever. She went on crawling, one pace at a time, hands and knees moving involuntarily because she'd lost the will to do anything else several minutes back.

Then the outline of Owen's body became visible, and a moment later, gray light made a circle against the blackness. Then she was out and falling to the floor, the beautifully solid steel floor a foot below the opening of the tunnel, and she crawled rapidly away from the nightmare and curled up in a ball, gasping for air as if she really had begun to suffocate.

Hands pulled her upright, and Owen took her in his arms and brushed earth from her hair. "Sorry," he whispered. "I've never known anyone as brave as you."

"What, because I'm unnaturally terrified of harmless small spaces?"

"Because you didn't freeze up, and you didn't refuse to go," Owen said. "I don't know if we have to do that again—"

Aderyn couldn't stop an involuntary whimper she hated herself for. She was tougher than this. "I'll be fine. It gets easier each time," she lied.

"I know that's not true, but I hope you hold to that," Owen said.

They waited for everyone to make their way through the tunnel. Livia looked blissfully happy when she emerged at the end of the line, followed by Akdukhur. "That was lovely," she exclaimed. "Too bad I said I wouldn't dig my own tunnels, because this place has tremendous potential."

Akdukhur made a shushing gesture. He pointed at another tunnel some distance from the first. There were four tunnels leaving this room in all, Aderyn noticed as she tried not to think about how many of them Akdukhur might expect them to use—four tunnels and one human-made door that wasn't closed all the way. With determination, she moved toward the tunnel Akdukhur had indicated, but the kobold barred her way and shook his head, chittering rapidly. Then he vanished into the tunnel himself.

"Well, what now?" Revelin said.

"I guess we wait," Owen said.

Akdukhur returned in only a few minutes. Now two leather thongs looped around his neck, each with a clear quartz crystal prism the length of his stubby forefinger dangling from it. Akdukhur removed one necklace and handed it to Aderyn. Then he gripped the quartz crystal he wore and held it to his lips. He breathed heavily across its surface, and it glowed blue with a light no brighter than a firefly.

Aderyn gasped. As Akdukhur's crystal glowed, hers glowed as well. "Synchronicity," she said. "They're made to respond to each other. This is how we'll coordinate our attacks." She pointed at herself, then at Akdukhur, and raised both her hands and gestured so they mirrored each other's movements. Then she breathed on her own crystal and smiled as Akdukhur's lit up.

Akdukhur gave a grunt that sounded like satisfaction and nodded. He brought out the **<Write-All>** again and drew on the floor this time, digging light grooves through the textured steel. Aderyn watched carefully. "That tunnel leads to a protected space," she said as he sketched. "A hidden entrance to the queen's lair—how is it still hidden? Oh, I don't know how to ask that, and I suppose it doesn't matter so long as it is. It brings us past the guards. Then we signal you that we're in place, and wait for your people to attack." She looked up at Owen. "It's not much of a plan, but there's no way to be more specific until we know the situation."

"There could still be too many to fight our way through," Embrus said. "I don't like the idea of abandoning the kobolds if it turns out to be too difficult. I don't know how we'd tell them to abandon the fight."

"It's this or nothing," Owen said. "And I choose to believe it's not impossible."

"Because a kobold thinks it isn't?" Revelin said.

"Because a kobold is taking a chance on us," Owen replied, "and Aderyn trusts him."

Akdukhur was watching them closely. On a whim, Aderyn extended her hand to him again and waited for him to press his palm against hers. "He's risking everything, too."

"Then we go," Owen said. "Which way, Akdukhur?"

Akdukhur led them, not through a tunnel, but out the door and down a short passage where most of the lights had been removed, making it even dimmer than the rest of the Enchanterium. Distantly, voices sounded, the faintest rising and falling noise of kobold conversation. Akdukhur stopped at a tunnel in the corridor wall and pointed. Aderyn asked, "Will this lead us to the waspnettle queen?" She knew she was stalling, but she needed a little time to nerve herself up to crawling into the dark again. She gestured, indicating a centauroid creature with a large stinger.

Akdukhur watched her for a moment, looking confused. Then he nodded. He pointed at the tunnel again.

"I have to go first for **[Improved Assess 3]**," Aderyn said, cursing the tremor in her voice. Before she could let it spread to the rest of her, she climbed inside and started crawling.

This time, she considered whether she shouldn't have let Livia cast *orb of light* so she could see where she was going. No, that was a bad idea, seeing exactly how close the tunnel walls and ceiling and floor were. She would keep moving, and eventually she would come out somewhere. That the somewhere was likely the center of the hive and the most dangerous place in the compound didn't change how relieved she felt at the prospect.

She counted seconds at first until she got to one hundred and it became too hard. Then she focused on putting one hand in front of the other, over and over until the tunnel was gray instead of black and she heard the whirring, buzzing sound of vestigial wings. She ducked her head and murmured, "We're close. Give me a moment," to whoever was behind her.

When she reached the end of the tunnel, she paused before exiting and listened again. The sounds of buzzing and the clicking of claws on metal didn't sound agitated. She glanced around. A wall panel had buckled here, making a small protected space she couldn't see around. She slid out of the tunnel and continued to crawl until she reached the edge of the panel, then peered around the side.

CHAPTER THIRTY-SEVEN

The room was smaller than the central chamber, though that might have been how the waspnettle wax secretions choked every wall and narrowed every door. They glowed eerily, unsettling Aderyn until she realized the glow came from the Enchanterium lights still burning behind the translucent wax. The whole room was barely as bright as a cloudy day.

An enormous golden shape sitting near where she crouched drew her eye. The waspnettle queen—it couldn't be anything else—had an enormous, bloated abdomen and a golden carapace that glimmered in the low light. Despite its wings being fully formed, they were clearly too small to lift the swollen body. It squatted over a pile of something irregularly shaped that Aderyn couldn't make out. She hoped it wasn't kobold bodies. Even if she hadn't thought of the kobolds as allies now, that seemed grotesque.

She Assessed the room, starting with the queen.

Name: Waspnettle Queen
Type: Magical beast, intelligent
Power level: 17
Attacks: claw x4, bite, special

Immune to: mind control

Resistant to: bludgeoning damage

Vulnerable to: *daylight, sunburst*

Special attacks: stinger (poison)

The waspnettle queen commands the obedience of the hive through both the low-level mental link all waspnettles share as well as the community's awareness that she, as producer of all offspring, is literally their future. While waspnettle queens do not fight on behalf of the hive, that doesn't mean they're not powerful in their own defense. Their poison is more potent even than that of the warriors and the elites, and they are capable of several claw attacks at once.

Waspnettles draw strength from their queen's presence and will fight viciously to defend her. This is also the hive's great weakness: killing the queen demoralizes the others, who are likely to scatter in search of a new queen or hive.

You know what you have to do.

Aderyn's skin crawled with a sharp, unpleasant full-body tingle. The last line seemed so final, and yet it wasn't at all unexpected. She swiftly Assessed the rest of the room. The description tag, nearly lost in the monster Assessments, read **[Shipping and Transportation]**. She had no idea how to use that, particularly with all the panels completely obscured by waxy growths. More important was the number of enemies: fifteen waspnettle elites, twenty-two warriors, forty-seven drones. Too bad she had no way to convey this information to Akdukhur.

She backed up and nearly shrieked as a hand went over her mouth and Owen whispered, "It's me, don't make a sound," in her ear. She nodded, and he removed his hand. He and Revelin had come through the tunnel and crowded into the space behind the buckled panel. There wasn't room for any more than the three of them.

"What now?" Owen whispered.

Aderyn scanned the room with **[Spot Weakness]**, hoping for an environmental advantage. The blue lines slid over the wax-coated floor and walls without coalescing into points of light. "We need to let Akdukhur attack first and draw the waspnettles' attention away from the queen," she whispered back. "Then we get into position and make our own assault. The queen is the weakness. If we kill her, it will break the others and they will likely scatter."

"'Likely'?" Revelin said, arching both eyebrows.

"It's the best we can do. We'll still have to fight some of them, but they'll be demoralized and that will work to our advantage as well. Pass the word back for everyone to be ready. I hate that half of us will still be in the tunnel when the fight starts, but there's no helping that unless we want to risk drawing attention to ourselves." Aderyn gripped the crystal and waited for Owen's hand to clasp her free one, indicating that everyone was prepared. Then she blew gently across the quartz. She didn't waste time staring at it; once she saw it light up, she turned her attention back to the room and waited.

The waspnettles were constantly in motion, she noticed, the drones crawling over the walls and ceiling, tending to whatever lay inside the cells, the warriors and elites marching in elaborate patterns that to her Warmaster's vision were training exercises meant to keep them sharp. For a moment, she saw them with an unjaded eye, how beautiful they were in an alien way. She shook herself, and the moment passed. Beautiful, true, but vicious and cruel and unwilling to make a truce the way the kobolds had. Their deaths would protect so many innocents.

A loud cry reverberated through the chamber, one voice that turned into many voices all *yip-yip-yipping* at a volume that made the wax quiver until some of the growths shattered and fell from the ceiling. Kobolds poured into the room, their browns and greens and blues and bronzes muted by the eerie light. Small fires from the kobold bushwhackers' breath attack lit their bodies with a warm light that contrasted with the cold light from the waxy walls. The waspnettles froze, startled. Then they rushed to meet the kobold attack.

The queen shifted and let out a buzzing noise that turned the kobold cries discordant. Almost instantly, a handful of white elite fighters surrounded her, brandishing javelins or swords. Aderyn ignored them in favor of watching the battle, listening to her inner sense of how well the kobolds engaged the enemy. She waved at Owen. "They're distracted. Get everyone out of the tunnel, now!"

This was the dangerous part, waiting to see if the queen and her elite bodyguards noticed them massing for a rear assault. Aderyn's hand hurt, and she realized she was still clutching the quartz crystal. She dropped it and massaged her hand without ever taking her eyes off the queen. The queen showed no other signs of agitation after that first buzzing shout, and the elites had their attention on the kobolds. This heartened Aderyn. The elites weren't as good as she'd feared if they weren't alert to a second threat.

The others had all gathered around her now, totally exposed. Aderyn spoke rapidly. "*Sunburst* first, to weaken them, then *thunderstomp*—they're vulnerable to being tripped. Owen, Revelin, Embrus, fight your way through to the queen. Remember the elites are a distraction. Weston and Inaya, keep the bodyguards preoccupied with [To the Heart]. Go for the body joints, waist and throat, and avoid their armor—I mean their carapaces. Cyanne, if you can isolate some of them with fire, we can take them out a few at a time. Ready? Then shield your eyes!"

Livia chanted a few syllables, and brilliant light burst across the ceiling, flooding the room and turning Aderyn's vision pink despite her arms flung over her face. She raised her head, blinking away pained tears. Light outlined every line and every creature like someone had traced them all with the brilliant <Sunsword>. Several waspnettle drones lay motionless where they'd fallen from the ceiling and upper walls, and most of the warriors were cringing from the kobolds—

Aderyn's heart sank. Many of the kobolds were also cringing in the brightness, and a few dropped their weapons and fled as she watched. She'd forgotten their allies were underground dwellers as well, and just as vulnerable to *sunburst* as the waspnettles. Nothing she could do about it now but press forward. "Go, go!" she shouted, and the rippling force of *thunderstomp* arrowed ahead of the others, racing toward the waspnettle queen.

Isold played a martial tune on his flute that filled Aderyn with confidence. Almost she ran after the others. But her only weapon was a staff that would be ineffective against the hard chitin, and she would just be a distraction to Owen and her friends. She and Isold circled the fight, staying close in case they were needed.

Fire erupted from the floor and spread rapidly in a line surrounding the elites to the left of the queen as if Cyanne had drizzled oil in a lopsided circle and set a match to it. The buzzing sounds of waspnettle fear and anger filled the air, but Isold's magic song was louder still, and the human fighters obviously felt its effects. Weston and Inaya fought like deadly dancers, moving lithely out of the way of stingers and javelins, slashing at enemy throats and abdomens. As they forced the elites not trapped by fire to retreat, Owen, Embrus, and Revelin made a more direct charge for the queen.

The queen lumbered to her feet and shrieked a challenge, or a summons, Aderyn couldn't tell which. "Watch out for reinforcements," she boomed out with **[Amplify Voice]**. Instantly Embrus turned his back on the queen, taking a defensive stance while Owen and Revelin continued forward. A dozen warriors led by two elites broke away from the kobolds and stampeded toward their queen. The floor buckled in front of them, and the wax layer shattered as metal plates twisted and rose up from beneath it. Three of the warriors stumbled, and one shrieked in agony as another metal floor plate whirled through the air like a razor-edged discus and neatly severed its spine. More of Livia's chanting filled the air, and the whirling plate returned to take the head off another waspnettle.

The fire raged higher, spreading inward to immolate the trapped elites. One of them threw its javelin at Cyanne, who didn't dodge fast enough. The heavy point drove across her shoulder, nearly taking her head with it. Cyanne screamed and collapsed to her knees. Isold's music stopped. "Come with me," he said to Aderyn.

They ran to Cyanne's side, and Aderyn supported her as Isold wielded the <**Wand of Healing**> over her wound. Cyanne was only barely conscious, her head lolling to one side, but she muttered, "Stupid bugs and their stupid weapons."

"You'll be fine," Aderyn said.

She raised her head and screamed at the sight of more waspnettle warriors, led by two elites, stampeding toward them, clearly intent on overrunning them. Before she could rise to face her doom on her feet, Isold put himself in front of her, braced himself, and let out a howl that chilled Aderyn's blood with a distant fear.

The waspnettles stumbled, hurtling into each other in their desperate attempt to turn and flee. Isold wiped his mouth and said, over his shoulder, "[Cause Fear]. It affects minds, but I took a chance that resistant was not the same as immune."

"It was worth the chance," Aderyn said.

"Aderyn!" Owen shouted. "I need [Outflank]!"

Aderyn swore under her breath. She'd been so convinced her weapon was useless she'd forgotten she had other skills that weren't. Gently, she laid Cyanne on the floor. "Concentrate on the reinforcements when you're up again," she said, and ran for the queen.

The first of the remaining reinforcements had reached Embrus, who was battling fiercely to keep them from overrunning him. Aderyn immediately saw she couldn't force her way past that crowd to reach Owen. Instead, she ran wide around the fire, which now extended nearly to the wax-coated wall. Its heat melted the wax, sending up stinking clouds that were probably toxic. Aderyn examined her options, then shouted, "Livia! I need—"

A gout of freezing water drenched her from head to foot. "That," Aderyn finished. She brought the hem of her shirt up so the wet fabric covered her face and, before her logical brain could tell her it was impossible, ran into the fire.

The heat scorched her skin, drying it rapidly, but she'd chosen a point where the fire field was narrowest, and she felt only slightly burnt when she emerged on the other side. Swiftly, she ran to meet Owen, the **<Laborer's Staff>** clutched in one hand. It might be almost useless against the queen's carapace, but **[Outflank]** didn't work if she didn't have a weapon.

Owen had gotten in a few good hits, she saw in the moment before she reached her position and **[Outflank]** tugged at her with its weird pressure, as if there was a connection between her and her prey. She brought the staff around and struck the queen with a resounding thwack.

With unexpected agility, the queen spun around and swiped at Aderyn with an enormous clawed hand—or would have if **[See It Coming]** hadn't done its job. Aderyn dropped so the blow sailed harmlessly over her head. Then the queen shrieked in mingled pain and fury as Owen slashed the narrow join between thorax and abdomen. The strike would have severed the queen's spine had it not been thicker than the average waspnettle's, but whitish ichor flowed, and when the queen turned on Owen, she didn't move as fast as she had before.

Heartened, Aderyn struck again. Without turning around, the queen lashed out with a hindleg that Aderyn dodged easily. The queen kicked at her again, and then a stinger the thickness and length of Aderyn's leg flashed past her face, close enough the wind of its passing ruffled her hair. She realized Owen was screaming her name just as she registered that **[Outflank]** wasn't working. Scurrying backward, she cast about frantically for her partner and saw Owen fighting a waspnettle elite that didn't cringe away from the light of the **<Sunsword>**. Owen's back was to the queen, and he didn't see the flex of her abdomen as she readied the stinger to stab him in the back.

Desperately, Aderyn scrambled forward, scuttling beneath the waspnettle queen as she reared up to strike. She shouted Owen's name, but the noise of the battle and Isold's flute soaring over it drowned her words out. She was too terrified even to weep.

Time seemed to slow as the queen's stinger cut an arc through suddenly thick air, aiming directly between Owen's shoulder blades. Aderyn screamed again, a wordless protest. Maybe the <**Ring of the Cat**> would save him, maybe not, but she couldn't bear to watch Owen die and she couldn't bear not to look.

A flash of movement from one side, Owen's name shouted by someone other than Aderyn, and then Owen was shoved to one side and nearly onto the blade of the elite he'd been fighting. The stinger didn't change its path, and in the next moment it impaled Embrus through the chest.

CHAPTER THIRTY-EIGHT

Aderyn was moving too fast to stop herself. She ran into Embrus, pushing his body off the stinger and collapsing on top of him. Embrus's wide eyes didn't seem to see her, and his mouth was frozen in a terrible rictus of pain. "No," Aderyn said, "no, get up, Embrus, we'll get you healed."

Embrus raised one hand to clutch Aderyn's shoulder. "Get away," he mumbled through rigid lips. Then his hand fell away, and his eyes stared up at nothing.

Aderyn backed away. The fighting had moved past them to the right, away from the dying flames, and the queen had shifted in that direction as well. That the monster had lost interest in them infuriated Aderyn. When a waspnettle warrior approached her, she rose and swung the staff's heavy crook at the creature with such strength it caved the monster's head in.

**Congratulations! You have defeated [Waspnettle Warrior].
You have earned [4000 XP]**

It was the first defeat notice she'd registered, though she'd been peripherally aware of them popping up here and there. It didn't matter. Her joke about Embrus not living to see his sweetheart again nauseated her now.

She stepped away from his body and rushed to meet the next warrior, dodged the javelin it threw, and aimed a blow at the place where its thorax and abdomen connected. A sword would have cut it cleanly through. The staff broke the joint so the warrior fell, twitching, as its upper and lower halves no longer communicated. Aderyn rejoiced at the new system defeat notice.

She worked her way to Owen's side. He and Revelin were back to fighting the queen, whose many wounds flowed with ichor and who was definitely moving slower now. "I can't get behind her for [Outflank]," she said.

"It's almost over," Owen said. Then, to her surprise, he lowered his <Sunsword>. Nearby, Revelin and Inaya fought in silence, Revelin directing blows at the queen that forced her onto Inaya's blade. He seemed to have a plan in mind, because his movement was all aimed in one direction.

The queen focused on Inaya, and in her moment of distraction Revelin vaulted onto the queen's swollen abdomen and dashed up it to where he could reach her head. With a powerful two-handed blow of his staff, he struck her throat with a terrible crack that resounded above the noise of battle.

The queen's head jerked. Then it sagged as if her neck no longer supported it. A cry went up from the gathered waspnettles, a clicking, rattling noise loud enough to bring more chunks of wax down. Then, like water hissing onto a hot plate, they scattered in every direction. Kobolds howled and ran after them, their deadly strikes not resisted by the fleeing waspnettles. Owen stabbed one of the elites through the thorax as it fled past him, but after that one blow and the system defeat notice that came after it, he let the monsters run.

"I hope that's not a mistake," Weston said as he limped to join them. Blood darkened his left trouser leg, but he seemed otherwise uninjured.

"If the kobolds are smart, and I think they are, they'll herd the waspnettles away from their lair," Aderyn said. "What I wonder is whether we'll see them again. We did help each other, after all, but we're not exactly friends."

"Owen," Revelin said. He leaped down from the waspnettle queen's corpse and approached them. "You did that on purpose."

Owen shrugged. "We fought together. Someone had to get the final blow."

"I don't need pity experience."

"It wasn't pity. Call it recognition of your goals. You did say you wanted experience—well, you got it." Owen didn't look angry, or scornful, or anything but perfectly calm.

"It doesn't matter, Rev," Inaya said. "We did plenty of damage. We earned that kill."

Revelin grimaced. "Where's Embrus? And Cyanne?"

With a sickening jolt, Aderyn remembered that still, paralyzed form. "Embrus died saving Owen's life," she said.

Revelin and Inaya exchanged puzzled glances. "He's not dead," Revelin said. "His name is still in my Codex."

Aderyn turned. "But I saw him—"

A short distance away, Isold knelt over Embrus, supporting his head while pouring a green potion into his mouth. Aderyn expected to see the potion spill over Embrus's lips, but instead, the Pathseer's throat moved as he swallowed. Then green fire exploded across Embrus's body as he convulsed, his back arched, the tendons on his neck bulging. Almost immediately, the green fire faded, and Embrus relaxed. He opened his eyes and worked his jaw a few times as if it felt stiff. "Interesting," he said.

"A <**Potion of Life**>," Revelin said in amazement. "And you used it on one of us?"

Isold put the empty vial away in his knapsack. "It's what we do for each other. If not Embrus, it would have been Owen."

"And I'm grateful," Owen said, offering Embrus a hand up. "Now, let's see about disconnecting this third system. After that battle, it should be easy."

"Oh, *don't* say things like that," Livia said. "You know that sort of thing is a jinx."

Owen clapped her on the shoulder. "We all lived through that battle. I'm willing to risk a tiny little jinx."

THE PATH to the third level control chamber showed signs of a rapid flight. The wax coating the panels underfoot was deeply scratched as from waspnettle claws, and chunks of broken wax littered the floor. All the cells that had been filled with liquid were slashed open, and the going was slippery where the fluid covered the floor. "That was the kobolds, I'm sure," Aderyn said the second time they found broken cells. "They wouldn't want any new waspnettles born in here."

"I'm worried that we haven't seen any of our allies," Owen said. "They shouldn't count on the waspnettles all going without a fight."

"They know to be careful," Aderyn replied. "So many of them died in that battle, they won't take chances." Akdukhur had not been among the fallen kobolds, something that relieved Aderyn's heart. He wasn't a friend, was barely an ally, but Aderyn liked him and was grateful he hadn't died.

No waspnettles remained in the control chamber, living or dead. Aderyn got out the <**Wayfinder**> and concentrated. Fears of having to chip away or melt all the wax to find the panel they needed distracted her, and it took several tries before she calmed enough to focus on her heart's desire. Finally, the spike glowed a warm pink, and she carried it around the room until the glow brightened and then went out. "This one."

The others joined her. "That is a lot of wax," Owen said. "And I'm not sure it's safe to melt it off. We might be at this for a while."

"It will be fine," Cyanne said. "Are you sure the rest of the room doesn't matter?"

Owen eyed her skeptically. "You're not thinking of destroying everything else, are you?"

"No, but what I have in mind could potentially damage the metal underneath." Cyanne flexed her fingers, and her left hand burst into flame, a hot white fire that burned afterimages into Aderyn's eyes. Cyanne extended her index finger and traced a line on the nearest wall, well away from the desired section. Wax smoked and melted, but the fire didn't spread. With her right hand, Cyanne inserted the tip of her belt knife into the groove her fire melted and worked the blade under the wax, then twisted her wrist. A large chunk of wax broke free, revealing undamaged metal beneath.

"Impressive," Livia said.

"If we all work at it, we can clear the panel quickly," Cyanne said. "I just need to know where to burn it."

Owen drew his <**Deadly Blade**> and scored a line that arched as high as he could reach, making a rough door outline. "That should do it."

Cyanne scored the line deeper, though she had to kneel on Weston's shoulders to reach the top of the arch, and the others attacked the wax with their knives. Popping chunks of wax away from the wall satisfied Aderyn. It felt good to free the Enchanterium of the wasp-nettle incursion, but there was also something viscerally pleasurable about breaking up the wax Aderyn couldn't explain. She kicked the loose wax away to get it out from underfoot and felt more satisfaction at seeing it go spinning across the uneven floor. Too bad clearing all the wax was impractical and unnecessary.

Finally, nothing obscured the panel, which looked exactly the same as the ones in the other control chambers. Weston turned the dial that made the blue and amber and red lights appear. The black glass scrying window turned pale gray, and the words *Authorization required* scrolled across its surface. Revelin and Embrus took involuntary steps back, but Inaya leaned forward to touch the screen curiously. "Who does the writing?"

"Some Spellcrafter's invention, probably," Weston said. He pressed buttons to spell out *Dulcia*.

More words appeared:

Dragon System 3: Flight Control

"If disabling this system hampers its ability to fly, that would give us a huge advantage," Revelin said.

Weston nodded. He flicked each of three switches, turning their lights amber.

The invisible hand erased the message, and new words appeared.

Deactivating flight control requires decoupling the system from the Enchanterium defenses. Do not attempt except in time of crisis. Please confirm decision.

Weston pressed the big green button and read aloud the words, "Decision confirmed, decoupling in process—they sure were fond of formality, weren't they?"

"How long does it take?" Inaya asked.

"Not long. Unless the automatic system fails." Weston fixed his gaze on the scrying window as if he could will it to display the right message.

Moments passed. Aderyn found she was staring at the window just as hard as Weston, hoping nothing would go wrong. Sure, they'd found the manual override before, but what if this system failed in a different way?

Finally, the letters faded, and a new message appeared.

Decoupling successful. Enter authorization to deactivate flight control.

Weston again spelled Dulcia's name. The window cleared again. After several seconds during which Aderyn thought she might scream with tension, more words appeared:

Flight control deactivated.

Almost immediately, a system message flashed in front of Aderyn's face.

You have received a [Cooperation] bonus of [6000 XP] for solving [Element 4] of the Lonely Tor mysteries. Experience bonuses increase with each element solved.

Aderyn and Weston both let out their breath at the same time, then laughed self-consciously. Owen put his arm around Aderyn's shoulders. "That's it, then. We can kill the dragon."

"Unless there's some other thing we don't know about," Livia said. "All right, don't look at me that way! I figured if I said it, it would tell the system not to bother throwing any more obstacles in our way. Sort of a proactive anti-jinx."

Weston grabbed her around the waist and swung her in a wide circle while she squawked her indignation. "Always thinking ahead," he teased.

"Put me down, you musclebound oaf," Livia said without rancor. "It's so undignified."

Owen faced Revelin. "We still have to find a way up to the dragon's lair, since I doubt the kobolds would live on the same level as it. You up to working together a little longer?"

"We still don't have a solution to the dilemma of whose quest takes precedence," Revelin said, once more impassive behind his beard. "And don't think you get any credit for letting us kill the queen. It's not a tradeoff."

"I didn't think that. But I still believe we're better off working together. What do you say?" Owen offered Revelin his hand.

Revelin didn't take it. He glanced at Embrus and Inaya, standing together beside him, and at Cyanne a few steps in front of him. Just as Aderyn realized they were all standing well away from her team, Revelin said, "I think we'll take our chances."

A sudden deep sleepiness filled Aderyn, making her bones ache with tiredness. She forced her eyes open long enough to see Cyanne gesturing in a complicated movement of both hands, and then the waxy, stinking floor came up to meet her. She was so exhausted she couldn't think about how strange this was for longer than two breaths of the stench, and then she was asleep.

She came awake with a jerk as if something had poked her. The pungent, old-cheese smell of the wax filled her nostrils, and she sat up and pinched her nose closed. It didn't help. Her entire body ached like she'd slept contorted, and her eyes were crusted over. She blinked until the world swam into focus.

Around her, her friends lay, as twisted into odd shapes as she'd imagined herself, though Isold was moving like he ached as much as she did. She tried to stand, and her legs shook so badly she had to balance with her hands to keep from falling over. Teetering from both weakness and the uneven floor, she made her way to Owen's side and shook him hard. Owen groaned, but he didn't open his eyes. "Wake up!" she demanded, shaking him again.

Owen's lips moved. "...sleep..."

"*Deep slumber*," Livia mumbled. "That bitch cast *deep slumber* on us."

"No," Owen said. His eyes fluttered open, and he managed to focus on Aderyn. "Where are they?"

"Long gone," Weston said. "Those thundering bastards betrayed us."

Owen groaned again and rolled to his hands and knees, then sat up fully. "I expected it, but not that soon. Stupid of me."

"I saw they were grouped out of reach of any spell Cyanne cast, but not in time, so I'm stupid too," Aderyn said.

"There's no point casting blame," Isold said. "We have to beat them to the dragon. Do we know how long we were unconscious?"

Livia shook her watch and swore under her breath. "Long enough for this to wind down. Call it ten hours."

"That is a damn long start," Owen said. "But they don't know how to get to the upper levels any more than we do. That's something."

A sudden dread certainty hit Aderyn. She grabbed the **<Purse of Great Capacity>** and upended it. A stream of small, useful objects poured out. "*No*," she said with feeling. "Inaya stole the **<Wayfinder>**. I can't believe she did that! I thought we were becoming friends!"

Owen gripped her hand. "That wasn't useful for finding the way up before, remember? It won't do her any good—"

"Except before, we were searching for things we didn't know enough about for the **<Wayfinder>** to locate," Aderyn said bitterly. "She just has to will it to find the dragon, and it will take her straight there."

They sat in silence for a moment. Finally, Owen said, "Crap."

"This is not over," Isold declared. He stood unsteadily and brushed himself off. "We have other resources. And there are those in the Enchanterium I would bet on knowing the way up. Follow me."

They ran through the empty halls, following a path on Isold's system map, until they were well out of the waspnettle territory. Aderyn didn't remember these halls, but she trusted Isold's memory. She was less certain about the plan they'd concocted, but it was really their only hope now.

As they neared yet another corner, Weston slowed. "I hear something ahead."

"Aderyn?" Owen said.

Aderyn let out a deep breath and walked around the corner. Ahead, a green kobold and a blue kobold blocked the way. They brandished their long knives at Aderyn, but stayed where they were.

"Akdukhur?" Aderyn said. She spread her hands wide to indicate she wasn't a threat. "I want to speak to Akdukhur."

The kobolds didn't react. Despairing, Aderyn said, "I spared his life—oh, you don't understand me! Please, I just need to see him."

Still, the kobolds didn't move. Then the blue kobold changed its grip on its weapon and banged the end of the hilt against the metal wall in an arrhythmic pattern. The clamor spread and echoed down the hall until Aderyn wanted to cover her ears like a child blocking out a thunderstorm. After about half a minute, the kobold stopped banging and resumed its guard position. Aderyn waited.

"Was that a signal?" Owen asked. "A signal of what? 'Here are the humans, come kill them'?"

"Stop being pessimistic, that's my job," Livia said.

Claws skittered across the metal floor, and a handful of kobolds emerged out of the darkness beyond the guards. Akdukhur was at the head of the group. He alone was unarmed, but having fought him, Aderyn didn't think that made him harmless. He stepped past the guards and stared up at her, the red lights on the walls winking in the depths of his large black eyes.

"Ehdern," he said, and followed it up with several barking syllables.

"Akdukhur," Aderyn replied. "We need your help."

CHAPTER THIRTY-NINE

A kdukhur regarded her in silence. Aderyn swallowed. Then she knelt to put herself on his level. "I helped you," she said, pointing at his bandaged arm, miming pouring water down her throat, pointing at herself and then at him again. "Help. You." She repeated the gestures.

Akdukhur let out a low growl and a couple of barking yips. He pointed at his wounded arm and said, "Ankoo."

"Yes, thank you," Aderyn said. She gestured at him, then at herself. "Now. I need you to help me. You. Help. Me." She repeated the gestures.

Akdukhur stared at her without moving. If he understood, he didn't care. Aderyn was sure he didn't understand. "How can I tell you?" she said in despair.

Akdukhur tilted his head. Then he extended the <**Write-All**> to her with a few more guttural sounds.

"Oh!" Aderyn was a terrible artist, but now wasn't the time to dwell on her shortcomings. She fumbled with the tool until she figured out how to open it, then hesitated. She might get only one chance.

Finally, she sketched a tall, lopsided cone and drew three lines across it, segmenting it from top to bottom. The **<Write-All>** dragged at the steel like she was writing in wet sand, difficult but not impossible. In the bottom, widest section of the cone, she drew a worm with sharp teeth. Akdukhur hissed when he saw it. "Yes, the deep delver," Aderyn said.

In the next section, she drew what she hoped looked like a kobold. Akdukhur nodded, but said nothing. Aderyn drew another kobold in the third section. She pointed at Akdukhur and the other kobolds. "You live here and here."

After another moment's thought, she drew a line cutting off the tip of the cone and drew an awkward winged creature she didn't think looked much like a dragon. "Dragon," she said, pointing. "Big dragon. Do you know about the dragon?"

A kobold behind Akdukhur let out a chittering cry that was taken up by the others until Akdukhur shut them up with a few curt words. He pointed at the dragon drawing, then spread his arms and flapped them like wings before breathing out flame that singed Aderyn's eyebrows. She jerked away, and Akdukhur subsided. "All right, you know," she said. "Well, see if this makes sense."

Remembering what Akdukhur had drawn before, she drew a little picture of Owen with his **<Sunsword>** next to the dragon, stabbing it. A few of the nearer kobolds shrieked and backed away as if the blade was real and could hurt them. Akdukhur stood his ground. He looked at Owen, then pointed at the picture. "Right. Owen," Aderyn said. She pointed at Owen, then at herself and her friends. "Kill the dragon."

Akdukhur traced the outlines, which left no ink on his hand. He muttered something Aderyn guessed was about the crazy humans who thought they could kill a dragon. Aderyn waved the **<Write-All>** in his face. "No, that's not it. Look." She drew a picture of five stick human figures on the third level, next to the kobold. Then she made a dotted line from that group up the side of the cone to the dragon. "We need to go there. Can you show us?" She pointed between the kobold and the stick humans, then between Akdukhur and herself. Then she jabbed the <**Write-All**> at the ceiling and pointed at Akdukhur again. "Do you understand?"

Akdukhur studied the drawing. Then he held out his hand for the tool. He drew a solid line paralleling her dotted one, beginning at the third level and reaching all the way to the top of the cone. Then he drew a human figure, more detailed than Aderyn's stick portraits, at the bottom of the line. He said something guttural and sharp in his language. Then he swiftly drew over his line again in one quick movement and stabbed at the other endpoint a couple of times before drawing a second human figure near it.

Aderyn, puzzled, said, "I don't understand."

Akdukhur grunted. He drew a circle around the lower figure, then used the <**Write-All**> to make a great arc like something leaping from point to point, ending at the upper figure. He did this a few times, glaring at Aderyn in between movements as if willing her to understand.

"I see," Owen said abruptly. "There's a fast way to the top of the mountain. Hang on." He dug in his knapsack and pulled out a chunk of hard bread. Gesturing, he got Akdukhur to hand him the writing tool, and with a few swift strokes he drew a stick figure even cruder than Aderyn's on the bread. The ink pooled on the hard crust rather than sink in, but when Owen brushed his fingers over it, it didn't come off on his hand.

Owen held the bread chunk over the lower humanoid figure for a second or two, then moved it rapidly to the top, following Akdukhur's line. Then he pointed at himself and the others and repeated the gesture. "You have a passage to the top."

Akdukhur spoke rapidly and pointed at the ceiling. Then he got up and walked back the way he'd come. When Aderyn and the others didn't follow immediately, he stopped and waved them onward with an impatient gesture.

"I guess we go," Owen said. "I hope this isn't a mistake."

"I trust Akdukhur," Aderyn said. "Yes, it's true we might still misunderstand each other. But we don't know how to get to the next level, and it's this or wandering until Revelin's team kills the dragon and it's too late." She strode off after the kobold bushwhacker, and Owen and her friends quickly followed.

Akdukhur led them through halls free of waspnettle secretions, so dimly lit Aderyn could barely see him in the gloom. She hoped his route to the top didn't involve more tunnels. Surely even kobolds couldn't tunnel straight up, right?

After only a minute, they came to the first closed door Aderyn had seen in the kobolds' territory, if that's what the halls were. It wasn't locked, because Akdukhur slid it open with only a little effort. He waved at Aderyn to stay back when she would have followed him inside, but he didn't shut the door, so she stood on the threshold and looked into the room. **[Improved Assess 3]** told her it was **[Transportation Hub 2]**.

The room was more brightly lit than the hall, though still dimmer than daylight. Still, it was enough for Aderyn to make out a space about as big as the **[Air Control]** room where they'd encountered their first kobold, but square instead of round. Holes of sizes ranging from the width of her two palms to big enough for her to crawl inside dotted the walls. They weren't kobold holes; all of them were square and looked intentional, like they were part of the Enchanterium's construction.

Five or six kobolds stopped in their tracks when Akdukhur entered. They glanced once at him and then stared at Aderyn, standing in the doorway. Akdukhur ignored them. He walked to the center of the room, where a big lopsided circle was painted in red on the floor surrounding a familiar rubbery round surface. Akdukhur didn't step inside the line. Instead, he walked wide around it to a panel on the far side of the room. The panel was covered with switches and dials and small glowing lights, with a large red lever in the "up" position taking up most of one side.

Akdukhur surveyed the panel for a few seconds. Then he barked out several syllables that made the other kobolds, who were still staring, return to whatever it was they'd been doing. Their activity involved taking things from a pile in one corner and sliding them into the holes. To Aderyn, their movements looked random, and the things in the pile didn't look like anything special: stones, chunks of steel, the occasional rough tool. But then Akdukhur called her name, and she hurried to join him, followed by the others.

Akdukhur barked sharply as they neared the circle, but Aderyn didn't need the warning, assuming this was another levitation device that was by Akdukhur's behavior active. As they approached the kobold, Owen said, "I have a feeling I know what he has in mind."

"What?" Aderyn didn't have any idea why Akdukhur had brought them there.

Owen pointed at the ceiling.

Aderyn followed the line of his pointing finger, and her mouth fell open. Directly above the red circle was an enormous round hole that led to a steel-lined tunnel extending beyond the limits of her vision. "I still don't," she began.

Akdukhur said, "Ehdern," and followed it up with a long string of guttural noises. He pointed at her, then at the circle, and finally at the hole.

"It's another levitation circle," Owen said. "It can send things through that tunnel to—well, I assume a higher level, maybe even as high as the dragon."

"That seems unlikely," Isold said. "Everything in this place works sporadically, if at all, and what are the odds a monstrous race would figure out how to operate this magic device?"

"They are known for their cunning," Aderyn said. "It's not so strange that they'd play around with the Spellcrafters' remaining devices, and if Akdukhur is representative, they're smart enough to work out their operation."

"These other holes are for transportation as well," Weston said. He'd lagged behind the others and now stood near one of the square holes, peering into it. "But it's horizontal movement, not vertical. They're sending things to different places in the compound."

Akdukhur suddenly grunted, an impatient sound, and took a stone from the pile of things. He tossed it into the levitation circle, gently so it wouldn't bounce back out again. It didn't move.

"So it *is* beyond them," Isold said. He sounded disappointed, though he'd been the one to question the kobolds' abilities.

Akdukhur returned to the panel and pulled the red lever down with some effort. A heavy clank sounded beneath the floor, like a huge piece of metal turning over. And the stone shot away from the levitation device, almost faster than Aderyn could follow, streaking straight up and vanishing into the tunnel's darkness.

Aderyn realized her mouth was hanging open and closed it. "Um. Was that—"

"Fast," Owen supplied. "Now *that* is something I can get behind."

Akdukhur shoved the lever up and yipped, waving at the circle in invitation. Owen nodded and took a few steps in that direction.

"Wait," Aderyn said, grabbing his arm before Owen could step over the circle. "Shouldn't we be worried? We don't know how high it will take us, and suppose whatever it moves doesn't slow down at the top? Smashing into the ceiling at that speed could crush us!"

"You're the one who trusts him," Owen said. "Do you think he'd suggest this if it was going to kill us? There are easier ways to do that." He turned, though, and bowed to Akdukhur, saying, "Thank you. I hope your people stay safe. If you venture out toward human —oh, never mind, you can't understand me." He bowed a second time.

"Once I'm at the top, I'll use [**Bonded Mind**] to let you know it's safe for someone else to go," he told Aderyn. "Which means you'll have to go last."

"I don't know about this," Livia said. "Couldn't I burrow to the top?"

"That might be too slow, dearest," Weston said. "This is fast enough you won't have time to feel disoriented. And if Aderyn could endure the tunnels—"

"All right, yes," Livia replied irritably. "But I'll go second. I want this over with."

Owen kissed Aderyn, took a deep breath, and walked to the center of the circle. Akdukhur hauled down on the lever, and the clunk of metal sounded again. With a shout of exhilaration tinged with fear that made Aderyn cry out in protest, Owen flew up and into the hole, vanishing in less than a second.

Aderyn stuffed her fist into her mouth to keep from making any more embarrassing noises. She couldn't help picturing Owen hitting a distant steel ceiling and falling back to earth as a shattered lump of flesh. Behind her, the sound of the lever shifting brought her back to herself. Owen was right; Akdukhur wouldn't send them to their deaths. Unless kobolds, smaller and lighter than humans, could survive this trip where humans couldn't...

She waited as the seconds passed, slow and stretched out with her anxiety. No one spoke. The only sounds in the room came from kobolds going about their business and pretending not to watch the humans or Akdukhur. Aderyn's body ached with tension. Surely Owen should have spoken to her by now. What if this tunnel led straight to the dragon's lair, and the monster had killed Owen?

The back of her neck tingled, and Owen's voice in her head said, *...sorry... slow... come now...*

Relief took the place of tension, leaving her feeling weak for a few seconds. She should have looked at the team roster for reassurance. "He's there, and he's safe," she said, though she didn't know if the second thing was true. He couldn't be in immediate danger, or that message would have sounded different. "Livia, you're next."

Livia marched into the circle and closed her eyes. "I'm—"

Akdukhur pulled the lever, and Livia's scream trailed her as she shot into the darkness.

"I'd better go next," Weston said. He gazed anxiously up.

Owen's response was quicker this time, and soon Weston and Isold were gone and only Aderyn remained. She held out a hand, palm first, to Akdukhur. "Thank you again."

"Ankoo," Akdukhur said, pressing his palm to hers.

Aderyn swallowed and stepped into the circle. She watched Akdukhur put his hand on the lever, not wanting the moment of ascent to be a surprise.

The lever came down. A powerful force grabbed Aderyn around the waist and threw her upward like she was a stone flung from a sling, so fast the movement dragged at her skin and her eyes like it wanted to tear them from her body. The speed thrilled through her, and she screamed with excitement. If this was flying, it was faster than any bird could manage.

After a few seconds of this, she began to slow, though she was still moving fast enough the wind of her passage stole her breath. Gradually, her speed diminished until finally she wasn't moving faster than a brisk walk and she was able to look up. A distant circle of gray light marked, she hoped, the end of the tunnel. The circle grew and expanded until finally she rose out of the tunnel and gently bumped against the ceiling. It was the steel she'd imagined when she'd feared Owen would smash into it, with hand rungs attached in a row so she could haul herself away from the tunnel to solid ground.

Owen waited there and reached for her hand as she approached the tunnel's edge. "Fun, huh?"

"That was *great*," Aderyn said, hugging him. "Is Livia all right?"

"I'll survive," Livia said.

Unexpectedly, a system message appeared.

You have received a [Humility] bonus of [6500 XP] for solving [Element 17] of the Lonely Tor mysteries. Experience bonuses increase with each element solved.

Owen blew out his breath. "Humility, huh? I guess that's what it took. Since it wasn't as if we'd have found it without Akdukhur's help."

Aderyn looked around. The round room was empty except for the tunnel mouth and another lever identical to the red one below. One door, currently closed, took up a large space on the wall opposite the lever. The door was big enough Aderyn could easily imagine carts coming through it with supplies to be sent below. As she thought this, Weston, who was kneeling beside the door, gave a satisfied grunt, and the door slid open.

"Well," Owen said. "Let's go dragon hunting."

CHAPTER FORTY

Unusually bright lights blossomed along the walls when they stepped through the doorway. The short hall outside the levitation shaft led after only a few steps to a wider corridor branching left and right. Owen stopped there. "What happened to that one item we found on those dead adventurers?"

"The <Traveler's Aid>," Aderyn said. "I meant to give it to Isold, but I forgot." She felt around in the <Purse of Great Capacity> until her fingers closed on a teardrop-shaped lump. When she pulled it out, the faceted peridot reflected the lights so it sparkled, cheering Aderyn with its simple beauty. She extended it to Isold. "I don't know how to make it work, but you probably do, if your <Identify Magic Items> skill knew what it was."

"It's not difficult if you're seeking a unique creature or thing." Isold held the item by its chain and let it swing free as he said, "Dragon." Rather than slowing, the movement sped up until the stone and chain were parallel to the floor. To Aderyn, it looked like the stone was straining to break free and go flying off into the darkness of the unlit corridor to the left.

"That's nice and obvious," Owen said. "We'd better run."

The <Traveler's Aid> took them along a passage that turned corners seemingly at random. Lights came on as they ran, brighter than anything in the rooms and halls below, with no dark spots where the magic failed. Their boots rang out against the steel flooring, the sounds echoing until the noise made Aderyn's teeth ache, but she ignored the sensation. She could endure a little discomfort.

Just as she realized they hadn't passed any doors, they came to a cross-corridor that branched left and right while the hall they were in continued ahead. Owen grabbed Isold's shoulder and brought him to a halt. "That's natural light ahead."

"It's where the <Traveler's Aid> directs us," Isold said. The gem still strained at the chain like an eager dog on a leash, pointing straight forward.

"Yes, and if that room is open to the outdoors, it could mean the dragon is there," Owen said. "We need to move cautiously."

"I don't hear sounds of battle," Weston said. "We might have beaten Revelin's team here."

"Or they've already killed the dragon, and we're too late," Livia said.

"I don't think so. The [Fire and Ash] quest hasn't been invalidated the way it would if there was no dragon for us to kill." Owen stared into the darkness ahead, a hallway that ended in dim but clearly natural light, as if he felt the pull of the dragon as clearly as the <Traveler's Aid> did. "Weston, take the lead. Aderyn, follow him, but not too close—let him get a look at what's there."

They crept down the hallway single file, Weston in the lead and Livia bringing up the rear. Now Aderyn cringed at every footstep, though they made practically no noise compared to the ruckus they'd caused while running. Every lamp that lit as they passed made her heart thump painfully in fear that the light would draw the dragon's attention. But nothing stirred beyond the end of the hallway. The narrow space didn't fill with fire or poison gas from the dragon's breath attack. Aderyn recalled that one of the things they'd disabled was Elemental Volley. The legends said dragons breathed elemental attacks, fire or cold or acid—maybe they wouldn't have to deal with a breath weapon, after all, if that's what Elemental Volley meant.

The light from the end of the corridor increased as they approached, but not by much; it wasn't much brighter than a cloudy day. The hall also grew colder, with occasional gusts of wind that reminded Aderyn they had been indoors for a long time. Air moving against her cheeks, even cold air, comforted her for a few dozen steps. Then it was just cold and damp, the sign of a storm rolling in.

Nothing blocked the end of the corridor, though stone hinges showed where there had been doors once. Weston gestured for Aderyn to stay back and flattened himself against one wall so he could peer around the doorway's edge. He remained perfectly still for so long Aderyn struggled not to fidget. She almost wanted to rush into the room shouting defiance at whatever was there, anything to break the tension.

After what felt like forever, Weston eased away from the opening and returned silently to the others. "It's in there," he whispered. "Apparently asleep, though I'm not sure Forged ever really sleep. Dormant, anyway. But I wouldn't count on it not being alert. Either it didn't notice me, or it saw me and is pretending to be unaware to catch us off guard."

Owen clasped Aderyn's hand. "You ready?"

Aderyn nodded. She walked slowly to where Weston had stood and, taking a deep breath, looked into the dragon's lair.

The domed chamber was at least twice the size of the control chamber where the deep delver lived, with a ceiling that wasn't more than a shadow in the light of the oncoming storm. Instrument panels occupied the walls at intervals, more widely spaced than below, which Aderyn judged meant there weren't more of them than in any of the control chambers—this room was just that big.

She saw all this in a glance before her eye fell on the dragon. At first, it seemed smaller than she had expected, not much taller than

Weston and a good deal less bulky than the deep delver. She realized this was an illusion caused by the sheer size of the chamber when she registered how much taller the dragon was than the instrument panel nearest it. That change in perspective took her breath away. The dragon was easily twenty feet tall, and although she couldn't see how long it was because it was curled on itself, its head was at least ten feet long from nose to crown.

A few teeth were visible in that jaw, fangs near the end of its muzzle that might as well have been daggers, and its mouth was big enough to bite an unlucky human in half. Aderyn had expected, since it was Forged, that it would have smooth metal skin and visible joints like the minions they'd encountered, but it had a pebbly hide of a bronze hue that gleamed dully. Enormous wings folded over its flanks were the only things about it that looked made rather than grown; the membranes looked like a fine mesh, and the ribs actually did look like they were metal.

Aderyn gazed at the creature for a moment more to calm herself. Then she Assessed it.

Name: Ymri
Type: Forged
Power level: ~~18~~ 15
Attack(s): Claw x2, bite, tail slap, special
Immune to: mind control, elemental acid attacks
Resistant to: bladed weapon attacks DISABLED, bludgeoning weapon attacks DISABLED
Vulnerable to: none
Special attacks: flyby strafe DISABLED; elemental breath weapon DISABLED
The Forged construct Ymri was created by Spellcrafters of the Enchanterium as a mobile defense against outsiders interested in claiming the compound and its contents for themselves. It's not nearly as effective as the other defenses they came up with, but it's dramatic and frightening and, frankly,

damaged the morale of attackers more than it did physical harm. There's something to be said for making your enemy soil his trousers and run screaming.

The Spellcrafters designed Ymri as the trigger for the Enchanterium's self-destruction system, on the assumption that anything that could destroy their Forged dragon was too much for them to defend against. Unless Ymri is disconnected from the system, killing it will cause the Lonely Tor volcano to erupt—but you know this. Disconnecting Ymri also disables its breath weapon, limits its flight capability, and eliminates the ablative component of its armor. This reduces its power level to 15 and will make it easier for you to defeat. The Spellcrafters wanted the disconnection to weaken it enough that they could destroy it if necessary, but there's a relationship between... you know, never mind, it doesn't matter to you right now.

There's not much more I can tell you. You've weakened it enough that killing it isn't impossible anymore. That's about the extent of what I hoped for. Just keep in mind that it's still dangerous, and don't get in the way of the tail slap.

That "what I hoped for" screwed Aderyn's curiosity almost to the breaking point. The system wasn't a person, because no one had ever suggested such a thing was possible. Aderyn refused to believe that out of all the millions of people who'd accepted the Call over the centuries, she was the only one who'd had this kind of personal contact with it to reveal such a thing. Someone else would have known. But—

She squeezed her eyes tightly shut and made herself focus. Now was not the time to analyze this strange development. Right now, it didn't matter if there was some person or entity out there who was talking to her through **[Improved Assess 3]**. What mattered was killing the dragon.

She opened her eyes and Assessed the dragon again, this time paying attention to what **[Discern Weakness]** revealed. Blue lines slid across one another over the contours of Ymri's body, intersecting and coalescing at the dragon's weak points. Some of them, she'd expected, like the joints where the wings met the torso and the base of the throat. Others were a surprise, such as the spot of blue light beneath the dragon's armpit that Aderyn suspected was mirrored on the far side she couldn't see. That might represent a thin point in the dragon's pebbly hide.

When she was confident she'd learned everything she could, she quietly retreated down the hall to the others and whispered, "We took out many of its defensive and offensive capabilities, but it's still immune to mind control abilities and elemental acid damage, though I don't know if that matters to us."

"Acid is my new elemental power," Livia said. "Stupid thundering ineffective new power."

Aderyn grimaced. "That's unfortunate. It's not immune to anything else, but it is still good at attacking with claws, teeth, and tail."

"So we either keep a safe distance or dart in and out of its reach, is that it?" Owen asked.

"Right. Aim for the wing joints, the base—"

A battle cry echoed down the corridor, picked up by more voices before being drowned out by a titanic roar. Owen cursed. "We're out of time. Go now!"

Chapter Forty-One

They all pelted through the doorway just as Cyanne's fire wreathed Ymri's head. The dragon roared again, this time in pain, and lashed out at the three figures racing toward it, weapons drawn. The fire vanished, and Revelin and Inaya struck as one, with Embrus close behind.

Owen grabbed Isold's arm. "You have to take her out," he said. "Circle around—"

"I understand," Isold said. "Aderyn, come with me."

Silently swearing a litany of curses over her destroyed sword, Aderyn followed Isold, casting only one backward glance at Owen as he led Weston in a charge at Ymri's head. With a sharp crack, the ground rippled, racing ahead of them in a wave of motion that struck not only the dragon, but the three members of Revelin's team flanking it. *Thunderstomp* made Revelin and Inaya stagger, but only Embrus fell. Ymri didn't do more than ride the wave of stone, but Aderyn guessed the humans had been Livia's actual target.

Cyanne aimed another blast of fire at Ymri, this time targeting its wings. She didn't react as if she knew Isold and Aderyn were closing in on her. Aderyn stopped Isold before he could approach the Flame-crafter. "I'll distract her. You won't get a second chance." When Isold nodded, Aderyn ran at full speed toward Cyanne, making as much noise as she could.

Her ploy worked. Cyanne turned to face her before Aderyn reached her and raised her burning hands as if to strike with her [Elemental Blast]. Aderyn didn't stop. If Cyanne attacked her with fire, there wasn't much she could do to defend against it. But Cyanne hesitated, giving Aderyn time to grab her and knock her to the ground, falling on top of her.

They tussled for a moment. To her surprise, Aderyn managed to pin Cyanne beneath her. Since she'd only intended to keep Cyanne's attention away from Isold, she hadn't planned for this outcome. She had no idea where Isold was or whether he would reach them before Cyanne wrestled free. "You didn't have to get us out of the way. We would have dealt honorably with you," she said, more as a distraction than because she cared.

"We need this quest," Cyanne said. She squirmed, but Aderyn had a better grip. "But we weren't going to kill you to get it. We're not monsters."

It suddenly occurred to Aderyn that Cyanne was flameproof, and there was nothing stopping her from setting herself and Aderyn on fire but her sense of honor. "If we'd worked together," she began.

Cyanne's jaw slackened, and her eyes went out of focus. From behind Aderyn's right shoulder, Isold said, "I used [Hypnotism], but I have to maintain eye contact and focus my concentration or she will break free. If you can think of a suggestion, I can use [Coercion] to keep her out of the fight indefinitely."

The crack of *thunderstomp* echoed through the vast room again, followed by the sound of Livia's voice chanting something incomprehensible. Aderyn didn't look to see what the effect was. The dragon roared in fury, and its heavy footsteps sounded a moment before muffled cries of pain told Aderyn Ymri had struck someone. It wasn't Owen or Weston, which was all she cared about.

She dragged her attention away from the fight and said, "You want something that won't put her in danger. Why not tell her to sit in the corridor?"

"I think I can improve on that. You will need to guide her." Isold helped Aderyn stand, then got Cyanne on her feet. Aderyn watched the battle, not listening to what Isold told Cyanne. Weston was fighting Inaya rather than Ymri and had driven her back from the melee, while Owen attacked the dragon from the front and Revelin and Embrus came at it from behind. At that moment, the dragon snapped its tail around, striking both men and knocking them to the stony ground. Owen took advantage of its distraction to drive the <Sunsword> deep into the joint of the nearest wing. Black blood flew in spurts, striking Owen's breastplate and face. Owen let out a pained cry and staggered back, swiping at his face as if the blood burned.

Aderyn screamed and took two steps toward him before Isold hauled her back. "Take her," Isold said, shoving a stunned Cyanne at her. Cyanne staggered, off balance briefly, before grabbing Aderyn's shoulder to steady herself. Once again cursing silently, Aderyn towed Cyanne after her, skirting the perimeter of the room until they reached the corridor. She shoved Cyanne through the doorway, then hesitated. Maybe she should have listened to Isold's command, in case she had to do something else with the stunned Flamecrafter.

Cyanne blinked. Aderyn froze. Cyanne didn't look as if she felt the effects of [Coercion]; her eyes were clear and focused. Then Cyanne said, "I'd better get started," and sat with her back against the wall. With her left hand, she pretended to pick up something small off the floor and deposit it into an invisible container held in her right. Aderyn stared in bewilderment. "One," Cyanne said, and repeated her motions. "Two. Three. Four—"

Aderyn shook herself out of the stupor her astonishment had created and hurried back to the chamber just as the dragon roared again, loudly enough to shake the walls. Aderyn kept from falling and examined the tactical situation. Owen still threatened Ymri's front end, darting out of the way of its jaws and returning blows that mostly glanced off the dragon's hide. But as Aderyn watched, Owen slashed across Ymri's face, scoring a line from its forehead across one eye. Ymri reared back and roared in pain, clapping one hand over its ruined eye so black blood trickled between its fingers. Owen didn't hesitate to take advantage of Ymri's distraction to thrust the <Sunsword> deep into the wound he'd made earlier at the joint of one wing.

With a shout, Revelin leaped over Ymri's tail to engage Owen directly. Owen deflected the first blow of Revelin's staff and struck back with a powerful swing aimed at Revelin's right arm. Aderyn bit back a cry of warning—Revelin was their opponent, but he wasn't evil—but it was the flat of the blade that connected, hard enough to make Revelin wince and step back.

"We shouldn't fight each other!" Aderyn said, using **[Amplify Voice]** to make her words reach every part of the chamber. Underneath that, she sent a **[Secret Message]** to Owen: "*Don't waste time fighting him, the dragon is fading fast.*"

Owen didn't react, instead pressing the attack against Revelin. He still used only the flat of the blade, but Revelin was driven slowly back. Then, with a move too fast for Aderyn to follow, Owen knocked the staff out of Revelin's hands. "Stay there," Owen said. He backed away several steps, then turned his back on Revelin and approached the dragon once more. Weston and Inaya had stopped fighting one another and were dodging Ymri's attacks, clearly looking for an opening to be the first to use **[To the Heart]**.

Aderyn saw Isold sneaking up on Revelin, and she hurried to put herself in Revelin's line of sight as a distraction. So she had a perfect view when Revelin left his staff on the ground and launched himself at Owen's back. With deft kicks and blows with the edges of his hands, he knocked Owen to the ground and vaulted onto Ymri's back. Owen didn't get up.

Aderyn sucked in a horrified breath and ran to his side. Owen was breathing raggedly, but was otherwise motionless. "Owen, get up," she said, shaking him violently. "You have to get up. The dragon—"

A hot wind stirred her hair. She turned and shrieked at the unexpected sight of Ymri's face barely a foot from her own. Ymri opened its mouth and blew out another painfully hot breath. Aderyn, unable to tear her gaze from the gaping maw, groped for Owen's arm and yanked on it, pulling him only a few inches.

Ymri paused. Aderyn guessed it was surprised at not having launched Elemental Volley at the puny humans who'd invaded its lair. Well, its breath attack might not work, but it had a mouthful of dagger-like teeth that would work all too well. Aderyn jerked on Owen's arm again, and this time Owen groaned and shifted his weight. "Get up, get up, get up," Aderyn chanted, still pulling.

Ymri's head jerked back, and it flinched from Aderyn. Why, she didn't know, because it wasn't as if she was a threat. Then she realized it had actually turned away because Revelin was perched on its back between its wings. Aderyn dropped Owen's arm and grabbed him around the shoulders, trying to lift him to any position that didn't leave him prone and vulnerable. Owen groaned again and pushed himself to his knees.

Revelin shouted a challenge and leaped out of the way just as Ymri slammed its head at him. His leap took him to the top of Ymri's head and then to its neck, where he swung himself to the base of the dragon's long, sharp-toothed muzzle. With another cry, he kicked the dragon between the eyes, not with his toes but with the heel of his boot. He spun around and kicked again, his momentum adding force to the blow.

Ymri swayed as if dizzy. Weston dove for the vulnerable spot at the base of its throat. Aderyn, supporting Owen, shouted a warning that boomed through the cavern, and Weston checked his movement as Inaya appeared from nowhere, blocking his path. Behind her, Embrus dodged the dragon's tail slap and readied a blow at Ymri's throat.

Aderyn found herself on her feet, running toward the combat with no idea what she would do—no weapon, not even the <**Laborer's Staff**>, which she'd dropped when Isold had handed Cyanne off to her, no mysterious Swifthands skills, and her Warmaster's vision told her nothing about how to keep Revelin's team from winning.

She was still ten feet away when Revelin dropped to one side of Ymri's head and punched it so hard it recoiled—right into the point of Embrus's blade.

The sword impaled the dragon through the throat, spurting acidic blood in every direction. Embrus let go of the weapon's hilt and flung himself backward with several stumbling steps. Ymri howled in anguish and slumped to the floor, hitting the stone with a thud that echoed off the walls. All around them, lights began blinking wildly in the instrument panels, as if the dragon's death excited them.

Aderyn sagged to her knees. Nearby, Weston lowered his sword as Inaya backed away from their fight. She watched Revelin walk wide around Ymri's motionless head and waited for him to stop and gloat. But he passed her without saying a word, instead going to Embrus's side and looking him over.

Footsteps warned her of someone's approach, and she looked up at Owen, who looked grim. "That's it," he said. "The end of the quest."

Aderyn checked her Codex, though she didn't want to see the message declaring the [**Fire and Ash**] quest was invalid. She blinked in astonishment. "It's not. The quest is still there."

Owen's eyes unfocused as he looked at his own Codex. "So it

wasn't the dragon," he murmured, almost to himself. "Then what is it?"

"It doesn't make any sense," Aderyn said. She read the [**Fire and Ash**] quest again. "A threat—maybe the waspnettles? Owen, suppose defeating them drove them out of the Lonely Tor and toward the settlements?"

"That would have invalidated the quest by causing a secondary threat." Owen shook his head. "Or increased the primary threat. It's not the waspnettles."

"But then—"

"I won't apologize," Revelin said, startling Aderyn out of her contemplation of the Codex. "Your needs aren't any greater than ours. You would have done the same."

"You can see we didn't," Owen said coldly. "Betrayal is a nasty word."

"It's not betrayal. We could have killed you while you were help-less—*that* is the act of an evil person." Revelin rotated his right wrist as if it pained him. "You can have the loot as compensation, if you want."

"I don't want anything from you," Owen said. "You got your experience. Get going."

"Don't be bitter, please," Inaya said, glancing swiftly at Revelin. "You know only one of us could kill the dragon. This was always going to happen, or something like it."

Inaya's voice reminded Aderyn of something. She stood and held out her hand. "Then you won't pretend you didn't steal the <**Wayfinder**>."

Inaya's face flushed red. She withdrew the metal orb from her belt pouch and handed it over. "Sorry. I wouldn't have kept it. I just needed it for long enough to fulfil our quest. If we both—"

"Don't bother. It turns out the dragon wasn't our quest require-ment," Aderyn said. "Not that that makes us trust you."

"Fair enough," Revelin said. "Like I said, you wouldn't believe me if I said I was sorry, but I hope you will believe it wasn't personal."

"What do you mean, it wasn't your quest requirement?" Embrus's face was pitted with acid burns, and his clothes looked tattered on the side the dragon's blood had sprayed him.

"None of your business," Owen said. "And now we're going."

Aderyn put a hand on his arm to stop him. He looked as bad as Embrus, with a spray of acid marks on his face and throat like black freckles. "Going where? There's a threat somewhere we don't know about—what are we supposed to do about that?"

Owen grimaced. "A threat from the Lonely Tor," he said. "The only other possible threat is if the volcano exploded, and we've prevented that."

"The waspnettles might overrun the settlements in their flight," Isold said. "But there's nothing we can do about that."

"And they ran long enough ago that if they *were* the threat, the quest would be invalidated already," Owen said again.

Livia joined them, stretching out her left arm as if it hurt. "But—"

"What?" Aderyn asked when she didn't continue immediately.

"Maybe nothing," Livia said. "But there are the kobolds."

"They're not a threat," Aderyn said. "They only fight to defend their home."

"That's true for now. What happens when they outgrow this warren? They might spread in the direction of the humans." Livia didn't look happy about this idea.

"That wouldn't happen." But Aderyn didn't feel nearly so confident as she sounded. Livia was right—there was no reason to believe the kobolds would always stay confined to the Lonely Tor.

"That's easy enough to deal with," Revelin said. "Fill the mountain with magma."

"No!" Aderyn shouted.

"Nobody asked you, Revelin," Owen said. "And that's not an option."

"I think it might be out of our hands," Weston called out. He alone hadn't joined the little group near the dead dragon's head, but was examining one of the instrument panels. He turned a dial and flipped a few switches, and the gray scrying window lit more brightly. Words scrolled across its surface:

Experiment 2703 catastrophic failure
Core collapse in 28 minutes 33 seconds

"Core collapse?" Owen said.

"The secondary defense system," Weston said. "The one that floods the compound with magma. We need to get out of here."

"What is Experiment 2703?" Inaya said.

Owen ignored her. He nudged Weston out of the way and stabbed at several buttons. The display changed.

Experiment 2703: Autonomous flying construct

"The dragon," Owen said. "How can the dragon be an experiment? Something's wrong." His fingers flew across the buttons. "Let's try... this."

Enchanterium defense no. 1: autonomous flying construct
See also: Dragon; Ymri; Experiment 2703

"Dulcia," Owen muttered, tapping more buttons.

Experiment 2703 detail: Upgrade to Elemental Volley in progress

Owen swore loudly and turned away from the panel. "Dulcia was messing with the dragon. That's why it's both the defense mecha-nism *and* an experiment."

"And we broke it," Aderyn said. "And when one of the experi-ments fails—"

"Magma will flood the compound in a little less than half an hour," Owen said. "The kobolds are doomed."

CHAPTER FORTY-TWO

"We can't let that happen," Aderyn said. "We have to do something."

"Do what?" Livia said. "I can't stop the magma core from overflowing. It's too big."

"Then we warn the kobolds. We can go back—that levitation pad works both ways, I bet—we'll go down—"

"That's suicide," Weston said. "And if the kobolds are the threat we're supposed to stop, we *shouldn't* try to save them. It would mean the end of the quest."

"Then it's the end of the quest," Aderyn said. "Because I couldn't live with myself if we succeeded at the cost of hundreds of intelligent lives. We can reason with Akdukhur—we can convince them to stay away from the human settlements—"

Weston grabbed Aderyn's shoulders and made her look at him. "Even if that's true, there's no *time*. We don't speak their language to be able to deliver a warning, let alone guide them to safety. And where would we take them? We couldn't ever save a few, let alone all of them. Aderyn, it's impossible."

"*No,*" Aderyn insisted. "They helped us. We can't abandon them."

As if in emphasis, the floor shuddered, and a great rumbling sound bigger than *thunderstomp* filled the air. Everyone flung out their arms for balance against the tremor. When it subsided, Owen said. "Maybe we don't have to."

He turned his attention back to the panel and stared at the buttons as if searching for inspiration. After a few seconds, he tapped out C-O-R-E-F-A-I-L-S-A-F-E.

"What's a failsafe?" Aderyn asked.

"It's a system that prevents something happening when the thing is triggered by accident," Owen said. "Those Spellcrafters had so many system redundancies, maybe they had this one."

White letters scrolled across the scrying window.

Enter authorization to cancel core collapse.

Owen let out a relieved breath. "Come on, Dulcia, don't let me down now," he muttered, and spelled out her name.

The invisible hand erased the white letters. Several seconds passed during which Aderyn stared at the scrying window, willing it to display good news. The longer the screen stayed blank, the harder her heart beat.

Finally, more words appeared.

Authorization accepted.
Enter secondary authorization.

Owen blew out his breath. "Quick, who remembers the other names?"

"Try 'Laralyn,'" Weston said.

Owen pressed more buttons. Again, the letters vanished.

Aderyn's eyes were dry from not blinking. Superstitiously, she feared the authorization would fail if she did.

"It's been nearly a minute," Livia said in a low voice.

Aderyn waved at her to shut up. Knowing how little time they had left wouldn't help.

A red light started blinking above the scrying window. More words scrolled into view.

> **_That user is not authorized to access core control._**
> **_Core collapse in 27 minutes and 1 second._**

Aderyn groaned. "No!"

"I'm not giving up yet," Owen said. He spelled out C-O-R-E-M-A-N-U-A-L-S-H-U-T-D-O-W-N.

> **_Manual shutdown of the core may be initiated from maintenance panels A-1-07 in level one command center, B-2-08 in level two command center, or C-3-09 in level three command center. Select HELP for further instructions._**

"That's it," Owen said. "The levitation pad will take us back to level three, and from there we just have to reach the central chamber. Let's go."

"Are you out of your minds?" Revelin said. "If you're too slow, the magma will kill you, too."

Owen rounded on him, getting right up into his face. "If you don't see why we have to try, then you really are the self-centered hypocrites you seem to be," he snarled. "You got what you wanted. Go tell the settlements how you're big damn heroes. But do it now and stop wasting our time." He turned to the others and said, "We have to run."

Aderyn scooped up the <**Laborer's Staff**> and caught a glimpse of Inaya's face. The Moonlighter's indecision was obvious. Aderyn thought about saying something, but the thought of magma filling the halls, of kobolds dying in agony, made her run after Owen without a word.

They reached the round room with the hole in the floor in what felt like it took forever. Weston immediately went to the lever on the wall and pulled it down. "Test it first," he said.

Aderyn found a coin in the <Purse of Great Capacity> and tossed it into the air. It flew in a graceful arc until it passed over the hole, where it changed direction and shot straight down, faster than anyone could throw.

"I guess we take our chances," Owen said. "I'll go first and let Aderyn know when I make it." Before Aderyn could protest, he leaped into the hole and vanished with a cry of excitement.

Aderyn wiped her sweaty palms on her trousers and waited, counting seconds—except she didn't know how long a second was for certain, so she was really just counting numbers and might be counting too fast or too slow. It was something to do that wasn't worrying about Owen crashing into the floor at the other end of the shaft.

When she reached "ten," the back of her neck prickled, and Owen's mental voice said ...*here... come...*

"Somebody go," she cried. "He's safe."

As first Weston, then Livia jumped into the shaft, Livia looking like she was going to her own funeral, Aderyn sent back, *"Are the kobolds there?"*

Owen's reply came almost immediately. ...*no... gone...*

That worried Aderyn. If the manual override didn't work, they'd need to gather the kobolds quickly and send them up to the top. But it was a big warren, and communication was difficult... no, she wasn't going to fret about possible complications until they became real.

Another tremor struck, not as strong as before, but lasting longer. Isold and Aderyn exchanged despairing glances. Then Isold disappeared down the shaft. Aderyn waited for Owen's confirmation that the pad was clear, then leaped into the air and let out an exhilarated shout as she dropped, cushioned only a little by a powerful force.

She stumbled coming off the pad when she alighted, and Owen took her hand to steady her. He was alone in the chamber. "I sent the others ahead," he said. "No point waiting, and Weston knows the way."

"I'm not sure I do," Aderyn said, pulling out the <**Wayfinder**>. "Let's hurry."

She took a few running steps before realization struck. "We can't use the third level chamber. It's covered with wax—clearing it will take too long."

"Damn. You're right." Owen stopped running and squeezed his eyes shut. His lips moved silently as if he was talking to himself. Then he opened his eyes and said, "It will take too long to fetch the others and then go to one of the shafts that leads to the second level. We have to do it ourselves."

"But they won't know where we've gone!"

"Weston will figure it out when he sees the blockage. They'll meet us there. Come on!"

They ran, staggering as more tremors shook the Enchanterium halls, with Aderyn's eyes on the <**Wayfinder**> and Owen's hand keeping her upright. Strange noises echoed through the steel walls, creaks and moans like metal under stress mixed with sharper, higher-pitched clamor. It wasn't until they rounded a corner and ran into several kobolds hurrying the other way that Aderyn recognized the clamor as kobold cries.

"Wait, stop!" she shouted. "Tell Akdukhur—"

But the kobolds rushed past and were gone.

"Don't worry about them," Owen said. "We have to reach the shutoff to save them. Stopping is a waste of precious time."

Aderyn nodded. She focused on their direction and started running again.

By the time they reached the shaft descending to the second level, the tremors were coming so regularly there almost weren't pauses between them. Aderyn stood at the top of the emergency stair in [Shaft No. 5] and contemplated how long a fall it would be. "We have to be careful or those tremors will knock us off."

"Crawl," Owen said, turning around and putting his advice into action.

Crawling was safer, but slow going, and more than once Aderyn had to stop and cling to a steel slab as a tremor went on too long. When they reached the bottom, she was shaking so hard she had to lean against the wall and wait to regain control of her limbs. Owen did the same. Finally, he extended a hand to her. "I remember the way. Hurry!"

Again, they ran, and now more and more kobolds thronged the halls, scurrying in every direction, too terrified to do more than glance at the two humans in their midst. After shoving their way through two crowds, Aderyn shouted, "Clear the way!" It didn't matter that kobolds didn't speak her language—[Amplify Voice] did the work for her. Kobolds disappeared through doorways and down side passages, leaving the main hall free.

[Central Control 2] looked exactly as they'd left it, with the fallen adventurers still where they'd been when they died. Owen hurried to the reference instrument panel and tapped a few buttons. "B-2-08," he muttered. "Come on, where is it?"

Lines appeared on the scrying window as if several hands wielding sticks of white chalk were all drawing parts of a single picture. After only a moment, it became clear the picture was an outline of the room and its many instrument panels. When the drawing was complete, more hands wrote tiny letters that to Aderyn looked like labels of the different components. "They're too small to read," she said.

"Just wait." Owen again tapped out B-2-08 and added H-E-L-P.

One of the labels turned red and began blinking. Owen's gaze shifted rapidly from the diagram to the panels, back and forth as he searched the room. "There," he said, racing to a panel directly opposite theirs. "It's right here." He ran his hands over the many switches and buttons and knobs until he settled on a large blue button and pressed it, hard.

Aderyn watched the scrying monitor for some sign the override had worked. Nothing changed on the display. The tiny label continued to blink red. "Owen," she began.

"That triggered something," Owen called out. "I think there are multiple steps. Which makes sense, since you wouldn't want to use this by accident." He raised up a T-shaped handle and turned it, then flipped up a series of toggles.

"Still nothing," Aderyn said.

Owen pressed another button. He hesitated, then jabbed it a few more times. "It's broken," he said. "There's no resistance. It won't work."

They stared at each other. "Can we get to the first level in time?" Aderyn asked.

Owen joined her and tapped out another sequence of letters.

Core collapse in 17 minutes 13 seconds.

"That's not much time," he said. "We have to run. No. *I* have to run. You need to see if you can get some of the kobolds out."

"I am not leaving you," Aderyn exclaimed.

Owen took her by the shoulders and kissed her. "This is our best chance, love. Go. I'll be fine. I know what to do—"

Aderyn threw her arms around his neck and kissed him hard, trying not to cry. "Go."

She watched him run down the corridor out of sight. Then she went in search of kobolds.

They weren't hard to find. After she'd scattered them with **[Amplify Voice]**, they'd regrouped a short distance away. The ones running in her direction recoiled from her, shifting nervously and edging against the walls in search of a way past her.

"Akdukhur?" she said. "I need to find Akdukhur. Take me to Akdukhur!"

The kobolds glanced at each other. One of the green ones said, "Akdukhur."

"Yes, please hurry!" Aderyn's hands trembled with nerves and fear. "Akdukhur!"

Another powerful tremor struck, and the kobolds clung to each other to stay upright. Aderyn grabbed the wall and pressed against it. This was a mistake. She should have gone with Owen. Shutting off the core collapse was the only thing that would save everyone, not trying to convince a monstrous species whose language she didn't speak that they needed to follow her.

The shaking subsided, and the green kobold stood erect, its thin tail lashing. "Akdukhur," it said again, and turned, beckoning her to follow.

The green kobold took Aderyn through corridors she was sure she'd never seen before, though it wasn't as if she remembered any of the places they *had* been. But these corridors definitely looked different: almost all the lights had been removed, and many of the steel panels making up the walls were missing. The edges of the round holes in the earth beneath glittered with shed kobold scales. Aderyn caught a glimpse of a kobold disappearing into one of the holes and had to make herself keep running after her guide, though her imagination supplied her with images of molten rock filling that hole, trapping the creature inside to suffocate, burn, and die. The thought firmed her resolve, and she sped up, hoping it wasn't already too late.

At the end of the hall, a metal door hung half open. Whatever lay beyond it was in darkness, but the green kobold didn't slow. It slipped through the crack and vanished. Aderyn didn't hesitate. She squeezed through the opening.

Something roared a challenge and leaped at her. She brought the

<Laborer's Staff> up in time to deflect a clawed hand aimed at tearing her throat out. "No, stop, I need to see Akdukhur!" she screamed.

Dim lights came on. Aderyn lowered the staff. Akdukhur stood in front of her, breathing heavily, his legs and arms planted wide in a defensive pose. The air was full of birdsong—no, that was wrong, the noises were high and shrill but too harsh to belong to a bird. Aderyn looked past Akdukhur at the far side of the room. Another kobold sat there, hunkered down in a pile of refuse. In the dimness, it gleamed, not bronze, but gold. Small gray creatures clambered over it, yipping shrilly. In the next moment, Aderyn realized they were tiny kobolds.

Aderyn took a step toward the golden kobold, and Akdukhur was suddenly in her face, growling. "Oh," Aderyn said. "*Oh*. Is that... is she... oh, Akdukhur, we have to get them out of here now." Without waiting for the <Write-All>, she drew a big cone outline on the exposed earth of the nearest wall, pointed at it, then threw up her arms and shouted, "Boom! This! The volcano will explode— boom!" There was no time to explain the difference between an eruption and magma overflow. She pointed at the cone again and repeated her gestures. Then she pointed at the door. "Go now. Go now!"

Akdukhur continued to face her, his expression unchanged. Then, without turning, he let out a long string of grunts and yips. The golden kobold lumbered to its—her—feet and tried to gather up her children. Akdukhur hurried to her side and picked up an armful of babies. The little kobolds' yips turned frightened, and one of them made a break for freedom. Without thinking, Aderyn dove and caught the baby kobold. It weighed almost nothing and wasn't much bigger than her two fists together. Breathless, Aderyn stared down at it as it started to cry.

Akdukhur barked an impatient cry. Aderyn moved to hand him the wayward child, but he shook his head. Then he detached another small kobold from his shoulder and without hesitation handed it to

Aderyn. He motioned with his head at the door. Aderyn took the hint and squeezed through the opening.

She retraced her steps as best she could, terrifyingly aware that time was running out. After a while, Akdukhur took the lead, with the golden kobold trailing him, both of them with their arms full of children as more kobolds joined their procession. Aderyn hoped Akdukhur knew the location of another of those levitation shafts, and that it could handle many people at a time.

But when the corridors again became familiar, Aderyn's heart sank. Akdukhur had led them to [Shaft No. 5]. Aderyn surveyed the steel steps of the emergency staircase with despair. Kobolds were already streaming up the stairs, but there was no way Aderyn could climb safely while carrying Akdukhur's children, not with tremors shaking the slabs. For a moment, she considered stowing all the baby kobolds in the <Purse of Great Capacity>, but that was a terrible idea. She didn't know if it contained enough air to sustain a living person, let alone ten of them.

"Akdukhur," she said, "I don't know what to do."

Akdukhur set one foot on the lowest step just as a powerful tremor struck the shaft. He flung out his arms for balance and then had to make a grab for one of the crying infants. His gaze fixed on Aderyn, and for a moment, they were just two people desperate to save a monstrous race.

"We have to get up there," Aderyn said. The back of her neck prickled, and Owen's voice said *...here... trying...* She shut him out. There wasn't anything either of them could do to help the other.

Akdukhur looked up. He hissed and drew back, sheltering the children he held as best he could. A shadow passed overhead, something falling to the ground. "Stand close together," Cyanne said. "I'll get you to the top."

Aderyn gaped. "Cyanne—"

"Weston says there's less than five minutes left," Cyanne interrupted, "so less talking and more flying, all right?"

She gestured and recited some long, flowing syllables, and Aderyn's feet left the floor as her weight seemed to fall away from her. She'd been levitated before, but this felt totally different, as if she was in control of her movement instead of being lifted. Instinctively, she willed herself to fly faster, and the ground shot away beneath her.

She reached the walkway and dropped to land lightly on it—and came face to face with Revelin. His bearded face was impassive. "Many of them are headed for that levitation shaft already," he said. "Cyanne will see about picking up the stragglers."

Aderyn shoved the two crying kobold babies at him. Startled, Revelin juggled them a little before securing his grip on them. "What am I supposed to—"

"Just take care of them," Aderyn said. "I have to get to Owen." She dove off the walkway and flew back the way they had come.

Chapter Forty-Three

Flying was so much faster than running. She sped over the heads of a few stragglers who stared at her in surprise, and then she'd left them behind and had the halls to herself. Surely that hadn't taken more than a few seconds, and she had at least four minutes to reach **[Shaft No. 1]** and then to fly to the central chamber. Plenty of time.

Her plan disintegrated almost immediately. The many turns of the corridors and their dimness meant she had to slow to keep from running headfirst into a steel wall. Chafing at this, she compromised by speeding up down the long, straight sections of hallway. She was so preoccupied with her flight it was a surprise when she flew through a doorway and discovered she had reached the shaft. She dropped straight down like a stone and sped on.

The shortest route was the one she and Owen had taken after meeting Revelin's team, through the library and the laboratories. She'd forgotten all the doors were shut between the shaft and her destination. Cursing, she hovered near the first door and pulled. It slid open, but so slowly she wished she could be immaterial to pass through all the barriers between herself and her goal.

The second library door moved more easily, but Aderyn felt the precious seconds slipping away from her. She ran rather than flew to the next door, which was only a few steps away. As if this one knew the urgency, it slid open at a touch, and from there it was only another handful of steps to the heavy steel door blocking the way to the central chamber. Aderyn grabbed hold and hauled it open, revealing the patchwork of lights interspersed with unlit panels and the rubble-strewn floor. The deep delver was gone, disintegrated the way all monsters did about an hour after being killed. Good thing it didn't respawn immediately.

Aderyn shot into the room, crying out Owen's name. "Over here," Owen said. He was standing in front of one of the instrument panels, staring at the scrying window. Aderyn rushed to his side, but he was so intent on what he was doing, she didn't want to distract him by hugging him in relief.

"Two minutes, seventeen seconds," Owen said. He pointed at a corner of the scrying window that displayed the numbers [2,17]. As he spoke, the number 16 replaced the 17. "I found the manual shut-down, but it's one of those panels that the deep delver destroyed in the fight."

"Then we need to leave," Aderyn said. This time, she did grab his arm as a tremor threatened to knock her off her feet. "Everyone's getting out—there's still time—"

"We won't make it," Owen said. "Maybe if Livia had come with us, we could teleport out of here, but there's just no time for anything else."

Aderyn felt numb. The fact that she and Owen were going to die in two minutes and eleven seconds didn't seem real. "What do we do?"

"I'm not giving up. What does your Warmaster's vision tell you?" Owen's blue eyes were fierce and focused on her.

Aderyn almost protested that it didn't work that way. Then she decided if Owen could still have hope, so could she. She surveyed the wreckage their fight had left the central control room. "Which one is A-1-07?"

Owen pointed, not at the panel they stood beside, but one a little way around the curve of the wall. A huge dent lay diagonally across its upper half, and sparks of what Aderyn assumed were magical energy occasionally sprang from the cracks radiating out from the dent. Aderyn flew across the broken, shifting ground and let [Spot Weakness] evaluate what she saw.

Blue light outlined the panel all along its edges and down the cracks. The light's brightness varied with the relative weaknesses of the panel, blindingly brilliant at the weakest points. Aderyn hesitantly touched one of these spots and jerked her hand back when magical energy surged there. She didn't feel pain, just cold. "We need to get the metal off," she told Owen.

Owen pried at the edges with the <Deadly Blade>. "It's not strong enough," he said, and activated the <Sunsword> instead. "I hope this works."

He inserted the blade of light into the crack Aderyn indicated. The <Sunsword> cut through the metal like a hot knife through butter, throwing off more sparks. Owen cut along the dent until he reached the edge of the panel, then followed that edge until, with a clang, half the metal sheet fell away, revealing the instrument panel's insides.

Fine silver wires in bundles traced an intricate pattern inside the wall, most of them ending in frayed edges where they'd pulled away from their switches or buttons when the panel fell. Some of the buttons remained, and one long row of toggles hung loose but still attached to the wall. "I don't know what I'm looking at," Aderyn said.

"Neither do I," Owen said. He ran back to the scrying window and tapped several buttons, spelling something Aderyn was too far away to see. A powerful tremor shook the room, knocking over loose metal sheets and making Owen cling to the panel to keep from falling. Aderyn shoved off the floor and floated lightly in front of the damaged instrument panel. The tremors were now so violent they made her teeth vibrate even when she wasn't in contact with the earth.

"Do you think," she began, and the next words froze in her mouth. The great hole through which the deep delver had emerged was glowing, a warm orangeish-red that pulsed like a beating heart. Aderyn realized she was sweating not from nerves, but because the room was warming up. "Owen!"

"I see it," Owen said, though he hadn't turned around. "Don't panic."

Fear gripped Aderyn finally, and she swallowed to moisten her dry mouth. "Tell me you have a solution."

"Almost."

"Are you lying to keep me calm?"

"Maybe. I don't know." Owen tapped a few more buttons, then ran, dodging debris, back to her side. "These two are why the manual override is broken," he said, pointing at a couple of bundles of hair-fine silver wires whose loose ends shivered with every tremor. "If I connect them, that restores the power to that button—" He pointed at a metal circle as big around as Aderyn's palm, painted a bright green. "And then it's just... press the button."

"So do it!" Aderyn shouted.

Owen's breathing was heavy, and he wiped sweat out of his eyes. "There's enough magical energy running through those wires that touching them could kill me."

"Oh," Aderyn said. "But you're not sure it will."

"No, I'm sure. I just didn't want to freak you out when it happened." Owen rubbed his hands together and reached for the wires.

"Owen! Stop!"

"It's all right, Aderyn. I have the <**Ring of the Cat**>." He smiled at her in a way that would have been reassuring if he hadn't looked so uncertain. "I just—I don't know how much it will hurt."

Aderyn threw her arms around him. "I'll be here. And I won't let you go."

"You have to. What if the energy overflows from me to you?" He gently detached her from him. "It's fine. I can endure it."

Aderyn blinked away tears. The memory of seeing him come back to life after having his throat slit didn't reassure her. But being pessimistic and soppy was the wrong thing to do. "You never flinch when it's a matter of saving others. It's one of the many things I love about you."

Owen nodded. "Thank you for the reminder. I love you, too." He blew out his breath, inhaled deeply, and gripped each wire bundle in one hand.

The ends of the bundles blazed with a yellow-white magical light like glowing water that spilled over Owen's hands. Owen grunted with effort and brought the two slowly together. To Aderyn, it looked like he was forcing two magnets together at the wrong ends. She floated higher as another tremor struck that made Owen stagger. By now the room was hot enough to make Aderyn gasp for breath. Instinctively, she reached for Owen as he bent double with the strain, but before she touched him, he made the two wires meet.

A blast of magical energy struck Owen in the face, and he screamed in agony so terrible Aderyn cried out with him. Owen's body sagged, and he landed in a loose-limbed heap, sprawled awkwardly over a chunk of stone in a pose no living human could have endured. Aderyn screamed again and dropped to her knees, but he wasn't breathing. Panic set in. She shook Owen, slapped him. He was clearly dead.

Dead. Right. The **<Ring of the Cat>**. She lifted off the ground to avoid being knocked over by a tremor that made the entire room shake and searched the panel for the green button. It took a moment for her numb brain to recognize it. Then she mashed it as hard as she could.

The room shook again, so hard it felt like the walls might collapse. Aderyn dropped to shield Owen's body from falling debris, but nothing struck them. The room stilled. The deep rumbling sound that had gone on so long it had almost faded into the background vanished, leaving only a ringing in Aderyn's ears. The reddish glow from the center of the room faded, though the control room was as hot as ever.

In the sudden silence, a tiny *ping* like breaking crystal sounded, and Aderyn backed up as a bright blue glow centered on Owen's left hand spread outward until it formed a dome over him. Seconds later, it vanished, and Owen groaned and rolled over. "I'm not doing that again. I actually felt my heart stop beating before I died."

Aderyn threw herself at him, wrapping her arms around his waist and burying her face against the side of his neck. Owen's arms encircled her, and he drew her close. "Sorry," he said. "I don't know what I would have done if I hadn't known I could come back from that."

"You're a hero," Aderyn said. "That doesn't change just because you knew you didn't actually have to give up your life."

"I don't care about being a hero. I'm just glad we survived. And saved the kobolds." Owen kissed her. "Even if we didn't complete the **[Fire and Ash]** quest. I was sure stopping the magma eruption would do it."

"There's still a threat from the Lonely Tor that puts the settlements at risk," Aderyn said. "And I think I know what it is. Come on. Let's find the others."

Owen got heavily to his feet. "Are you *flying?*"

"Just a little. Revelin's team came back to help. I guess they weren't as self-centered as I thought."

"Or that guilt trip I laid on them worked." Owen drew in a breath and coughed deeply. "This air is hot enough to fry my lungs. I wonder how long it will take to cool off?"

"I'd just as soon not find out," Aderyn said.

THOUGH THEY DIDN'T DAWDLE on the return journey, they didn't rush, either. The limp weakness that always followed mortal peril made Aderyn's bones ache. For the first time since entering the Lonely Tor, she looked forward to a long sleep somewhere safe and quiet. But the adventure wasn't over yet. She hoped she'd guessed right about the quest. It wasn't even a guess so much as a suspicion that made logical sense. Well, if she was wrong, her team would figure out the truth. They always did.

They were halfway up [Shaft No. 1], Owen climbing and Aderyn keeping pace with him by flying, when they heard shouts from above. Three heads poked over the platform. "You're alive," Weston said. "Thunderation, but we were worried."

"You ought to be careful, Aderyn," Livia said. "Cyanne said the *fly* spell doesn't last more than half an hour at her level."

The thought of falling from this height chilled Aderyn like being drenched in icy water. She swiftly flew to the step above Owen and drifted above it. "Thanks for the warning."

"I still say flying is madness, but it looks like it helped." Livia stood, moving out of sight momentarily until she came into view again at the top of the stairs. "Everyone else is in the dragon's lair, or near it. There aren't as many kobolds as I thought, but there are still a lot."

Aderyn's stomach lurched, and she dropped a few inches onto the last steel slab. She flung out her arms for balance and then stepped cautiously away from the stairs. "I guess it's obvious we stopped the magma core collapse. Saying it feels so anticlimactic."

"We realized the third level control chamber was unusable right as we reached its doorway," Isold said. "We took a chance that you two would have gone for the second level, and we intended to join you there, but we ran into the kobolds and Revelin's team, and Revelin said *you*, Aderyn, had said something about finding Owen. Meaning you weren't in the second level chamber either."

"I had a feeling if we tried to find you, we would be too late," Weston said, "and we decided not to go running all over the Enchanterium searching. Instead, we helped get everyone to the top—"

"Hoping all the time that it was high enough," Livia muttered.

"And when the tremors stopped, we came back," Weston continued, ignoring Livia's grumbling. "Was it as simple as the instructions said, or did you race against time running out?"

"Some of both," Owen said.

Aderyn grabbed his left hand and showed them the two empty sockets where gems had once adorned the <**Ring of the Cat**>. Only one stone, an emerald, remained. "Owen gave his life to save everyone."

"Aderyn, you make it sound so dramatic," Owen said, turning red.

"And *you* make it sound like nothing," Aderyn snapped. "Let's meet in the middle and agree that it was a selfless act even if you came back from death."

"And don't mention it to anyone else," Owen said. "Never mind that I feel awkward, I don't want anyone knowing I have this advantage and killing me to prove it works."

"That's a good point." Weston glanced over his shoulder as if watching for eavesdroppers. "We should head back. We still have to figure out what the solution to the quest is."

"Aderyn says she knows." Owen slung his arm around Aderyn's shoulders and hugged her. "You ready to tell us the secret, or are you waiting for the dramatic moment?"

"It's not really a secret, just an informed guess," Aderyn said. "And this moment is as good as any, because it's going to take some work."

CHAPTER FORTY-FOUR

The halls of the topmost level showed no sign of the cataclysm that had nearly destroyed the Enchanterium. When they reached the great cave, the dragon's body was still crumpled in death the way they'd left it. No kobolds remained, but Revelin, Inaya, Embrus, and Cyanne stood grouped together near the wide opening, looking out. They didn't approach the team. Owen strode toward them, his hand loosely gripping the hilt of the **<Sunsword>**.

"You survived," Revelin said. He still didn't look as if he felt guilty about anything.

"I understand you stayed to help," Owen said. "Changed your mind about what honor means?"

"I deserve that." Revelin extended a hand to Owen. "I should have been more open with you about finding a solution to our dilemma."

Owen gripped Revelin's hand firmly. "I choose to move forward. And, since our quest wasn't about killing the dragon, it all worked out in the end."

"So, what *is* your quest?" Inaya asked.

Owen glanced at Aderyn. Aderyn said, "We need to find the kobolds a way to expand without interfering with the human settlements."

"How can you be sure that's it?" Cyanne sounded genuinely confused.

"It was simple when I thought about it," Aderyn said. "The quest has two victory conditions that both have to be met: protect the settlements from a threat from this mountain, and do it without creating a different threat. There are only two possible direct threats the Lonely Tor presents to the surrounding settlements. One is the dragon. The other is the kobolds. You killed the dragon without invalidating our quest, so it wasn't that. If the dragon wasn't the threat, the kobolds were, and *their* threat was the possibility of them spreading so far they'd come into contact with the human settlements."

"Which we discussed," Revelin said.

"Right. But that was misleading. See, the Spellcrafters who designed and built the Enchanterium set it up so it was easy to destroy any internal threat without making the mountain explode. That made the solution obvious—cause the core to collapse, fill the mountain with lava, destroy anything inside. Just like drowning rabbits in a warren."

"Which we would never do," Livia said. "We're not monsters."

"Anyway," Aderyn said, shooting Livia a quelling look, "we would have taken that route, and it would have fulfilled the quest. But then I met Akdukhur, and discovered the kobolds are anomaly monsters, not abominations, and that meant the obvious solution was the wrong one."

"You couldn't know that for sure," Revelin said. "They're still monsters, and the system cares more about human life than monsters."

"Then why did the system put us in the path of the kobolds, and show me they weren't hostile?" Aderyn shot back. "I don't think it's a good idea to assume we know what the system wants, especially since—" She stopped herself before revealing how personal the system's messages to her had become. "The point is, we chose to save the kobolds, and the Fated One quest isn't invalid, which proves we made the right decision. So now we just have to communicate to the kobolds that they should stay away from human settlements, and that completes the quest."

"That still sounds unlikely," Embrus said. "You could barely express the concept of the volcano blowing up and killing all of them, as I understand it, so how do you expect to explain something far more complicated?"

"I admit I don't have everything solved," Aderyn said, "but I know enough to make a start. So we're going to find Akdukhur. But we wanted to thank you first. For staying around."

"We could hardly do otherwise." Revelin shot a quick glance at Owen, who looked impassive to everyone but Aderyn. To her, the set of his shoulders and the tilt of his head revealed his smug satisfaction at putting one over on the dour Swifthands.

"Well, we're grateful anyway." Aderyn shook Revelin's hand. "Where will you go next? Obsidian?"

"We got experience for killing the dragon and for completing the Lonely Tor quest," Inaya said. "We're going to travel overland to Obsidian and see if we can't gain one more level before reaching it. And then... I think we're all ready to retire. There's not much we could do to top this quest."

"Understandable," Owen said. "Good luck to you. Um, how are you getting out of here? The door we came in by below is locked from the other side."

"There's a lift that goes to the bottom from here," Embrus said with a grin. "Looks like those Spellcrafters didn't like the idea of walking all the way to the bottom."

ADERYN STOOD at the top of the lift passage and watched the lift descend out of sight. "I'm not sure if I like Revelin or not," she said to Owen standing beside her, "but he did the right thing in the end."

"That doesn't earn him as much credit as you think," Owen said. "Let's finish this."

The rumblings seemed to have damaged some of the lights, because the corridors were dimmer than Aderyn remembered. Livia created several *orbs of light* and drew them along with their little group. The light cast funny shadows, but Aderyn felt no uneasiness about the smallness of the space and the weight of the mountain pressing down on her. She'd faced real danger, potentially lethal danger, and that made her irrational fears unimportant.

This time, they knew they'd entered kobold territory because brown and blue and green kobolds showed themselves immediately, peering out from within rooms or dropping out of holes in the ceiling and scampering away. A few of them, bronze bushwhackers, stayed in sight, pacing the companions ahead and behind like an · honor guard. None of the kobolds spoke, not even the high-pitched chittering noises that Aderyn thought might be more for orientation in the tunnels than speech.

After a while, Aderyn realized the kobolds were leading them into halls she'd never seen before, and the wall lights were dimming. Livia's lights looked brighter by comparison. Owen said, "Maybe we're wrong about how much space they take up, if their territory goes this far."

"I'm sure their expansion is the threat," Aderyn said, "but it might happen decades or even centuries from now. The system has a longer perspective than we do. If it wants us to control their spread now, there must be a reason for it. Like the quest is about us, not about them."

"You say that like it's a person," Weston said.

"I—" Aderyn still didn't know what it meant that the system had begun addressing her so informally and personally, but it wasn't something she wanted to discuss. "I don't know."

At that moment, the kobold bushwhackers in the lead scampered ahead, through a doorway into a space dark enough to look endless. Owen and Aderyn exchanged glances. Then they walked through the doorway.

For a few seconds, the room remained dark, with only the indirect light from Livia's orbs shining in from outside. Then Livia sent the lights flying forward, and at the same time, lights blossomed along the walls, pale blue like the lights making patterns on the walls of the levitation shafts. The combined radiance revealed an enormous octagonal room filled with makeshift benches in tiers that rose halfway to the ceiling. Kobolds crowded the benches, their colors muted in the overall dimness. Every one of them had its fathomless black eyes fixed on the companions.

Directly opposite the door, in a round depression lined with furs, sat the golden kobold. Her children lay curled close beside her or in her lap, their small sides heaving as they slept soundly. Akdukhur stood beside the golden kobold, leaning on a staff—no, a sword sheathed in black leather with a black-wrapped hilt and tarnished quillons and pommel. None of the kobolds moved. In the face of the massed tribe, Aderyn's words deserted her temporarily.

She glanced at Owen, who raised his eyebrows and jerked his head toward Akdukhur. Aderyn nodded. She stepped forward and said, "The kobolds are safe from the volcano now. Boom! No." She gestured as she said "boom" to suggest a huge explosion, then shook her head dramatically.

Akdukhur regarded her closely. Then he repeated her gestures and pointed at the kobolds surrounding them. "Ankoo," he said.

"Yes. But that's not the end." Aderyn pretended to write on the floor, which was a patchwork of steel slabs and bare concrete where some slabs had been removed, before extending a hand to Akdukhur.

Akdukhur handed her the <**Write-All**> as quickly as if he'd expected her request.

Aderyn drew a picture of the Lonely Tor and again drew lines across it to show the bottom three levels. She drew little kobold figures on the second and third levels. Then she drew human figures, not much more than stick pictures, well to one side of the mountain. "Not us," she said, gesturing at herself and then at the picture. "Other humans." She drew more humans until she reached the edge of the concrete square.

Akdukhur walked slowly to her side. "Ehdern," he said, pointing at Aderyn. He pointed at the humans in the picture and shook his head. "Ka Ehdern."

Aderyn watched him, puzzled. Akdukhur scowled and pointed at himself. "Akdukhur." He pointed at the golden kobold. "Trimka. Ka Akdukhur. Trimka."

"Not Akdukhur," Aderyn said. "I understand." She circled the humans in the picture and said, "Humans. Ka Aderyn."

"Hoomn," Akdukhur said.

Giddy excitement at being able to communicate better threatened to carry Aderyn away. She controlled herself and said, "Kobolds can't attack humans." With the tip of the <**Write-All**>, she pointed at Akdukhur and then at the gathered kobolds, then pointed at the stick figures. Akdukhur didn't react. Aderyn thought for a moment, then drew many kobolds between the stick figures and the mountain. Then she mimed swinging a sword at Akdukhur and pointed at the picture, shaking her head.

Akdukhur snapped his fingers at her and gestured. Aderyn handed him the <**Write-All**>, and he erased the kobolds attacking the humans, shaking his head and saying, "Ka, ka." With a few swift strokes, he drew more kobolds inside the volcano and pointed at them with his free hand, gabbling something in his own language. Aderyn nodded.

"Are you sure he understands?" Weston said. "It's one thing for them not to deliberately attack, and another if they breed so much they run up against the humans accidentally."

"I know." Aderyn pointed at the baby kobolds, but Akdukhur took on the expression he wore when he didn't understand and was waiting for Aderyn to figure out an explanation. Daringly, Aderyn stepped closer to the golden kobold, Trimka, causing a wave of muffled gasps to surge through the watching kobolds. Aderyn pointed at one of the babies without touching it, just coming close enough to make it clear what she meant. Then she indicated a creature the size of an adult kobold and pointed again. "They will grow up," she said, though of course her words meant nothing to the kobolds. "Where will they go?"

Akdukhur glanced at the small gray kobolds, then knelt to draw again. Aderyn watched him sketch more kobolds inside the Lonely Tor, then continue drawing so kobolds filled the space on the other side of the mountain from the humans. He sat back on his haunches and let out a few inquisitive yips.

"Yes," Aderyn said, nodding vigorously. "That's acceptable. Now for the other thing."

She took the <**Write-All**> and moved to another section of floor. Again, she drew the cone of the Lonely Mountain, and beside it she drew exaggerated human figures armed with swords. "Ka Aderyn," she said, pointing at the figures. Then she drew an arrow from the figures into the mountain and drew a kobold there. "Danger," she said. She erased the kobold and drew another one lying down with a sword impaling it, and finished by indicating as best she could the concept of other adventurers entering the Enchanterium and killing what they thought were evil monsters.

Akdukhur let out an angry hiss. Then he stared at Aderyn as if to ask "what do you suggest I do about this?"

"All right," Aderyn said. She drew holes at the base of the mountain and near its top. Then she pointed at Akdukhur and, one by one, erased all the holes until only the one at the top was left. "You will have to seal the mountain," she said.

Akdukhur pointed at the mountain's top. He mimed traveling very fast from the base of the mountain up to the hole Aderyn had drawn and said something that sounded like a question. "We will destroy that one," Aderyn said, pointing to herself and her friends and then erasing that hole.

Nodding, Akdukhur stood and laid the sword on the floor. He spread his arms wide and roared loudly enough that two of the baby kobolds stirred and let out little cries of dismay. Trimka gathered them into her arms, shushing them. She glared at Akdukhur, who ducked his head as if embarrassed.

Aderyn had gotten the point, though. "What about the dragon —yes, that would draw adventurers." She spread her own arms, then crumpled to the ground and pretended to be dead. "No more," she said. "Ka dragon."

She and her friends had discussed this before seeking out the kobolds. "The system regenerates most monsters," Isold had said, "so more than one adventurer or team of adventurers can gain experience by fighting them. But Ymri was made by Spellcrafters, not the system, and even though the system took advantage of Ymri's existence to make it part of a quest, it's unlikely the system had enough control over the dragon to make it a true monster. So I believe the Lonely Tor quest, or Enchanterium quest, is no longer available to anyone."

With that in mind, Aderyn felt confident in her assertion. "Ka dragon," she repeated. "No more adventurers."

Akdukhur nodded as if satisfied. He accepted the <**Write-All**> and put it away in a pouch he wore at his waist. Then he picked up the sword and extended it to Aderyn. "Ehdern," he said. "Taktuk. Ankoo."

"What—" Reflexively, Aderyn took the sword. "For me? What is 'taktuk'?"

Akdukhur tapped the sword. "Taktuk. Ehdern ka taktuk."

She hadn't realized he was aware she'd lost her sword. She drew the short sword a few inches, expecting to see a blade as tarnished as the pommel. Instead, the sword shone bright like silver, its surface unpitted and its edge honed perfectly. A warm thrill of pleasure suffused her at the sight. "Thank you," she said. "This is a magnificent gift." She bowed to Akdukhur. Akdukhur bowed back.

The others bowed as well. Owen took Aderyn by the elbow and steered her back the way they'd come. "You can admire your new toy later," he said. "For now, I think they'd rather we didn't intrude on them more than we already have. Akdukhur might not be afraid of us, but all the other kobolds were nervous. Except the golden one. Her, I could see tearing us apart if we threatened her children."

"You're right." Aderyn's chest still ached from tension. Success had not at all been a given. "That almost seemed too easy."

"Those kobold bushwhackers were as nervous as anyone, and they were armed," Weston said. "If that was easy, it was only by comparison to everything else we've done these past few days."

"And it's not over," Livia said. "Not for me, at any rate. I'm guessing sealing this place will take all my resources, so we'd better get started."

CHAPTER FORTY-FIVE

She was right. Aderyn had promised the kobolds they would be protected, but only an Earthbreaker could make good on that promise. The others watched Livia fill the top half of the levitation shaft like plugging a bottle, then they brought steel sheets from all over the upper level to conceal that anything odd had ever been there. They located the stairs Revelin's team had used to get to the top, and Livia collapsed the earth on those as well, in case some flying adventurer found their way to the dragon's lair. Owen suggested not destroying that.

"If adventurers come here and find nothing obvious, they'll search harder and maybe find a way in we haven't covered," he said. "Leave the dragon and its lair so it gives them something to discover."

Livia was nearly exhausted when that was finished. She leaned heavily on Weston as the team climbed into the lift and descended to the base of the mountain. The ride wasn't as spectacular as the levitation shaft, because the lift tunnel was narrow and closed in on Aderyn enough that she had to close her eyes and hold tight to Owen's hand. But in only a few minutes, the ride was over, and Aderyn gratefully climbed out.

She'd lost track of time there under the mountain, and the sun rising in the east surprised her because she'd expected it to be night-time. Facing the rising sun, she breathed in chilly air and stretched her arms as wide as they would go. "I'm glad it's over."

"Not quite," Livia said. She took a solid stance and clasped her flesh-and-blood hand over her stone fist. Her voice sounded tired at first, but as she spoke the words of her *move earth* spell, it grew firmer and louder until she was shouting over the sound of the volcano shifting and filling in the tunnel. When she stopped, and the stones stopped rattling down the mountainside, there was no sign that any entrance had ever been there.

Congratulations! You have completed the quest [Fated One's Destiny: Fire and Ash].
You have been awarded [50,000 XP]

Welcome to Level Sixteen

Livia sagged. Weston caught her and lifted her into his arms, but she said, "I didn't push beyond my limits, I'm just really close to unconsciousness. I need food and I need sleep. I don't care if it's sunrise. I was convinced we were close to midnight down there."

"So was I," Weston said. "It's going to take time to adjust to a schedule governed by the sun and moon."

"Let's set up camp," Owen suggested. "We have some decisions to make."

Aderyn volunteered to activate the <**Soldier's Friend**> and help Isold with meal preparation. Impatience sped up all her actions—impatience to look at her own advancement, impatience to see where the **[Fated One's Destiny]** would lead next, impatience to know if the sword Akdukhur had given her was special. Though, receiving a sword from an intelligent non-human race as thanks for saving them made the weapon special on its own. She still hoped it was magical.

Finally, everyone had a mug of hot tea and food from the <**Forager's Belt**>, and Aderyn settled beside Owen and let the tension bleed out of her. In between bites of beef jerky, she whispered, "Advancement."

Name: Aderyn

∞ **Jacob Owen Lindberg**

Level: 16

Class: Warmaster

<u>Skills</u>**: Bluff (15), Climb (13), Conversation (14), Intimidate (11), Sense Truth (16), Survival (9), Swim (1), Knowledge: Monsters (15), Knowledge: World Lore (8), Knowledge: Demons (1), Unite**

<u>Class Skills:</u> **Improved Assess 3 (27), Awareness (19), Knowledge: Geography (13), Spot (16), Discern Weakness (26), Dodge (16), Improvised Distraction (16), Outflank (20), Draw Fire (12), Keep Pace (19), Amplify Voice (16), See It Coming (21), Basic Weapon Proficiency (Swords) (14), Read Body Language (13), Basic Map Access (6), Compel (9), Spot Weakness (6), Secret Message (4), Bonded Mind (4), Sense Ambush (1), Reposition (0)**

She read over her class skills a second time, focusing on her skill ranks. She was sure no one in the world had twenty-seven ranks in [**Improved Assess 3**], if only because no other Warmasters had reached level sixteen. The thought excited and saddened her at the same time. She hoped her time in Finion's Gate, demonstrating through action what a Warmaster could do under the right circumstances, meant other Warmasters would find partners and help prove the common wisdom wrong, but it was hard not to remember just how bad the prejudice against her class was.

To keep from feeling despondent, she Assessed her new skill.

Reposition: Move an enemy combatant a short distance from its current position, either to stop it threatening an ally

or to put it within reach of another ally. Additional ranks increase the distance an enemy may be repositioned.

That seemed related to **[Compel]**, though Aderyn didn't see how it was an improvement on that skill. **[Reposition]** sounded like she would have to get right up close to an enemy to use it. Well, if it wasn't as exhausting as **[Compel]**, which still tired her as much at nine skill ranks as it had at one, it could be a useful tactical tool.

"**[Anatomist]**," Owen murmured. "What is that, Aderyn?"

Aderyn Assessed him and focused on his newest skill. "It gives you a variation on **[To the Heart]**. That skill shows Weston where to strike for a kill shot, but **[Anatomist]** draws your attention to any weakness in an enemy you've already done damage to. Like guiding you to improve your effectiveness."

"That and **[Weapon Mastery]** ought to make me nearly unstoppable," Owen murmured. "Will you Assess **[Weapon Mastery]** and tell me if it does anything more than give me information about the longsword I wield?"

"I don't have to. My father talked about it often." Aderyn settled herself more comfortably against Owen's shoulder and touched the hilt of the inactive <**Sunsword**>. "**[Weapon Mastery]** means you gain advantages based on the weapon type you've used most. When you're wielding a longsword, for example, you can't be disarmed, and your attacks are more powerful and do more damage. They also sometimes do elemental damage, like fire or ice or lightning—the type is based on your fighting style."

"Wow." Owen lifted the hilt and turned it over in his hands, examining it. "I wonder what my fighting style is. I never thought about it before."

"You're a methodical fighter who never lets his emotions control him," Aderyn said. "You look like you're following your instincts, but not in a wild or erratic way. I would guess ice, based on that."

"Too bad there aren't any monsters around for me to test that theory." Owen set down the hilt and added, "And I can't be bonded to your sword, because it's not a longsword. What an amazing gift, Aderyn."

"Yes, and I feel guilty that what I really want is to know if it's magical. The fact of the gift should be enough."

"It's magic," Livia said. "Isold?"

"Yes, is it a long-lost artifact of monster beheading?" Weston asked with a grin.

Isold smiled back. "I'm afraid not. It has enhancements to the damage it deals and to its accuracy in combat, but nothing extraordinary. However, there is something odd about it."

"You said if an item is too powerful for your skill, you can't identify it, but it niggles at you," Aderyn said.

"This isn't the same feeling," Isold said. "That is, I do feel as if there is knowledge about the sword just out of my mental reach, but it's not knowledge about magic. It's knowledge about history."

"So it *is* a long-lost artifact," Weston said.

"Possibly. My guess is that it either belonged to someone famous, or played an important role in a well-known historical incident." Isold gazed at the sword as if willing the knowledge to come to him. "We may need someone to cast *heritage* on it before the mystery is resolved."

"And, speaking of mysteries," Owen said, "it's past time we discovered what the next part of the quest is."

Everyone fell silent as they examined the quests in the Codex. Aderyn focused on the glowing gold dot so it enlarged to fill her vision with silver lettering.

A new quest is available: [Fated One's Destiny: Crush the Horde]
An army of monstrous orcs has emerged from the Blighted Range, intent on conquering the southern human lands.
Destroy their leaders and push the army back into the mountains.

Reward: [75,000 XP] plus any XP gained through actions taken to complete the quest.
Accept? Y / N

Aderyn's breath hissed out of her in surprise. "That's a lot more specific than the others. I mean, even the instructions about the Sarnok said 'defeat' instead of 'kill.'"

"It makes sense," Isold said. "Since the beginning, we've had options for how to fulfil the quests that determine what future quests are available. We defeated the Sarnok through cleverness instead of killing it. We could have killed the kobolds, but we chose... compassion, I suppose you could call it. If the system is testing the Fated One's responses, perhaps, having demonstrated cunning and compassion, we are now expected to show strength."

"Strength, fine, but we're talking about an army," Weston said. "How are the five of us supposed to defeat an army?"

"Strength isn't just about beating on something until it surrenders," Owen said. "Wars are won through strength in numbers, intelligent use of resources, and wisdom in tactical deployment. You want to bet we'll have to either build an army or convince someone to give us theirs?"

"Owen, I don't know about this," Aderyn said. "My tactical understanding is for small groups—what if it doesn't apply to armies?"

"I don't see why it wouldn't," Owen replied. "You can already Assess large groups, you understand how to position people for an ambush or a defensive maneuver, and you have a sense for what the enemy intends to do. I bet once you are in a position to Assess a battlefield, you'll see the truth of that."

Aderyn wasn't nearly so sure, but she said, "It doesn't really matter, does it? Since we have to complete all the quests. We'll go south, and I'll have time to practice those skills before it's an issue."

"Actually," Livia said, "we can be there by tomorrow."

The others stared at her. Livia shrugged. She already looked better than she had after closing off the Lonely Tor. "I took *world door* as my eighth-level spell. Combine that with *scry*, and I can get us anywhere in the world. Within reason. I'm still limited by my magical resources, and *world door* is hard at level sixteen. But if I rest all day today, I'll have just enough energy to get us all south. It would help if I had a target—is there a large city in the southern part of the continent, Isold?"

"The largest city in the south is Ikharatia," Isold said after a moment in which his eyes lost focus. "It is about the size of Finion's Gate. However, it is as far from the Blighted Range as one can get and still be in the southlands. If the orc army has just left the high risk area—"

"Which makes me wonder how much time we actually have," Owen said. "I find it hard to believe that an orc army has been massing on the border, waiting for the system to signal it to advance. Maybe they're still gathering."

"Regardless, we should not waste time," Isold said, "which is why I think we should consider trying to locate something closer to the mountains."

"We need an army of our own," Aderyn said. "That means finding a city with a standing army—oh, crap, I can't believe I just said that. How in thunder are we supposed to convince some foreign city to give us control of their military forces?"

"That's something to decide when we have a better idea of what we face," Owen said. "Don't freak out, okay? We don't have to go from town to town handing out the king's shilling to recruits. We will figure this out."

Aderyn nodded. Again, she didn't feel all that confident, but Owen was right that there was no point panicking over the unknown.

Owen clasped her hand reassuringly. "Then are we agreed? Rest for the day, and head south in the morning?"

"It's an exciting new adventure!" Weston said, grinning.

Livia punched him lightly on the arm. "You know armies are famous for having dysentery outbreaks, right? You planning to be excited about that?"

"I choose to anticipate a future in which the runs do not feature prominently, yes," Weston said. "Besides, I've always wondered what the southlands look like. With the high risk area of the Blighted Range cutting them off from the north, you almost never see southerners in the safe zone or the northern cities."

"That *is* exciting," Aderyn said, perking up. "And think of all the stories we'll have to tell our children someday."

"That is the kind of enthusiasm we need," Owen said. He raised his half-empty mug. "Here's to another quest!"

Aderyn saluted her friends and drank deep. True, this adventure sounded like they would lean heavily on her Warmaster skills, and that made her nervous, but in the end, they all depended on each other. And a trip to the mysterious south!

"To another quest," she exclaimed. "And to one step closer to our goal."

Appendix: Character Sheets

Name: Aderyn
∞ Jacob Owen Lindberg
Level: 16
Class: Warmaster
<u>Skills</u>: Bluff (15), Climb (13), Conversation (14), Intimidate (11), Sense Truth (16), Survival (9), Swim (1), Knowledge: Monsters (15), Knowledge: World Lore (8), Knowledge: Demons (1), Unite

<u>Class Skills</u>: Improved Assess 3 (27), Awareness (19), Knowledge: Geography (13), Spot (16), *Discern Weakness* (26), Dodge (16), Improvised Distraction (16), *Outflank* (20), Draw Fire (12), *Keep Pace* (19), Amplify Voice (16), See It Coming (21), Basic Weapon Proficiency (Swords) (14), *Read Body Language* (13), Basic Map Access (6), Compel (9), Spot Weakness (6), Secret Message (4), *Bonded Mind* (4), Sense Ambush (1), Reposition (0)

*italics are paired skills with partner

Name: Jacob Owen Lindberg
∞ **Aderyn**
Class: Swordsworn
Level: 16
Skills: Assess (12), Awareness (15), Climb (12), Conversation (14), Sense Truth (13), Spot (12), Survival (6), Swim (10), Knowledge: Demons (1), Unite

Class Skills: Superior Weapon Proficiency (27), Advanced Armor Proficiency (20), Knowledge: Monsters (13), *Exploit Weakness* (26), Dodge (16), Parry (17), Improved Bluff (15), *Outflank* (20), Trip (6), *Keep Pace* (19), Disarm (7), Intimidate (13), Charge (7), Two-Weapon Fighting (9), *Read Body Language* (13), Basic Map Access (6), Overrun (7), Demoralize (7), Sunder (2), Shatter Confidence (2), *Bonded Mind* (4), Weapon Mastery (longsword), Anatomist (0)
*italics are paired skills with Warmaster

Name: Weston
Class: Moonlighter
Level: 16
Skills: Assess (14), Climb (15), Conversation (13), Intimidate (11), Survival (5), Swim (3), Knowledge: Social (13), Knowledge: Demons (1)

Class Skills: Pick Locks (17), Advanced Sneak Attack (15), Superior Weapons Proficiency (13), Advanced Armor Proficiency (13), Improved Detect Traps (17), Disable Traps (14), Improved Spot (19), Awareness (16), Dodge (15), Stealth (18), Improved Bluff (14), Dirty Fighting (11), To the Heart (15), Hide (10), Improved Thrown Weapons Proficiency (11), Disguise (2), Hide in Plain Sight (6), Evasion (8), Basic Map Access (6), Escape Artist (4), Unarmed Combat (2), Improvised Weapon (2), Glibness (1), Improved Sense Truth (14)

Name: Isold

  Class: Herald

  Level: 16

  <u>Skills</u>: Assess (11), Awareness (15), Bluff (11), Climb (7), Conversation (8), Intimidate (5), Sense Truth (17), Spot (15), Survival (5), Swim (2), Knowledge: Demons (2)

  <u>Class Skills</u>: Perform (singing) (18); Knowledge: Magic (14); Knowledge: Monsters (14); Knowledge: History (12); Knowledge: Social (10); Knowledge: World Lore (14); Identify Magic Items (16); Charm (17); Distraction (12); Map Access (16); Inspire Courage (13); Fascination (10); Persuasion (10); Perform (drum) (12); Suggestion (9); Resist Magic (7); Shout (5); Hypnotize (9); Find Object (4); Coercion (3); Break Enchantment (5); Perform (flute) (3); Cause Fear (2); Sleep, Mass (0)

Name: Livia

  Class: Earthbreaker

  Level: 16

  <u>Skills</u>: Assess (6), Awareness (8), Bluff (7), Climb (3), Conversation (9), Intimidate (13), Sense Truth (10), Spot (10), Survival (4), Swim (3), Knowledge: Demons (1)

  <u>Elemental Powers</u>: Earth, stone, acid

  <u>Class Skills</u>: Knowledge: Magic (14), Elemental Blast (earth spray, shower of small stones, rain of large stones, stone sphere shrapnel) (13), Earth to Mud/Mud to Earth (8), Mage Armor (shifting stone slabs) (8), Excavate (7), Summon Elemental Hammer (6), Basic Map Access (6), Tremorsense (3), Sculpt Earth/Stone (3), Speak with Stone (1), Pass Through Stone (0)

Spell List

0-level spells: Daze; Drench; Light; Telekinesis, minor; Mending; Freezing Ray, minor; Root, Spark

1st Level spells

Air Bubble; Break; Force Shield; Grease; Heat Metal (slow); Loose Bonds; Mudball; Sunder Weapon; Thunder Punch

2nd Level spells

Create Pit; Dust Cloud; Earth's Endurance; Thunderstomp; Mirror Image; Mud Minion; Improved Mending; Protection from Fire, Mass (big earth dome); Skip

3rd Level spells

Iron Spike Attack; Thunderstomp, Greater (directed); Clairvoyance; Dispel Magic; Immobilize; Telekinesis, Greater; Daylight

4th Level spells

Stone Ladder; Stone Sphere; Transport, Minor; Invisibility (self); Earth Glide; Stone Fist; Daze, Mass

5th Level spells

Hungry Pit; Dismissal of Demons; Scry; Lighten Object; Darkvision; Passwall; Burrow

6th Level spells

Move earth, major; Stoneskin, Mass; Invisibility, Mass; Dispel Magic, greater; Truthspeak

7th Level spells

Immobilize, greater; Sunburst; Reverse gravity; Acid ray

8th Level Spells

World door

AND NOW A SPECIAL MESSAGE...

Did you enjoy this book? Want more LitRPG adventure goodness? Then the LitRPG Books Facebook group is for you! Find new recommendations, connect with fellow readers, and more!

About the Author

In addition to the Warmaster series, Melissa McShane is the author of many fantasy novels, including the novels of Tremontane, the first of which is *Servant of the Crown;* The Extraordinaries series, beginning with *Burning Bright;* and *The Book of Secrets,* first book in The Last Oracle series.

While her home remains in the mountains out West, she currently lives in Kerala, India, with her husband and two rambunctious Persian cats who believe they own the house. She wrote reviews and critical essays for many years before turning to fiction, which is much more fun than anyone ought to be allowed to have.

You can visit her at her website
www.melissamcshanewrites.com
for more information on other books and upcoming releases.

To subscribe to her newsletter, which is published monthly, visit **www.melissamcshanewrites.com/contact-me-2/join-my-mailing-list**

ALSO BY MELISSA MCSHANE

WARMASTER

THE BOOKS OF THE DARK GODDESS

THE LAST ORACLE

The Book of Lies

The Book of Betrayal

The Book of Havoc

The Book of Harmony

The Book of War

The Book of Destiny

THE LIVING ORACLE

Hidden Realm

Hidden Enemy

Hidden Pursuit

THE EXTRAORDINARIES

Burning Bright

Wondering Sight

Abounding Might

Whispering Twilight

Liberating Fight

Beguiling Birthright

Soaring Flight

Discerning Insight

THE NOVELS OF TREMONTANE

Pretender to the Crown

Guardian of the Crown

Champion of the Crown

Ally of the Crown

Stranger to the Crown

The God-Touched Man

Emissary

Warts and All: The Deluxe Expanded Edition

The View from Castle Always

Winter Across Worlds: A Holiday Collection